D0897874

HUNTING THE
KING

REVIEW

Ever since Dan Brown published his bestselling *The Da Vinci Code* in 2004, thrillers about religious history have become a lucrative, if predictable, staple of the publishing world. To stand out from the stacks, it seems, would take an act of divine intervention.

Peter Clenott proves the skeptics wrong with an intelligent debut about the race to uncover the most prized archaeological find of all time: the tomb of Jesus Christ. The tale begins on the eve of the 2003 Iraqi invasion, when a museum curator stumbles across a cryptic guide to the messiah's remains, allegedly buried somewhere in the Iraqi desert. As the chaos of war ensues, the secret spreads across the globe, eventually reaching the protagonist, American archaeologist and biblical expert Molly O'Dwyer. With the backing of a Polish financier, Molly soon embarks on an action-packed adventure to find Jesus' tomb with the U.S. military, Iraqi fighters, and a slew of other "bad guys" on her trail.

Fans of intellectual thrillers and historical fiction will find a worthy new voice in Clenott. With the ease of a seasoned novelist, he takes readers from the bowels of Abu Ghraib and the streets of ancient Jerusalem to the stuffy offices of Boston academia and the desert enclave of a devout imam. Like *The Da Vinci Code*, *Hunting the King* is based on the premise that Jesus had a child by Mary Magdalene, with descendants that survive to this day. But by blending religious intrigue with contemporary politics and an eclectic cast of characters, Clenott manages to create a story that is entertaining and wholly his own.

The author's best invention may be Molly O'Dwyer, a genuinely likeable heroine who more than holds her own in a man's world. An ambitious scientist, she is also an observant Catholic whose heart and mind don't always agree. Her quest to find the truth without sacrificing Jesus' soul "and the soul of every other human being on this planet who believes in him" adds a provocative layer to the story. Molly's spiritual searching sometimes bring her into contact with supernatural phenomena, which may put off some readers. Her own natural skepticism provides a fitting counterbalance.

For fifteen years Clenott has worked in social services aiding victims of fire, flood and domestic abuse in Massachusetts. This is his first published book in a planned series featuring Molly O'Dwyer. Given such an auspicious start, the sequel can't come too soon.

—Aimee Sabo, *ForeWord*

HUNTING THE
KING

A NOVEL

PETER CLENOTT

KÜNATI

LARGO, USA

HUNTING THE KING

For information, contact Kunati Inc., Book Publishers in both USA and Canada.
In USA: 6901 Bryan Dairy Road, Suite 150, Largo, FL 33777 USA
In Canada: 75 First Street, Suite 128, Orangeville, ON L9W 5B6 CANADA,
or e-mail to info@kunati.com.

FIRST EDITION

Designed by Kam Wai Yu
Persona Corp. | www.personaco.com

ISBN-13: 978-1-60164-148-9   EAN 9781601641489
FIC000000 FICTION/General

Published by Kunati Inc. (USA) and Kunati Inc. (Canada).
Provocative. Bold. Controversial.™

http://www.kunati.com

TM—Kunati and Kunati Trailer are trademarks
owned by Kunati Inc. Persona is a trademark owned by Persona Corp.
All other trademarks are the property of their respective owners.

Library of Congress Cataloging-in-Publication Data

Clenott, Peter.
  Hunting the king : a novel / Peter Clenott. -- 1st ed.
      p. cm.
  Summary: "Explores the existence of the Gospel of Hannaniah, the alleged
daughter of Jesus in the form of a thrilling fictional thriller that explores the Middle
East against a backdrop of scandal, schemers, spies and scientists who seek to
obtain the greatest prize the world has ever seen"--Provided by publisher.
  ISBN 978-1-60164-148-9 (alk. paper)
  1. Apocryphal Gospels--Fiction. 2. Arab countries--Fiction. I. Title.
  PS3603.L476H86 2008
  813'.6--dc22
                        2008000913

Dedication

With profoundest thanks and love

to my mother and father,

Esther and Martin Clenott,

who were with me

every step of the long journey.

CHAPTER 1

March 17, 2003: Baghdad, Iraq

Sun and Moon have always risen over Babylon. In their magnificent garden, Adam and Eve first spoke to the God of the Habira where the Tijra and the Uphra unite before entering the open waters to the south. Great temples, towers, and stepped pyramids were built to worship Sun and Moon and their children. In the fertile land between the two rivers, creation itself took root.

When Abraham, the father of all the fathers, left Ur to lead his Hebrews into a promised land, Babylon remained. For two thousand five hundred more years, even as empires came and went, as the Prophet Mohammed was born and died and his faith spread among the people, Babylon lived. Even when the sands of the desert buried the temples, and the towers and the cities, and the Ottomans came to power, and almost a thousand more years passed, Babylon remained. Its treasures lay hidden, its history whispering in the warm winds above, its spirit flowing in the blood of its children.

But everything comes to an end.

"O Daughter of Babylon who are to be destroyed," the psalmist cried, urging destruction upon those who had destroyed Jerusalem, "happy the one who repays you as you have served us! Happy the one who takes and dashes your little ones against the rock!"

And sooner rather than later.

If the American president was to be believed, and Imran Fawzi had no doubt the most powerful man in the world was not given to exaggeration, the little ones of Iraq were going to have their heads bashed against the mighty rocks of the American military in forty-eight hours.

"Allah! Allah! Allah! Why tonight of all nights?"

Fawzi's breath came in the shortest of gasps as he left his telephone dangling from its cradle and rushed out into the warm spring night. As a young man, he had been rugged, an adventurer, a world traveler, an archaeologist who feared no mountain or desert. But he had been chief curator of antiquities for the Iraqi National Museum for the past ten years, appointed by Saddam Hussein, and in those ten years he had gone to fat and poor health.

Why now? Why? He cursed the missiles that in two short days would rain down upon his city, upon his museum. He cursed his car, as well, his lovely blue Citroen, whose door ripped a hole in his pants and in his shin as he jumped into the driver's seat.

Forget the blood, he thought. There'll be more than enough blood in two days. Two days? Maybe even tonight.

Not five minutes earlier, Professor Mohamoud Jama had called him, screamed in his ear to hurry, hurry, *hurry* to his home!

"Thieves! Looters! They're breaking in! My discovery, from the desert, Fawzi! It's here! Here!"

Momentarily, Fawzi had been befuddled. What discovery? And then he remembered in a flash of recollection. Jama had hinted years before about a find he had made, something that had appalled and terrified him. Something that had made him do what he had never done before in his professional life—rebury it. Cover it up. Pretend it had never seen the light of day. Now what was Jama saying? That he hadn't buried it after all? That he had kept it? Smuggled it into his house? Kept it a secret for all these years from even his most esteemed colleagues?

Fawzi screeched in reverse out into the street, cell phone to his ear, one hand on the steering wheel, both eyes on the road ahead. Worse even than Romans were Iraqi drivers. One day on the road, and his C2 sports car had more nicks and scrapes than his face after shaving with a dull straightedge. That destruction at least he could control to some extent. It was even partly his fault. What made men such as himself and Jama scream in the night and fight off rising panic was what would happen to ten thousand years of artifacts in the National Museum and in the thousands of other historic sites throughout the country when the Americans started their assault. But in Jama's case, there was something else—something special— that Fawzi could only guess at.

"Habib! Habib!" he shouted into his cell phone.

Overhead, the constellations, Greek, Roman, Sumerian, ancient, everlasting. Ahead, the Tigris and the Fourteenth of July Suspension Bridge that spanned the river where it abruptly hooked west past Saddam Hussein's Command Headquarters, connecting the south of Baghdad with the north. Traffic, heavier even than usual, defied the American threats. The bridge had been damaged by bombing during the First Gulf War, but too many Iraqis trusted their great leader who named the bridge for the day his Ba'athist Party came to power. Restaurants still served fine foods along the street. Dance clubs still enticed the young and well-to-do. Fawzi lived in the exclusive Al-Zawiya neighborhood of the city in between loops in the ancient river. Sunni Arabs dominated. Rich Shi'ites could pay their way in—at least for two more days. Unfortunately, Professor Jama lived north of the city at Aadhamiya near the College of Science, where he sometimes taught. That meant Fawzi had to shoot his precious 2003 Citroen C2 sports car through the heart of the downtown, nicks, scrapes, and full-scale broadsides aside.

"Habib!"

"Yes, I heard you the first time, Uncle!" came Habib Al-Nazariiy's voice over Fawzi's cell phone. Habib lived a ten-minute drive from Jama and could reach the elder archaeologist before Fawzi could.

"I got a call from Jama!" Fawzi wheezed.

"Who?"

"Mohamoud Jama, you fool! You must meet me at his house!" Fawzi shrieked as a car leaped out at him from his right, honking madly, the driver shouting, cursing. Fawzi had dashed through a red light to dart through a busy intersection. Pedestrians jumped, dived, averted disaster, swearing in the wake of the expensive European car. Fawzi saw all, heard all, couldn't care less. On he sped, an Iraqi missile on wheels.

"People are looting already," Fawzi told his nephew. "They broke into Jama's house while we spoke! We must stop them. At all costs! Do you understand, Habib? At all costs!"

How could Habib understand? Even Fawzi was unsure what Jama was hiding, why he was so frightened. Here was an old man who had seen everything in his day, withstood months of torture at the hands of Saddam's Secret Police in the infamous Abu Ghraib Prison. One thing alone scared him, that his secret—his terrible secret—would be leaked to the world. But what was it?

Fawzi spun his steering wheel with such an abrupt twist that he felt the tendons in his left arm stretch painfully. Whole sections of the city were black and lightless, electrical power in such disrepair since the First Gulf War that neighborhoods took turns living without power, turning Baghdad into a checkerboard of light and dark areas. Fawzi barely noticed. The Citroen squealed into the Fourteenth of July traffic rotary oblivious to the taxi it forced into a streetlight. Once Fawzi reached the main street again, a long straightaway into the northern suburbs, he flattened his foot on the accelerator and took off.

Fourteen years ago, just after the first American invasion of Iraq, Mohamoud Jama, distinguished professor of archaeology at the College of Science in Baghdad, had been notified of a find in the Syrian desert, southwest of the Iraqi capital. The Iraqi oil ministry had been exploring the region for new reserves when American missiles struck. One fortuitous explosion exposed an ancient buried structure. Jama, naturally, was called in to dig further.

Driving like a madman in and out of traffic, Fawzi recalled the morning ten years after the discovery when Jama, clearly under the influence of alcohol—forbidden under Islamic law, but Jama, a Christian, didn't give a damn about Islamic law—stumbled into Fawzi's office at the museum.

"You must help me, Fawzi!" he exclaimed, slurring his words and sinking into a leather chair in front of Fawzi's desk. "I have desecrated the Holy of Holies!"

"What are you talking about, Mohamoud?" Fawzi had asked, anxious about the drunken university professor inhabiting his office. The obligatory photograph of Saddam Hussein stared down at them. One never knew what the omnipresent dictator saw or had reported to him.

"I have found the truth!" Jama had exclaimed. "Out in the desert! It will destroy my faith! Destroy it, Fawzi!"

"Get a hold of yourself!" Fawzi had tried to calm the old man, but Jama would have none of it.

"At first I took it to be nothing more than a common burial mound," Jama said. "We have so many of those. Worthwhile, interesting, yes. Little did I know ..."

"Little did you know what? What, Mohamoud? You are babbling nonsense!"

"The deeper I dug, the further in I ... My God, she was there!"

"Who, Mohamoud? For God's sake, what are you talking about? Who was there?"

"The American, O'Dwyer. She has corroborated what I found. It all makes sense now. She translated what I was afraid to touch. But now I know what she does not."

Fawzi had tried to coax more of the mystery out of the drunkard, but Jama had gotten sick then and there, vomited all over Fawzi's desk and important paperwork. Fawzi had unceremoniously thrown the archaeologist out of his office at that disgusting moment.

Jama had apparently buried whatever he had found without Fawzi's assistance, and had not spoken of it since. Until tonight, drunk again by the sound of his voice, but in a panic that Fawzi could not ignore.

Fawzi fought his way to the north of the Iraqi capital, crossed the looping Tigris one more time until he reached the Aadhamiya section. Pallid streetlights wavered, flickered, a testament to the energy crisis in the capital. Jama shunned wealth and prestige by neglecting to curry favor with Hussein. As a result, the elderly professor contented himself living among students in a shabby middle-class, one-story brick home painted white. A white Fiat almost as old as the man who owned it sat in the driveway beside the house. The door to a shed was open, ominously so, for a trail of tools led from the garage to the front door of the house, which was wide open to the night air and to anyone who chose to gain entry. A gray van was parked on the street, its doors open and guarded by a youth of about twenty. From where he sat in his car, Fawzi could see that the back of the van had been loaded already with artifacts. The looting of Jama's house had begun in earnest.

"You!" The youth gestured for Fawzi to move on. "Get out of here, if you know what's good for you!"

Fawzi knew what was good for him better than most. But before he could even turn the key in the ignition of his Citroen, his nephew Habib Al-Nazariiy screeched to a stop in an Italian import built for urban terrorists, small and fast. The young thief standing at the rear of his van reached for his pistol too late. From the passenger side window of his automobile, Habib sprayed the looter with rifle fire. Blood splattered the van, the street, the brick patio in front of Mohamoud Jama's house.

"You're late!" Fawzi shouted.

"I had to go to the bathroom."

Habib aimed his Kalashnikov assault rifle, 5.45 caliber with a magazine of thirty tiny missiles, at the young man, now dead.

"Forgive me?" Habib asked.

"Hurry!" Fawzi admonished.

A cool evening breeze blew dust off the street in through Jama's open door. Fawzi could hear nothing coming from inside the house, but he was glad he had thought to call his nephew. Habib, a manly thirty-five, with the dark eyes of an Arabian hawk, had served in the Iraqi army, knew how to use the Russian weapon, commonplace now, highly effective. At the door, they peered into the front room. Jama's body lay sprawled on a carpet in a pool of blood. The phone was clutched in his rigid hand.

"Allah be merciful," Fawzi whispered.

"Allah's a little too late for Mohamoud," Habib said. He pushed into the room at a crouch, his assault rifle poised, one finger on the trigger, another to his lips. Then he pointed.

Fawzi followed his nephew's finger toward a door that led down into Jama's basement. Heart pounding out of control, sweat trickling down his bald head past what once was a hairline, into his brown eyes, he made sure to keep his nephew's body between him and the doorway. They crept forward.

"Downstairs," Habib whispered.

Fawzi heard scraping and hammering downstairs, voices. The thieves had ransacked the main part of the house. Furniture was overturned. The contents of desk drawers were spilled across the floor. Even the walls had been struck as if by pickaxes, the looters leaving nothing to chance. Jama not only stole from his own archaeological expeditions but had been a collector of items from around the world, as well.

Who would have known about them? Fawzi wondered. Other faculty. His loyal students probably. Fawzi reminded himself to consider his own friends and his own notable collections.

Slowly, quietly, Habib pushed the basement door wider. The looters worked by lantern light, their shadowy effort playing on the concrete walls of the cellar. The wooden steps to the cellar creaked slightly when Habib stepped down. Wisely he gestured for the heavy Fawzi to stay off them, then positioned himself, his right foot on the third step down, his left foot on the top stair. Taking quick and deadly aim, he ignored the priceless artifacts that the thieves were loading.

"*Allah akbar!*" Habib shouted and squeezed the trigger until every last bullet in the cartridge of his Russian-made assault rifle was spent. Fawzi stuck fingers in his ears to deaden the sound of the screams and the thunder of the bullets. Habib breathed heavily when the rifle clicked empty. He glanced back at his uncle who had buried his head in his arms.

"You can come down now, Uncle," he said, inserting a second cartridge. "It's done."

"Your father was smart to send you into the army," Fawzi said, wiping the perspiration and tears of fright from his eyes. "Better still your engineering degree for the days ahead."

Well, what was blood after all? Fawzi had seen enough of it in his time. He'd seen the devastation wreaked upon the Kurds in the north when they angered Saddam. What were a few deaths in a basement compared to thousands in a communal dirt grave?

Clutching his nephew's shoulder, he followed Habib into the basement. Blood and pieces of three dead men had splattered the dirt floor of the cellar and the many trunks and boxes that lined the brick walls. Light from a single lantern reflected off the glass cupboards, now empty of the artifacts that Jama had collected over the years. These were now in boxes and trunks. Fawzi opened one and was astonished to find, among other things, a Sumerian vase he guessed to be seven thousand years old, casually dumped into a crate without even paper wrapping to protect it.

"Villainy!" he muttered and could only imagine how bad it would get once the Americans invaded.

"Uncle."

"Blasphemy!" he swore.

"Uncle."

"The fools. They deserved to die!"

Fawzi looked about. In his hurry to assess the damage, he had forgotten all about his nephew. The looters had been exploring what was hidden beneath the floor as well as what was obvious on the shelves. The dirt was pitted with holes. Poor archaeological technique, Fawzi thought.

"Uncle," Habib repeated. "What is this?"

Fawzi glanced at his nephew. Habib stood beneath the cellar stairs, pointing his empty rifle at a hole in the ground. Beside the hole were a pickaxe and a shovel. Within the hole, covered in shadow and dirt, Fawzi could just make out the tip of something buried within.

"What do you think it is?" Habib asked him.

"What do I think? What do I …?"

Suddenly Fawzi knew. As if he'd been hit by one of his nephew's bullets, he knew. Jama's secret. The one the old man had hoped to hide from the world. The one he had bequeathed to the darkness and the ages. The one he had mistakenly kept from everyone but Imran Fawzi, a man who knew how to shift as well as the desert sands.

"Dig it up!" he ordered.

"We should leave, tell the authorities," Habib advised.

"No. Dig it up!"

"We've just killed …"

"Dig it up!"

So determined was Fawzi to discover what it was his old colleague had buried that he plied the shovel while Habib scraped away at the hole with the pickaxe. It took them more than an hour to expose the hidden relic, an hour of careful digging around what appeared to be a clay vase, so heavy it took the two of them and a pulley they rigged from ropes to drag it out of the hole onto the dirt floor.

"My God!" Fawzi whispered when the ancient clay urn lay at his feet. The pot was fat, as round as it was tall. This was no amphora for wine. Around its equator, running along a band that may have once been painted red or brown, Fawzi detected letters. Excitedly, he knelt in the dirt.

"Help me roll it into the light," he told Habib.

They had to shove bodies aside to push the heavy artifact into the center of the room, then heft it onto a table directly under the light. "Can you read it?" Habib asked.

"Hebrew," Fawzi said, his fingers trembling as they caressed the letters. Around the circumference of the urn, Fawzi translated the letters carved into the clay at least two thousand years before. Fawzi struggled with the wording until finally his eyes widened. For a moment he couldn't speak or utter a sound. When he did, he broke down in tears. Leaning his heavy frame on the table, he ignored the dizziness and nausea that threatened to topple him.

"Open it!" he managed to spit out.

"Here?"

"Yes!"

"It's sealed," Habib said, noting a plug of hardened wax and clay that filled the opening.

"Break it!" Fawzi said, uncaring. "Hurry! Hurry!"

Habib picked up a hammer. "Are you sure?" he asked.

"Break it, I don't care! It's not the outside that matters. It's what's inside."

Shrugging his shoulders, Habib hefted the mallet and struck at the rim of the ancient vase. The tool bounced on impact but tore a hole into the plug. Two hits, three, four—Habib pounded away, chipping at clay, and wax and mud, dislodging material to spray into the air, cracking the vase that had held together for twenty centuries until at last it gave way. Like a river freed from a dam, the mouth of the jar and all its contents gave way, falling out of the darkness into Imran Fawzi's waiting palms. But even he was unprepared for what he held in his hands—the two-thousand-year-old skull of an infant.

Fawzi's jaw fell. Habib Al-Nazariiy stared at the tiny head and at his uncle, who looked as though he held the keys to the kingdom of heaven.

"Well," he said, "what is it?"

"This, my dear nephew," Fawzi said, when at last he could calm his hammering heart, "could be the salvation of Iraq."

CHAPTER 2

March 17, 2003 Badghis Province, Afghanistan

Technically, Molly O'Dwyer should never have crossed the border into Afghanistan. Her passport permitted her to work on an archaeological dig in neighboring Turkmenistan. But technically, she didn't give a rat's ass.

What's a few kilometers? she figured. Who's going to know? Until it's too late for them to do anything about it.

She lowered her binoculars, and the cold mountain breeze blew her red hair across her eyes. Badghis Province wasn't called the Home of the Winds for nothing. She tucked her floppy canvas hat into the belt of her jeans to keep it from flying away. The valley below echoed with the spit of small arms fire and the occasional boom of heavier artillery.

Molly puffed out her cheeks in exhaustion. That's who's going to know, she thought. The goddamned Afghani military. Brushing her hand over her grimy cheeks, she knew this was no time to back down or stop digging for the find they were preparing to steal across the border.

"Molly! Come quick!"

Giving one last glance through her binoculars down the forested slope, north toward the Turkmenistan border, she prayed the fighting between government forces and local Muslim insurgents would stay at a distance until she got what she had come so far and waited so long to obtain.

Five years before, near the Valley of the Kings along the west bank of the Nile, burial site of pharaohs, she and the Iraqi archaeologist Mohamoud Jama had made the discovery of a lifetime. A community of ascetics had established residence outside the ancient Egyptian city of Thebes. What made these first-century Jewish monastics so special, what had drawn both Jama and Molly to this site in the first place, was that their religious community was post-crucifixion. It had thrived in the time of the Roman occupation of Judea, built along similar lines as the one at Qumran, where the Dead Sea Scrolls had been found. But unlike the site at Qumran, this one had not been abandoned in the wake of the Roman destruction of Judea. Rather, it was an indication that the newly established faith of the followers of Jesus had taken root elsewhere, beyond the reach of Rome at the very time that Rome was brutally putting down a Jewish insurrection and burning Jerusalem.

Then Jama had become excited. He had found something, but he would not, or could not, divulge it to Molly no matter how much she interrogated him. She maintained a distance then, dispassionate, wondering why he would invite her on the expedition and then keep her in the dark. Until one night, she awoke and stumbled out of her tent, still half asleep, and wandered into the desert away from camp. As if directed by the foot of God, she had tripped over a shrub, rolled down a dune into a shallow depression and landed against a large flat rock exposed by the desert wind. The rock had Hebrew markings on it. The scrolls that lay beneath changed Molly's life forever.

"Molly, 'urry!"

"Coming, Anicet! Coming!"

Her breath was a fine mist in the thin air of the Firozkhoi highlands as Molly raced across the path that had taken her expedition from the plain below into the Afghani foothills ten kilometers from Turkmenistan where they should have been.

She trotted past the tents they had pitched into the hillside, past the horse-drawn carts and tethered horses that had drawn them, pushed through the dozen local tribesmen that a generous grant had afforded her to hire. What lay beneath that rock in Egypt had ultimately led her here, to war-torn Afghanistan.

"Wait'll you see, Molly!"

What the hell could it be?

Anicet Kashimura had followed Molly from their Boston college campus into this remote region of South Central Asia. Risks be damned, they were friends as well as colleagues, and Molly knew nobody could map and lay out a site better than Anicet.

Molly had never intended to dig in Turkmenistan. The scrolls from Thebes had led her here. After three weeks of intense search, she and her team of Afridi and Pashtun laborers had encountered the remains of limestone stairs that seemed to lead directly into the face of the hill. A fire in the woods had exposed the soil to flash flooding and mud slides, which had, in turn, exposed the stairs to the light of modern day. With time running out on their visas, Molly and Anicet had set up camp and begun to dig in earnest, setting their workers to forming three trenches in a box pattern enclosing the stairs. Now four feet into the rocky earth, Anicet peered up at Molly, her long Jamaican dreadlocks beaded with dirt.

"What do you have, Ani?"

"A door, Molly!" her friend exclaimed. "You were right! A freakin' door!"

Molly leaped into the trench behind her friend, nearly knocking her into the stone slab that they had unearthed after five days of digging.

"There's writing on it!" Molly hunkered closer and brushed away centuries of earth with a small paintbrush.

"Ebrew?" Anicet asked.

"You betcha!" Molly could hardly believe what she was reading. She had been right! By God, she had been right!

"Behold you, all who enter here," she read, her voice shaking. *"Eternal life is given to those who believe. To those who don't, death."*

"Good news for you at least," Anicet said.

"Better than that." Molly caressed the Hebrew letters with her calloused fingertips. "This proves the Egyptian community Jama and I found branched out, set roots everywhere. Everywhere! But history wiped them out." Molly wiped away a tear. No more. No time for that.

"Coincidentally, Jama and I made our own discoveries. Both indicated that a powerful movement existed just after the crucifixion of Jesus. That's why he invited me on his Egyptian dig." Molly removed a brush from her belt and swept away dirt to expose more ancient writing. "But the movement we were interested in isn't the one reported in the gospels. Not Paul or Peter or any of the other apostles had anything to do with it."

"Oh, oh. I'm 'earin' Satan's footsteps, Molly. Heresy?"

"Let's just say the future leaders of the Church didn't want anyone to know anything about it." Molly shoved her brush back beneath her belt.

"Shovels!" she shouted suddenly. "Hurry!"

Hauling herself up and out of the trench to give her laborers access to the door, Molly watched them pick and shovel around the edges and dig deeper to expose the bottom half of the entry which went further into the ground. Every so often the sound of battle in the valley thundered and rattled her concentration. It was getting closer. Insurgents typically hid in forested slopes like these to escape pursuit by the more heavily armed national troops. When an explosion rocketed into the hillside only a hundred meters below them, Molly nearly rocketed out of her sneakers.

"Molly."

"It's all right, Anicet," she lied. "We're fine."

She trained her gaze on the trench and on the soil that was flying out of it as the Pashtun laborers dug deeper and deeper into antiquity. At last when they had reached the bottom of the stone slab doorway, Molly leaped back into the trench. In one hand she held a chisel, in the other a hammer. Inserting the chisel point into a crack between the door and the timber that held it in place, she battered at it. Wood chips flew. Dirt peppered her unprotected eyes.

"The crowbar, damnit!" she yelled. The damned stone was holding tight. "The three-foot mallet!"

"You're gonna ruin the door," Anicet warned.

"Fuck the door! I want what's inside!"

Molly crouched and caught her breath. Five years she'd been waiting for this moment. Three years to decipher the long-dead author's scrolls. Two years to raise the funds. Even then she'd had to lie to her backers that she was planning to dig in Turkmenistan.

As she waited for the tools, she brushed away more dirt from the doorway. Her fingers traced markings in the stone, etched by chisels centuries ago. Wiping the debris away, she was struck by the figure of a Star of David. More puzzling was what was within the central hexagram of the Jewish symbol: three holes clearly and purposefully hammered into the rock in the shape of a triangle. Beside the Jewish star another symbol had been carved that resembled a jagged V.

Where have I seen that before? she wondered. Thunder seemed to rumble across the sky overhead. *Seven*, she counted. Seven holes shaped in a jagged V. *I know I've seen it.*

Molly stopped and looked up. Another blast of artillery, closer now, but not about to stop her. A young Pashtun, a teenager, jumped into the trench beside her. With a smile he proffered a stick of dynamite.

"Fuck the door," he said.

Glancing up at a worried Anicet who looked over her shoulders toward the slope and the valley below, Molly took the dynamite. "Anicet, you smoke."

"Yes."

"Match, please."

"Molly, you're crazy! We haven't got time!"

But Anicet struck her match and Molly stuck the lit explosive into the base of the door then scrambled up and out of the hole. Seconds later, before she could even dive to the ground, the dynamite went off and archaeological shrapnel whistled through the air and over her shoulders. Before anyone else, she was back in the trench, crunching over shattered stone, peering into the darkness that lay beyond the open entryway.

"God, let this be it," she whispered, then coughed on the stale air that poured out. "Anicet, a flashlight!" she yelled.

"Who am I, Dora the Explorer?"

The young Pashtun boy followed Molly into the trench. Anicet dropped down next and aimed her flashlight into the lightless space beyond. "You feel it, Anicet?" she asked.

"I feel a boding sense of doom," her friend said. "And a little cold."

The Pashtun boy hung back. "It's all right, Abdimajid." Molly shone the light around the space as she made her way in, keeping her head low, for the beamed ceiling was only five and a half feet above ground level.

"Molly," the boy said, "my father says we must go."

"Tell him to wait."

"But the soldiers …"

"Wait."

Even down here, they could hear the fighting, though duller and less frightening. Molly's beam focused on the walls of the room. "You notice anything peculiar, Ani?"

"I'm walkin' around in a two-thousand-year-old tomb. Bombs are goin' off over my 'ead. Everything's fuckin' peculiar."

"It's a circle," Molly said. "I count twelve passageways running off it. I've never seen anything like this. They must go deep into the hill. Come on."

The floor had once been smooth limestone, but the ceiling had collapsed in places leaving a carpet of debris, manmade and otherwise. Tiny creatures, accustomed to the dark, skittered by Molly's feet as she swept the light around the full circumference of the room.

"More writing?" Anicet asked, pointing at the stone lintels that jutted above the entries into the twelve passageways.

"Hard to tell."

At one time the lintels must have been higher or the floor lower. Now they were positioned at eye level for Molly to study.

"The writing's been worn away," she said. "If we had time …"

"Which we don't."

But Molly had become oblivious to the fighting on the surface. When a mortar shell struck so close that the shockwave rained dust into her face, she merely coughed it away and kept looking.

"They aren't words, they're symbols," she whispered. "But what do they mean?"

Without hesitation and on gut instinct alone, she chose the centermost tunnel and entered it. She'd been inside Egyptian tombs before, and this place gave her the same eerie chill. She could almost shut her eyes and walk as the original inhabitants of this place had walked, utterly familiar with its secret niches and chambers.

"Molly!"

Her light followed a line of symbols at eye level to her right along the length of the narrow tunnel, deeper into the hill. Familiar. So familiar, and yet she couldn't put a finger on what the symbols might mean. So entranced was she that she lost track of where her feet were heading. When the ground abruptly gave way and she tumbled into a void, the flashlight flew out of her hand and everything went dark.

"Molly!"

"Anicet! Get your ass in here!"

"Get my ass in where? Molly, we got trouble, and not in River City!"

Molly scurried around on hands and knees, feeling blindly for the lost flashlight. She had fallen a good four feet and banged her head on the wall behind her, temporarily disorienting her. In scrambling to her knees, she head-butted something else even harder and sharper.

"Shit!"

"Molly, where'd you go?"

"Central passage, damnit."

Molly's fingers latched onto the flashlight. Her head throbbed and blood trickled down her scalp into her eye.

"Be careful, Anicet. There's a drop-off." Then she flicked on the light. "*Jesus!*" Her eyes widened. Crawling around in the dark, she had banged her head on a sarcophagus.

"It's a burial chamber, Ani!" And by the size and appearance of the stone grave, whoever was buried inside had been an important member of this community. The most important. Molly focused the beam of her light. More symbols adorned the foot of the tomb. But only three words. In Hebrew. A name.

"Anicet?"

"Molly," her friend coughed and spluttered, making her way into the burial room. "Tanks!"

"For what?"

"No! *Tanks!* Artillery! Our workers 'ave all run off! Abdimajid. They're all gone! There's a fucking tank climbing up our ass!"

For a single moment, Molly considered backing out. Then her eyes locked on the tomb, on the symbols, on the name, and she said, "Help me!"

"What?"

"Just do what I say. Please. Help me pry off the lid. I want to see who's inside."

"It better be the Prophet Mohammed," Anicet said, "or we're in deep shit."

She laid the flashlight so that its beam tilted toward the ceiling. Molly on one end, Anicet on the other, put their full strength behind the stone seal of the sarcophagus and pushed. Gritting her teeth and growling, forgetting about everything else, Molly shoved and ground stone against stone. They heaved and felt the heavy limestone lid slowly give way until it dropped with a loud crash onto the floor. She retrieved the flashlight and peered inside.

"Wooden coffin," she said. "Local pine probably. More writing."

"What's it say?"

"Can't tell. But I know it's a she. Leah, daughter of Hannaniah the Prophetess."

"Hannaniah."

"Yuh. The author of my Egyptian scrolls."

Molly climbed up onto the sarcophagus to get a closer look. Outside, the shelling had stopped, but there was movement in the outer room that she paid no mind to. "Let's get this out of here," she told Anicet.

"The coffin?"

"We're not going back empty-handed. We might not get this chance again. You take that end. I've got this one. She's not that big."

Anicet looked about. There was noise in the outer chamber. Sweat dripped off her worse than it ever had in the muggy Jamaican summer. "I hope you know what you're doin'," she muttered to Molly.

"Do I ever?" Molly worked her fingers under the coffin of Leah the daughter of Hannaniah the Prophetess. Anicet did the same at the feet.

"Ready?"

Anicet grunted.

"Lift!"

Slowly they raised the six-foot coffin out of its stone cradle. It was surprisingly light, but the stone Molly braced her feet on for leverage was damp. Her feet slipped and the coffin tilted hard against Anicet's knees.

"Jesus!"

"Hold it!" Molly shouted.

"I can't!"

Molly tried to slide her knee under the falling coffin. Instead, she slipped and the coffin went with her, over the side of the sarcophagus, onto the ground with a bang. Her jeans and the flesh of her upper thigh split open in a bloody gash. Her head slammed against the floor. Her flashlight was knocked over and the light went out.

Anicet screamed, but she wasn't the only one terrified by the unexpected sound of the coffin lid striking the ground. An armed gunman burst into the chamber, fell through space just as Molly had, and came up firing at everything that moved.

"Anicet!" Molly could see nothing but the burst of ammo as the gunman's bullets blew up against the walls of the crypt.

Molly dropped in a heap beside the sarcophagus, protected by its solid stone bulk.

"*Istany! Istany!*" she shouted with the little Arabic she knew. "Stop!"

But when Anicet screamed again, Molly didn't think twice. She darted out from behind her protection, cried for Anicet, groped and grabbed her friend's hand when she felt it reaching for her in the dark.

"Anicet! Here!" She pulled with all her might and, as the gunman's aim redirected toward them, dragged her friend behind the safety of the sarcophagus.

"I'm hit," Anicet told her. "My arm. My legs."

"I'm sorry. I'm sorry. You'll be all right. I promise."

Even then the soldier's screams almost overwhelmed the noise from his weapon. Molly cradled Anicet in her lap, her head braced against the cold stone of the tomb, fighting off her own fear. She felt Anicet's blood on her hand. "*Istany! Istany! Ihnna American! Ihnna American! Stop, we're American!*"

But the shouting and shooting didn't stop. More voices filled the tomb and echoed around the chamber. It was their laughter that finally prodded Molly to peer over the sarcophagus. Afghani government troops had entered the tomb and were comforting their panicked cohort, kidding him, retrieving his spent cartridges.

One of them flashed a beam toward Molly. In its light she looked down at the coffin, its lid dislodged by the fall from the sarcophagus. The light glinted on the skull in the coffin, topped by the copper and bronze tiara of a high priestess, her gaping death smile a warning to the armed intruders.

Eternal life is given to those who believe. To those who don't, death.

The men stopped laughing. Anicet moaned. "Molly, you okay?"

And Molly rose, bleeding and wounded. In her best Arabic, she said, "Can somebody get us the bloody hell out of here?"

CHAPTER 3

March 20, 2003 2:00 AM Baghdad

It had taken two days for Imran Fawzi to contact his good friend Ghazi Al-Tikriti. Titles meant nothing these days. History. Reputation. If you weren't military, you were nothing. Try to shove your way into an important ministry, and you were shoved back out. Try screaming into the telephone, and the sound of the click on the other end immediately put you in your place. Contacts in the Special Republican Guard were useless. Acquaintances in the Ba'ath Party were worse. Their bags were already packed. At least the military was sticking around to fight it out with the Americans. Panic had taken Baghdad by its scrawny neck and shook it about like a vulture with a tasty bit of Iraqi intestine.

Not only was Ghazi an important officer of the Iraqi Intelligence Service, the Mukhabarat, he was a Tikriti, a relative of the dictator Hussein. Now, if Fawzi had been a cousin or a nephew, he might have been able to amble into Ghazi's fancy office at the Iraqi Intelligence Service Headquarters, reach into Ghazi's liquor cabinet, help himself to a splendid French Bordeaux, vintage 1930, pull up a chair, and get down to business. But Fawzi hadn't been thinking clearly since he and his nephew Habib had found the infant's skull in Mohamoud Jama's basement. Allah be blessed, who would?

Then, in a moment of desperation, as the American president's deadline approached, Fawzi had a brainstorm and called the one person who would know how to get Ghazi Al-Tikriti's attention immediately. Fawzi's cousin, a banker. One little white lie later—

something about a Syrian bank account being emptied—and Imran was on the phone with his hard-to-reach former college classmate. Two hours later, with dawn and the American troops three hours away, the Director of Antiquities at the National Museum of Iraq paced outside the office of General Ghazi Al-Tikriti, Chief of Directorate 23.

As at Mohamoud Jama's house, looters were hard at work even here at the center of Saddam Hussein's secret service. Except that these looters were not thieving neighbors or treacherous students. These were soldiers of Hussein's elite guard, carting off anything they thought might have black-market value. No one, least of all Fawzi, tried to stop them.

He would have thrown himself into the intelligence officer's arms when the door to Ghazi's luxurious suite of offices opened, but Tikriti's arms were already filled. "Ghazi!" he cried. "It's about time! Have you any idea why I have been trying to reach you?"

Tikriti's arms clasped a Styrofoam box normally used for storing picnic food. This evening the box contained state secrets Tikriti would either hide from or sell to the American troops.

"Have you any idea what my last two days have been like?" Ghazi replied. He laid the box down on the carpeted floor, breathing hard. The elevators in the directorate weren't working, and this was not the first box of stolen state documents he had carried down three flights of stairs to his waiting escape vehicle.

"Why are you wasting my time, Fawzi? I could have you shot for that pathetic trick of yours. Do I look foolish enough to keep my money in a Syrian bank?" While Al-Tikriti was, like Fawzi, in his fifties, he had maintained his college-age stature. He was tall and hard with a black moustache setting off a darkly suntanned face, drenched in sweat from his labors. Tikriti was no office-bound clerk.

He preferred leading his troops, being where the action was, not only making orders but carrying them through on the front lines. He had done so in his role of Chief of the Southern Command, punishing the rebellious doomed foes of Saddam after the 1990 war. He, for one, Fawzi thought, would not back down from any confrontation with the Americans.

Fawzi raised his hands in an attempt to placate his old friend. "I am sorry. I appreciate what you have been going through. All the more vital that I speak to you. Had I been able to reach you two days ago, much of this might have been avoided."

"As you can see, I'm busy." Ghazi evidently had no intention of bringing Fawzi into his private rooms. From a plate-glass window, he could see the skyline of Baghdad, the winding Tigris River, the moon hanging overhead, a bright nosy neighbor peering over a starry fence at a city about to be bombarded to hell. Handing the Styrofoam box to Fawzi, he ushered the museum director out the door, down a hallway, and toward a staircase leading to a parking garage three floors down.

"You know that Mohamoud Jama is dead," Fawzi huffed.

"Immaterial."

"He was murdered by looters. Students from his own classroom! Colleagues who knew what priceless artifacts he kept in his house."

"So much for tough grading. So what?"

"So, it is what they were trying to loot that brings me here. You must contact Saddam! Now! This very minute! I have in my possession something that will stop the Americans in their tracks! I swear to you! Go back to your office! Get on the phone!"

Fawzi had little maneuvering room on the staircase. Looting soldiers and clerics, untrammeled by military protocol in the last moments of Hussein's rule, ignored rank, flaunted theft, and shoved past the museum director and the intelligence commander, coming and going, up and down, heisting their own precious treasures. Fawzi had to speak at the top of his voice at Ghazi who bulled his way down the stairs, clearing a path to the garage.

"Where are you going anyway? What's in this box? Who's going to defend the city?"

"Don't be a fool, Fawzi! No one is!"

Indeed, Al-Tikriti's white button-down shirt, open at the collar and cuffs, his Adidas running shoes and khaki pants might have been worn to the races on a mild Sunday afternoon. His uniform no longer mattered, and he was prepared to pawn his gold military medals in a camel's heartbeat. The only uniform that mattered now was the standard military pistol he would never sell nor the more useful Kalashnikov assault rifle. The boastful Americans didn't have the slightest idea what lay in wait for them on the streets of Iraq.

"I'm a tired man, Imran," he said. "Get to the point."

At the bottom of the last staircase, at the entry to the parking garage lit only by a single flickering light, Fawzi set the Styrofoam box down.

"Jesus of Nazareth," he said.

"Jesus of Nazareth," Tikriti repeated. "Pick up the box, Fawzi. That's the last one. I have no more time for this nonsense."

"It is not nonsense, Ghazi. Of that, be assured."

"Then what does the Christian prophet have to do with us? Now of all times."

Fawzi sucked in a breath, hefted the box of intelligence material, and followed Tikriti into the parking garage. Military vehicles were interspersed with expensive personal cars. Ghazi pointed to an SUV.

"Just after the First Gulf War," Fawzi said, struggling with the weight, "Jama stumbled upon a find in the Syrian desert. I don't know exactly where because he buried the place up again. So far as I know, he never told anyone what he'd found. With one possible exception."

"Jama was a drunk. He was also manic-depressive and on more medication than my wife. Perhaps he was delusional."

At the American-built SUV, Fawzi laid the Styrofoam box on the concrete floor and sagged against the vehicle. He didn't ask how Ghazi would know all of this. Intelligence knew everything. He said, "I myself considered those factors when he barged into my office one day, ranting about what he had discovered. Then two nights ago, he rang me up while his home was being broken into. My nephew Habib and I raced over as quickly as we could, but by the time we got there, he was dead and thieves were ransacking his cellar."

"Habib is a capable man."

"He was that night. In the basement we found something that Jama had hidden. A burial urn, two thousand years old. Inside were the remains of a baby along with this."

Fawzi reached into the folds of his light blue silk jacket. From a pocket he handed Tikriti a necklace from the dead child. The medallion was of gold hammered into the form of a Star of David, about two inches across. In the center was a triangle. At each of the six points the goldsmith had sculpted symbols, arrangements of dots meaningless to Tikriti who studied them briefly.

"Jews," he said dismissively. "They will save Iraq?"

"Only in the remotest sense," Fawzi said. "I was able to estimate the age through writing on the urn, a name, a lineage. The deceased infant Rivkah, child of Leah, daughter of Hannaniah, daughter of Yeshuah bar Yushef."

Tikriti slammed the SUV door shut. "Yeshuah bar Yushef being ..."

"Jesus of Nazareth." Fawzi let the implications sink in before finally overcoming his fear of Tikriti and clasping the intelligence officer by an arm. "You must believe me, Tikriti. Jama was Christian. After we made the discovery in his cellar, I happened upon some of his journals."

"Just happened upon them?"

"He truly believed he had stumbled upon the burial ground of the family of the Nazarene."

"In Iraq?"

"Yes!"

Tikriti took back the little Star of David necklace and swung it before his face, trying, like any competent intelligence officer, to figure the angles presented by this piece of information. "First of all," he said at last to a breathless Fawzi, "you don't know this Yeshuah is *that* Yeshuah. And even if it were, what of it? You have people claiming to be descendants of the Christian prophet. They might or might not be. How does this stop the Americans from attacking us?"

Fawzi paused. They were not alone in the garage. The shadows and footfalls of other military men stealing from the city before they stole out of the city made Fawzi lean in close to Tikriti and speak in a whisper.

"I might have thought as little of this information as you were it not for an American archaeologist named Molly O'Dwyer. Jama's discovery in Iraq somehow led him to another dig in Egypt. This Professor O'Dwyer accompanied him. Along with remains, they discovered a veritable library of scrolls she called the Gospel of Hannaniah. The selfsame Hannaniah, I presume, whose name Jama found on the buried urn."

"Go on," Tikriti said.

"In her gospels, Hannaniah claimed to be the daughter of

the messiah. She was very explicit in her details about their life together."

Abruptly, Tikriti and Fawzi looked around. Outside the building an air raid siren blared, loud enough to be heard underground. Anxious to push Fawzi to the point, Tikriti glanced at his Rolex. It was 2:30 AM. Perhaps the American blitzkrieg had begun already.

"To the point!' he cried. He had to leave now! The Mukhabarat headquarters would be one of the first targets destroyed.

"The known gospels," Fawzi explained as Tikriti headed to the driver's door of the SUV, "say that Jesus was resurrected after the crucifixion. But ..." Now the Iraqi archaeologist, like the poorest of ham actors, paused for the dramatic effect. "Hannaniah's gospel was far more detailed and far different. Jama believed that Jesus survived the crucifixion and that his followers settled here! In Iraq! The remains he found belonged to one of Jesus' descendants, Tikriti! Can you imagine what the Americans would do if we told them that here in Iraq is Jesus Christ's family plot!"

Yes, Tikriti could imagine. They would laugh at the Iraqis and then bomb them some more. But he had been in the intelligence business long enough not to show Fawzi what he was really thinking or feeling. While Fawzi stood just outside the door, Tikriti climbed in behind the wheel of the SUV and shut the door between them. He held the Star of David pendant, swung it even as he stuck the key in the ignition. Then he asked the most logical of questions.

"If this plot is out there somewhere, where is it?"

"I don't know."

"Then what good will it do us?" Tikriti turned on the engine, which roared to life as if equally anxious to flee Baghdad. "Without proof," he said, "we're only bluffing. And you can't bluff Americans, not when they're dead set upon destroying you."

"But we can find them!" Fawzi cried. "Not in three hours, no. Call Saddam. Tell him to contact the American president. Tell him we have proof of the remains of a descendant of Jesus. Perhaps of Jesus himself! Tell him we've run DNA tests and can pinpoint the age of the body. Tell him accompanying evidence will lead us to even more. Jama kept a diary, Ghazi. Buy me time and we will save our country! You will save it!"

Shifting into reverse, Tikriti paused. "A diary?" he said.

"Yes!"

"You are being completely honest?"

Fawzi hesitated.

Tikriti shot one more glance down at his wrist and his expensive timepiece. Fawzi had nothing, he thought, but what the hell. "Where is it?" he asked.

"At the museum."

"I'll be there in an hour." Tikriti leaned out the window. "If you have nothing, you understand I will have to kill you."

"Understood, Ghazi."

Fawzi watched the intelligence officer peal out of the garage. The siren outside had not stopped wailing. Tikriti would be impressed, Fawzi had no doubt of it. Jama's diary spoke of what he had found in the desert, a body, a whole graveyard of bodies, and the key to a map, which would lead them elsewhere, perhaps to the final truth of the man called Christ. Now if only he could figure out a way to abduct the American archaeologist who had been like a daughter to Jama. She would add credence to the story. But how?

As for Ghazi, once he had sped into the Baghdad night, he picked up his car phone. Oh, yes, he would make a call, all right.

But it wouldn't be to Saddam. As the Americans would say, fuck him. Instead, Ghazi Al-Tikriti, Chief Intelligence Officer, General in the Iraqi Army, Commander of the Southern Division, placed a call to Warsaw to a man who could buy and sell anything, a man who moved in the highest of diplomatic and corporate circles, a mobster.

At precisely 5:30 AM, the first of three dozen Tomahawk missiles was launched at Baghdad, targeting military and intelligence sites, government buildings, and the private residences of Saddam Hussein and his family. At 5:34 AM, forty satellite-guided cruise missiles sped from American warships stationed in the Red Sea and zeroed in on the Iraqi capital. All told, over three hundred missiles struck the city while Imran Fawzi locked himself in his office in the Iraqi National Museum wondering why the hell Ghazi Al-Tikriti had betrayed him. The looting of the National Museum began even while the Tomahawks were flying.

Of course, Saddam Hussein was no longer in Baghdad. Nor was Ghazi Al-Tikriti, who had gathered up his wife, ten daughters, their spouses and children and fled south in the very direction American and British troops were advancing. He didn't care. He had a plan. So did the United States. It was called Operation Iraqi Freedom. And so much was to occur over the ensuing months to prove everyone wrong about everything.

Not five minutes after the first missile struck in the heart of downtown Baghdad, an excited crowd of Iraqi villagers left their mud-brick and straw homes and stood on the west bank of the Shatt Al-Arab, the waterway through which the combined might of the Tigris and Euphrates rivers flowed into the Persian Gulf. The Shatt Al-Arab served as the southeasternmost border separating the nations of Iraq and Iran, and the villagers raised their voices in praise and prayer as a small, unadorned dhow crossed the water from the western Iranian side to the eastern Iraqi.

No sooner did the craft touch Iraqi soil than the cheering villagers, marsh Arabs as they were known to the world, survivors of Saddam Hussein and Ghazi Al-Tikriti, raced down the sandy embankment to the shore of the river to swarm around the dhow's primary occupant.

Imam Abdul-Azim Nur, holy man, wise beyond his thirty-six years, embraced his thankful followers then sank to his knees in the soil of his homeland and kissed it.

"Allah be praised," he said. "I am home."

Behind him, a second, shorter but younger man, waded through several inches of water onto the shore. Iranian by birth, he watched Nur swallowed up by the pigeons of his homeland. Like Nur, he was an educated man, a religious man. But unlike Nur, he carried a blank book and a pen wherever he went and wrote down almost everything he witnessed. It was his obsession with detail and his undeniable loyalty to the Islamic Republic of Iran and to its holy supreme leader Ayatollah Khamenei that had led to Barid Shamkhazi's latest assignment: to follow Abdul Azim Nur wherever he went, to transcribe all that he saw, to admonish and guide the Iraqi imam, and to make sure, with the full support of the government of Iran, that Nur helped to establish an Iraqi Islamic republic in complete and full partnership with its neighbor to the east.

Such an honor bestowed upon him by Ali Hoseini Khamenei himself filled Barid with so wonderful a sense of purpose that he could not help but feel an overwhelming and perhaps unholy pride when Nur turned to him for approval before reaching within the folds of his black burnoose and withdrawing a leather-bound copy of the Qur'an and an Iranian hand grenade.

When Nur told his flock of pigeons, "Let us take our homeland back from the infidel," Barid Shamkhazi had no doubt that he meant it.

CHAPTER 4

April 8, 2004 Boston, Massachusetts

Smoke. That was always the first thing she saw. And smelled. Enough fire, black and toxic, to blind her and choke her. To kill her. She was five years old again, a desperate child, screaming for her mother. But her mother was gone, lost to the dark and the flames, long, long gone.

"Molly, do you hear me?"

She did, though she was far away from the man who had spoken to her. Thirty years away.

"Molly, where are you?"

"In the house!" Five-year-old Molly coughed out the words as if she were forcing them against the cloud of smoke that was trying to kill her.

"Mama!"

"She's gone, Molly. You've been in that basement alone for years. Come forward in time. Leave the past to the past."

Father Ray Teague, a Jesuit instructor in psychology at Mt. Auburn College, leaned over his patient. She lay in a semi-hypnotic state on a couch in his campus office. She'd been his patient and colleague for many years, and it saddened him to see her stuck in a horrible moment in her life, a moment best left as buried as the earthbound artifacts she sought to bring to light.

"I can't leave!" she hollered. "Mama!" Her cry was so loud Teague feared she'd frighten passersby in the hall beyond his door. Her hands clawed at the invisible smoke as if to part it, and she raked her fingernails across Teague's bearded cheek.

"Damn, Molly, that's enough," he said. "I'm bringing you forward."

With a gentle but forceful palm, he held her head down against the pillow on his couch and avoided her struggling hands.

"Picture yourself floating out of the darkness," he told her. "Out of the smoke and into a clear night sky."

That was how regression worked. Simple instructions, a progression of restful images taking the patient in a trance from the present into as deep a past as the patient and doctor wished to go, then back again, all ghosts and demons hopefully exorcised. Obviously, the technique wasn't working with Molly.

"The stars tonight are brilliant," Teague suggested. "Look at the constellations. Orion. The Big Dipper. Let their light guide you. You rise high into the night sky and float on a breeze that carries you. There's Boston. The Prudential Tower. The Hancock. The Sox are in town. The lights at Fenway are golden. And on you float, down Commonwealth Avenue, the long tracks of the C Line leading you out through Brookline into Newton. At the end there's Mt. Auburn College, the Admin Building, the Psych Department. In through the open window you float, down onto my couch. You open your eyes and you're home."

And Molly opened her eyes, green and moist, but she wasn't home. Briefly disoriented, she looked about Father Teague's office, at the framed degrees, the shelves of books, the prized photo of Teague with Red Sox pitching legend Pedro Martinez. She shook her head clear of the smoky cobwebs, rubbed her eyes and grunted, "Well, that helped."

"We tried," Teague said. He laid his notepad aside, stretched and yawned. They'd been at it for two hours, beginning right after her last class. Now it was nearly midnight, past Teague's bedtime. He felt as exhausted as Molly, and she had done all the work. "The next time we might get where we want to be," he said. "Regression doesn't work in one or two sittings, Molly."

"You're being kind." She sat up and set her bare feet on the floor. "What you're not saying is, it's not the fault of the technique. It's the fault of the patient. She's nuts."

"She's troubled," Teague corrected.

"Troubled and nuts. You're right. I should just let the past stay in the past, move on. This is ridiculous." Molly slipped her feet into sandals, mindlessly brushed off the lap of her green skirt.

"But you're still having those dreams."

"Yes. Every night." Nightmares actually. The fire. The black smoke. Her mother disappearing, dying. And that sickening feeling that it had all been her fault. Ever since Turkmenistan, the dreams that she thought she had left behind had returned with a vengeance.

"You understand, of course, where all this is coming from."

"Herr Freud," Molly said, smiling at her therapist and friend. Patting his cheek, she noted the blood that came away on her fingertips from the scratch she had given him. "Oh, did I do that? Ray, I'm sorry."

"You're a demonstrative patient," Teague said. He stood up, handed Molly her backpack laden with heavy textbooks and a laptop. "Guilt is controlling your life. It shouldn't."

"I'm Catholic." Molly strapped the backpack over her strong shoulders, strong from years of hard fieldwork.

"Yes, well, you've confessed, and I'll be damned if I know for what. If the Red Sox had sinners like you, they wouldn't keep us waiting eighty-six years to win a world series."

Teague walked her to the door. In her mid-thirties, she was his junior by some twenty-five years. He had known her mother quite well, known Molly from the day she'd been born, christened, and welcomed into this mad world. No one knew who her father was. So, upon the unexpected and tragic death of her mother some thirty years before, Teague had taken it upon himself to keep an eye on her. And she was and had always been an eyeful.

"Guilt sucks," Teague said, shucking off his professional cloak for his paternal one. "I pray to a God that understands His creation in all its frailty."

"I thought you didn't believe in God, Father."

"Shhh!" Teague raised a finger to his lips, and Molly laughed, a nice way to bring her back from her despairing past. "All I'm saying is," he said as he ushered her down the empty school corridor to the main entrance, "you focus too much on guilt. True faith is not founded on guilt but upon love. You mistake me, Molly. I haven't gotten to where I am today by being faithless." As they reached the door and stood on the steps leading to the verdant campus common beyond, Teague pointed to his head. "I do believe in God. But He's here," he said before pointing to the stars. "Not there."

"There we part company, Father. I think He's in both places."

Molly kissed the scratch she'd put on Teague's cheek, thanked him and bounded down the stairs like a twenty-year-old student, anxious to get home, jump into a warm bath, and throw off her cares with a *National Geographic* or Oprah's magazine. Tomorrow was Friday, Good Friday in fact. She had no classes and could sleep late before heading to the campus chapel for services. Father Ray would be there, more by act of political/academic pressure than by act of faith. Molly, God bless her, still believed. Hell, she still looked forward to Christmas and the clop clop of reindeer feet.

The night sky was glorious, as full of stars as it could be, given the brilliant Boston backdrop. Two thousand years before, over the Galilee, Hannaniah had gazed upon these same stars. As had her father, if indeed Jesus of Nazareth, Yeshuah bar Yushef, was her father. Having spent six years deciphering the gospels of Jesus' only child, Molly believed he was. That meant, of course, that the hack scientists and pulp fiction writers who proclaimed Jesus' survival may have been right after all. That not only had Jesus survived, but so had his line of descent, perhaps down to this very day. If so, who would they be?

Pulling her car keys out of her backpack, she paused in the nearly vacant faculty parking lot. Her refurbished green 60s VW Beetle waited under the spill of lamplight. Only one other car stood in the lot, uncomfortably close to her own, a white Volvo S80 with tinted windows. She couldn't see inside, if it were occupied or not. As peaceful a campus as Mt. Auburn might be, rape happened. Be suspicious, she knew, be safe. So when the door to the Volvo opened, and a figure all in black stepped out into the light, she guessed it wasn't by coincidence.

"*Buona sera.* Molly O'Dwyer?"

"Who wants to know?"

The mitigating factor, what kept Molly from turning her keys into a weapon, was that the stranger who emerged from the Volvo was a woman, smaller than Molly. Dressed in high heels, though, she could stand eye to eye with her.

"Nina Cavalcante," the woman said, and instantly Molly's fears were swept away. In fact, the name, the heavy Italian accent brought a wide smile to Molly's face.

"Oh, my God!" she squealed and hurried across the three spaces separating their cars to gobble the newcomer in the embrace of old friends. "Dr. Cavalcante!"

They weren't really old friends. They had never met before. Yet when Cavalcante pried herself free of Molly's arms, she, too, was beaming like a little girl reunited with a favorite playmate.

"I read your paper!" they exclaimed in a single voice, laughing with delight. Children.

"Afghanistan! Molly, how did you dare?"

"Don't ask," Molly said. "I spent six months explaining to the State Department how I took a wrong turn. I loved your letters. Thank you for writing. Thank you for your support."

"We girls have to stick together. Your translation of Hannaniah's Gospels deserves a Nobel Prize."

Cavalcante stepped back to make an unapologetic study of the American woman, head to toe, then toe to head. She nodded her approval.

Molly was well aware of Cavalcante's renown, or infamy, in academic circles, as a pop culture archaeologist, a digger into the mystical and fantastic. Vampires. Witches. The occult.

Molly looked over her Italian counterpart's shoulder, as a second person exited the Volvo. He didn't leave it so much as he swung his long legs out, planted his feet on the parking lot, and sat where he was, gazing up at Molly.

"Teodor Kwiatkowski," Cavalcante said.

"Archaeologist?"

"Not quite."

"Friend?"

"*Una collega.*"

"He doesn't look like any archaeologist I've ever known. To see me?"

"To assist us." Dark hair tomboyishly short, dark-complexioned, Cavalcante was a wisp of a woman, thirties, slender, with catlike nervousness. Her large, lovely brown eyes dominated her otherwise small features, and she used her hands constantly to express herself. Here was a woman, Molly thought, completely open, incapable of dissimulation. But then you'd have to be if your primary focus in life was exploring the history of the paranormal.

Cavalcante didn't bother to invite her male companion over. "We waited for you over two hours," she said.

"Are you visiting?"

"No."

"Staying at a local hotel? Stay with me."

"*Non possiamo*. We are flying to Warsaw on Sunday."

"Warsaw?" Molly said. "On Easter?"

Cavalcante made the sign of the cross then smiled. But when she suddenly clasped Molly's elbow and drew her close, the smile was gone. "You must come with us," she said, whispering as if afraid someone would hear. But there was no one else in the lot Molly could see, other than Kwiatkowski who disinterestedly played with the laces of his shoes. "I can't tell you everything yet. But I promise you, Molly, no expedition you've ever been on will be like this."

"In Warsaw."

"That's just the beginning," Cavalcante insisted. If possible, her owl eyes widened even more as if to mesmerize or seduce Molly. She spoke so close that Molly could smell the roasted garlic and onions Cavalcante had eaten for dinner.

"What did you find in Afghanistan?" she asked.

"Catacombs. A burial site," Molly said.

"More specific. You held back in your report. I know you did. You didn't divulge everything."

"I've been snake-bitten in the past when I was too honest, too open. The catacomb was a Jewish one. Approximately two thousand years old. Under the circumstances, we were lucky to get out alive. Except for a few quick photographs, I have nothing left of the dig. State confiscated everything else."

"In your paper, you tied it to an earlier discovery with Mohamoud Jama in Egypt. The Gospel of Hannaniah. One doesn't go to Afghanistan on a hunch. You knew you were going to find something there. How?"

Molly looked past Cavalcante at Teodor Kwiatkowski who was no longer fixated on his shoelaces. Rather he stared at Molly as if he could hear what they were saying. Something disquieting about him—his Aryan looks, his silent attentive manner—made him appear more a bodyguard or hired assassin, someone who would not have liked to hear her say *no* to Cavalcante.

"The Gospel contained a poem, a lamentation actually," Molly said. "The Old Testament Lamentations were written in the wake of the destruction of the first temple, filled with longing and despair. I couldn't figure why Hannaniah would include them in her gospel. They were out of character for her. She was, in my mind, a very positive, upbeat woman despite all she suffered."

Cavalcante squeezed Molly's elbow. "You lived Hannaniah for five years," she said. "I envy you. But that is your style. You inhabit the people you explore. You bond with them as though they were your kin. Like me. We are like blood sisters, you and I. What pleasure is the search if, in the end, you can't dance with the ghosts? What did the poem say?"

"I believe it was written for her children as a remembrance and a guide, so that generations after her death, her descendants would be able to find her."

"My God. It took you five years to get the money to go?"

"It took me nearly that long to understand what Hannaniah was doing. Lamentations are acrostic poems. The first letter of each verse follows the Hebrew alphabet, letter by letter in sequence, aleph to tav, forming some kind of theme. Hannaniah used the form but not the alphabet. She was trying to hide something. It took me a while to figure out what."

"Yes?"

Molly smiled and wagged her finger. If Cavalcante could be secretive, so could she. Cavalcante turned and snapped her fingers, a gesture that brought Kwiatkowski out of the Volvo, a locked briefcase in hand. Without a word, he handed it to Cavalcante who opened it quickly. Then he stepped back out of the way, out of deference, it seemed to Molly, to the document Cavalcante withdrew.

"Here," she said to Molly, "take it. This was faxed to us several months ago."

Molly glanced at Cavalcante, time of night completely forgotten in this unexpected and disturbing meeting. She took the paper from Cavalcante and saw immediately that it was a faxed copy of a document that had been originally written on other, perhaps far older, paper. The glare from the streetlight interfered with reading the document, so she turned her back on Cavalcante and headed to her car. Sitting in the front passenger side seat, she opened the glove compartment and read by the overhead light.

When at last Molly looked up, still clutching the document, her hands were shaking. "Where did you get this?" she demanded.

"Our funder had it," Cavalcante said. "As you can see, it is only part of some whole."

"Don't be coy with me, Nina Cavalcante. Do you know where this originated?"

"Yes. Mohamoud Jama."

"Mohamoud?"

"Although he is not the person who sent this to us."

"I worked with Mohamoud in Egypt."

"I know."

"He was with me when I found the Gospel."

Molly shut her eyes. Nina's letter ... her document ... appeared to be a fragment of ancient parchment with Hebrew lettering. It couldn't be. Impossible. The Gospel of Hannaniah had stunned the world. Briefly. Purported to be written by the illegitimate daughter of Jesus, experts called it a hoax, the delusion of an overzealous female disciple of Christ, completely unprovable. And, frankly, Molly was just as glad to accept that interpretation rather than have to advocate her own. The scientist in her was fascinated. The loyal Catholic was deeply troubled by the implications of her discovery. Not to mention that the publicity had nearly killed her career. More disturbing, the dreams— her nightmares—had begun shortly after Egypt and had not deserted her, subsequently driving her back to the psychiatrist's couch.

Yet, despite all, she had returned to the hunt, illegally entered Afghanistan to validate her Egyptian find, opening the door yet again to all of the harsh academic criticism, the calls for her resignation, the vilification by theologians from around the world, the whispered phone calls late at night at home and at her office, the death threats, all of the outpouring of anger that had followed in the wake of Hannaniah's discovery. Under such overwhelming pressure, Jesus' daughter's gospels might have passed into history, briefly interesting, harmless, leaving Molly to get on with her life in a comfortable academic niche, secure in her talents, ready to explore other archaeological mysteries. But Molly, try as she might, couldn't abandon her search. Just as Jama had fearfully covered up his discovery in Iraq only to pursue his quest with Molly in Egypt, she had been unable to give up her search.

And now this faxed evidence from Mohamoud Jama, her mentor in Egypt, the man who had warned her what was to come now that they had uncovered the truth as he had called it. While there wasn't a hell of a lot to go on, the few words she could translate told her more than enough. Her heart raced. The door that she had reopened in Afghanistan was about to be blown off its hinges.

Leah to her dearest Mother. I have found a new home for us among good people.

"Oh, my God!" she said. "Addressed to Hannaniah in Thebes. That's how Jama knew where to look."

"And there's more," Cavalcante told her. From her Aryan guard's briefcase, she withdrew a document of more recent stock, yet in its own way even more puzzling.

"What's this?" Molly asked.

"A page from Professor Jama's diary. The sender meant to entice us without giving us every detail."

Molly eagerly snapped the faxed paper out of Cavalcante's hand and was immediately swept away on a journey of six thousand miles, to the far side of the planet, to a hole in a hill in distant Afghanistan. On the paper, Jama had drawn a Star of David, made up of two counterfacing triangles. At each point, he had drawn symbols composed of dots in varying number, five, six, seven. One symbol looked like a house with a triangular roof. Another looked like a squiggly letter w. A third, a jagged v. Hebrew letters accompanied each symbol. And there were six more letters attached to each line of the central hexagram.

"Afghanistan," she whispered, her heart beating with excitement.

"You know this figure?" Cavalcante asked.

Molly looked up at Cavalcante who had lit a cigarette and was nervously puffing it into the night. From around her neck, Molly unchained an amulet, a Star of David necklace, two inches across, that she had retrieved from her site in the Afghani highlands. Worn around the neck of the Jewish high priestess, it bore the exact symbols as the Star of David in Jama's drawing.

"Where …? What are we looking for?" Molly asked. "If I decide to go."

"What are we looking for?" Cavalcante watched the smoke tail up towards the stars. "Dream the dream of all archaeologists," she said. "It's what you knew six years ago in Egypt. The ultimate truth. That's what we're looking for, Molly. Hannaniah."

CHAPTER 5

Good Friday, Abu Ghraib Prison, Baghdad

The eight of diamonds. A minor playing card. Nice to have if you've got four other diamonds and you're playing gin rummy or three other eights and you're sitting at a poker table in Las Vegas.

Andrew Milstein twisted his eight of diamonds between his fingers, rolled it up, occasionally held it against the bridge of his nose, pressing it against his head to thwart the insidious migraine that always seemed to begin the moment he entered the gates of the Abu Ghraib Prison. The Naprosyn he had taken an hour ago was proving useless. Probably he could convince one of the medical people assigned to the 800th Military Police Brigade at the prison to give him a shot of something stronger. But then he'd just fall into a stupor and wouldn't be at all effective in this interrogation. Then again he had to wonder if he even wanted to be part of this interrogation.

Two dogs barked, their shrill screams driving a spike of pain through Milstein's brain. Damned dogs, he thought, and damned soldiers using them. The prisoner was strapped to his cell bars, stripped naked, his genitals dangling between his legs, a tempting target for the snarling Dobermans straining at their leashes to get a piece of him. The eight of diamonds.

Before this war to start more wars, the eight of diamonds was just a card and a dull one at that. Now, because of some military mind's atypically clever concept of placing the faces of Iraqi war criminals on them, such cards had become fodder for news briefs, comedy sketches, and gambling freaks. Who would be the next criminal brought to justice? Who would be the last? The ace of spades and his sons, the aces of hearts and clubs, had been dealt with. But they didn't interest Milstein the way the eight of diamonds did. Ghazi Al-Tikriti.

"Fuck you!" Ghazi yelled at the dogs in excellent English. His head, face, and genital area had been shaved clean. Blood trickled from wounds to his ribs where one of the dogs had managed to sink his teeth before being pulled off by his army controller, a young female little better than twenty years of age, a sadistic little bitch.

It amazed Milstein that under these degrading circumstances Tikriti had held out for so long. He looked bone thin, and his eyes drooped from lack of sleep. Milstein shouldn't feel overly sorry for him. After all, Tikriti's history was well known to him. After the southern Shi-ites and Marsh Arabs had rebelled against Hussein in the wake of the Kuwait disaster, Hussein had hand-selected Tikriti, his cousin, to punish them. And punish them he had, in ways far more insidious than this. But Milstein couldn't help think that his side should behave better, not use a woman soldier to lead the disgusting assault on this prisoner, the eight of diamonds. The military high command and Washington's elite knew exactly what was going on here but chose to turn a blind eye when their sadistic female interrogators smeared menstrual blood on their Iraqi prisoners' faces or nicked their testicles with knives.

Tikriti's prison mate had fared even worse. Hands and ankles bound together behind his back, a pillowcase over his head with a cloth jammed into his mouth, he hadn't stirred since Milstein arrived that morning. And no one had bothered to look in on him.

The man who should have stopped all this, who had the authority to prevent it, sat back, legs dangling over a desk, and ate a decent breakfast of sausages, eggs, toast, and orange juice. He chewed slowly with the occasional "Mmm-mmm" to make the starving prisoner salivate then talk so he could finally eat.

Forcing aside the blinding pain in his head, Milstein could no longer take the torture and stepped in between the closest canine and Tikriti. God only knew how the American commanders could knowingly disavow what they knew full well was going on. "All right, stop it! Stop it!" he exclaimed.

The soldier holding her dog at bay frowned but didn't back off. She let the angry canine leap on Tikriti's chest and stick his slobbering mouth in the Iraqi prisoner's face. "Just doin' my orders," she said.

The man in charge of the interrogation jumped off the table, placed his hands on his hips and shook his head. "Milstein," he said, "this is not your domain."

"I'm the one MI sent to talk to him. For God's sake, give me the chance before you kill him." Milstein raised a cup of cold water to Tikriti's mouth. "Take some," he said. Then to the woman, "Untie him."

Tikriti sagged upon release. Milstein gave him the full cup of water then entered the cell to see to the second bound prisoner. Immediately upon pulling the pillowcase hood off the man, he could see that he was dead. Vomit had spilled out of his mouth into the hood, at least that which had made its way past the cloth muzzle. The rest of his stomach waste had caught in his throat and suffocated him some time during the night.

"Jesus Christ!" Milstein hollered. "You fucking killed him!"

The chief interrogator, Richard Jackson, sweat dripping from his narrow Marine-cut head, signaled his female associate off and stepped into the cell. He was not military though he had served his country previously in Military Intelligence. Milstein had done so as well, and the two had known each other in passing from their days in the First Gulf War. But while Milstein had returned to civilian life to teach Middle Eastern history at Amherst, Jackson had gone into the private sector, specializing in prison security and transport. He had been awarded this plum contract in Iraq through high-placed connections in the Pentagon. In fact, they had asked for him specifically. Wars can be very good for the pocketbook.

Jackson said, "They're killin' our people, Milstein." Slicing the bonds that held the dead man's hands to his ankles, he seemed to be showing the deceased a kindness. Milstein found it bizarre, particularly when the dead man's stiffened appendages didn't release comfortably to his side but held their distorted, painful position. "This man," Jackson said, "took out one of our transports, killed three of our people. What would you have me do? Tickle him?"

"People under torture will say anything. It's proven that other methods of interrogation work better. How the hell do you know I won't report this to the high command?"

"Go ahead. You think it'll surprise 'em?"

Milstein looked up at the taller man. At five feet seven inches, the history teacher from Brookline, Massachusetts, was no match for the six-footer from Tennessee. His Semitic features and dark complexion made him resemble Tikriti far more than he did the all-American rough-and-tumble Jackson, whose gray eyes studied Milstein as if to determine whose side the interloper was really on.

Milstein turned away to look back at Tikriti. "You got the directive from MI. This man has special non-military information that could be vital to our efforts. This kind of abuse is beneath us."

Jackson shrugged. "His story is absurd. He's bluffin' to save his skin."

"That's for me to decide, not you," Milstein said. "I outrank you."

He stepped out of the cell. Jackson followed him.

"Any logical mind can see that he is tryin' to buy his freedom with a story so outrageous it's laughable."

"But you are here," Tikriti said. "And you aren't laughing." Tikriti raised his head to gaze wearily at Milstein. "Get the woman out of here," he said. "I won't talk until she is gone and I have my clothes back."

Milstein nodded. Men of Tikriti's culture were frightened more by emasculation at the hands of a woman than by the truncheons, knives, and electric wires used by professional male torturers. Milstein ordered the woman, her dog, and everyone else besides himself and Jackson from the area. Then he personally wiped Tikriti's wounds and helped dress him.

"Milstein as Christ," Jackson grunted.

"Milstein as human being," Milstein replied. He waited as Tikriti gulped down a cold can of Coke left by one of the soldiers. Tikriti had eluded authorities for a year before a Shi'ite architect who had been sodomized with a cattle prod by Tikriti's men, identified him. Almost immediately, Tikriti had begun to babble about bodies, artifacts and Jesus. That was when Milstein, originally sent to Iraq to help in the recovery process of that nation's looted antiquities, became involved. Once Tikriti seemed recovered enough to take his questions, Milstein began.

"It is my understanding that you have possession of items that belonged to Imran Fawzi."

"Yes."

"Imran Fawzi has disappeared."

Ghazi shrugged. "Your missiles frightened a lot of people."

"Maybe he was killed because of things he had in his possession," Milstein said.

"Looters." Ghazi gazed at his interrogator with cool self-assurance that had been severely lacking only moments before.

"If you stole Fawzi's items, archaeological artifacts, then you are a looter," Milstein said.

"He gave them to me of his own free will."

"You mean you tortured him."

"No, we met as your bombs were hurtling down on us. He wanted me to contact Hussein. He figured Saddam could use them as a bargaining chip to keep you Americans from attacking us. I knew better."

"You still have them?" Milstein asked.

"Of course."

"Where?"

Tikriti managed a smile and kept his silence.

Milstein pulled up a metal folding chair and sat in front of Tikriti who had slumped to the cold concrete floor. Like Jackson, Milstein had been in Iraq before. As a multi-lingual member of Military Intelligence, Milstein had been assigned to Iraq during the First Gulf War to encourage the southern Shi'ites and the Marsh Arabs to rebel against Saddam. When the first Bush administration bailed out, the insurrection failed and everything went to hell. Ghazi Al-Tikriti had been largely responsible for that hell. As far as Milstein was concerned, he had a grand opportunity to make amends.

"Tell me about the things Fawzi showed you," he said.

"The skeleton of a child. He called her by a Hebrew name, which was etched into the urn I also have. As well as the name of the child, the urn described her lineage. Do you mind if I smoke?" Ghazi reached into the pocket of his shirt and pulled out a pack of Gauloises cigarettes. "The names meant nothing to me," he said, holding the cigarette out for Milstein to light. "Rivkah. Hannaniah."

"Hannaniah?" At the sound of the second name, Milstein bolted to attention. His migraine evaporated and his eyes fastened on Tikriti. "Are you sure?" he demanded. "Hannaniah? That was the name Fawzi mentioned?"

"The daughter, if I am to understand correctly, of your prophet Jesus."

"Mr. Milstein's Jewish," Jackson said. "His prophet is Chase Manhattan."

Milstein ignored Jackson. "Can you confirm this?" he asked.

"Yes. There was a body. The urn had Hebrew letters on it. And something else. A diary. Mohamoud Jama kept a diary."

Both Milstein and Jackson hooked Ghazi with sharp stares.

Unfazed by either of them, Ghazi nodded toward Jackson. "In due course the diary," he said. "In surety for my freedom and as proof of my story, you might ask Mr. Jackson for the medallion he plucked from my clothes yesterday. Fawzi found it on the child's skeleton."

"Mr. Jackson?"

Milstein held out his hand to an embarrassed and slightly reluctant Jackson who fished Tikriti's medallion from a shirt pocket. Milstein swept it out of Jackson's hand then held it up to the light. A Star of David, two inches high, two inches long, and rather heavy for its size. Six mysterious symbols had been carved at the points. Milstein stared at them. Almost immediately, his head throbbed again, the migraine lashed at him, the whips of his constricted blood vessels routed pain throughout his body. A sun of intense light exploded before his eyes, and the interrogation room disappeared.

"Milstein!" someone called, but the voice was so distant as to be nearly imperceptible.

When he opened his eyes, he was no longer in Abu Ghraib Prison in the western suburbs of Baghdad. He was no longer in Iraq or, for that matter, in the twenty-first century.

He stood outside the white walls of a magnificent city. The sky was blue. Orchards of olive trees stretched down into a lush, beautiful valley. All around him people mingled, hauling goods to market, fetching water, all dressed in robes or rags. There were donkeys, sheep, dogs. Milstein needed no brochure or map to tell him where he was. Or when. He had been here before, though he had admitted this to only one other person.

Jerusalem.

Glancing down at his arms, he saw that he no longer wore a suit coat and tie but was instead, like many around him, dressed in the robes of a pilgrim with a woolen hood protecting him from the hot sun. When he heard his name called, he was stunned to be recognized. But the person did not call him Milstein. She shouted someone else's name, yet it was so obviously his that he turned around and almost called back to her. Would have, had his voice not caught in his throat.

She was so lovely to look at. Red hair. Green eyes. No woman in this lifetime or any other had captivated him so. And when he finally managed to blurt out her name, he cried out in Hebrew, and Tikriti and Jackson heard him as well. "Hannaniah! Hannaniah, it's me!"

"Milstein! You all right?" Jackson shouted, shaking him. "What in the hell was that all about?"

Milstein glanced at Tikriti who had risen to peer down at him. Milstein had toppled off his chair onto the floor like an epileptic in the throes of a seizure. Bracing himself on a table, he pulled himself together as best he could. What could he tell his colleague or the other that they would possibly believe? He smiled reassuringly and told Jackson, "I'm all right. It's these damned migraines. Do you mind …?"

Milstein left Tikriti and walked down a long hall past the two subdued Dobermans and their military masters to a water bubbler for a cold drink. There was no doubt in his mind now that Ghazi Al-Tikriti was telling the truth. He could never explain to Jackson just why he knew this was so. Only one other man would understand. Perhaps one woman, too. The woman he had seen in Jerusalem. Or, at least, the woman who bore such a strikingly similar face to Hannaniah, daughter of Jesus, that she might as well be the same person. Molly O'Dwyer.

Milstein crumpled the paper water cup and tossed it into a trashcan. Somehow, some way, he was going to go after the greatest artifact ever found, the one that Ghazi suggested lay at the end of the archaeological rainbow. But first he needed to take a trip, because he couldn't possibly make the next journey alone. He would convince his military handlers to let him go. He would go back to Boston, where he had been raised, where he had gone to college, and where he had first run into the woman of his dreams. He would bring back Molly O'Dwyer one way or another.

CHAPTER 6

Good Friday, Boston, Massachusetts

"Let us pray for God's ancient people, the Jews, the first to hear His word."

So worshipped the congregation of teachers and students at the afternoon Vespers service on Good Friday in the Mt. Auburn College chapel. The pews were filled, standing room only in the back hall and in the balcony overlooking the podium. Faith had never exempted itself from the academic community, not even here in liberal, ungodly Boston. Professors taught quantum mechanics. Students prepared for careers in medicine, business, law. But even amongst the most cynical atheists, faith of one kind or another resided beneath the veneer of intellectual skepticism.

Molly sat right up front in the first row beside her analyst and friend, Father Ray Teague, and directly behind the college president. The presiding priest's version of this old prayer was the result of reforms made at the Second Vatican Council. The traditional prayer went, "Let us pray for the perfidious Jews: that our God and Lord may remove the veil from their hearts." But the change, Molly suspected, still contained a subtle anti-Semitic message. While the Jews had been the first to hear His word, they had also been the first to reject it. Perhaps she was reading too much into the restructured prayer. Then again, she had translated the Gospel of Hannaniah, she who claimed to be the daughter of the messiah. Hannaniah was a Jew who hadn't rejected her father's words. But Molly's interpretation of them was far different from the Vatican's. *Some things change*, Molly thought, but oh so slowly and in general not nearly enough.

The Church—her Church—had been embroiled in so much controversy lately that it required effort to defend it against many of her academic colleagues who belittled it as archaic and incapable of growth and change. Priestly pedophiles and apparent church forbearance for the perpetrators had tied the Boston diocese up in budget-killing litigation. Aggressive opposition to gay marriage, the threat of withholding church sacraments to Catholic politicians who supported abortion as a choice, the failure to recognize women as equals of men, all of these pulled dangerously at the straining strands of her faith. There were those lay Catholics who were organizing and fundraising to build a counter-movement to the conservative hierarchy that controlled the Church. But while Molly opposed her Church on all matters that seemed unjust to her, she had never lost faith in what really mattered.

Molly shifted in her seat. Light streamed through the stained-glass windows above and to her right. Father Ray was nodding off. And if truth be known, Molly's mind was anywhere but here.

They had called her into the chancellor's office five years ago and begged her not to publish, cajoled her, threatened her. Three powerful men. The chancellor, an eminent scholar himself; Bishop Braddock, representing the Boston archdiocese; and a state senator with strong ties to Washington. Each one in turn had made his point that it was one thing for gold-digging writers to speculate on such things as Noah's Ark, the whereabouts of heaven, and the humanity of Jesus. It was something quite else for an academic of Molly's standing to bring to light things that should never be revealed.

Sitting in church five years later, Molly could still feel the heat in the chancellor's office where she had been forced to sit in the hot spill of June sunlight pouring through the window to fall directly into her eyes and onto her lap. She felt as though she had walked into a trap and sat before a board of inquiry despite their initial polite gestures and offers of tea.

"You are an amazing woman," the chancellor had told her, a very tall man, who sat erect in his chair behind his desk out of the sunlight. "You are a respected member of this community. But, as you know, we have procedures, long-standing protocols. No one publishes, whether in biology or literature or any field, without putting their ideas before a body of their peers for review. It benefits the writer and safeguards our standing in the academic community."

"I sent my manuscript to you, Chancellor," Molly had told him.

"Yes, but after the fact. It was done. You were ready to go with it, with or without our approval."

"It is not a matter of academic credibility," Bishop Braddock said, stepping in. He had recently been brought into the archdiocese from New Orleans, an outsider, to clean up the publicity nightmare created by the pedophile priests, a controversy which was nothing, in his mind, to the one Molly was about to kindle. "Your work is of the highest repute. But that is the problem. Your word will be accepted as truth."

"As it should. I only report what I find. I am a good Catholic, Father. My work will not hurt the faith. It will only bring new light to it."

"That is where we part company, Ms. O'Dwyer," the third man, the politician, had said. "Please understand, we don't take freedom of speech lightly. But you can't yell fire in a movie theatre. You can't parade a swastika through a Jewish neighborhood. And you can't tell Christians that the Son of God is not the Son of God. Not without consequences."

Molly hadn't had time to think about those consequences. The chancellor threatened her tenure. The Bishop threatened her soul. The politician threatened a lawsuit. In the end, it was too late anyway. She had sent her manuscript to a friend, who had forwarded it to a publisher, who was so enthusiastic that the manuscript was practically on the presses ready to be printed and marketed globally. Fortunately for the Church, only a few copies had been distributed for review before the chancellor, the bishop, and the politician could put a to stop it. Unfortunately, someone had pirated the manuscript, reproduced it for Internet consumption, and made it available for anyone with a computer to read, print, and pass along.

Molly had survived, but only because she had retracted publicly, recanted, gone against all she believed in, explaining to the world that Hannaniah was still only a vague distant figure, perhaps real, perhaps not. The Vatican had come out strongly against works of fiction that dealt with such controversial matter, let alone academic publications such as hers. For a member of the Catholic faith to read such works was deemed sinful by Rome. And so, like Galileo four hundred years before her, Molly had retreated and placed her faith before her science. Then she secretly began plotting her trip into Afghanistan. And now, with the chancellor retired, the Bishop promoted, and the state senator unseated, she had jumped back in again with both feet, not a single lesson learned.

Molly shifted and squirmed in her seat. Father Teague was right about her suffering from guilt. Even before she went into Afghanistan. She had been raised by a mother who, by all accounts, was as unchristian as she could be. Jane Stratton had been a Ph.D. at twenty-six, a prodigy, a pagan, a counterculture faculty member at Mt. Auburn, the single unmarried mother of a daughter she loved above all else. She had lived to profane the establishment and she had died as a result. Her fate weighed heavily on Molly's mind. Such were Molly's genes. Such was her pedigree.

But Molly could hardly remember her mother, who had died when Molly was five. Molly had been raised in the home of her mother's sister and brother-in-law, the O'Dwyers, good people, faithful Catholics who brought Molly into the Church. And the Church and Molly had been a good fit in those days. The Church had saved her life, kept her sane, showed her how her mother could still live, and live forever. It was the Church, in fact, that had led Molly into archaeology, introduced her to and nurtured her fascination for places biblical and mysterious. In the thirty-odd years since her mother's death, she had remained loyal to that Church despite all.

But life knew full well how to complicate things. Now came Nina Cavalcante and her incredible proposition, one that, if true, could overturn everything, change the world in such a way that it would never be the same again and probably not for the better.

Bishop Braddock had told her that the Church is not a democracy, that Church leaders need to be able to control the mass of lay worshippers to avoid chaos and a descent into immorality.

Partly for that reason, Molly had turned down Cavalcante's offer last night. It was one thing to translate scrolls purportedly written by the illegitimate child of Jesus. That was an intellectual pursuit of a drama that, in truth, could have been a work of fiction. The daughter's account might be impossible to corroborate, although Molly's find in Afghanistan was a step in that direction. Finding the actual remains of Hannaniah, though, would be different, beyond the intellectual into the spiritual realm. Bodies might contain DNA. DNA might fingerprint a real human being who had walked with Jesus, sat in his lap, cuddled with him, cherished him, and knew him for what he really was.

Molly's faith was strong enough to accept whatever she found, but she was less certain about the strength of those whose faith led them to see Jesus or the Virgin Mary in the shadow on a window. Wasn't she obligated to them? To sustain their fragile beliefs?

Why then did she squirm uncomfortably in her chair, mind not at all on Vespers, but instead on the faxed document and Mohamoud Jama's Star of David drawing, clues that might corroborate Molly's feeling that Jesus' resurrection had not occurred, and that Good Friday was a tradition based upon apostolic spin?

"We have established a community by the rivers," Hannaniah had written to one of her children. "I have returned to the father of all to finish my days. But all is not done. You will hear more from me. My words are as my father's. Listen to me and establish your rule based upon his wisdom."

Molly would never forget those words. She was an archaeologist first and foremost, a seeker of truth. From the moment she had first stumbled upon Hannaniah on the fringes of the Sahara, she had left her faith behind and plunged into a different world. She could never have made Bishop Braddock understand. Hannaniah had set Molly's world to spinning, so much so that Molly would have forsaken all—her academic career, her personal life, the comfortable relationship she had with her Church—just to know more. Would have and almost did. What's more, Hannaniah had penetrated Molly's dreams.

Yet she had turned Cavalcante down and now she was sleepless and irritable. She could not betray her Church. She could not undermine the faith of hundreds of millions of people. Her own didn't matter. Her own prejudices and beliefs aside, she would never shatter another person's very hold on reality.

And yet, the blood that coursed through her veins, nourished her body, fed her intellect, would not let her sit still. If the truth was out there, she needed to be the one to find it. When it came down to it, she was her mother's child, not the Church's.

She had to follow Cavalcante. Hannaniah compelled her. Touching the decaying scrolls, Molly could almost see and feel Hannaniah, breathe her and be her.

Nina Cavalcante, Teodor Kwiatkowski, and whoever was funding them, were unconcerned about whose faith would be trampled. They were willing to unleash a tsunami against the exposed shores of Christian faith and would do it with or without Molly.

But if I went with them …

"Molly."

She looked up. The chapel was empty except for her and Father Teague who was shaking her shoulder. "I don't suppose you remember any of it," he said. Molly frowned. "The service. Where were you?"

"Oh, nowhere." Molly stood up, embarrassed and a bit dazed. She brushed off her blue skirt, the closest thing she had to Sunday best, and accompanied her friend down the central aisle of the chapel to the campus common.

Outside, a warm afternoon sun sent her shadow down the walkway just ahead of her. Hers was just a little longer than Teague's. "What if I told you," she said, "that someone handed me a fragment of a parchment, an ancient letter, written by Jesus' grandchild to his daughter, asking them to join her in a newly established community, after the crucifixion? Would you tear it up? Would you publish it? Keep it a secret? What would you do?"

"I'd probably go out and get drunk," Teague said. "Why? Has such a letter come into your possession?" He waited, studying her face. "Does such a thing exist?"

"Apparently," Molly said. "I saw it last night. Or a fragment of it. I suspect there's more. Lots more."

Teague stopped dead in his tracks. Around them students walked, jogged, and biked, taking advantage of the beautiful spring day.

"A fraud, a forgery," he said.

Molly shook her head, resting her chin in her hand. "I don't think so."

"A joke. A mistake. Another Shroud of Turin. Medieval, yes, but not biblical."

Again, Molly shook her head. "I trust the source, for one thing. For another, it corroborates my findings in Afghanistan. Whether Hannaniah was Jesus' daughter or just some love-struck convert, she relentlessly pushed his ministry, far more than he was able to. Thirty years after the crucifixion, the Jews rebelled against Rome. Rome won, sacked Jerusalem, burned and destroyed it. The survivors fled Israel. Hannaniah established settlements throughout the ancient world not just to keep her people bound to each other, but bound, as well, to her father's ministry. Wherever these settlements exist, of course, there are graveyards. And bodies."

"My God."

"That's not the half of it."

"Do I want to know the other half?" Teague said.

"The people who possess this letter want to look for those bodies." Molly looked up. A young couple passed with two little girls in tow. She recognized the mother as a lecturer in anthropology and had often seen her daughters cavorting in the playground just outside their offices. Seeing them always reminded her of her own biological clock. At thirty-five, she felt the ache of motherhood unfulfilled.

"Who is 'they'?" Teague asked.

"People I trust. Well, at least one of them. I don't know who they are."

"My God."

"You said that already, Father. But that doesn't answer my question. What do you do?"

Teague had no answer. "What did you do?"

"I said, no. Now I'm not so sure that's the right answer. They'll go without me."

Molly sighed and walked on. Teague accompanied her in silence down the tar path, through the campus green. Mt. Auburn was a Catholic Jesuit college. Because of her mother's status as a professor here at the time of her death, Molly had been a fixture of one kind or another for more than thirty years, as a child, later as a student, and finally as a professor. Mt. Auburn wasn't just a college campus to her. It was a familiar neighborhood. It had been her home, her turf, her hangout. She had practically grown up here while living with an aunt and uncle, studied here, found and lost love here, become a woman. More important, the whole blood and spirit of her life had been watched over by the selfsame Church that now employed her to teach here. Going after the bodily remains of Hannaniah and possibly other descendants of the man she knew as the Son of God could destroy it all.

At the entrance to the science building, Molly said goodbye to Teague. She spent the rest of the day in her office reading through her translation of the Hannaniah gospel. In the evening, having skipped dinner, she headed home in darkness. Her headlights played off the maple and oak trees that lined her home street in North Dorchester. Her windshield wipers worked against a fine mist that blew off the ocean nearby. A storm headed in from the south, but Molly's mind was elsewhere.

She was unprepared to find Nina Cavalcante camped out on the front porch of her house, smoking a cigarette, and holding an umbrella overhead. Molly looked around for any sign of a car or

Cavalcante's Polish bodyguard, Kwiatkowski, but she saw neither.

"This reminds me of London," Cavalcante said as Molly exited her VW and headed up the stairs onto the porch of her modest two-family house in its modest neighborhood of mostly white working-class families. People here tended either to go to church on a regular basis or pretend to. They prayed for the Red Sox, put their money on the Patriots, and watched their favorite reality TV shows, all too well aware that reality normally sucked while living out the credo 'better them than us.' Molly would have raised a child here, much as her mother had, even without a dad. But unlike her iconoclastic mother, Molly preferred the retro ideal of mom, dad, and Sunday afternoon with the kids. Her life just didn't seem ready for it yet.

"I haven't been to London in years," Molly said. "I've never been to Warsaw." Unlocking a briefcase, she handed Cavalcante the Hannaniah document. "I believe this is yours. It wasn't written by Hannaniah, you know."

"It wasn't?"

Molly unlocked the door into her front hallway. "Hannaniah has a very distinct scroll, very florid, very romantic. I think one of her children wrote it. I wish you had told me about these correspondences in your letters to me."

"For reasons that will become clear to you, I couldn't. You don't mind, do you?" she asked, hesitating at the door.

"Of course, come in. Where's your significant other?"

"I gave Teodor the night off." Inside the foyer, Cavalcante folded up her umbrella. "If you seriously want me to come with you, Nina, to Warsaw or wherever, you have some damned difficult explaining to do."

Cavalcante brightened. "You mean you'll come? *Brava!*" Under the chandelier light in the hallway, Cavalcante looked like a brown-haired fawn, a young girl in jeans and an 'I Kissed the Pope' T-shirt. She looked more like a student than a teacher, more like a roommate than a colleague, a waif with the energy to climb mountains.

"But you see," she said excitedly, following Molly down the hall toward the kitchen, "that is just my point. You've seen something none of the rest of us ever has! Hannaniah's fingerprints. Her style. Her way of thinking. We can't succeed without you!"

"I'd like to know who that 'we' is. Is Mohamoud Jama in on this with you?"

"Mohamoud Jama is dead."

"Dead?"

"Killed in Iraq. I don't know the circumstances. *Mi scusi.* I know you were close to him."

"Close until Egypt."

In the kitchen, Molly took a small white metal box from the refrigerator. Inside the box was a bottle of insulin. From there, she led Cavalcante into her bathroom where she kept a box of non-reusable syringes. Unabashedly, she lifted her shirt to expose the flesh of her taut belly. In went the needle.

"Diabetes," she said. "Controllable but annoying."

"I haven't used a needle in years," Cavalcante said with a shrug. "But that was years ago when I was a kid. Amphetamines. Bad for the body, good for the mind. I had my first *allucinazioni* then. Dreams. Visions. Ancient ghosts that go bump in the night."

Molly eyed Cavalcante through the mirror over her bathroom sink. The Italian archaeologist certainly had a way of throwing out surprising morsels of information.

"Have you eaten?" she asked. "Ebenezer Scrooge believed his ghosts were a product of bad pudding."

"I eat like a pig. I'm one of those people who can eat and eat and stay as thin as spaghetti, but I'm not hungry now. No, dear, my visions aren't induced by food poisoning. They are real."

Molly avoided Cavalcante's eyes, thinking of her own visions, her nightmares, and what they might mean. Reality gone haywire. "Do you mind if I eat while you talk?" She returned to the kitchen and scrounged in her refrigerator for two cold slices of pizza that went into her microwave. "Egypt was a remarkable moment for me. But it's screwed up my life royally ever since. For Mohamoud, I think, it was even worse. I think he went a little bit mad."

"I heard," Nina said. "He never dug again."

"No. He pursued other interests." As the timer went off, she asked, "Where do we think Hannaniah is buried?"

"You must have some ideas," Cavalcante said.

"I asked you first."

Cavalcante sat at Molly's small kitchen table. Her briefcase lay at her feet. "Iraq," she said.

"What?" Dropping into a chair opposite Cavalcante, Molly ignored the bubbling slices of pizza. "You are kidding, right?"

"A year ago our funder got word through a friend that Mohamoud Jama had made an historic find somewhere in the desert between Baghdad and the border with Syria."

"He did? He never said anything to me. In any case, we are at war in Iraq," Molly said. "Does that ring a bell?"

"Apparently Jama had been so upset by it, he kept it a secret from everyone for many years."

"Including me," Molly said. She didn't even feel the sizzling mozzarella cheese and tomato sauce slide down her throat. "Jama wasn't Muslim. He was Syrian Christian. Devout. Tolerated by Saddam, but just barely. The discovery of Hannaniah's Gospels meant as much to him as to me."

"But whereas you published an in-depth account of your discovery, Jama went further, *si?*"

"I was fucking naïve. Mohamoud was rattled."

"Rattled? Or exhilarated? What did he do, Molly?"

"Went out and got drunk. Besides the scroll gospels, we also found the remains of an adult female buried in an urn. The remains may have belonged to a child of Hannaniah's, a grandchild of Jesus himself. Once he was sober again, Mohamoud insisted on taking DNA samples of everyone within eyeshot looking for descendants of the messiah. Because he thought they might be able to perform miracles, too? Who knows? He went crazy. Some things science should just tiptoe around and leave well enough hidden."

"But you're the one who got published. You're a scientist, Molly. A good one. *Il migliore.* The best! Truth must always be revealed. Why do you have reservations now?"

"About Iraq?" Molly asked. "Christ, yes, I have reservations! I didn't publish my book on Hannaniah! It was stolen and reproduced without my permission. I took hell for that, am still taking hell for it."

"But you went to Afghanistan."

"I'm a masochist. In any case, how the hell would we get into Iraq? Now of all times."

"Through Poland. With their troops."

Cavalcante rested her elbows on the table and stared across it into Molly's eyes. It was only then that Molly noticed the cross pendant that hung around Cavalcante's neck. Molly wore a similar one. "We have to go in, Molly," Cavalcante said. "No matter what. Iraqi intelligence got their hands on the find. The officer who was trying to sell the information for his freedom was taken prisoner. What he knows, American intelligence may know as well. The philosophical question of whether or not we should disturb Christian faith is of no matter. Who do you want to find Hannaniah's remains? Us or U.S. military intelligence? The thinkers or the fundamentalists?"

"That's some choice."

Molly hardly tasted her pizza. She nibbled at the edges and gazed at Cavalcante's unopened briefcase.

"Even after the Iraqi intelligence officer, a relative of Saddam's, contacted us," Cavalcante continued, "we didn't know what we had. The buried remains of a child, entombed in an urn with Hebrew writing, the name Hannaniah included. If accurate, it might be interesting but not enough for us to move on it. Then you published your findings from Afghanistan and, *voila*, connections were made, information was validated. Hannaniah established communities throughout the old world to spread her father's faith. Your own interpretation of Hannaniah's scrolls says that Jesus, Yeshuah, may have survived the crucifixion. If he did, then perhaps he died in one of those communities. Who knows? Anything is possible. We think the location of that community is what Jama discovered."

Molly's heart fluttered. "And Jesus?"

Cavalcante shrugged.

Molly took in a deep breath.

"In Iraq," she said, the cool scientist in her trying to nudge aside the faithful unsettled Catholic. "Any idea where?"

"Jama didn't tell you?"

"I told you, he was either drunk or distracted. He wasn't the same man I knew. He was desperate, and he wouldn't answer my questions. Only that he'd made a find that Egypt substantiated. Once he saw my work on a goddamned hacker's website, he no longer trusted me. It seems I angered everyone."

"Not me." Nina leaned across the small kitchen table and took Molly's hands in hers.

"The Iraqi intelligence officer said that Jama kept a diary. That's all we know. We don't know the contents except for that single page you saw. We don't know if the Iraqi intelligence officer was telling the truth or bluffing. Jama is dead. The other man who might have been able to help us, Imran Fawzi, has vanished."

"Great. We're already cursed and we haven't left Boston." Try as she might, Molly couldn't control the rapid thumping of her heart. Above, her brain urged caution. *Say 'no,' Molly. Jama's dead. Fawzi. You'll be next. Or institutionalized.* But tugging from below, her gut, the very core of her being, demanded, *Go! It's your destiny. Yours and no one else's.* The wobbly metal legs of the table rattled as Molly's knees hit them. "You're flying blind," she said at last. "Iraq is a big country. Where do you start digging?"

Cavalcante smiled, gripped Molly's hands, for it was clear which side in Molly's struggle had won out. "That's where you come in," Nina said. "My colleagues think they know where to begin. I think you know. I think you know the same way you knew where to dig in Afghanistan. I think it is inside you, the same way Mohamoud Jama knew it was inside you."

"Me?"

"Your dreams, Molly. You have them, too, don't you? As I do and Jama did. Christ is reaching out to us from beyond the grave."

"Then you're not only flying blind, you're flying crazy."

Abruptly, Molly stood up, separating from Cavalcante. And yet she knew that Nina wasn't crazy. Not at all.

Shutting her eyes, she rolled back her head and let herself relive the moment she had stumbled upon Hannaniah's scrolls near Thebes. It was as though she had been struck by lightning and cast through a portal in time to return to that same spot two thousand years before. Hannaniah had lived and breathed and produced a library of literature. She must have been an explosive force, a powerful figure, yet one that history had chosen to ignore, until Molly had come along and deciphered Hannaniah's lamentations. She was no longer in Boston in the twenty-first century. She was back, far back in time, at a place that the daughter of Jesus might have known.

"Ur," she said, suddenly opening her eyes. "Ur of the Chaldees."

"Molly, you are a genius!" Cavalcante exclaimed. "That's what I predicted!" Startling Molly, Nina pulled her down and planted a kiss on her forehead. "I told them!" she said. "I told them! I, too, said it would be Ur. Jesus returned to his roots beyond the borders of the Roman Empire, safe from the carnage and reprisals of the Jewish revolution. It all makes sense, Molly!"

Crouching, she took Molly's face in her hands and held her with her eyes.

"Molly, trust me!" she whispered. "We are sisters. That's what my heart says. That we have been and will be. No matter what happens, no matter what else you learn, trust me in everything!"

Trust? If Molly was taken aback by Cavalcante's unexpected emotion, she didn't show her surprise. After all, she had secrets, too.

Hannaniah's Gospels spoke of the child Hannaniah's life with her father, a controversial enough concept, but did not go further. It took a considerable leap of logic to conclude that Jesus had survived the crucifixion. The Hannaniah that Molly knew could easily have invented a father for political purposes. Women fell in love with charismatic men. Maybe Hannaniah had concocted a story for attention or power. Yet everything that Molly had found since then was leading her to believe otherwise, that Hannaniah hadn't been playing with history, that she had been telling the truth all along. That her father was Jesus and he had survived the crucifixion. The remains found in the urn in Egypt, Hannaniah's scrolls, the lamentation poem that led her to Afghanistan, the Hebrew writing on the tomb in the Afghani foothills—all led Molly to conclude that Hannaniah was more than a first century con artist.

Cavalcante released Molly. She put her briefcase on the table and opened it.

"This is the only other piece of information we received from Iraq. A photograph of something found in the urn with the child. Does it look familiar?"

Molly wiped her greasy fingers on a paper napkin before allowing herself to touch the photograph. Holding it close to her face she studied the picture. The color photo showed a clay fragment in a black desk rack. Cavalcante handed Molly a magnifying glass for closer inspection.

"It was on the urn found in Jama's house," Cavalcante said. "You can make out in Hebrew the name Rivkah. Above the name, though, you see …? Some kind of symbol. Have you seen anything like it before? A jagged V."

Molly nodded, breathless. "The Star of David has similar markings." She handed the photograph back to Cavalcante. "And you have something else? You must have," she said, abrupt and too anxious to tolerate any further avoidance. "Nina, if we're going to work together, you need to be more forthcoming than you have been. So far, you have information that leads you to conclude that Hannaniah persisted, but you have nothing that proves her father did. Yet something led you to consider Ur, too. What is it? What other information do you have?"

With a sigh, Cavalcante shut and locked her briefcase.

"We have the other half of Hannaniah's gospels."

Andrew Milstein landed at Logan Airport on Easter Sunday morning. He had tried to take an earlier flight, begged his bosses to scramble a jet to get him back to the States asap, but the best they would do was a military flight to Berlin and a connector civilian flight to Boston. Against his wishes, the civilian interrogator, Richard Jackson, was ordered to accompany him. Their mutual boss, Army Intelligence Major General Jim Eisenstadt, had demanded it.

"I've got 130,000 American soldiers in the line of fire here," he had ranted after Milstein had brought him Ghazi's tale. "I've got fourteen hundred dead already and bodybags that ain't goin' away empty. And guess what: elections be damned, we ain't goin' anywhere. Fact is, we're gonna be addin' more troops."

Sitting in Eisenstadt's spacious office in the safe Green Zone of Baghdad, Milstein hunched forward, elbows on knees, not particularly paying attention to the command staff's complaints, wishing the chain of command had ended with the State Department, which would have been more receiving of his request.

Jackson was cleaning his Glock 21 pistol, capable of firing off thirteen deadly rounds before reloading, while taking in everything Eisenstadt said.

"The President will never forego his responsibilities to the people of Iraq," Eisenstadt assured them. "But frankly, this shit's a mess. And it ain't goin' away. There are only so many fires you can put out. Men get tired, frustrated. They want to go home." Eisenstadt turned to Milstein. "We need something to counter all this bad publicity. If what you say is out there," he said, "that may be our counter. The people who support the president won't let us abandon it to Muslim terrorists. They'll demand we hunker down as long as needed to find and protect it."

Milstein looked up, horrified. "You're not going to leak this to the press?"

"Hell, no," Eisenstadt said. "I'm not even tellin' the president until it's a done deal. You just get that young lady back here, if you think she can get the job done. Don't let her say no, y'understand?"

Milstein had no intention of letting that happen.

After Milstein had left the office, Eisenstadt pulled Jackson aside. "Make sure she doesn't say no, Rick. The lady, as I understand it, can be awfully hardheaded. I don't think Milstein's got the legs to do what has to be done."

Jackson, of course, had enough for both of them, as he'd shown the stubborn Tikriti. He departed Baghdad with a smile, and he was still smiling as he stood outside Logan Airport beside Milstein though it wasn't the thought of action that pleased him. It was the money. Civilian life had been good to Richard Jackson. Iraq was going to make him a multimillionaire.

Milstein was thinking similar thoughts, though not with avarice. There were four major religions in the Middle East: Islam, Christianity, Judaism, and Capitalism, the latter being by far the oldest and most cherished. Dollar signs moved everyone. The bottom line. Profit. If what was buried in the Iraqi desert was worth a few unplanned dollars, who wouldn't buy in? Of course, the contractors could always write it off as a military necessity, Milstein thought, and let the president pay for it.

Throwing a fifty-dollar bill at a taxi driver, Milstein said, "Newton. Mt. Auburn College." Then he and Jackson hopped into the back seat, Milstein carrying the only suitcase he'd taken. Holding up another

Ulysses S. Grant for the driver to see through the rearview mirror, he said, "This is yours if you get us there in a half hour."

"Guess you haven't been to Boston lately," the cabbie said.

The two intelligence contractors could easily have connected to Newton via the transit system, Blue Line to Green Line all the way out to the collage. But Milstein was in a hurry. As traffic on I-93 flew by and the taxi entered the new harbor tunnel into Boston, he opened his suitcase and pulled out the manila folder that contained the FBI's dossier on Molly O'Dwyer.

Milstein cringed at how much private information the government had on her. If they had an inch-thick file on Molly O'Dwyer, imagine what they had on him. But then he had always been a pretty good boy, from a respectable family, served his country, paid his taxes. Molly, on the other hand …

He gazed at her face, a file photograph from the *Boston Globe* taken after her last publication. My God, he thought. She has the exact same face. They could be clones.

He loved that face and found himself staring at it as the taxi rose up out of the tunnel and headed west on the Massachusetts Turnpike, emerging from the heavily-trafficked underworld within home run distance of Fenway Park.

Reluctantly he put Molly's picture back in the file and reviewed the material he'd already pored over on the flight across the Atlantic. If he knew his Molly, he'd catch her on campus, in the chapel, at Easter services. The FBI was well aware Professor O'Dwyer had many contacts in the Muslim world, had traveled to the Middle East frequently, had entered Afghanistan illegally, for which she had been reprimanded but little else, and had supported many liberal causes in the past. They didn't consider her a threat, but they took no chances. Regrettably, their analysis of her hadn't ended there. They knew what movies she preferred, where she ate lunch, what books she took out of the school library, who her friends and lovers were. In short, Milstein surmised, somebody at Mt. Auburn College had ratted her out.

He closed the suitcase. "You'll let me do the talking?" he asked Jackson.

"She's all yours. I'm just along for the ride."

"Good. You and the Dobermans worry me."

Many a would-be athlete lived in the western suburbs of the city, which were just awakening in pinks, whites, and greens from the long winter. Easter Sunday meant that the Boston Marathon was a week away. Joggers were out in packs, stretching, dreaming of crossing the finish line first. Milstein had been an all–Ivy League swimmer. He preferred the water to inhaling car exhaust, whereas Molly had been a long distance runner at Mt. Auburn. He had graduated the same year she had, a transfer from Dartmouth, and as the taxi turned onto the college campus, Milstein directed the driver to the chapel.

Damn, he thought. People were already coming out, but the taxi driver had earned his extra fare. Milstein threw him the second fifty then carried his suitcase up the sidewalk and down the asphalt path to the chapel. Jackson had sent his bags ahead to their airport hotel.

It had been a while since Milstein had visited his alma mater. He wondered if he might recognize anybody. He did. Father Ray Teague.

"Ray!" he shouted. "Ray!"

"Andrew?" Teague looked up from a conversation he was having with two of his students, in short sleeves and cut-offs the day was so mild. Jackson hung back at a respectable distance as Milstein offered a smile and a hand.

"Captain Milstein," Teague said, looking up into the blue eyes of

HUNTING THE KING ■ 83

the Jewish boy. "I heard you were in …"

"Iraq, yes, sir."

"Just now?"

"Just now. But as a civilian, not military." Milstein lowered his suitcase, looked past Teague to the entrance of the chapel, New England in its simple white beauty. But that wasn't what interested him. "I'm hoping to meet somebody," he said. "I figured I might find her here."

"And you brought a suitcase?"

"I was in a hurry."

"Apparently. I hope she's worth it."

"Molly O'Dwyer," Milstein said, and Teague's smile vanished.

"Molly? Why Molly?"

"I can't tell you, Ray. Wish I could. Did you see her at service?"

Teague shook his head. "And that's unusual. She's a pretty orthodox kid when it comes to things like that. Much better than me, I have to say."

"Hell, I was hoping to talk to her." Milstein looked about, catching Jackson's unreadable eyes, anxious what to do next.

"If it'd help … Is it so important, it can't wait?"

Milstein sighed. "It probably can."

"You know, come to think of it," Teague said, "I did get a call from her yesterday. A message really. I didn't speak to her."

"Yes?"

"You may be out of luck."

"Out of luck? How?" Milstein's heart sank. He couldn't have come all this way for nothing.

"Well, she said she was going out of town. Today."

Now Jackson stepped in. "Any idea where?" he asked.

"I don't know," Teague said. "She sounded like a birthday girl. Very excited. Said the college had approved it. Sounds like she might be gone for a long time. If the college gave its consent, knowing Molly, I'd bet she's off on another dig."

Milstein and Jackson exchanged a look.

"Where does she live?" Jackson asked.

"We can't …"

"Sure we can. Where does she live, Father?"

"I can take you there, if you like. But I think you're going to be disappointed."

"Let us decide that."

Teague drove, but without the abandon of a Boston cabbie and without a working knowledge of Boston streets. By the time they reached Molly's two-family in North Dorchester, it was one in the afternoon. The first sign was good: Molly's VW was parked in her driveway. But when she didn't answer Milstein's buzzer, he had the gut feeling that someone else had gotten to her first, maybe the people Tikriti had originally contacted.

"Father," Jackson said to Teague, "do you mind standin' back?"

"Why?"

Jackson's right foot answered for him, crashing into the door at handle level. It took just two hard karate-style kicks to snap Molly's lock, chain, and door so that it crashed inward and gave Jackson, Milstein, and Teague the run of the place.

"Molly!" Milstein hollered. "Dr. O'Dwyer!"

A cat raced by his feet. On the refrigerator in the kitchen, Molly had left a detailed note to someone named Anicet on what and how much to feed Tabby. Teague accompanied Milstein who searched drawers and cupboards for any clue to where Molly had gone, when, and with whom. Jackson was less thoughtful, leaving plenty of debris on the floor for Tabby to play with.

"Nothin', nothin', nothin'," he cursed. "A woman doesn't just pick up and disappear like that without tellin' somebody somethin'."

"Unless," Milstein suggested, "she didn't want anybody to know."

"Yuh, well …" Jackson took out a cell phone and punched in a few numbers.

Suddenly Molly's phone rang. When Milstein reached for it, Jackson grabbed his hand to stop him and pushed the conference call button. "Just listen," he said as Molly's taped message to incoming callers played.

"Don't wait up for me. I'll be gone for a bit. You know, the usual. Try me in four weeks. *Do widzenia.*"

"*Do widzenia?*" Jackson wondered.

Milstein swiveled and headed for the door. "It means good-bye," he said. "In Polish."

They brought the two prisoners before Abdul Azim Nur at three in the morning, bound by ropes, heads covered in black hoods. According to their captors, they were a French engineer and his Iraqi lover. They had been kidnapped in the act out of a so-called safe area for foreign workers in Baghdad.

Nur was an early riser. He always had been, even as a child, going with his father and the other fishermen of their village to net the catch of the day, and later, as an adult, rising for early morning prayer. But this morning, his visitors had awoken him from a very sound and disturbing sleep. He would never have related to them the bizarre nature of his dream.

Sex was a troublingly common theme. Tonight he had been dreaming of engaging in intercourse. In it, Nur was not Nur. The female was unfamiliar to him. She was simply beautiful and every bit a hungry tigress, passionately embracing and kissing him under the imposing night skies of some barren desert wilderness. That he was having extremely pleasurable sex with her was not what bothered Nur. He was educated enough to understand that what the body desires but is denied will exclaim its frustration in dreams.

It was what happened after their sexual encounter that bothered him. The woman bore a litter of cats with red fur. He might have laughed this off were he not like Pharaoh, believing in the mythical power of dreams and needing a Joseph to interpret them. The litter of red-furred cats, as soon as they left their mother's womb, scattered in all directions, but wherever they went they cried for the man Nur was in his dream. And although they meowed as cats should, Nur understood what they were calling him. Father.

Groggy from sleep, he was miffed to be pulled out of the mud-brick hovel he called his temporary home in the Iraqi marshlands. The Iranian, Barid Shamkhazi, never seemed to need sleep. He would accompany Nur everywhere he went during the day and spend all night writing voluminous notes that he would copy, also by hand, to be sent by courier back to Tehran. Nur would just as soon have left Shamkhazi in Iran, but, after all, it was the ayatollahs' money that was funding his efforts, so he had little choice but to accept the young man's companionship.

"What have we here?" he asked as he stepped out the wooden door of his shack, fixing glasses on the bridge of his nose. "Who is it? Why have you brought them to me at this hour?"

"Prisoners," Barid explained. "One is a whore. The other a traitor."

"And they couldn't wait? Take off their hoods. Unbind them. We aren't Americans."

Nur forbade his followers, known by the Americans as insurgents, to engage in kidnapping. If a war must be fought, then so be it. But kidnapping blurred the line between war and terrorism, and Nur was no terrorist. He approached the two prisoners. Both trembled. The European was short, young, probably in his twenties. He emitted a volley of French once his gag was removed. Nur's reassuring reply relaxed the Frenchman.

"*Vous parlez francais?*" the man asked, praying this would mean he would not be executed.

"*Ne vous inquiétez pas.* Don't worry," Nur told him, turning his gaze on the second, much older man.

"Homosexuals," the Iranian cleric Shamkhazi said, as if nothing else needed to be said. "The foreigner, at least, is worth money."

"What need have I of money when I have you, Barid?"

"He is also connected to Rochefort Française, the largest European construction firm in Iraq. He can get us plans for all the engineering and reconstruction work being planned by the invaders."

Nur didn't care. His was a religious and political mission, not a scientific one. His attention was firmly on the older Iraqi male, who couldn't look Nur or anyone else for that matter straight in the eye.

"I know you," Nur said in such a harmless way that it shouldn't have frightened the man. But it did.

Dropping to his knees, the Iraqi prostrated himself before his captors and begged for his life. "I did nothing wrong," he said in Arabic so the Frenchman couldn't understand. "This man tricked me. He told me he had found an artifact, one of those stolen from the National Museum. I am Imran Fawzi, the director."

"Ah," Nur said non-commitally.

"Take his head," Barid advised. "He's no good to us except as an example to other collaborators."

"Besides which, he is homosexual," Nur said.

"Wicked in the eyes of Allah," Barid agreed.

Fawzi looked from one man to the other, begged for mercy from the holy man, and told him what he knew about Ghazi Al-Tikriti and Jesus buried somewhere in Iraq. Nur stared at him, angry that Fawzi would surrender his French lover to save himself and bothered beyond reason about his fanciful story of Jesus.

Barid Shamkhazi was not so conflicted. "You have told us the truth?" he asked. Fawzi nodded.

"You have told us everything?"

Again, Fawzi shook his head, not looking at the Frenchman, who understood none of this.

Barid turned to Nur. "You know this Tikriti?"

"The Serpent of Allah? Yes," Nur said. "Saddam's assassin. Why? He is now where he belongs. Abu Ghraib."

"Then he mustn't stay there." With a snap of his fingers, Barid signaled for the guards who had captured the Frenchman and the museum director to take them away. "We can free him. We have the power."

"No."

"Imam, Jesus is within the palm of your hand."

"If this coward is telling you the truth. And if you can trust that dog Tikriti. I say, no."

"Imam! Jesus!"

"I said, no!" Nur whirled about, fixing the Iranian with a cold glare, anger barely in check. "Mine is a holy mission. I won't desecrate it even for your money."

Barid gaped at the retreating back of the Iraqi holy man as it disappeared into the mud-brick shack. Nur himself couldn't explain why he had lashed out in such a manner. Something about the dream, something about the man in it and the woman. Maybe he was just overtired, sleep deprived. Or maybe it was something in Imran Fawzi's eyes when he spoke of Mohamoud Jama, a woman named Molly O'Dwyer, and Jesus.

What in the name of Allah, he wondered, could they possibly have to do with me?

Nur was slipping back into his dream when the shot rang out that ended Imran Fawzi's life.

"Witac do Warszawa."

Welcome to Warsaw. The hand that shook Habib Al-Nazariiy's belonged to a young man who had been studying chemistry at the University of Warsaw for two years. The airport hummed around them. Imran Fawzi's nephew, Habib Al-Nazariiy had just flown in from Baghdad. It had taken him a while to get a passport and permission to travel abroad from the American authorities, but he had always been on good terms with them. A graduate of the University of Texas, he had worked for the Iraqi Oil Ministry before the war, and his expertise and knowledge were appreciated by the American occupying forces and their civilian counterparts. The oil must flow, after all.

But Habib had not come to Warsaw to bring home such educated young men as the one who had met him at Warsaw Airport. A month earlier, Ghazi Al-Tikriti had contacted him by phone, just prior to Tikriti's capture.

"A pity about your uncle Fawzi," Tikriti had said. "I told you not to trust the Americans. And you. Are you getting a high-level position with the ministry, or are you fetching coffee for some American who knows nothing about our pipelines and facilities?"

"What do you want, Ghazi?" Habib had asked.

"Your uncle handed over to me the things that the two of you found in Jama's cellar. Foolishly, I turned them over to a contact in Poland. I trusted him to use them wisely."

"To buy your freedom?" Habib had just as wisely guessed.

"Without freedom, what good is life, yes, Habib?"

Tikriti had gone on to explain what he had sent and to whom. Rather than using these archaeological wonders to help Iraq, it turned out that Tikriti's Polish contact had connections he preferred. Iraq would be plundered anew by another entity. But it wasn't too late. If Habib could collect these treasures from Poland, he and Tikriti could still work out a deal with the Americans.

"We have something they want," Tikriti had told Habib. "Desperately. So we make a trade. Our country for their god."

And so Habib had made up his tale of oil industry politics and had finagled a passport to Poland. Now, as he followed the Iraqi student, whose chemical skills had taught him how to build substantially destructive explosives, he imagined what he would do once he got to their target. He hadn't been able to sneak a weapon on board the flight from Baghdad, but there were guns aplenty in Warsaw.

Their target was a mere three hours away, in a city called Torun.

CHAPTER 7

For Molly, science was all about honesty, truth, getting to the cold hard facts of a dig through rigorous search and careful unbiased appraisal and reappraisal. But she was also fully aware that beyond integrity science was also often about secrecy. Who knew what, when. Whose theory was proven correct. Who should get credit. Molly had never been allowed to see the complete Gospels of Hannaniah. Frustrated, she had beaten her head against a wall of scientific jealousy and mistrust until Nina came along. Given the documents she had been waiting so long to examine was Christmas morning to Molly. She couldn't get enough of them.

Like the more famous Dead Sea Scrolls, divided among teams of biblical scholars for translation, Hannaniah had gone to two teams of archaeologists for further study. Molly had taken half, entrusted to her by the leader of the expedition, Mohamoud Jama. Jama had been willing to part with his portion only because he trusted Molly, trusted her scholarship, trusted her loyalty to him, trusted her faith.

The two archaeologists had met many years before while Molly was a grad student studying abroad and he a visiting lecturer. Over tea many times, the two would discuss their religion in the context of their scientific pursuit. Both loved the exploration, both identified with the past, and both cherished their belief in God. In return for her youthful enthusiasm, which enthralled and captivated Jama, he took her into his confidence as much as he would take anyone. Hence his anger when her translation and explanation of Hannaniah appeared in public in such an outrageous way. Hence her shame and anger for being made to feel the betrayer when all she had tried to do was bring to light a new understanding of what Jesus may have been trying to do. All undone thanks to the faceless and the faithless.

From Boston to Warsaw via LOT Polish Airlines took eight hours. Travel by car from Warsaw Airport to the northern town of Torun added another three hours by which time it was after midnight. During the whole trip, sitting beside Cavalcante while chauffeur Kwiatkowski drove, Molly seethed.

"He said you'd be furious," Cavalcante said as the dark Polish countryside passed them at a leisurely pace. Kwiatkowski drove as though in no hurry to get anywhere. "That's why he sent me and Teodor."

"He is an asshole!"

"True enough, but he's a highly distinguished and very connected asshole."

The "he" that Molly and Cavalcante were referring to was André Leveille-Gaus, the third member of the Jama-O'Dwyer expedition in Egypt.

"He stole my discovery!" Molly raged. "Then he had the fucking nerve to deny me access to it. I found it! He was just along for the ride!"

Cavalcante rested a calming hand on Molly's knee. Her hair blew in the breeze from her open window. Kwiatkowski ignored them both. A Chopin *polonaise* played from a CD in the front. "You wouldn't even have been in Egypt and found Hannaniah if he hadn't invited you in the first place, yes?"

"Jama invited me," Molly said. "Leveille funded the expedition. He barely spoke to me. 'Oh, you can't possibly translate it all. We'll talk, we'll share. Don't worry, Molly. I wouldn't keep you in the dark.'

Bullshit! That's exactly what he did. And why? He hasn't published a fucking thing!"

Cavalcante tapped Kwiatkowski on the shoulder.

"Five more minutes," he said.

"Good. We're tired."

Then she turned her attention back to the simmering Molly. "His portion of the scrolls was potentially far more sensational. He has hesitated to publish them. Yours should never have been published."

"Not in the way they were. You've seen them?"

"Some of them," Cavalcante said. "I shared things I had. He shared some things that he had. Regrettably, that's how it works sometimes."

"I was more than willing to share," Molly said. "His door was always closed to me."

Molly laid her head back against the car seat. She was more than tired. She was exhausted. The trip hadn't been so bad, but she hadn't slept in two nights with the anticipation of what lay ahead in Iraq, of meeting Leveille-Gaus face to face for the first time in five years, of finally getting a look at what he had stolen from her. She had no intention of going anywhere until she saw his segment of the Hannaniah Gospels, the originals, nothing less. Copies could be edited in any of a hundred ways, and nothing was beneath Leveille-Gaus.

Molly allowed her feelings to cool a bit as they entered the outskirts of Torun, a medieval Polish city, one of only two cities in Poland that escaped destruction in the Second World War. The Old City was a living archaeological exhibit where families and businesses inhabited gothic and baroque structures that dated back eight hundred years.

At one point, the usually quiet Kwiatkowski turned in his seat and pointed to a four-story building with a brick façade. "Copernicus lived there," he said proudly.

"Really." Molly leaned out her window to look at the church-like structure. She could imagine the famous Polish astronomer peering from one of the top-floor windows, looking up into the night sky, conjuring his visions of the solar system that ran counter to the beliefs of the time and the Holy Church.

"Some time," Kwiatkowski told her, "I must show you my telescope."

Molly gave a new appraisal of the man who had hardly spoken a word to her since they had met in Boston. On the plane, he had spent his entire eight hours with his nose in a mathematics book, which meant that he was hardly the goon she had suspected.

Outside the city they turned onto a narrow country road wide enough for only one car. Tree branches scraped the roof of the car and leaves poked inside their windows. Cavalcante smiled, turned gleaming eyes on Molly.

"Reminds me of Transylvania," she said.

"Transylvania?"

"The first time I ran away from home, I was thirteen. I hung out with a group of kids in the forest outside Vlad Dracul's castle. We did coke mostly. Got high, had sex, drank each other's blood. It was a kick for a while. But I never got over the romance of the unreal. This is wonderful, don't you think?"

"We'll see," Molly said.

And then the first turret of the castle appeared above the treetops, and she understood what Cavalcante was feeling. "This is yours?" she marveled.

Kwiatkowski couldn't restrain a broad smile as he looked at Molly through the rearview mirror. "Father's. After the communists fell, he made a fortune in computers. He always wanted to be a king."

"Looks like he made it."

Molly and Cavalcante gaped at the castle as it came into full view on the far side of a stream. They each counted the turrets and exclaimed, "Ten!" at the same time. There was a moat, a drawbridge, an iron portcullis over a gateway, and stone walls that rose at least twenty feet. Lights blazed inside. As the car approached, the drawbridge descended and the gate lifted. Kwiatkowski's car bumped over the wooden timbers of the bridge and entered a cobbled courtyard that included a stable and a guesthouse. The elder Kwiatkowski greeted them outside. Several men armed with automatic weapons accompanied him.

"Teodor!" he shouted. Michael Kwiatkowski looked gigantic, every bit as tall as the turrets of his castle, with a pile of white hair that blew this way and that in the night breeze. He threw his arms around his son and did the same to Cavalcante, hoisting her small body up in his exuberance. She coughed when he released her. Molly used her colleague to keep Kwiatkowski at bay and held out her hand instead.

"Welcome! Welcome!" he cried, unabashedly appraising her much as Cavalcante had when they had first met. "You are beautiful for an archaeologist," he said, "Hunh, Teodor?" He winked at his offspring. "We are about to embark on the most glorious mission of all time! Welcome to my home!"

Teodor tossed a quick embarrassed look at Molly. "My dad," he said.

Kwiatkowski led the team of archaeologists into the main building, an echoing front hall filled with medieval furnishings including the requisite tapestries, suits of armor, and a family coat of arms. A carpeted stone staircase led to the second floor, but Kwiatkowski ushered his charges into a room to the left of the entrance. Two chandeliers glowed brilliantly over a thirty-foot-long table covered in steaming platters of food. A fire gave warmth from a huge fireplace opposite draped windows.

"I assumed you'd be hungry," Kwiatkowski said. "Pasta and vegetables if you are vegetarians. Meat for the rest of us. And wine."

Molly had no qualms about looking like a pig. She would have pulled up the closest chair and dove in to the first platter, whether it contained quiche, linguini, or hot dogs, had André Leveille-Gaus not made an unannounced appearance from a doorway on the far side of the room. As soon as she saw him, her hunger vanished, her face flushed, and she had to brace herself on one of the dinner chairs to keep herself from taking a bite out of him.

"Molly!" he said. "It's been too long, much too long." He approached, hand outstretched as if there were no ill feelings between them. Red-haired like Molly, he was twenty years her senior, with large hands calloused from years of digging, face a light Mediterranean tan, freckled from childhood, and as wrinkled as the Alps of his native country. Molly avoided his grip and did her best to control her anger.

"For five years," she said, "you have brushed me aside. Now you want me again. You must need me pretty bad."

"The world needs you, Molly. Nina has told you everything?"

"Enough to bring me here, obviously. Also, obviously not everything."

Leveille-Gaus nodded, glanced at his host. "There is much to tell, much to share," he said, "and very little time in which to do it. Tonight we rest. Tomorrow we prepare. The day after, we are gone."

"To Iraq," Kwiatkowski said.

Cavalcante was the first to grab a plate and work her way down the table, loading her plate with sausages, pierogies, fish in horseradish sauce, stuffed cabbage rolls, sauerkraut, chrusciki pastries. Kwiatkowski filled a plate for Molly, pulled out a chair, and more or less pushed her into it.

His father said, "You two are old friends, I take it."

"We met in Egypt five years ago," Leveille-Gaus said. "Her reputation as a relentless explorer was well-known even then. But I liked her work so much, I invited her to join me."

"Mohamoud Jama invited me. You paid for the tickets."

"The Hannaniah Gospels," the younger Kwiatkowski interrupted, having sat beside Molly, his dish piled to the edges. He held her gaze briefly in a way that she understood. *Lay off him for now. Let's keep the peace.*

She stuck a blini in her mouth.

Cavalcante said, "The Hannaniah Gospels are an autobiography really. The life of a woman who claimed to be the daughter of Yeshuah bar Yushef, Jesus of Nazareth. Such a discovery might have set the world on fire, except that, aside from accurate dating of the scrolls, nothing that she wrote could be corroborated. Alone, they could be an honest piece of history or they could be an imaginative work of fiction."

"A number of other gospels have been discovered," Leveille-Gaus added, searching with meticulous care through the containers of food for just the right breast of chicken or the moistest looking roll. "The Nag Hammadi Gospels are authentic but less noteworthy. They make no claims about Jesus' identity, but they are considered heretical, the product of early Christian sects that, among other things, believed in a female deity."

"Good for them!" Cavalcante exclaimed. "No wonder they were considered heretical."

"They were the imaginative workings of people who came to Jesus from what you would call the counter-culture of the times."

"But you," the younger Kwiatkowski spoke to Molly, "believe

Hannaniah."

Molly swallowed a piece of fish, wiped her lips dry, and laid down her fork. "Her work is too meticulous, her descriptive passages of life with and without her father, all too precise to be fictitious."

"Maybe she was a first century novelist," Michael Kwiatkowski said.

"No." Molly looked up from her plate. "For five years, Hannaniah was uncorroborated. But not anymore."

"Afghanistan," Kwiatkowski senior said.

"And apparently Iraq." Molly looked at the older man seated at the head of the long table like the patriarch of an extremely rich family. She wondered how much he knew, not only about the expedition but about her.

"You are a brave woman," he remarked, staring back at her. "You remind me of my wife, Teodor's mother. Tell me what you found in Afghanistan."

"Proof that Hannaniah was more than a writer of fiction. Of course, had I been allowed access to the section of the Gospels that Professor Leveille kept, it might have saved me a lot of time and effort."

"If you knew what was in that section, you would understand."

"Tell me then. Be brief if we have little time."

Leveille-Gaus took his time chewing and swallowing a piece of chicken swimming in thick white gravy. He showed no sign of annoyance or concern. "Meaning no disrespect, Molly," he said, looking toward the funding source of this expedition, "I answer to a higher god than academia. I will not undermine or destroy a people's faith for the sake of academic accolades."

"That was never my point!" Molly blurted.

"Perhaps not. But that would have been the result had brakes not been applied to your research."

Molly stormed to her feet. "Brakes?" The younger Kwiatkowski tried gently to settle her back into her seat, but she was having none of it. "Then you admit it! You purposely sabotaged my research!"

"The work never stopped. I spent five years translating the scrolls. I'm a busy man and had other work on my plate as well."

"Then you should have entrusted them to me."

"And have them all end up on the Internet before any other scholar had the chance to review and critique your work?"

"That was not my fault!"

"But it happened."

"I sent you a copy. Perhaps you were the one who leaked it to the world. If the translations had proven to be disturbing in any way, I would never have published without lengthy discussions with you and other people in the field. Accolades mean nothing to me!"

"Then what does?" Leveille-Gaus asked. "What drove you to Afghanistan?"

Under the bright light of the chandeliers, under the watchful gazes of Cavalcante, and Leveille-Gaus, the Kwiatkowskis, and their bodyguards, Molly suddenly found that she couldn't speak, couldn't utter a word. She had no idea what to tell them. Or, she did, but couldn't. Father Teague would understand. In those ancient scrolls, in the thousands of lines of literature, in the wonderful imagery, in the heart-wrenching testimony of a woman who held nothing back, Molly had found in Hannaniah what she had lost herself thirty years before. Her mother.

The Polish highway was quiet two hours after midnight. As far as Habib Al-Nazariiy was concerned, his Polonez sedan and the van being driven by the chemistry student were the only two cars on the road. With his own driver, there were four men in all, each armed with assault rifles. They had scouted out the Kwiatkowski estate the day before and expected some trouble. But Habib knew what the bomb in the van was capable of doing. A bomb of similar size in Nairobi, Kenya, set off outside the U.S. embassy, had injured over a thousand people and killed dozens. The American troops and their counterparts, the national security forces, certainly had learned what nasty business car bombs could be. But that was only to be the distraction.

An hour from Torun, they pulled over to the side of the road, checked their map, drank hot coffee, and reviewed their plans. Habib was well aware that Ghazi Al-Tikriti was now in American custody. But the former Iraqi intelligence officer wasn't the only man in Iraq who would be interested in obtaining the archaeological relics from the Kwiatkowski castle. Habib didn't hate Americans. They disappointed him. They frustrated him. They cost him work and financial security for his family. And they would be in Iraq for a very long time unless their dead made a mountain of corpses so high their friends and families forced their government to bring them home. And so, they were going to pay.

Settling back in the passenger seat of the Polish-made automobile, Habib rested his automatic weapon on his lap. He had never had the opportunity as a soldier to use it against Americans in the First Gulf War. Regrettably, he was probably going to have to use it against them now.

After dinner, Molly had been tired enough to sleep but too restless to sleep well. Each of the guests of Michael Kwiatkowski had been afforded a bedroom with a huge bed. Molly's bed had a canopy with sweeping drapes and a cloth cord for ringing the maid for breakfast in bed. But after another all-too-familiar nightmare of fire and death, Molly fled her silk sheets and down comforter and walked out onto a small balcony that gave her a lovely healing view of the forest and farmland and a winding river beyond the walls of the castle.

She had fallen asleep in her black cotton bathrobe, a gift from a former lover, a paleontologist, and the pleasant early morning air blew the robe around her ankles. While it was still dark, the twittering of birds on the castle towers and balconies foretold dawn. Molly glanced skyward above the turrets and trees to the stars that shone in as great a multitude as they had on the desert the night she had discovered Hannaniah.

"It's beautiful, isn't it?"

The voice took her by surprise. As it was masculine, she quickly tied her bathrobe belt around her waist. Then she looked along the castle walls to the other balconies that jutted out toward the courtyard two floors below.

"Up here," the voice said. "To your left."

Molly obeyed the voice, Teodor Kwiatkowski's. Cavalcante's friend stood on a balcony one floor above hers. His telescope was aimed at the stars. His eyes were fixed on her. "Come on up," he said. "I have the moon in my scope."

"How do I get there?" Molly called to him.

"Just follow the stairs. Mine is the third door on the left."

Why she felt no hesitation or qualms about taking up his offer, Molly couldn't say, but she quickly donned jeans and a shirt and headed barefoot out her door, up the lavish staircase, and onto the lengthy fourth floor hallway. Perhaps it was because she knew she wouldn't be able to get back to sleep anyway. Or because Kwiatkowski, unlike any of the others, including Cavalcante, didn't seem to be hiding anything from her.

Out onto his balcony she stepped. She smiled at him, took him in more intensely if quickly, noted a scar above his right eyebrow in the shape of a crescent moon. He stepped aside to give her a view through his telescope.

"It's a Sky View Pro 120 mm EQ Refractor," he said.

"Wow!" Molly felt as though she were circling the moon from a few miles up, like an Apollo astronaut. Craters, mountains, the great seas and plains of the moon were within finger reach. Foolishly, she extended her hand towards the object in her sights.

Kwiatkowski chuckled. "It's good, isn't it?"

Molly blushed. "Sorry. Instinct."

"No apologies necessary," Kwiatkowski said. "I did the same thing the first time I looked through a telescope, and it wasn't nearly as good as this one."

Molly took another look at the silver moon above them. "Someday," she said, "I wouldn't mind going there. Even if there aren't any archaeological sites. Are you a would-be astronaut, Mr. Kwiatkowski?"

"Me? I'm not as brave as you."

Molly looked at him, dressed already for the day ahead in tan khakis and a white buttoned-down shirt. He was several inches taller than she, broad in the shoulders, slender, his blond hair styled in a military crew cut. His brows were darker and made his light blue eyes stand out. Nordic, she thought. Nice.

"Then, what are you?" she asked. "The strong silent type? A mathematician? Former prison guard?"

Kwiatkowski's smile had a pleasing shyness to it. He bent down to take a peak through his telescope and shifted the view looking for something else. "Military, actually," he said. "Major. I will be leading your team into Iraq. We have a small Polish contingent there helping out your forces. Dr. Leveille believes your site is within the Polish Military Sector."

"Lucky for us," Molly said as Kwiatkowski moved aside to let her peer into the scope. "Mars?"

"The god of war."

"I'm used to looking down into the ground," she said as she moved the apparatus to study the red planet. "What awaits us in Iraq?"

"Hell," he said. "I advised my father against it. My father does as he pleases."

"And you always do what he wants."

"He's rich. He's earned the right to tell people what to do."

Molly looked away to give Kwiatkowski an opportunity to view Mars. Down below in the courtyard, she heard activity. Lights in the guesthouse were on, and there was movement outside near a parked black limousine. Beyond the walls of the castle, the sky was brightening to a deep blue. Molly thought she saw vehicles approaching from the access road. One moment the moonlight reflected off something moving. The next all was dark again, blocked perhaps by the overhanging trees.

"Do you believe in God, Molly?" Kwiatkowski asked, turning to look at her.

"Why? Do you think we'll be desecrating the faith if we go into Iraq?"

"In civilian life I'm a mathematician," he said. "I worship numbers."

"A lapsed Catholic, huh."

"You're not?"

"No," Molly said. "Not at all. Numbers may define the known, but they can't explain the unknown."

"Then why are you here?"

She looked away, unable to answer immediately. Below, the guesthouse door opened and two men exited. One hefted suitcases and loaded them into the trunk of the limousine. Michael Kwiatkowski came out to speak with the second man. Even from a distance, there was something familiar about the man. His silver hair. The cane he used to help him walk. Couldn't be, she thought. The two men hugged and laughed. Doesn't anyone sleep around here, she wondered?

"I'm a moth, Mr. Kwiatkowski."

"You don't look so fragile to me. Iraq is the flame you're drawn to?"

"Not Iraq," she said. "The truth. About myself. About who I am and where I fit into all of this. Don't you ever feel lost?"

"All the time. That's why I love numbers. They're fixed, comforting."

Molly leaned over the railing of the balcony as the black limousine engine came to life and the man talking to the elder Kwiatkowski entered the car. Familiar, uncomfortably familiar. From Boston.

She said, "When my mom died, I was really screwed up for a while. My aunt and uncle put me into Children's Hospital to have me evaluated. But I wasn't crazy. Just miserable. The Church brought me back to life. I won't say I'm devoted to it. I am a reasoning, thinking person who feels free to disagree with the holy fathers when she pleases."

Molly swung the telescope to tilt down toward the courtyard and the face in the limousine as the automobile moved toward the gate. The portcullis lifted and the drawbridge lowered. The telescope focused on the license plate of the car.

"Your father, I assume," she said, troubled by the vision of the man in the car, "isn't a lapsed Catholic either."

Kwiatkowski laughed. "My father? Hell, no. He's a lapsed communist."

Just then, the driver of the limousine blasted his horn. Molly looked away from the telescope. The limousine had been making its way toward the bridge over the moat and onto the access road when something suddenly blocked its way. The driver had to be leaning on his horn he was making such a racket. In the courtyard, Michael Kwiatkowski hurried over to the car. Several of his armed guards followed.

"What the hell?" Molly said. She was just about to step into the younger Kwiatkowski's room, when a van sped across the drawbridge and slammed into the limousine. The impact hurled the limousine into Kwiatkowski senior, crushing him beneath its wheels. His two guards were tossed aside as well. Before they could regain their feet and their weapons, the invaders opened fire.

" Cholera jasna!" Kwiatkowski junior shoved Molly off the balcony and into his room. "Stay here!" he ordered. He snatched a pistol that had been holstered and strapped to a bedpost and ran into the hall. He hadn't been gone ten seconds when an explosion tore apart the Kwiatkowski estate.

Molly thought of a tornado, the roar people often equate with a passing locomotive. But this was worse. The ground shook beneath Molly's feet, and she pitched forward. The balcony she'd been standing on moments before was ripped from its metal brackets and hurled down. Glass, brick and metal shrapnel flew into the room, shredded her clothes and tore her flesh in dozens of wounds. She gagged on dust and dirt and tried to rise but could only get to her knees before the façade of the castle facing the courtyard gave way and a debris-filled cloud of hot air poured in.

"Jesus Christ!" she hollered and pushed herself with all her might out into the hallway. The building seemed to be collapsing beneath her. It swayed but held together. The darkness of early dawn was now matched by a lightless corridor, the explosion knocking out the electricity. In the darkness, Molly heard distant shouting and gunfire. Closer by she heard other frightened voices.

"*Aiuto! Aiuto! Cos'è successo? Dov'è tutti?*"

"Nina! Over here!"

Molly crawled toward the sound of Cavalcante's cry for help. From somewhere else she heard Leveille-Gaus shouting, "What's going on? What the hell happened?"

She tried to call to him but could only manage to choke on dust and cough. Finally, she managed to touch Cavalcante's hand, and the two archaeologists fell into each other's arms.

"Jesus Christ, Molly!"

"My sentiments exactly. Stay here. I'm going to try to find Dr. Leveille-Gaus."

The gunfire was much louder now. Molly felt her way through the black corridor, her bare feet crunching painfully on shards of wood, plaster, and brick that had been blown into the hallway. What had happened? An explosion obviously. But why? A personal vendetta against the amiably immoral Michael Kwiatkowski? Or something else, something to do with them.

At the top of the stairs leading down to the main hall, Molly paused, afraid that a stray bullet might find its way up those stairs and into her, or that some black-hooded figure wielding a machine gun would come racing through the doorway. In that instant, she recalled the terrible accident that had preceded the explosion—the black limousine, the man who had entered it from the guesthouse, and the license plate she had seen through Teodor's telescope. The plate had three letters and one number on it: S C V 2. Molly had visited Rome often enough. The letters referred to the Stato della Città del Vaticano. And, of course, it all made sense. The familiar face in the back seat, the man with the silver hair and the gold walking stick, now surely dead: James Braddock, the very bishop who had threatened her with excommunication, apparently representing the highest of the high among Catholics. After all, what was the nationality of John Paul II, if not Polish?

Richard Jackson wasn't a happy man. Most people who knew him considered him to be a man of the world. After all, he had sold his professional services to governments all over the planet—the Congo, Indonesia, Peru. Wherever governments were embroiled with their civilian populations and needed security advice and assistance, he was their man. But Richard Jackson, for all his international experience, hated to fly. He particularly hated to fly on little sleep. And his flight from Boston with Andrew Milstein restlessly moving about beside him had not been conducive to restful shut-eye. When they touched down in Warsaw, it was 11:00 AM and Jackson hadn't slept for two days.

"Jesus, Milstein, can't it wait a couple hours?" he begged. He had booked a room at a nearby hotel. Molly O'Dwyer had not had that much of a head start on them that he was overly concerned about losing her.

But Milstein was insistent. "You can rest if you want," he said. "I'm not letting Molly get away from me again."

"Molly?"

"O'Dwyer. Molly. Whatever." Milstein's cheeks reddened.

Jackson knew all he needed to know about their mission to find Molly O'Dwyer. He certainly didn't need to know Milstein's personal attachment to it.

Guessing from the message Molly had left on her answering machine, Milstein had contacted all local air services to find out if someone named Molly O'Dwyer had booked passage for a flight to Poland. Indeed she had, on a flight that had arrived in the Polish capital Easter Sunday night. It wasn't difficult after that to trace who had accompanied her on that flight. They hadn't bothered to cover their trail, not suspecting anyone would be interested.

Milstein had recognized one name. Nina Cavalcante. Like Molly, she was a familiar figure in the international archaeology community. She was, in fact, an archivist at the Vatican, a specialist in areas supernatural—miracles, exorcisms, and all things mystical and historical relating to the Church. Interpol had a file on her as thick as the one the FBI had on Molly, and Milstein had access to Interpol through his connections at the Defense Department.

Nina Cavalcante had known Imran Fawzi, who had been under surveillance by the international police agency. She had shown him the sights in Rome, which had included those places where he might meet and pick up young Roman men. Milstein figured Fawzi liked and trusted Nina Cavalcante. And when it came time to tell someone about Mohamoud Jama's historic find, he had entrusted her with the information. And from her to Molly O'Dwyer. The Roman connection had been quick to act, gathering Molly up, then using their Polish contacts to find a way to get into Iraq. Milstein hoped to God he could reach her before they had a chance to sneak into the war zone. Fortunately, Interpol had an even thicker file on Michael Stanislaus Kwiatkowski.

At an airport car rental agency, Milstein chose a Fiat to take them to Torun. When he headed for the driver's seat though, Jackson said, "Throw me the keys. I'm drivin.'"

"You didn't sleep."

"Perfect. Puts me in the right mood. You navigate."

Michael Kwiatkowski had been one of those post–communist bloc phenomena who jumped at the free market experiment like a shark after free food. While chaos ruled, he had used all his skills, made use of all his old connections, legit and otherwise, to buy, sell, cajole, and bully his way to the top of the money chain. He had friends who would kill for a *zloty*. He had friends who held the pope's ear. Most important, he had money up the wazoo. And he owned a castle, which was where Milstein was directing his associate.

"You didn't think this was serious before," Milstein said as Jackson floored the Fiat out of the airport, dodging an elderly newspaper vendor, just under Mach speed. "Look out for the old man."

"I saw him."

"If the Vatican is somehow involved with this, you can be damn well sure there's something in the Iraqi desert."

Jackson glanced into his rearview mirror at a milk truck that he had barely missed, squeezing between it and a tour bus in his hurry. "Why the Vatican?"

"It stands to reason, doesn't it?" Milstein said. "The pope is Polish. Cavalcante works for the Vatican."

"And the Poles have troops in Iraq."

"An Najaf." Milstein spread a map of the Polish highway system on his lap. A red line in marker with a large black dot showed where he had traced their route and final destination. "They'll use the Poles to get into the country unless we can get to her first."

"And when we do?" Jackson asked, squealing a hard right onto an entry ramp, following Milstein's order.

"We appeal to her patriotism."

Jackson grunted. "And when that doesn't work?"

Milstein didn't answer, so Jackson pulled out his cell phone.

"Who you calling?"

As an important Defense contractor and former military operative, Jackson knew the right people to call anytime, any place. For example, he knew the American NATO commander in Poland. To Milstein he said, "Back-up."

What had taken Kwiatkowski in the middle of a quiet night three-plus hours to drive, Jackson gobbled up in just over two. A kilometer south of Torun they were met by a lone army transport vehicle. It was early afternoon, a warm Monday. The two vehicles, the Fiat and the transport, pulled over to the side of the road. Milstein had navigated successfully so far, but Jackson didn't want to progress any farther until he had laid out his plans with the officer in charge of the half-dozen men NATO had lent him for this assignment.

Milstein stretched, leaning against the hood of the Fiat. Jackson and the army officer were deep in discussion at the back of the NATO truck. The men inside were armed with rifles, and Milstein thought they were a bit of overkill. Gazing once again into Molly O'Dwyer's file, he couldn't get over how much she looked like the red-haired girl in his vision. If he had believed the likeness to be sheer coincidence, he wouldn't be here now. But he didn't think so.

A long time ago, Molly, he said to himself, we met. A long, long time ago. In Jerusalem.

Plan set, Jackson approached him. "All right," he said. "We're good to go. Are you armed?"

"I've got a pen," Milstein said.

"Does it have a serrated edge?"

"No."

"Then stay back if there's trouble."

Jackson zoomed down the road before Milstein could buckle his seat belt. The NATO truck stayed close behind. At first, Milstein missed the access road, little more than a farm road meant for wagons carrying hay and produce to market. There were no signs, no opulent front gates. The small convoy turned back and wasted almost an hour making wrong turns before they found the correct road into the Kwiatkowski estate. It was two o'clock before the turrets of Castle Kwiatkowski came into view. Almost immediately, Jackson could tell something was wrong.

"Jesus Fuck," he said, slowing the Fiat down as he approached the drawbridge. He stopped the car and waved the military truck to a stop behind him. "Jesus Fuck!" he repeated, unholstered his Glock pistol, and leaped out of the car.

The drawbridge was down. The iron portcullis had been blown clear of the gate. The gate itself had been reduced to stone rubble. The rubble had collapsed onto a van.

Jackson signaled with his hand, distributed the NATO soldiers to his left and right. "Stay behind me," he told Milstein.

"Who the hell did this?"

"Let's hope there's somebody left alive who can tell us."

At a trot, Jackson led Milstein and the troops across the drawbridge, covered in debris. No vehicle could have gotten through now anyway. They had to climb a mound of metal and stone to get a peek into the compound beyond.

Milstein gasped at the site. My God, he thought. *Molly.*

The sturdy medieval castle had withstood the impact of the explosive fairly well. All the windows had been shattered. The balconies that had not been hurled from their embrasures hung by metal threads to the walls. There was nothing left of the vehicle that had carried the device, but the remains of a black limousine had been propelled into and wrapped around a tree that had been uprooted by the blast. A headless corpse lay beneath a tire. The guesthouse and stables had been utterly destroyed, the remains of horses mixed in with those of humans scattered from one end of the court to the other.

Jackson led his soldiers with silent gestures. He bolted from the gatehouse into the courtyard, kept low, skirted the crater that the blast had dug out of the cobbled yard and headed for the nearest cover, another fallen tree. The NATO troops fanned out, well trained, and cautiously closed in on the main entrance to the castle. Milstein paused over the body of a man with a gaping bloody hole in his forehead.

"Middle Eastern," he said to Jackson.

"You're positive?"

"Unofficially."

"Then someone survived the explosion and returned fire."

That was good news. But who? The courtyard was dead still. Milstein dashed from cover and ran straight for the castle entrance.

"Milstein!" Jackson shouted. "Don't be crazy!"

But Milstein had no intention of stopping. Molly O'Dwyer was more to him than an expert archaeologist who could uncover a remarkably significant biblical find. She was imbedded in his past, both recent and distant.

"Molly!" he yelled. "Molly O'Dwyer!" as he leaped over fallen mortar, metal gutters, and roof tiles. His cries echoed in the empty hallway. His feet left deep impressions in the fine powder and dust that coated the first floor. "Molly!" he shouted and rushed up the staircase to the second floor just as Jackson and the other soldiers galloped in behind him.

"That was probably the stupidest thing you've ever done," Jackson told him when he found Milstein in a demolished bedroom on the third floor.

"There's nobody here," Milstein said. "They're all gone."

"We haven't found all the bodies yet." Even so, Jackson holstered his gun and looked about the ravaged room. The remains of a telescope had been spun across the open space to land comfortably on a canopied bed.

"So, what do we do now?" Milstein asked. "Where could they have gone? Who could have done this?"

Leaning out the rectangular opening that had at one time led onto a balcony, Jackson covered his eyes from the strong sun that ennobled this devastation in a halo of light. "Well, Mr. Milstein," he said, "whoever did it don't like your Molly O'Dwyer as much as you do. Let's hope to God she doesn't plan on goin' to Iraq."

Milstein slumped onto the debris-blanketed bed. He was tired physically and emotionally and, wouldn't you know, his migraine was returning in its own terrific blast of pain. "That, Mr. Jackson," he said wearily, "is exactly where she's going."

Abdul Azim Nur was a deeply religious man and, though only thirty-six years old, held in awe by those who fished the waters of the rivers south of Baghdad or who scraped a living out of the Iraqi soil. Born among the marsh Arabs, he was raised by a father who could neither read nor write, to become an imam, well-educated, a man of the world far beyond the boundaries of Iraq's famed marshland, a devout believer in Allah and in His prophet Mohammed.

But he was also a man who liked German pretzels, who played soccer like a fanatic, who read biographies and historical novels, and who dreamed unusual dreams. Often these dreams were of an erotic nature, something he would never have confided to anyone. He was thirty-six years old and had never had sex with a man or woman. Didn't intend to. It was part of his belief that, to serve Allah properly, he needed to remain chaste, much like the Catholic priests. But that just heightened the intensity of the thoughts he had while asleep.

Women, naked, large-breasted rubbing against him, sharing his bath, ravaging his bed, undermining his faith and his devotion to God. He awoke in the middle of the night panting from the exertions of sex, wet like a child, embarrassed, needing to cover up his damp sheets before his sin was discovered.

Lately, though, he had suffered another sort of dream. It did not bring pleasure like the others, yet there was definitely an erotic quality to it that made him lie awake pondering its meaning. In these dreams, he was not Nur but someone like Nur. The sex was violent, bloody, often engaged with men as well as women. In these dreams, Nur felt he was being pulled apart, his nakedness both sexual and perverse. But what struck him most of all, what lingered longest in his memory far into the day, after morning prayers, after breakfast, was the face of one woman in particular.

Abdul Azim Nur woke up with a splitting headache. He slept in a tent pitched among the reeds of the marshes south of Baghdad. The early morning air was warm, the breeze without comfort, but at least he slept alone so that no one could hear his cry as he burst from the nightmare that had been fed by his migraine.

The woman, he thought. Always the woman. Red-haired. Beautiful. Grabbing for him, trying to save him from the mobs.

"Hannaniah!" he shouted, and wondered where in the name of Allah he had heard it before.

CHAPTER 8

Kwiatkowski knew an abandoned farm house several kilometers from his home. He limped now but not from any gunshot wound. After he had killed three of the assassins who had murdered his father, he had given chase to a fourth. He cursed himself for slipping on a dislodged cobblestone, twisting his ankle, and letting the remaining attacker get away. But at least he had saved the others. Molly, Cavalcante, Leveille-Gaus.

His father had dismissed all the household staff except his personal bodyguards, given them time off so that they would be unaware of and unable to talk about the unusual guests his father was putting up. That meant that the destruction at Estate Kwiatkowski would go undetected for several days, time to get the archaeological team out of Poland before anything else could happen to stop them.

"You mean we're still going through with this?" Molly asked as they followed the banks of the stream that became the moat around Kwiatkowski's castle. The sun edged above the horizon giving them enough light to travel by. Kwiatkowski had allowed them time to gather what they could of clothes and equipment before hurrying them along. Molly had managed to salvage one suitcase, which contained, most importantly, her insulin, packed in an insulated cloth bag, and medical supplies.

"We have to go on, Molly," he told her. "We're obligated."

"To whom?"

"To the world," Leveille-Gaus told her, kneeling by the stream to take a drink. Sweat and grime had reduced his academic mien to that of a peasant. His damp red hair was plastered to his head. His frayed gray suit coat showed two missing buttons.

"By the world, you mean the Vatican?" Molly asked.

Cavalcante sat with her knees up to her chin, reading from a thin black binder that she had salvaged from the rubble. She had sacrificed clothes for her precious books and scholarly material.

"Don't you think it's time you told me the full truth, Nina? Sister to sister? One of the men who died back there was Bishop Braddock, he who threatened my soul with eternal flames for publishing Hannaniah. What was he doing here? Am I supposed to believe he supports me now?"

"The Vatican never closes any door," Leveille-Gaus said.

Cavalcante looked guiltily at Leveille-Gaus. A slight dawn breeze tussled her hair covered in plaster dust.

"But how did you get involved with the Vatican?" Molly asked.

"I worked on the Dead Sea Scrolls for the Church," Leveille-Gaus explained. "Whereas Nina's interests tend to be more ... bizarre."

Cavalcante stood up. On tiptoes she struggled past five feet, but there was something so alive about her, like a ballet dancer with every move balanced between the delicate and the athletic, that Molly couldn't help watching her. Cleopatra reincarnate. One of the Greek Muses. All of the above. When Cavalcante came to sit beside her, she snuggled into Molly like a best friend at a sleepover.

"As a girl, I was attracted to the far out," she said. "Even as an archaeologist. What was Christianity at the outset after all? A cult. A sect whose members believed in a mythical figure who could cheat death and rise to life immortal. His followers were mostly counterculture, preaching liberalism, feminism, communism. One sect practiced free sex. They worshipped a male/female Christ figure. It was in looking for them that I first came across Hannaniah."

"When *you* first came across Hannaniah?" Molly glanced at Cavalcante, stunned. "When?"

"About eight years ago."

"That's not possible! I discovered her existence *five* years ago!" Molly looked to Kwiatkowski and Leveille-Gaus, wondering why they would conspire against her.

"I know what you're feeling, Molly," Cavalcante tried to reassure her. "Don't be alarmed. Your discovery was everything. All we had were bits and pieces."

"As you have said, Molly," Leveille-Gaus put in, "Hannaniah was prolific. The Vatican Archives have many scattered references to her, documents either authored by her or mentioning her by name. But until your discovery, she was just another shadowy biblical figure with little or no significance.

"Hannaniah cataloged the various sects that sprang up after the crucifixion. In fact, in one sect she was considered a demi-god, the female half of a holy spirit, while her father, Jesus, was the male half."

"Heretical," Kwiatkowski muttered.

"Certifiable," Cavalcante said. "Much as you, Molly, I began my own lifelong pursuit of Hannaniah. I saw much of myself in her. And where was the best place to work to get information about her? The Vatican. In Jerusalem, I uncovered what might have been the remains of Nicodemus. Hannaniah's writings led me to him. I think she'll lead us elsewhere, too."

Molly shut her eyes to keep from crying. All along, all along, she had considered Hannaniah her own gift to the world. More than that, she felt she had established a personal relationship with Hannaniah across the centuries that she didn't want to share with anyone. A blood bond almost. Somehow, despite her affection for Cavalcante, she felt robbed of that relationship now.

"Both Nina and I have read letters from her to St. Peter," Leveille-Gaus said, "in which she calls Yeshuah her father and chastises Peter for going astray. Independently of one another, we surmised that he had survived crucifixion. Then you discovered the treasure trove out in the desert. It unlocked everything. Everything!"

"Or almost," Molly said. "Because if it unlocked everything, I wouldn't be here now."

"Open the binder," Cavalcante told her.

"What is it?" The binder contained lined paper two inches thick filled with computer-generated print.

"It is a poem," Leveille-Gaus said. "You wanted the other half of the Hannaniah Gospels. Well, there it is, translated into English."

"This can't be all of it," Molly said, flipping through the pages. "Are you holding out more on us, Dr. Leveille?"

"It is the relevant part."

"There is nothing irrelevant about Hannaniah. I want to see all of it."

Kwiatkowski abruptly stood up, interrupting the conversation, and strapped on his backpack, which, besides his gun, was all he had rescued from the castle. "I'd rather we argue on the run. Despite everything, we have a plane to catch. We have to get to Warsaw."

"Just a minute, Teodor." Molly returned to the first page of the binder. Cavalcante read beside her.

"It's a lovely poem, a sad poem, an odyssey written by a very unusual young woman."

"Hannaniah," Molly said quietly.

"Yes. Like the lamentations, you will notice they are written in stanzas of three lines each. There are six such poems, each with the same number of stanzas."

"Six." Molly got it. "Hannaniah loved to play with numbers.

She was an academic like us. I'd have preferred to read the original Hebrew. Her nuances will be lost in the translation."

"All well and good," Kwiatkowski said, practically lifting Cavalcante to her feet in order to get everyone going. He walked to a path that ran along the riverbank. The others could discuss the fine points of biblical poetry all they wanted, but they'd damn well do it on the fly. Molly would have held onto the binder but couldn't carry it and her suitcase. Reluctantly, she entrusted it to Cavalcante's keeping.

"Molly!" Kwiatkowski yelled from up ahead.

"Yes! Yes! I'm coming!" She eyed Cavalcante, fixed her with a look that said, No more games between us. Tell me everything.

"Why are you out here, Nina?" she asked. "What's in it for you?"

Cavalcante smiled. "The end of the world, my dear. As we know it."

Like any astute, worldly-wise man, Ghazi Al-Tikriti was ambivalent about the press. The news media could be helpful or harmful depending upon how gifted you were at manipulating them. Even under Saddam when the Iraqi press had to toe the line, Tikriti had used his contacts to his advantage. At home, he had convinced the media to portray his destruction of the marshlands along the Tigris and Euphrates rivers and the annihilation of the resistance fighters hiding within them, as a controlled military action in defense of the homeland. Abroad, he had used AP and UPI sources to leak a story that he hoped would pave his way to asylum: the rape and scarring of his youngest daughter at the hands of that true monster, Uday Hussein.

Oh, yes, Ghazi Al-Tikriti's captors knew full well that he hated Saddam Hussein, his sons, and all their clan. Distant cousin though he was, he would have plucked out Uday's eyes with a fork if the opportunity had presented itself. But his captors didn't want to hear any of that. At the moment, they were caught up in their own media fiasco.

"What did they do to you?" a prisoner named Aden asked him as they were led, cuffless and shackleless, through the Abu Ghraib courtyard, past snapping foreign cameras, to a convoy of military vehicles that would take them to a more humane facility in Al-Hillah.

The world now knew in all its horrific pictorial glory how some American troops treated their prisoners within the walls of Saddam Hussein's former jail—the same way *he* had treated his enemies, real and otherwise.

"I won't even tell you what they did to me," this Aden snarled into Tikriti's ear, walking behind him. "But if I ever get my freedom, every American woman I see will pay."

"Then let us hope," Tikriti said, "you don't get that chance."

For Ghazi Al-Tikriti was not an awful man. He had raised ten wonderful daughters, hadn't he? Ten. No sons. A beautiful wife whom he adored. Every Westerner he had met remarked at how European his attitudes were toward his women. Well, didn't the Qur'an say to respect females as you would respect yourself? As he marched through this media show for the benefit of the flag-waving Marge and Homer Simpsons back in America, he could honestly convince himself that he was a good man who had fallen in with the wrong people, who would have killed him and his entire family if he hadn't obeyed their orders with a smile.

At the back of the military transport truck, Tikriti was loaded in with Aden and the other prison evacuees. The cameras followed him as he turned to give one final wave to the idiots who didn't realize this convoy wasn't going to make it to Al-Hillah.

Once seated on a bench in the truck facing Aden on the other side, Tikriti had his legs shackled again to a chain on the floor. His hands were also cuffed, and he was frisked by a male American soldier to make sure he hadn't slipped something dangerous from his cell. Then the convoy of trucks and humvees set out through a heavily-defended front gate, past coils of barbed wire, and a phalanx of armored vehicles capable of rapid response to the mortar fire that often penetrated Abu Ghraib's defenses to kill guards and prisoners alike.

The back canvas flap of the truck was closed, so Tikriti couldn't see the neighborhoods of the city he had once traveled freely as a military bigshot. These were the exclusive neighborhoods open only to the elite Sunni and Shi'a: Al-Khadra, Al-Mansur, Al-Rashid, Al-Ma'mun. Escorted by the army reservists of the 264th Military Police Battalion out of a place called New Jersey, the convoy pushed south toward Al-Hillah, reputedly friendly territory, first on Rabia Street, then southeast down the so-called Airport Road that led westward, to Saddam International Airport.

The Iraqi prisoners kept their silence under the watchful eyes of two young reservists, armed, fingers to triggers, sitting on either bench of the truck, their backs to the flap. Tikriti looked across the narrow space to the woman-hater Aden, whose wounds were not apparent to him. Aden looked back, puzzled, because each time the convoy made a turn, Tikriti silently moved his lips counting *wahid, ithnein, thalatha*, one, two, three. At six, Tikriti did a strange thing. He slipped off his bench and fell to his knees as if he were initiating a Muslim prayer service. Aden frowned. Then he heard a distinctive whine, rising in volume, and understood. Almost too late.

The first explosion came up front, striking the forward vehicle of the 264th military convoy. "Mortar fire!" one of Tikriti's American guards screamed. "What do we do?"

"Stay with the truck!"

Then the second blast came, so close the canvas of Tikriti's truck was riddled by the shrapnel, holes were torn in the side. Anyone who hadn't ducked, as Tikriti and Aden had, was ripped apart as viciously as the canvass. Blood sprayed Tikriti, but he stayed on his knees until the third mortar landed directly in front of their vehicle. The detonation deafened Tikriti. It shattered the windshield and propelled hundreds of fine particles of glass down the driver's throat, killing him instantly. The truck swerved, smashed against a light post, and came to rest on its side.

By the time Tikriti had opened his eyes, the two American soldiers were gone. The Iraqi prisoner to his right was dead, mouth agape, eyes open, a piece of canvas stuck to the gooey mess that was his exposed brain. Others were dying. Aden moaned.

"Help me. Help me." Aden hung upside down, his head almost in Tikriti's lap, his ankles locked in their fetters.

All Tikriti could do was mutter a few prayers. First, for the friendly Iraqi police officer who had managed to alert him of this attack. Second, for the followers of the holy man Abdul Azim Nur who had carried it out. And third, for Allah whose greatness Tikriti had been known to question in the past.

The explosions persisted, then died out to be replaced by the unpleasant familiar chatter of small arms fire. When the canvass flap of the truck was suddenly shoved aside, Tikriti jumped, not knowing whether the Americans had survived to shoot him or whether an untrained Iraqi freedom fighter would gun him down by mistake.

He was pleased, upon second look, to see the friendly face of an Iraqi teenager, his black hood pulled off his face, giddy and giggling, fulfilling a dream. The boy held a Kalashnikov rifle in one hand

and a key in the other, and he shouted, "I killed a marine! I killed a marine!"

"Fine," Tikriti told him. "Good boy. The key."

"With one shot!"

"You're a brave lad. The key."

With Tikriti's urging, the young Iraqi mujahedeen did Tikriti's bidding, then released Aden and the other Iraqi prisoners.

"God is good," Aden said, rubbing his bruised and bleeding ankles.

"He better be," Tikriti replied. "And Iraqi to boot." Then without pause he scrambled out of the truck, out of his bonds, to freedom. Since asylum was now out of the question, he had other business to attend to.

CHAPTER 9

Once more, O City of Life, your daughter cries for you. Seven tears.
A lone flame, darkness's guide, shines in the desert
Leading her, the king, his queen, to the Father of all.

Mother, your people fly before you. Six children.
Romulus and Remus breathing fire upon the king's crown,
We are lost. We are separate. We are rootless and mad.

Molly hunched over the black binder that Cavalcante had given her. She had opened it the moment their Polish troop transport plane left the ground from the Warsaw Military Airbase, and for nearly six hours without interruption her eyes had remained fixed on the six stanzas that composed the verse. From a distance of two thousand years, Hannaniah, daughter of the Messiah, spoke to her in a poem that was far more than a poem.

Blow the ram's horn, Father. It is Yom Kippur. Five notes.
Your daughter plays the lute. Your wife sings her song.
Praise the shepherd who dies, she sings. Adore the world
that is born.

"We're almost there." The male voice that spoke to her didn't even cause her to glance up. "I said, we're almost there, Molly. Baghdad."

"Really?" When she did shift her attention to Teodor Kwiatkowski, dressed in the uniform of a major in the Polish armed forces, she was dazed, adrift in another place and time. "It feels like we just left."

"You've had your face in that binder for six hours. Everyone else has been sleeping."

Kwiatkowski held a cup of steaming black coffee and a plate of scrambled eggs, bacon and pancakes. He raised the tray at Molly's side. "Should I feed you?" he asked.

"That's probably the only way you'll get me to eat." She smiled but didn't close the binder. "Once I get into something like this, I can't put it down. Hannaniah is trying to tell us something. I'm either too sleepy or too stupid to get it."

Cavalcante lay beneath a blanket on the carpeted floor of the passenger cabin, a pillow under her head. Molly had been so immersed in her reading that she hadn't heard her friend's cavernous snoring. Leveille-Gaus had fallen asleep sitting in his chair on the opposite aisle, his glasses clinging to the bridge of his nose. Kwiatkowski was the only other passenger in the passenger section of the aircraft. A dozen Polish soldiers who would accompany them into the Iraqi hinterlands, lay asleep in a segregated section of the plane. Sitting beside her, Kwiatkowski took a fork and ate off her plate.

"We arrive in half an hour," he said.

"Then?"

"We'll be met by Polish troops. They'll escort us to the Polish embassy. You'll be introduced as journalists covering a story of Polish involvement in the war. We want as few people as possible to know what you're really doing. Even my soldiers aren't aware. From there, you people have to decide where we go. The equipment for the dig has already been arranged, along with trucks, food, and ammunition. I'm sorry this is all so rushed, but we are under time constraints."

"At least you got us military fatigues to wear." Molly eyed the food on her plate. It looked typically tasteless, but she was famished.

"How about leaving some for me?" she said.

"Sorry." Kwiatkowski handed her the fork.

The mountains of the Turkish-Iraqi border, the home of the Kurds, came into view outside. History here was older than Noah's fabled ark. It was Molly's first trip into Iraq. Apparently, it was to be a fast and furious one.

"What exactly is the push?" she wondered. "I mean, I understand we are going into a dangerous situation and need to proceed with caution. Hell, after what happened …" Molly paused. "Oh, Teodor, look, I'm sorry. None of us … your father …"

"It's all right," he said. "Men grieve in silence. It's like a code of honor. My single purpose now is to carry out my father's wishes and take care of you while you are in Iraq."

"You do understand that archaeological expeditions can take months, even years. People make careers out of a single dig."

Kwiatkowski stood up to rouse the other sleeping passengers. "You can take all year if you like," he said. "I just don't think you'll have the chance. Others will know we're here. They'll be looking for us. They may already have found us. Whatever you do, you must do with all due speed. Or we may end up like my father."

Kwiatkowski shook Cavalcante's shoulder while Molly returned to her reading. Think, think, she ordered herself. If Teodor is right, Hannaniah, I need your help.

Upon the back of a horse the savior rides. Four legs.
The fisherman sinks, the bearer of life disappears.
What rises is the Trinity to welcome home the reborn.

The plane lurched violently. Molly's breakfast, untouched since Kwiatkowski's departure, slid off her tray onto the floor. Looking out her window, Molly watched the plane descending, saw buildings and streets appearing out of the desert, a large city sprawl. Baghdad. God, she'd let the last half hour slip by in deepest concentration the way she had let the first six hours of their flight vanish.

"All right, everybody," Kwiatkowski said. "Time to buckle in. We'll be landing in five minutes."

"Molly." An excited Cavalcante, eyes alight, clasped Molly's shoulder before she fastened her safety belt beside Molly. "Are you ready?"

"Like a zombie at a bar mitzvah." Briefly, she took one final look at the two remaining stanzas of Hannaniah's lamentation.

In the corpse of the night we unite again as one. Three hearts.
Mother, Father, your children have come home.
At their daughter's fingertips, the fisherman will plant his seed.

Rest where he casts his nets. Two lamps alight.
And where your daughter's arms reach out to her people
There in the heart of David we wait for you in silence.

Six verses, Molly thought. Six children. Six points on the Star of David. Five notes. Four legs. Hannaniah, you're going to give me migraines.

No sooner did the Polish transport set down than a Polish army truck drove across the tarmac of Saddam International Airport and parked at the ramp into the plane. To bypass normal entry into the country through the airport terminal, Kwiatkowski had the passengers exit the plane and enter the army truck without going through Customs. Officially, none of them ever entered Iraq.

What Molly saw of Baghdad on the nearly one-hour trip into the city center was obscured by canvas. On any normal day, the distance from airport to hotel could have been covered in a quarter of the time.

"There was a terrorist attack on this road yesterday, a prisoner escape," Kwiatkowski explained, peering into the back of the vehicle from a window to the front seat. "They're always cautious, but today they're stopping every car."

"Are we in trouble?" Leveille-Gaus asked.

"I don't think they'll bother us. But just in case, don't make yourselves obvious."

In her years in archaeology, Molly had traveled often to the Middle East, knew Cairo almost as well as she did Boston, could walk the streets of Jerusalem blindfolded. She'd never been to Baghdad but had studied its history.

Five million people called the Iraqi capital their home, three quarters of them Shi'a Muslim, one quarter Sunni. Since its founding in AD 762, the city of Abu Jafar Al-Mansur had been a center of Islamic faith and scholarship. While Europe was plunged into dark ages of plague and cultural decline, Baghdad of the 10th century could well have been called the cultural capital of the world.

But history has a way of toppling the mighty, and Baghdad had seen its share of topplers, from Tamerlane the Mongol, to the mighty Ottoman Empire, to the even mightier British Empire that seated its favorite Muslims on the throne and dug for oil. And now, apparently, it was America's turn, under the pretense of securing democracy for a freedom-starved population.

Molly longed to peek out through the back flap of the truck. Baghdad was no Boston and deserved a long curious look. No American city could claim the age or the architectural diversity of

Baghdad. Saddam Hussein had done his damnedest to destroy it, sinking his nation into a decade-long war against Iran, following it up with the Gulf War and an international embargo that strangled its economy almost to death. But he had managed a building boom, as well, financed by Iraq's huge oil reserves.

A modern skyline of high-rises paralleled both rivers of the capital, with community housing projects and luxury hotels now inhabited by foreigners. Scattered throughout the city were beautiful turquoise-tiled mosques and minarets, the Baghdad of myth and faith. The main streets were wide enough for as many as eight lanes of traffic. On the afternoon that Molly and the other archaeologists arrived in the city, clouds of wind-blown sand from the desert curtained the city from a brownish sun. Soldiers wore special goggles. Civilians wrapped scarves and kerchiefs around their faces. In Molly's mind, it was the perfect magical entrance into the city that gave the world Scheherazade and the 1001 Arabian Nights.

"So?" Cavalcante sat beside her as they crept through the stop-and-go traffic, Leveille-Gaus on the opposite bench, several of their Polish guards immersed in a game of cards. "You've been reading almost non-stop. Any thoughts?"

"It's definitely not just a poem," Molly said. The chopping sound of low-flying helicopters nearly drowned out her words. Their rotors kicked up more dust, and the soldiers closed the canvas flap tighter. Leveille-Gaus crossed the space between them to settle on Molly's left. She held the black binder open on her lap.

"If I had had the opportunity to study these documents, I might be able to give you a reasonable response. As it is, this environment isn't the most conducive in which to decode Hannaniah. She is intentionally difficult."

"Some of it is fairly obvious," Leveille-Gaus suggested. "We know that the Second Temple was destroyed in AD 70, on the tenth of August, six hundred and fifty-six years to the day after the first temple was destroyed. The Jewish people were scattered to the wind. Romulus and Remus is Rome chasing them out into the desert."

"Yom Kippur occurs in September," Cavalcante added, looking at Molly for some sign of agreement. "That would signify the blowing of the ram's horn. But what do the five notes mean? Or the seven tears, for that matter."

Molly sat motionless and stared at the lined paper in the binder. Outside the truck, now at a complete stop, voices shouted in Arabic.

"Hannaniah loved numbers," Molly said. "Three is a common theme for her. Mother, Father, Daughter. They have a special meaning. The Holy Trinity to her is her family. Understandable for a girl whose father was Jesus and whose mother may have been Mary Magdalene. Her father is crucified. Her mother goes insane. She has no one else. She is an outcast, the product of an illegitimate relationship. All she has, all she can hang onto, is the love she has for her parents. My guess is she was obsessed with them."

And Father Ray, she thought, would say the same of me.

Abruptly, she looked up. Kwiatkowski shouted in Polish. His men in the back of the truck leaped to his command, jumping into dusty daylight, guns drawn. When Cavalcante rose in panic, Molly grabbed her wrist and sat her back down.

"Trust him," she said. "We're all right." She turned her attention back to the binder. "There's nothing in this poem that specifically leads me to conclude anything about where Hannaniah went after the Temple was destroyed. Though it may be here. Dr. Leveille, maybe you can tell us what she wrote in the Gospels I haven't read."

"They were forming communities, like seeds," Leveille-Gaus told her. "But you know that."

A gunshot exploded. Leveille-Gaus, Cavalcante, even Molly instantly fell to the floor of the truck, belly to metal. Molly could no longer hear Kwiatkowski. Dozens of voices screamed at once. The first gunshot sparked an eruption of firing.

"We'll never get anywhere this way!" Molly shouted.

"Keep down!" Leveille-Gaus ordered.

Molly handed the binder to Cavalcante who protected it against her chest. Molly didn't give a damn about herself. She crawled forward and risked a peek out the window and through the windshield to the traffic ahead. A frightened crowd of Iraqi civilians ran helter-skelter into and across the boulevard and into shops bordering either side. Polish soldiers, using their truck for cover, returned fire, aiming toward the third-story window of an apartment building where a sniper fired into the street then ducked behind a concrete wall. Molly couldn't see Kwiatkowski anywhere. What she saw instead caused her heart to leap in a panicked burst.

A little girl dressed in a white burnoose, apparently separated from her parents, was caught on the side of the road, screeching, face buried in the asphalt, one arm reaching uselessly for someone to help her. Molly envisioned herself as a child doing the same thing for the mother who never came.

She jumped from the back of the truck.

"What the hell are you doing?" Leveille-Gaus yelled at her. "Don't be crazy, O'Dwyer! This is not Rome."

Molly ignored him. Like the long distance runner she used to be in college, she pitched forward, arms and legs straining for the finish line, lungs screaming, focused on the prize. She saw the little girl and nothing else. Bullets from both sides flew past her. The heat of the day was nothing compared to the heat of the gun barrels firing hundreds of rounds of ammunition in the few seconds it took her to reach the child, scoop her up in her arms, and run headlong into an Iraqi man who had come running out of nowhere for the girl with the same thought in mind.

"Let her go!" the man yelled over the gunfire.

"She's a child!" Molly shouted back.

"She's Iraqi. She's mine," the man said in perfect English.

Looking into his fierce, bright green eyes of a man who could probably have ordered her instant death. Then she realized that the gunfire had abruptly ceased. Silence surrounded the man who had appeared as if by magic from the surrounding buildings with his small circle of bodyguards.

A Polish soldier lay bleeding and moaning in the street. The sniper had achieved his goal. The little girl clung to Molly as if she'd never let her go.

"Give her to me," the man insisted. He was dressed as a common pedestrian out for a stroll with several burly friends.

"Are you her father?"

"That is none of your business. Give her to me."

Molly held the child tight.

Kwiatkowski strode to her side. "She's not yours," he said. "Let her go."

"Teodor ..."

"Let her go. I've got a man wounded. If she's not hurt, she's not our concern."

Molly scowled at the Pole, then reluctantly pried the child's fingers from her shoulders and kissed her on the forehead before offering her to the arms of the Iraqi.

"It'll be all right," she whispered even if the girl couldn't understand. "It'll be all right." They were the words that would have comforted her thirty years before if her mother had been able to speak them to her. She turned away and wiped a tear from her eyes.

"That was pretty stupid," Kwiatkowski told her after the Iraqi had left with the child in his arms. Then he squeezed her shoulder and guided her back to the truck. "Don't do anything like that again, okay? You meant well. Just remember where you are at all times. For your own good."

"She was a baby."

"This is Iraq, Molly. Get used to it."

At last, the traffic moved again. As they passed through the checkpoint, Molly dared a glance out the back flap of the truck. The road was drenched with the blood of a dead civilian who lay in open view. Hastily, she shut the canvas and glanced at her companions.

"I need one night by myself. With the gospels," she said. "Tomorrow I'll tell you where we're going. Ur or otherwise. If we're still alive."

Before Saddam Hussein's rise to power, a half million Shi'ite Arabs inhabited twenty-thousand square kilometers of wetlands in southeast Iraq straddling the border with Iran. These loyal Iraqis had fought and died for Hussein in his war against his neighbor. The marshes were their home as well as the home to a great diversity of aquatic animals, water buffalo, and migratory birds. It had been their lives and their culture for over five thousand years. They fished the waters, hunted among the reeds, tended their sheep, and lived at peace. Then they rebelled against Saddam Hussein, foolishly assuming the Americans would come to their aid.

Now, as Abdul Azim Nur gathered his worshippers in a small mud-brick mosque to perform the noon Salaah, the marshes had been replaced by salt-pans, and only ten thousand Arabs called the land their home. Forty thousand others had fled to Iran and lived in refugee camps. The rest were dead. While they all rejoiced at the departure of the dictator Hussein, they shared a profound frustration and cynicism toward the liberators. What good were all the promises when the marshes were gone forever?

Loyal to Abdul Azim Nur, his faithful commenced the second prayer ritual of the day, standing and facing their holy leader, the man who had led them in their collapsed insurrection against Hussein. The ritual hadn't changed for hundreds of years. Each man raised his hands to his ears before folding them over his chest, right hand over left. Then, bowing, they placed their hands upon their knees.

"*Laa ilaaha illallaah*," Nur chanted. There is no God but Allah. "*As-salaamu alaykum wa rahmatullah*." Peace on you and the mercy of Allah.

The men prostrated themselves on the brick floor then finished their ministrations by coming to a sitting position on their individual mats. Nur was about to address his followers when Barid Shamkhazi came to the mosque's entrance and signaled to him. Nur rose, turned the services over to an assistant, and headed out into the humid Iraqi afternoon, offering expressions of gratitude as he went. He came to a halt at the sight of Shamkhazi in heated discussion with a newcomer who had arrived with a phalanx of armed bodyguards.

Ghazi Al-Tikriti smiled at Nur. "Oh, God, You are Peace," he said, quoting The Prophet. "From You comes Peace, To You returns Peace."

"I'm so glad you feel that way, Ghazi," Nur said with a glance at Barid. His black robes and turban protected him from the sun. His spectacles reflected the light so that his eyes could not be seen.

"All true Muslims believe in Peace. I have been in Abu Ghraib."

"And you look no worse for wear, Allah be praised."

Tikriti gathered the holy man under his arm and directed him to the shade of one of the only trees remaining in the village. Shamkhazi kept his distance. A stone well rested in the shade, too, its water undrinkable. Rifles were stacked against the well as they were not allowed inside the mosque. Perched on the lip of the well like a vulture who hadn't eaten in weeks was Aden, the woman-hater.

"My humble thanks to you, Imam," Tikriti said. "I would not be here if not for you."

"It was not my decree that freed you, but the will of the ayatollahs, apparently. The people here haven't forgotten your role as Saddam's dog."

"I have ten daughters, Imam. What was I to do?"

"Fall on your sword," Nur said. A fly landed on Tikriti's moustache, which he did not seem to notice, as oblivious to his own evil nature as to the fly.

Tikriti said, "We are all Iraqis now, united in our hate for the invader. I saw things in prison that I did not see under Saddam. I have come to beg your forgiveness and to ask for your help."

"You interrupted the Salaah."

"As long as the Americans are in Iraq, all is profaned. Will you help me, Imam?"

Nur watched the fly clean itself on Tikriti's face then go after the human vulture poised on the well. "Help you do what, Ghazi?"

"The Americans control the cities, barely. But you control the deserts," Tikriti said. "From Iran to Syria, from Saudi Arabia to Jordan. The people follow you. They will rise if you say rise, sleep if you say sleep. For now the turmoil is all in the cities, but it won't stay there, if only because the oil they want so desperately is not in the cities. Ultimately, they will come to you."

"You want me to lead a holy war over oil?" Nur asked. He folded his arms across his thick paunch and waited for what Ghazi was really leading to.

Tikriti leaned in closer to whisper. "I want you to give me some men," he said. "The Americans are planning an expedition into the desert. They are looking for something far more valuable than oil. If they are successful, you will never get them out of the country. They must be stopped."

Abdul Azim Nur had not attained prominence as a holy man by being stupid. He had known Tikriti for many years, even before Tikriti had become an officer in Saddam's army. He knew that Tikriti was not a stupid man either. He had risked coming here, of all places, to beg forgiveness and to ask help from people whose children he had slaughtered. Even Barid Shamkhazi's cloak of protection would not keep the man alive if the men of the marsh wanted him dead.

Nur had returned from exile in Iran principally to defend his Marsh Arabs, to carve out territory for them in this new Iraq. He trusted no one—not the surviving Iraqi elite, nor his Iranian mentors, nor the Americans, nor Ghazi Al-Tikriti. But this Tikriti was a snake and he bore watching.

"What is it the Americans are after?" the holy man asked the snake.

"Their god," Tikriti replied. "The remains of the man called Jesus."

What happened next was a blur to Nur. One moment, he stood and faced Ghazi Al-Tikriti, the next, he fell to the ground in a faint. And then he vanished. That is to say, he lay at Ghazi Al-Tikriti's feet physically, but in mind he was propelled to another place, another time, brought to the walls of an ancient city. From a twenty-first century Iraqi imam he was transformed into a man familiar with this new environment. He tried to utter Tikriti's name, hoping that would return him to where he belonged, but no words came out of his mouth. He couldn't speak. He couldn't move. He watched in amazement as a host of snarling red-furred cats, their claws bared, closed in on him. He considered running, but even such movement appeared beyond his current ability.

When he saw the young woman with red hair, he knew that something terrible was about to happen to him. He screamed out her name, not knowing how or why he knew it. But it was that sound that saved him and returned him to the marshes of southeastern Iraq and to the feet of Tikriti and Barid Shamkhazi who had rushed to his aid with a drink of water.

"Imam! Here! Drink this! What happened?"

"Imam," Tikriti asked, "are you all right?"

Nur propped himself on one arm and sipped the water, too dazed to respond to Tikriti.

"Do you give your consent?" Tikriti pressed him.

Nur shook his head.

Barid interpreted for Nur. "Go," the young Iranian told Tikriti.

"He gives his consent?"

"I do." Barid signaled to one of Nur's lieutenants to accompany Tikriti. "Go and do what you must."

Tikriti strode away.

Who is she? Nur wondered, this red-haired American woman he'd confronted on the streets of Baghdad the day before and then again just now, somehow, under the historic walls of ancient Jerusalem.

Who is she?

Still dazed, he managed to yell after the departing former Iraqi intelligence officer. "Tikriti! The woman! Bring me the woman!"

Major General Jim Eisenstadt had survived the jungles of Viet Nam, the First Gulf War, Pentagon infighting, which was arguably more brutal, and a Democratic administration. He'd been married. Three times. Paid child support for three kids. One per marriage. He'd been shot at, blown out of the sky, kicked in the shins, thrown out of court, but he'd never faced the almighty shit he was going through now. All because a couple of damned fool PFCs had gotten themselves photographed climbing a hill of naked Iraqi prisoners. And if his ass was on the line, everyone's ass was on the line.

"Including yours," he told Milstein and Jackson. "What the hell happened in Poland?"

"A car bombing," Jackson explained. They talked on the fly, heading toward a chopper pad outside the former Presidential Palace Command Center a hundred meters from the Tigris River. Eisenstadt was heading back to the States for debriefing, and he wasn't in the best of moods.

"But why the hell was there a car bombing in Poland, for God's sake? What's in Poland?"

"Molly O'Dwyer," Milstein said. He held on to his sunglasses. One of the earpieces was loose, and the jog to Eisenstadt's helicopter threatened to knock it off. "We counted three dead terrorists."

"Arabs?"

"Probably. They weren't carrying ID."

"So you don't know who's behind them," Eisenstadt said. At the chopper pad, he stopped to catch his breath. The rotors of the helicopter were in motion, so they held onto their hats and glasses. "I can't be involved with this, boys. I have too much on my plate, and this is fast getting out of control. And for what? Some archaeological dig? What is your plan of action?"

"Stake out the Polish embassy," Jackson said. "Look, I was skeptical at first, too, General. But somebody wants what O'Dwyer and the others are after. If Tikriti was right …"

"Tikriti is no longer under our jurisdiction."

Eisenstadt's words stopped Jackson cold. "What do you mean, sir?" he asked.

"One of our prisoner escort convoys was attacked outside Abu Ghraib. We lost five men. Tikriti and a few other Iraqis got away. Do you think that has anything to do with what happened in Poland?"

Jackson and Milstein looked at each other. "Can't be sure," Jackson said.

"So what can you do for us, General?" Milstein asked.

"What do you need?"

"Soldiers. Trucks. We need to provide for a full archaeological operation with supportive troops."

"No can do," Eisenstadt said. "I'm stretched enough."

Milstein raised his voice. "Do you know what is out in that desert, General?"

"No, sir. Do you?" Eisenstadt started for the helicopter bay.

"Jesus of Nazareth!" Milstein hollered. "That's who!"

That stopped Eisenstadt, who eyed Milstein as he if were staring down a journalist from MSNBC. "You better not be fucking with me, Mr. Milstein You better be on the button with this one or near enough a cow can fly through the buttonhole. I'm not losing my head over some crazy claims."

To Jackson, whom he knew and trusted, he said, "One truck. You gather the people you need. Civilians, no military personnel."

"But how do we dig?" Milstein asked.

"Your problem," Eisenstadt said. "Compromise the Poles, if that's what it takes. Just don't leave a trail."

"Compromise?"

"You never heard any of this from me," were Eisenstadt's final words, coming from the steps into the helicopter.

"Compromise?"

"You heard him," Jackson said, watching the general disappear into the craft. It ascended in a windstorm of sand that forced Milstein and Jackson to duck their heads and cover their faces.

"You did tell him Jesus, didn't you? You don't know that."

"The only thing I know for sure is compromise is out of the question," Milstein said as soon as the roar of the departing chopper had died to silence. "Whether it is or isn't Jesus, this is a holy mission, not some Vin Diesel flick."

Jackson laughed and slapped his Jewish companion on the back. "Milstein, life is a Vin Diesel flick. Might as well enjoy it. The intermission sucks."

As the two Americans headed back across the lawn of Saddam's former command headquarters, two other men watched them from three floors up. One had arrived from the States only an hour before and was exhausted from the long trip. The other was native-born but had also arrived only recently from a flight into Saddam International Airport. What they had in common was that they both knew Andrew Milstein, and both knew that they would be of inestimable value to his expedition into the Iraqi heartland.

Father Ray Teague breathed on the lenses of his glasses and wiped the dust clean on his shirt. "I don't know about you," he said to the other man, "but I hope we know what we're doing."

"Don't worry," said Habib Al-Nazariiy. "I know I do."

CHAPTER 10

Movies always get it wrong. Fires aren't bright. They don't light a path through smoke-filled hallways, conveniently providing an escape route through scattered flames.

Fires are dark. They are black. They are pure death. Escape routes do not exist. Anyone who hasn't fled the fire when it is still smoldering and static is as good as dead. Molly knew that better than most. She had escaped a fire. Her mother, who had gone back inside to look for her, had died. Now, years later on an almost nightly basis, Molly relived that dark black hell. Sometimes she escaped it. Sometimes she did not.

When she woke up in the night screaming, the darkness and unfamiliarity of the room frightened her. The hand that abruptly sealed her mouth shut only made her struggle more violently. She tried to kick her way to freedom, to scratch the face of the man who held her down, but he was too strong. Both of them panted with the struggle.

"Molly!" he whispered. "Calm down! It's all right! You were dreaming!"

Kwiatkowski pulled his hand away to study the bite mark on his palm. "I hope you've had your inoculations," he said.

"I'm sorry."

Molly sat up in the bed she had chosen, in the room overlooking a tiled courtyard and an empty swimming pool. As her eyes adjusted to the darkness, assisted only by moonlight filtering through diaphanous white curtains, she saw the black binder on the floor beside her, open upside down. She must have fallen asleep reading it, though she couldn't remember turning off the lights. Then she recalled that the private walled estate Kwiatkowski had led them to was deserted and had no electrical power.

"Did I wake everybody up?" she asked, bending to retrieve the binder.

"Only me, it seems. But you never know. We're not supposed to be here."

Molly, her companions, and their Polish guards had slipped out of Baghdad with the military orders to join their Polish division near An-Najaf south of the capital. But Kwiatkowski had made other plans, choosing to hole up in the private compound of an Iraqi businessman his father had known. It was an expensive retreat on the banks of the Tigris, built as a retreat from the crowds and the suffocating presence of Saddam Hussein and his sons, a paradise of cool water, warm breezes, and shade trees whose dates and figs guests could pluck at their leisure.

It was a place where Iraqi men with money could enjoy the companionship of lovely Iraqi women, neither of whom were interested in The Prophet's injunctions against such behavior. It was the kind of exotic place Michael Kwiatkowski would have visited whenever he made a profitable business transaction with the Hussein government, even while the international boycott was in force. The son, unlike the father, remained loyal to his mother, dead ten years. He came only because the place was long abandoned.

"Are you hungry?" he asked Molly.

"No. I really should get back to work on this. What time is it?"

"You don't wear a watch?"

"No watch. No rings. *Nada*. Except these." Underneath her shirt, clasped around her neck, she wore the Star of David pendant that

Hannaniah herself might have worn two thousand years before. Although the size and weight of the medallion indicated that it might have had a purpose other than adornment, Molly had attached the pendant to the same necklace on which dangled her crucifix. She liked the juxtaposition of the two spiritual symbols.

Kwiatkowski flicked on a flashlight and focused the beam on the translated Hannaniah gospel open on Molly's lap. "It's two o'clock," he said. Outside, his men would be keeping watch along the iron-barred walls and gate of the compound. Since none of them had come at a trot to the main house, he assumed Molly's scream had gone undetected. He sank into the comfortable if dusty mattress beside her.

"Anything new?" he asked.

"I would prefer to curl up with this back in Boston for a couple of months," she said. "Your father equipped us nicely, but all the tools and maps in the world aren't worth a thing if Hannaniah doesn't tell us where to look. I thought at first of Ur, the birthplace of Abraham. But there was no scientific reason for speculating that."

"How do we know Hannaniah's trying to tell us anything?" Kwiatkowski asked. "I know the others think so. My father did. Do you?"

Molly looked up from her reading to Kwiatkowski's thoughtful face, and for a fleeting moment her heart raced like that of a young girl feeling a primal attraction as old as humanity. But it was more than that. More than, *God he's good-looking.* More than the heat of the moment. In the moon-washed semi-darkness, his features had ever so briefly looked familiar to her, like she had known him before. Closely. Intimately. But where? And how? The urge to forego Hannaniah and kiss him was so powerful, she had to force her attention back to the book. And she hardly knew the man.

"I begin with the assumption," she explained, "that Hannaniah was not making all this up. Yeshuah bar Yushef, our Jesus, was her father. She was born out of wedlock," much, Molly thought, as I was. "Her life was difficult but not impossible. She tells a very stark tale. No frills. No dramatic leaps. Sometimes reading her I feel guilty because it's like reading the private diary of a young girl."

"But you read."

"I'm compelled to. It's like Anne Frank's diary. Very personal, very painful. And yet the world is a better place for having known her. Hannaniah was no more a liar or a deceiver than Anne Frank. If she says her father was Jesus of Nazareth, then he was."

Molly took the flashlight from Kwiatkowski and shone it on the binder. She turned several pages to a poem. A warm breeze rustled her bedroom curtain. Kwiatkowski withdrew a Bic lighter from his pocket and lit up a cigarette.

"Please, not around me," Molly said.

"Sorry." He crushed it out against the metal bedpost. "Bad habit. Can't stop."

"Try gum." Molly flipped a page. "I've only had a short time to scan Dr. Leveille's portion," she said. "But it's very different from mine. More hyperbole. More verse than prose."

"Maybe it's a different author," Kwiatkowski suggested.

"Or poor translation. I've thought about that. Maybe one of her children took up her pen. But Leveille, much as he has angered me, is an expert in Aramaic and Hebrew. He's not likely to have screwed up that badly."

"Leading you to believe …"

Molly gazed again into Kwiatkowski's pale eyes, searched them briefly, could have sworn they were darker before, sighed. Whatever familiarity had swept swiftly across his pale face before was gone.

"She was in a hurry," Molly said at last. "Like we are. The gospels I translated she wrote at her leisure. What Leveille read was written by Hannaniah in a matter of months or even weeks. One was the product of youth, the other of middle age. Judea was in crisis. The Jews were rebelling against Rome. The Romans were responding as the Romans always did. The Jewish community in Alexandria was massacred. She and her father fled across the Sinai with a plan. Jerusalem was about to be destroyed, the remnants of the militant movement wiped out at the fortress of Masada, their people scattered to the winds."

"The Diaspora," Kwiatkowski said.

"Yes. The modern version began then." Molly ran her fingers over the pages in the binder as if, like a ghost hunter, she could pick up Hannaniah's scent and follow her on her journey east. Oh, if only she had the original scrolls!

"Their plan," she said, "was to establish permanent Jewish settlements beyond Rome's borders, safe havens where their people could rebuild, regrow, perhaps return to the Holy Land but not as they had left it. They would be different, more tolerant, less encumbered by the rules and regulations of the priests. Jesus hated regimentation. His brilliance was in seeing what lay at the core of every religion of his day—love—and founding his ministry on that. Everything else—rules, regulations, laws, taxes—had nothing to do with faith and God, and he emancipated his followers from them. He and his daughter would plant the seed of a revived faith, nurture it in these new communities, then bring it back to Jerusalem. This was the messiah's plan. This was the resurrection. A new world built upon a foundation of love rather than edict, an acceptance of all people, a philosophy of intellect welded to faith, a ministry developed by Yeshuah and modified through experience by him and by his daughter Hannaniah."

By the time she had finished speaking, Molly was on her feet pacing to the rapid march of her ideas.

"So," she said, "they fled east. With a plan. Remember that. Hannaniah loved numbers, like you, played at astrology and magic. Three, the trinity, mother, father, and daughter, the most important of all. Ten for the lost tribes of Israel and for the holy commandments. Seven. Seven holes in a jagged V. Six for her children. Five notes. Four legs. Three hearts. Two lamps. God, she is telling us something!"

Molly lifted the Star of David from around her neck. "Hannaniah was also a scientist, trained by her father and by Greeks to think rationally. They knew where those communities were going to be located. Jama and I found the first in Egypt. I found another in Afghanistan. People in India have a tradition that Jesus traveled to the Ganges and died and was buried there in Srinigar. There may be a grain of truth to that, though I suspect their grave doesn't hold Jesus but one of his disciples."

"Thomas, perhaps," said a shadowy figure in Molly's doorway. "No," he said, "Jesus is not buried in India. Or in France. Or in Cleveland, Ohio. He is somewhere else."

"You don't believe in the resurrection?" Molly asked.

Into the room walked Leveille-Gaus, quiet, shoeless, his red hair unkempt from sleep. "Well, either Jesus was the Son of God or he wasn't, yes? If yes, we're on a fool's mission. If no, we have work to do. The Jews and the Christians can't both be right, can they?"

"I believe they can." Molly stopped her pacing and stuck her hands in the back pockets of the military khakis Kwiatkowski had provisioned for them in Warsaw. Leveille-Gaus' point was a powerful one, and at the heart of the abyss between all of the world's great religions. Can only one religion be right and all the others wrong?

Was Jesus the Son of God, crucified, and resurrected? Or was that myth, first century religious spin?

"Religion is faith," Molly said, "not dogma. That was Jesus' point. That was why he fought the temple priests and consorted with outcasts. With all due respect to your rules and regulations, all that matters is faith, love, respect for others."

"But that's not the point," Leveille-Gaus said. "You can believe Jesus was divine all you want. Either he was or he wasn't. Somebody's got to be wrong."

"I look at the stars every night," Kwiatkowski said, "and I can't imagine God. It is too much for me. The concept of always and forever. It is arrogant of us to think we truly understand it. And if we don't understand, how can we say with any true authority what is right and what is wrong about anything? We live and we die. That's it."

Kwiatkowski lowered his head into his hands and quietly wept.

As if drawn by his emotions, the fourth member of the expedition came in and stood over the Polish officer and massaged his shoulders. "Shame on us all," Cavalcante said, "for ignoring Teodor's sacrifice."

"I'm all right," Kwiatkowski said. "I only cry because it is more soothing than prayer."

"I suppose since we are all awake now," Leveille-Gaus said, "we might as well make plans for the morning. Are you any closer to deciding where we start, Dr. O'Dwyer?"

"I know where we have to start," she said.

"Ur of the Chaldees," Leveille-Gaus said.

"Yes, as a starting point. Not necessarily the goal."

Leveille-Gaus glanced in Cavalcante's direction. "That's exactly where we would have gone. Hannaniah was not being as obtuse as she might have been. Even if she wanted to keep the locations of the Jewish settlements secret from outsiders, she had to leave clues her people could understand. The poem and the star both lead us to the Father of us all. Abraham. At Ur."

"Then why did you need me?" Molly asked. "You had Teodor's father's backing. Or the Vatican's. You had your portion of the gospels and Nina's information from the Vatican archives. Why am I here?"

"Because, Molly," Cavalcante said, "Hannaniah speaks through you. She didn't write a Fodor's of Ur. And Ur, as you suggest, may only be the starting point. Mohamoud Jama made his discovery in the Iraqi desert somewhere. Not at Ur. You know Hannaniah better than any of us. You've gotten inside her head. And she's inside you."

"Nina, please."

"We have proof, Molly!"

"Proof of what?" Molly confronted Cavalcante and only then realized that her Italian associate was holding a manila folder crammed with documents. "Proof of what? That she's inside my head? You are crazy."

"Not at all," Cavalcante said. "Here. Look." She offered Molly the manila folder.

"What? More of Hannaniah's gospels?"

"No," Leveille-Gaus said. "Science."

Molly glanced once at the Frenchman before snatching the folder from Cavalcante. She had never doubted the two were holding out on her.

"What are these?" Molly asked, perusing the documents.

"DNA tests," Cavalcante said. She spoke gently, softly, but with the excitement of a child waiting for her mother to unwrap the greatest of Christmas gifts. "You said yourself, Mohamoud Jama went off on a wild goose chase using the DNA samples you had recovered from the body in Egypt. He tested all the local villagers, hoping to find someone who bore the genetic markings of a descendant of Jesus.

He went to Israel, too, to the area he believed Jesus had been born, and tested as many residents there as he could."

"Yes. I know. So what?"

"In order to convince the Egyptian people to take the necessary tests," Leveille-Gaus said, "he started by testing everyone on the archaeological expedition with him. Me. You."

"And?"

Cavalcante pulled a sheet of paper from the manila folder and handed it to Molly. "It wasn't such a wild goose chase after all, dear. Jama was stunned to discover that of all the people he tested the only one who matched the Egyptian sample—the only one who appeared to be a direct descendant of Jesus of Nazareth—was you."

In the darkness in the room once used by wealthy Iraqi men to unveil and unwrap poorer Iraqi women, Molly tried to read Cavalcante's document. She slumped onto her bed.

"Turn off the flashlight, Teodor," she said. Moments later, she began to cry.

"Molly?" he asked.

Cavalcante sat beside her and rubbed her arm. "You knew all along, didn't you? Jama told you." Molly didn't have to answer. "I don't know if it's science, Molly, but somehow, if you are dreaming of Hannaniah, it may be because your mind contains her memories, passed down through the generations. It's real, Molly. You hold the key."

"Damn it!" Molly threw Cavalcante off and stormed to her feet. Heading out the door, she turned about-face. "How did you know? How did you find out? Why weren't you up front?"

"Jama asked for your help," Leveille-Gaus told her. "After the First Gulf War, Iraq had no facility to test the DNA samples he had taken. He wanted you to provide a lab for him. When you turned him down, he came to us."

"Bullshit! It's all bullshit! I'm not her! I'm not some holy goddamned descendant of the Messiah! This is crazy!"

Kwiatkowski offered his arms for her support, and Molly buried herself in his chest and wept.

"You are all trying to make me something I'm not," she said. "Every kook on the planet will come after me, and I have nothing to offer them. I'm as faithless as the rest of you."

Molly shook free of Kwiatkowski, aware for the first time how empty her faith had really been all these years. She was still very much that little girl who had sworn at the world, cursed it for eternity, when the one person she loved most in the world had died.

"It doesn't change anything," Leveille-Gaus suggested. "Except that you may be able to help us find him in ways that no one else can."

Molly grunted and pushed away from Kwiatkowski, rubbing her eyes against the sleeve of her shirt. "I doubt it," she said. "And this is not to go anywhere, do you understand? No one finds out about this." Bending down, she retrieved the black binder that had fallen off the bed onto the floor. "Can we be in Ur by sunset today?"

"No problem," Kwiatkowski said. "Barring mishaps, we can make it in about four hours."

"Good." Molly headed for the door. "By this time tomorrow night, we'll know where to start looking. And it won't take any hocus pocus."

André Leveille-Gaus was used to the terror and chaos of war. His father had been a career diplomat for the government of France, a low-level bureaucrat in the French embassy in Algiers during the bloody years of the Algerian war for independence. Not unlike the Middle East today, that Muslim nation had been rife with terrorism, kidnapping, murder. As a middle-schooler, Leveille-Gaus remembered tucking a loaded pistol into his book bag and walking the streets of the Algerian capital with his friends, eyes flitting back and forth, anticipating at any moment the shriek of braking tires, the sudden opening of a door, the quick grab and the permanent disappearance.

Some things, he thought as he left Molly's room, you never forget. He had every reason to dislike and distrust Muslims. His father had been assassinated in a car bombing much like Kwiatkowski's. The world hadn't changed one bit. The violence had simply shifted.

And yet it was in Algeria that Leveille-Gaus had found meaning to life, in exciting expeditions into the hinterlands while the world was at peace, with his mother the teacher and her brother the geologist. He had met his future wife in Algeria, made their first child on a honeymoon there on the twentieth anniversary of his father's death. The land was beautiful, the history alive. And it was in Algeria on a dig ten years earlier that Leveille-Gaus had first read the name Hannaniah.

Oh, yes, he thought as he quietly left the main building and walked among the palm and fig trees, I have known Hannaniah far longer than you have, Molly. But not as well.

He would never speak of the bizarre dreams he had had ever since he uncovered Hannaniah's name in the desert, dreams so real he could have sworn he was back in Jerusalem at the time Hannaniah lived. Cavalcante had them, too. She had written to him once about them. Dreams that she had been Hannaniah's lover, dreams that Leveille-Gaus would normally have found amusing, had he not been so ensnared by the mysterious Hannaniah himself. Who, in God's name, was she to have such a hold over us? Maybe, like Molly

O'Dwyer, they all had their own genetic connection to the Messiah of the Jews, and like pawns of God were being put back into play after two thousand years.

Finally pausing under a tree at a far corner of the estate, he unzipped the fly of his pants and directed the stream of his urine into the tall grass near the trunk. He had passed one of Kwiatkowski's armed soldiers going in the other direction toward the estate. He felt safe enough, once he was done, with the moon hidden by the waving palm fronds, to pull out a small transmitter, to raise its antenna, and to speak softly into it.

"Tomorrow it begins," he said. "At sunset. I'll keep you apprised. Just have a helicopter ready, and make no mistakes. When it's over, I'm the only one coming out."

CHAPTER 11

Three million times the sun had set on Ur since the first people had built the first walls of the ancient city. In those days, the waters of the Arabian Gulf had extended farther north, almost as far as Baghdad. Rivers carrying silt from the mountains to the sea deposited a plain of rich and fertile soil that farmers farmed and herders grazed. Here around 6000 BC the Ubaid people established their kingdom, to be followed in turn by the Sumerians and the Babylonians. Abraham, the patriarch of the Hebrews, was a pup, a newcomer, who left the land of the Chaldees for Canaan four thousand years after the region had first been inhabited.

Driving from the north down a highway largely empty but for the occasional military vehicle, Molly longed to jump onto the roof of the armored truck that carried the archaeologists to Ur, but ambushes notoriously picked off trucks, humvees, or tanks, killing the careless passenger who thought all was safe. A person didn't have to see his murderer, who could be hiding far off the side of the road with a shoulder-mounted grenade launcher or a homemade multiple rocket launcher. She pestered Kwiatkowski so much that he finally let her ride in the passenger seat while he drove. A second armored vehicle, carrying supplies and the rest of the crew, followed them.

Molly was practically standing in her seat when Tell el-Mukayyar first came into view. "That's it!" she said. "God, look at it!"

"Sit down!" Kwiatkowski insisted.

Molly pressed against the glove compartment, elbows on the dashboard, forehead touching the windshield. "Can you imagine how old this place is, Teodor?" she said. "I envy Woolley."

Woolley, the British archaeologist, had excavated the site over a period of ten years in the 1920s and 30s. Back then the Tell, the archaeological mound, had been a hill of debris. Buried beneath it, now visible to the eye across the desert plain from as far as a mile away, was the famed ziggurat of Ur-Nammu, the temple to the moon goddess Nanna, rising about seventy feet above the arid flatland.

Molly surrendered to Kwiatkowski's urging and fell back into her seat. "Remember," he told her, "American soldiers guard the site. You're part of an international team of archaeologists surveying sites to make sure they are properly safeguarded. We are here to safeguard you."

"Don't worry, Teodor. I'm not going to drop my pants and moon anyone."

"Just checking."

Instead of dropping her pants, Molly unzipped a backpack between her feet on the floor. From it she withdrew a laminated document Cavalcante had given her. Outside, the mid-morning temperature was breaching one hundred degrees. Inside, the air-conditioning ran full throttle.

"This is a letter," she explained to him, "that Nina found in the Vatican archives. A copy at any rate. From Hannaniah to Peter in Rome. Basically, it chastises him for making false claims in regard to her father. By this point, it seems Yeshuah is dead and she has taken over his ministry. That is neither here nor there for our purposes. What is important is that she tells him to come here, 'to the place of our birth,' she says, and to cease and desist preaching until he does. Remember, family means everything to Hannaniah. The birth of her family, the Jewish people, was Ur, that place, she tells Peter 'near where the Mother and Father rivers converge to the sea.'"

"But Ur is a large place," Kwiatkowski said, "and as you said, it's already been excavated. What's left that hasn't been found?"

"Everything Woolley overlooked."

As Kwiatkowski slowed to make a left turn off the main road onto the drive that would take them to the former tourist attraction of Ur, Molly held her breath.

The great stepped pyramid, built four thousand years before, rose out of the desert like a mud-brick Fort Knox, a solid structure one hundred and fifty feet wide, built on three levels, three rectangles set on top of one another with a temple at the very top. Stone stairs led up from what several thousand years ago would have been a spacious and busy courtyard. The stairs ran from just beyond the American military encampment up the front of the pyramid to the highest level. Two more staircases reached up from the right and left corners, forming a sort of cross and meeting the main staircase in the middle. The Englishman Woolley had not only managed to uncover this archaeological wonder but had unearthed four square miles of the city of Abraham that surrounded Nanna's temple, its warehouses, shops, schools, homes. Royal tombs filled with wonderful artifacts had competed for headlines with the magnificent finds of King Tut's burial chamber in Egypt. Teodor was right, Molly thought. Unless Hannaniah had left them the correct clues, they could search Ur forever and not find what they were looking for.

Their vehicles drove toward a small U.S. military encampment, tents billowing in the hot desert winds. Temperatures in the summer could far exceed one hundred degrees, turning Ur into an oven whose mud bricks could have baked in the open air. But it was peaceful, a reasonably safe and quiet assignment away from Iraq's violent cities. Even the nearby city of Nasiriyah was passive, and the cooling water of the Euphrates was a short bouncing ride away on a humvee.

Before Kwiatkowski had parked his vehicle at the military compound's front gate, two American soldiers of the 241st Military Police out of Florida approached him. Molly watched from inside the truck. When the two armed Americans laughed, she knew Kwiatkowski had been successful. He waved to her.

"I hope you have your sunscreen, ma'am," one of the soldiers told her, giving her an appreciative once-over. "And a hat would do, too."

"I have my old trusty," she said, dusting off a Red Sox cap, which she perched on her head above dark-tinted sunglasses. "When can we begin?"

"Right away, ma'am," said the second soldier. "Your orders look good. It's pretty damn quiet here, if you want to know the truth of it. What are you looking for?"

"Damned if I know," Molly said with a wink. "But I'll let you know when I find it."

Out of the back of the second truck jumped Leveille-Gaus and Cavalcante, who took a swig of water from a canteen before sharing it with Leveille-Gaus. They came to stand beside Molly and Kwiatkowski as they gazed up at the ziggurat, which lay across a barren stretch of ground half a football field from the military encampment.

"Do we wait until sunset?" Leveille-Gaus asked. "Or do we have enough to go on to start a methodical search?"

"How about lunch?" Kwiatkowski asked, ever pragmatic. "I couldn't work in this heat without something inside me."

"Great idea," Molly said. "You get it ready. I want to take a little walk."

She headed for the ziggurat. Cavalcante tugged on a backpack and walked beside her. Molly took a drink from her own canteen. "Forty acres," she said. "I didn't realize the dig site was so large."

"Is that going to be a problem?"

"I hope not."

One hundred and twenty-two steps up the side of the ziggurat, Molly and Cavalcante panted their way through the heat to the top. Once there, Molly looked back at the figures in the military compound. Down below, Leveille-Gaus waved to them. Cavalcante waved back.

Molly said, "How far do you trust him?"

"He's a superb archaeologist, Molly."

"That doesn't answer my question."

Cavalcante shrugged off her backpack, unzipped it, and pulled out a video cam. She aimed it at Molly and looked through the viewer. "Did anybody ever tell you you're quite photogenic, Molly?" she asked.

"My last boyfriend. A paleontologist. He said the same thing about himself."

Laughing, Cavalcante redirected the camera and walked west toward the edge of the ziggurat.

"Woolley did a hell of a job," Molly said. "But when Hannaniah and her followers came here, they didn't see what Woolley did two thousand years later."

"The ziggurat must have been more evident," Cavalcante agreed. "Even much of the city. There are historical accounts as late as the third century BCE of Arabs inhabiting the site. Hannaniah wouldn't have had to dig in the way Woolley did."

"No, definitely not." Molly crouched and gathered pebbles, which she tossed over the side onto the second level of the pyramid twenty feet below. Shutting her eyes, she tried to view Ur as Hannaniah must have, the long-deserted ghost town where the winds of the desert hunted the spirits of the dead and chased them through the empty buildings. The streets were so narrow and the shops and residences so concentrated that even in its heyday Ur must have been a chaotic, confusing warren of activity, easy to get lost in.

" 'Come to the place of our birth,' she told Paul," Molly said. " 'Walk the straight and narrow path. Where our mother joins our father, there we will open our arms to you.' "

"A double meaning?" Cavalcante asked, laying her video cam aside to sit next to Molly. To the south and west Iraq lay before them, flat and arid all the way to Saudi Arabia or Syria.

"Straight and narrow. Trite but to the point," Molly said. "Paul is the greatest salesman of all time, Yeshuah's most important disciple, if you liked what he was selling. Guilt. Hannaniah didn't. But she also meant something else."

"A map."

"I think so."

Molly stood up. A strong gust of hot air spiraling atop the ziggurat nearly caused her to lose her balance and fall over the side. But holding her ground, she pointed west. "If Ur is the father," she said, conjuring an image of Hannaniah doing this very same thing on the roof of the temple to the moon goddess Nanna, "then the mother lies in that direction."

"The setting sun?" Cavalcante asked.

"Jerusalem."

The red sun arrayed its dying light across the desert from west to east, from the distant horizon to Ur. Molly and the others had spent the rest of the day using Leonard Woolley's original site map to explore the old city. Now she, Cavalcante, Kwiatkowski, and Leveille-Gaus stood on the western side of the ziggurat watching the last rays of the sun, the last stretch of its motherly arm, touch the reborn walls of Ur. At that point where the mother bid goodnight to the father, Molly thought, taking into account the change in the earth's axis over the past two thousand years, is where we'll begin to look for Hannaniah.

Woolley had managed a thorough and patient reconstruction of Ur. Beside the royal tombs and cemetery south of the ziggurat, he had excavated enough artifacts to help him determine what was a warehouse and what was a residence or shop—cooking vessels, pottery, jewelry, cuneiform tablets containing records of commercial transactions, law, war, and dynasties that went back beyond the construction of the ziggurat four thousand years ago. Thanks to Woolley's diligent and painstaking work, Molly hoped that her team's effort would be far less rigorous and time-consuming. Even so, much depended upon Hannaniah, and her own ability to read Yeshuah's daughter.

"Are we ready?" Leveille-Gaus asked. All four members of the expedition carried powerful military flashlights. Cavalcante checked her video cam. They had made a copy of Woolley's site map for each person. Kwiatkowski and Leveille-Gaus wore holstered pistols.

Molly indicated the spot where the sun had finally surrendered Ur to darkness. "We'll start there," she said. "I believe that is the Ishtar Gate. In Hannaniah's day, it would have been an obvious point of entry into the city."

"Just exactly what are we looking for?" Kwiatkowski asked. His soldiers would tag along with them just in case, though no one anticipated trouble. They would also serve, if and when the time came, as laborers bearing shovels.

Molly started down the one hundred and twenty-two steps of the central staircase, her flashlight beam playing off the stone steps. The

American military encampment below was quiet.

"I'm sure Woolley didn't miss anything on or in the ground," Molly said as she carefully maneuvered the steps. "But my guess is there wouldn't have been anything for him to find. At some point, Hannaniah's followers abandoned the site. They may have taken everything with them."

"Except their dead," Cavalcante said.

"True. I found dead in Afghanistan. But Woolley didn't find anyone here. At least none he could date to that time period."

"He wasn't looking for anyone from that time period," Leveille-Gaus reminded her.

Molly nodded. She had thought all these points through. "People bury their dead with telltale artifacts," she said. "If Woolley didn't find them, they weren't here. Mohamoud Jama did find them. Somewhere out there in the desert."

"So, how are we going to find them without Jama's help?" Kwiatkowski asked.

"Look on the walls. Look on the lintels," Molly said. "Look for anything the people couldn't take with them that Woolley might have overlooked. Tomorrow. There's no point in trying tonight."

But Molly could hardly sleep and slept fitfully when she finally managed to doze off. With a stomach full of Polish K rations, she settled into a sleeping bag inside a tent pitched among the Americans, Cavalcante snoring peacefully beside her. Some time during the night, she rolled over, moaning "Fire!" then burst awake.

"Who's there?"

Her heart raced. The flap of the tent moved gently as though someone had been peeking in. A shadow moved past the canvas outside.

"Who's that?" she called.

Her mind clouded by her dream, she shoved her sleeping bag aside and groped in the dark for her flashlight. Cavalcante remained blissfully unaware of the intrusion.

Flashlight in hand, Molly exited her tent. A wave of dizziness forced her to shut her eyes briefly. When she recovered, she shot the beam toward the ziggurat, in the direction the figure seemed to have gone. "Great. Ghosts."

The low murmur of soldiers caught her ear. She looked about to see two of the Americans sharing a smoke and a bit of conversation. She waved to them as she headed toward Leonard Woolley's excavation. They made no move to stop her, only waving back. It was the wolf whistle that got her attention. Only then did she realize that she had dashed out of her tent without pulling on her khaki pants. She wore only a white tee shirt and baggy men's underwear.

"Shit." Torn between running after the ghostly night stalker and returning to the tent for her pants, she opted for modesty. Cavalcante was sound asleep, but Molly's suitcase had been opened. Without giving it a thought—she might have left it open when she took her last dose of insulin—she ran back outside and toward the ancient city.

The night sky was brilliant. Four thousand years ago, standing atop the ziggurat, the high priests of Ur may have sacrificed victims to their moon goddess on a night such as this. A silver crescent hung over the city, the proper lighting for ghosts to haunt the shops and streets of the town. Why Molly insisted on trying to find the specter that had entered her tent, she couldn't say. Keeping her flashlight trained on the ground before her feet, though, she pursued her quest beyond the pyramid, into the city itself.

It is lovely, she thought. What a magnificent work of architecture. The ancients may have lacked the technology of the twenty-first century, but they certainly didn't lack the engineering and creativity. Their geniuses developed the alphabet, designed mammoth building projects, irrigated the land, and formulated the first laws of science.

As Molly entered the city uncovered from the desert eighty years before, she felt a little like a rat in a maze. In daylight, the old streets would have been difficult to maneuver without a map. At night, she had to trust her instincts. Her flashlight beam played off mud-brick walls, arches, and courtyards. Like the City of the Dead in Egypt, once teaming and alive, it was now lifeless. And yet, if she paused, eyes shut, and let herself go, she could envision the people at work, the caravans of camels laden with goods, the women baking bread or breastfeeding their infants, the men off-loading the boats onto wharves where the waters of the Arabian Sea had once come right up to the walls of the city. In the air she could imagine the smells of people who worked where they slept, who ate where they played, made love and fought within inches of where she stood, not one night ago but tens of thousands of nights ago.

She heard a sound and spun about, flashlight beam sweeping across the mud brick wall of what once may have been a pottery shop. The sound was familiar, the flap of leather against stone, like the lazy heel of a sandal padding upon the ground. *There!* To her left! Movement! She held her breath. Disappearing under an arch.

"Hey! You!" she called. "Stop!"

She hurried after it. At the archway, she paused and leaned against the wall. The dizziness would not go away. She cursed, shook it off, and followed across an open courtyard, lit by the moon and stars, to the far end. There she flashed her beam left and right and on a hunch went right, deeper into the city.

I'll find you, she thought. Ghost or human, I'll find you. Another right and then a left, down a narrow unpaved alley, residences or shops on both sides, empty square spaces, barely two arms' length apart. Thank God she wasn't claustrophobic.

And then again, a sound, tantalizingly close, as though it were leading her on, just beyond reach, but drawing her deeper and deeper into the city. Finally, she had to stop.

She was in great shape, always kept herself that way. She could run a 10K this afternoon if she had to, climb a mountain, swim the width of the Charles and jog up Massachusetts Avenue all the way to Harvard Square without losing her breath. But tonight, her head and her body fought her. She felt drugged and sick to her stomach. Closing her eyes, she pressed her hands to her hammering head. What the fuck? she wondered. That was when someone called her name.

"Molly. Molly."

Her eyes flew open. Her headache vanished. "Mama?"

"Molly."

The beam of her flashlight shot down the length of the alley toward a corner, a turn into another narrow passage. "Where are you?" Her heart pounded. For the first time in many years, she was as frightened as a child left alone in a lightless house.

Then she saw. As clear as the moon.

"Stop! Stay there!" Molly called. But the figure, a woman dressed in a white robe, did not stop. She gave one last glance in Molly's direction and moved to her left, floating, it seemed, on the air. Molly followed.

At the juncture of the two alleyways, Molly turned after the rapidly moving female. Her beam of light caught the hem of a robe as it swished around another corner. Thus went the chase, for five minutes, ten minutes. Not only was she losing the race to the shade, she was weakening, feeling the effects of whatever was ailing her. She stopped to catch her breath, bent over at the waist and fighting back nausea.

When she looked up, she gasped. The shadow woman stood not more than five feet from Molly. She held out her hand.

"Do not stop," she said. "I am she whom you seek."

Oh, my God! Am I dreaming?

The world spun. Molly gaped, her vision a blur. She felt faint and unsure of anything her senses told her. Had the woman really spoken to her, or had the wind carried some sound from the desert. The woman was dressed like a figure from the time of Jesus, robed from head to foot.

The woman turned and hurried down a dark passage as if afraid the sun would soon rise to send her atoms back to oblivion. Molly struggled to follow, wondering if perhaps she were really back in her tent, lying next to Cavalcante, dreaming it all. But she kept going and glimpsed the woman, like a ghost in white, vanish into a room. By the time Molly reached the entrance, the woman was gone. A hallucination, it had to be.

"I need to give up K rations," she muttered, barely conscious now. Bile rose in her throat. Staggering into the building, she stumbled down a stair into a small square chamber. A small amount of light entered through a circular hole in the roof, perhaps an outlet for a cooking fire. She fell onto a raised brick platform that may have served the resident family as a bed or as a place separated by height from their livestock. She could barely raise her head off the ground. The beam of her flashlight struck something etched into a wooden beam above her. With the last of her strength, curiosity driving her, she pushed herself up to her knees, and focused the beam on the image carved in the wood.

It can't be.

A wave of intense heat swept through her. She faltered, dropped her flashlight, then dropped to the floor in the dark.

Molly woke up in a truck highballing it up Highway 1 to An-Najaf where the Polish contingent of the allied forces was stationed and a hospital could be found. It took her several moments to realize where she was, lying under a gray military issue blanket on a mattress of sleeping bags. When she tried to rise, dizziness and the jouncing of the speeding truck took her back down again.

"Lie still," Cavalcante advised, kneeling beside her. The Italian archaeologist took a damp cloth and held it lightly against Molly's forehead.

"You gave us a scare." Kwiatkowski sat on her other side, arms folded across his raised knees. "How are you feeling?"

"Like I just climbed Everest without an oxygen mask. What happened?"

"We found you in Ur," Cavalcante said. She looked anxiously into Molly's face, hoping to see irrefutable signs of recovery. "When I woke up and found you gone, we began a search. It took hours."

"Maybe we're the ones who should be asking what happened."

Molly opened her eyes to gaze at Kwiatkowski who studied her without a hint of feeling. "Where's Dr. Leveille?" she asked.

"Back at Ur," Cavalcante said. "When he saw you were all right, he figured one of us should stay behind to look for Hannaniah."

Molly grunted. "No need to. I found her."

Kwiatkowski and Cavalcante shared a glance across Molly that she understood quite clearly. "No, really, I did," she said. She pushed herself up again, first to her elbows, then to an upright seated position. It was only then that she noticed her left arm was attached to an IV drip. "Oh, damn," she said. "My insulin."

"You forgot to take it?" Cavalcante asked.

"Hell, no. I never forget to take it. Or almost never."

"How about last night?" Kwiatkowski asked. "Was that one of those times?"

"No," Molly said. "Absolutely not." She shook her head, angry with herself. "No wonder I was so dizzy. Anybody have any water? Preferably cold." She licked parched lips, then opened them to receive the canteen of water Kwiatkowski offered her.

"There was somebody in our tent last night, Nina. You didn't hear them? See them?"

"No. Who would go into our tent?"

"I don't know," Molly said. "But I grabbed my flashlight and followed. Nina, I thought it was ..."

"Who?"

"My mother."

"She's dead, Molly."

"I know that. I was hallucinating. I know that, too. But, God, it was so real."

Molly tugged on the IV line. Kwiatkowski scolded, "No wonder you have visions. You don't take proper care of yourself. You're lucky the American soldiers are part of a Med Evac unit. You had no insulin left in your supplies."

"Impossible. I always carry enough."

"Not this time. The Americans saved your life. If I had known you were insulin-dependent, this might not have happened."

"I didn't see it was any of your business," Molly flared.

"With my father dead, I say this expedition is my business," Kwiatkowski flared back. "Your getting sick, dying, jeopardizes it!"

"Well, thank you for caring!"

Under normal circumstances, Molly would have stormed out on

the Pole. Diabetes was a weakness, and she didn't like her weaknesses exposed for public consumption. Unfortunately, tied to an IV drip in a truck barreling through war-torn Iraq at ninety kilometers per hour, she had little choice but to sit where she was.

"I saw her," she insisted. "Dream, fantasy, whatever. She stood as close to me as you two. Spoke to me. It wasn't my mother, Nina. It was Hannaniah. I know it was."

Cavalcante, for one, was willing to believe. "You see, Molly? She is in you. The closer we get to her, the more your mind focuses on the memories she has left behind inside you. Hannaniah has found her way into your head, and she won't go away until you find her. I've had dreams of her, too," she said to Kwiatkowski. "Ever since I began reading her letters. Something is drawing us all together again. Do you have dreams of her, Teodor? Something far more powerful than we are has chosen us."

"Wonderful. And what drugs are you on?" Kwiatkowski got up to tap on the window to the cab.

While he was up, Molly whispered to Cavalcante. "She looked like me. Red hair. Green eyes. Obviously, I was seeing things. But when I followed her, she took me to a place …"

"Where we found you." Cavalcante leaned in excitedly to whisper back, two girls sharing an intimate secret.

"I remember some of the details," Molly said. "A hole in the ceiling, perfectly round. On the floor, a place for animals, a place for residents. It's all kind of fuzzy. But then I noticed something, markings cut into the beam above my head. The beam wouldn't have originated at Ur. Newcomers might have used it to prop up a crumbling ceiling."

"We didn't bother to look," Cavalcante said. She caressed Molly's cheek, gazed into her eyes for a quick moment. Her cheeks flushed. "We were worried about you," she said. "You hardly had a pulse."

Molly smiled. The truck slowed down. She looked up as Kwiatkowski rejoined them. "Military checkpoint," he said. "We're almost in An-Najaf."

"Isn't that where that religious leader is causing trouble? Nur?" Even before arriving in Iraq, Molly had read a lot about the Shi'ite cleric who had sparked anti-American violence in that holy city.

"We don't have a lot of choice. There's a kind of truce in force now. I just want you to see a doctor, one of ours, make sure you're okay. Then we head back to Ur."

"Fine," Molly said. "Except, we don't have to go back to Ur."

"What?"

"What I saw in Ur is what I saw in Afghanistan. A jagged V symbol and a Star of David." She waited for a reaction from her two colleagues. Seeing that they still didn't understand, she said, "A map."

Staff Sergeant Kevin Nieves of Saco, Maine, U.S. Military 101st Police Reserve Unit, would have let the Polish vehicle through to An-Najaf without a hitch, but he had been ordered to be thorough, searching all non-American military vehicles entering and exiting the city. No exceptions. So, when he opened the rear door into the armored Polish truck, he was surprised to see two women inside, one attached to an IV.

"Wow. Ladies," he said. "Is she all right?"

"A casualty of the heat," Kwiatkowski lied.

"I hope she's all right." Nieves shut the door with a smile and a finger wave that Molly returned. "She's a real looker," he said.

"Don't let her hear you say that."

Kwiatkowski returned to his place in the truck, and soon the

Polish vehicle was on its way, headed into the unsafe, unstable battleground of An-Najaf. Staff Sergeant Nieves watched the truck edge back into the slow-moving traffic. On the horn to Military HQ, he spoke to his commanding officer.

"That woman you asked us to be on the lookout for?" he said. "I just saw her, sir. With the Poles, just like you said."

On the other end of the radio call, Nieves's commander thanked his vigilant soldier before turning to Andrew Milstein and Richard Jackson and saying, "Got her."

CHAPTER 12

Someone should have known.

Defiling the holy cities of Islam is like defiling the very faith of the followers of Mohammed, desecrating it, violating it. Even if you consider yourself a friend, you do not track mud into the House of God. You do not run in when you should bow down. You do not wink when you should show deference. Whatever differences exist between you and the faithful are unimportant. Respect matters, a reverential distance, patience. The invaders understood none of this. Someone should have known, but apparently no one did.

Situated south of the infamous Sunni Triangle, Najaf should have been friendly territory to the allied forces. Najaf was the burial site of Ali, the son-in-law of Mohammed and the founder of the Shi'ite sect of the Muslim faith. Saddam Hussein, secular politician though he was, had been born into the Sunni Islamic sect. The Sunnis, who rejected Ali and who were the minority Islamic population in Iraq, nevertheless had held control of the government through Saddam and his political party, the Ba'athists. If anyone should have been delighted with the toppling of Saddam, the Ba'athists, and the Sunnis, it would have been the Shi'ite citizens of An-Najaf.

But the honeymoon between liberated and liberators had ended months before. Too much doubt, too much suspicion, incompetence, arrogance, violence. When Najaf erupted in counter-liberation violence against American and allied troops, it should have come as no surprise, though clearly it did.

Entering the city, Kwiatkowski was prepared for hostilities. His pistol was unholstered, and those of his soldiers who had come with them vigilantly kept their eyes on the passing houses and shops and on the road ahead and behind. One man was seated in a gun turret at the top of the vehicle, but nothing could have defended against a launched rocket or a buried IED, an Improvised Explosive Device.

A fragile truce had been agreed upon by the American peacekeepers and the followers of the militant holy man, Abdul Azim Nur. But Kwiatkowski took nothing for granted and wasn't overly upset when he was stopped at a second American checkpoint.

"We've taken several casualties," an American marine told him. "Suicide car bomber. We've pulled back to let the Iraqi police see what they can do. You'd be advised to pull back, too, to Camp Eagle III. Your injured can get medical help and evac there."

"No, thanks. I'm familiar with the city. I want to join up with my people." Kwiatkowski smiled and the marine nodded.

"Suit yourself, Major. It's your call."

And so Kwiatkowski accessed An-Najaf; plans, however, slightly modified. "The Polish consular office is out," he told his passengers through the connecting window. "Nur's followers are out in force in that area. How are you doing, Molly?"

"Don't worry about me," she insisted. "Unhook me from this damned machine and let's get out of here. I told you, I found a map."

"Tomorrow," Kwiatkowski said. "If Dr. Leveille and Nina are right, you're our map. We go nowhere if you die. Let's make sure you're okay."

With a sigh, Molly lay back. As the Polish truck headed into a section of the city policed by Iraqi nationals, looking for a hospital, Molly removed her Star of David pendant, borrowed a magnifying glass from Cavalcante, and scrutinized the star. "It was actually Jama who suggested the possibility," she told Cavalcante. "It's all in the dots, you see? Or, at least, I thought it was."

"The dots?"

Molly focused her attention on the jagged V symbol on the upper right point of the star. "Jama's drawing, do you happen to have it, Nina?"

"It will be with Dr. Leveille, I'm afraid. Why?"

Molly didn't answer immediately but continued to study the various symbols on the star.

"The dots represent the communities that Hannaniah set up?" Cavalcante asked. "Is that what you're saying? But what are the other symbols? The house. They aren't letters. The squiggly *w* is not the Hebrew letter *shin*. It must mean something else. And the thing on the bottom looks like a dog's snout."

"Two of the symbols on the bottom appear to be structures of some kind. Houses perhaps. But this … I didn't see this before."

"What, Molly?"

"Look." Molly held the gold star for Cavalcante to study. "The dots aren't all the same size. On each symbol, one dot is slightly larger than the others."

"Are you sure? Maybe it's just a flaw."

"No. The workmanship is too good. There is precisely one flaw in each symbol. See for yourself. On the house, it's the rooftop. On the jagged V, it's the dot on the top right. Jama thought the V represented seven communities established by Hannaniah. It was a map whose bottom point he placed in Egypt at our dig site. The legs of the V traveled east to Jerusalem, where the cult began, and into Iraq to Ur, the birthplace of the Hebrew patriarch. The V divides going south into India and further north, where I went, into Afghanistan. Beyond Rome's borders, Hannaniah intended to spread her father's faith to the world."

Cavalcante handed back the medallion and the magnifying glass. "But following that logic, why isn't there a dot for Jama's unknown site in Iraq?"

"I don't know. Maybe that one wasn't planned. My translation of her gospels accounts for six children, starting with Leah, her oldest. In the wake of the destruction of Jerusalem and the Diaspora of the Jews, I'm guessing she created six communities, one to be headed by each child. But why the hell did she go out of her way to enlarge one dot out of each symbol?"

A shot rang out. The two Polish soldiers jumped to their feet as the truck came to an abrupt halt. Cavalcante nestled against Molly as Kwiatkowski slid open a metal partition covering the window.

"Change of plans," he said quickly but with no sign of concern. "Keep down. There's a hotel a block ahead. We'll make for that, stay till dawn, then leave."

"Great, I can use a vacation," Molly said. "What happened to the hospital?"

"Let's just say it's under reconstruction." Kwiatkowski slid the metal partition shut again, not a reassuring sign, then leapt down to the street before the truck recommenced its journey.

Turning her attention to the Star of David pendant, Molly reflected upon her supernatural follow-the-leader game with Hannaniah at Ur. The scientist in her subscribed to the notion that she was nuts, that she was conjuring the ghost of Yeshuah's only child because she wanted so badly to believe in her. But Molly was Catholic too, ever devout and devoted. And didn't Catholics believe in miracles and saints and bodily possession? Why couldn't Hannaniah be some sort of miracle produced in part by scientific fact as yet unexplained and in part by faith? If birds retained species memory of migratory routes they had never flown, why couldn't she possess ancestral memory, handed down through her genes, stored in that vast untapped library of her mind, accessible now only because the drama of her life had forced them from their long hidden shelves?

Molly was retracing each step of her journey in Ur when the explosion drowned out everything—thoughts, words, even screams. With the second concussive blow, their armored truck shot ahead, accelerating so unexpectedly that everyone in the back pitched over. Molly's IV tore painfully from her arm.

"You're bleeding!" Cavalcante hollered over the din outside.

"It's all right," Molly said although she wasn't sure it was. Kwiatkowski didn't magically appear like the mighty Oz to explain anything. The truck merely careened through traffic Molly couldn't see, shaking and bouncing everyone inside. A sudden left turn spilled everybody across the floor, then a right tossed them back the other way.

"Now I'm better," Molly said as the truck finally stopped, depositing everybody on their behinds. Before Molly could say a word, Kwiatkowski had the back door open and yelled, "Everyone out! Hurry! Hurry! Molly, you need help?"

"It's a little late for that," she said but didn't reject his arm as she leapt from the truck onto the pavement of a parking lot. Directly ahead, through a palm-lined walkway, was the entrance to a concrete slab of a hotel ten stories high, fringed in palm trees and armed guards and sporting a waterless fountain filled instead with a toppled statue of Saddam Hussein. "Wait a minute," Molly suddenly said. "What about my insulin?"

"Got it!" Cavalcante exclaimed, showing Molly her metal medical box.

Behind them a wrought iron gate closed and machine guns

scattered a mob who threw rocks, bricks, and anything else they could find over the barrier. Some wore black ski masks. Others held aloft placards bearing the likeness of Abdul Azim Nur.

"I thought there was a truce!" Molly shouted.

"There is," Kwiatkowski said. "Lucky for us."

The hotel lobby was filled with frightened foreigners who had not evacuated the city, a scattering of Polish and Italian soldiers and armed Iraqi police trying to keep everyone calm.

"I lost one of my people back there," Kwiatkowski said. "I sure as hell hope you know what you're doing, Molly!"

"Me? As I recall, you two practically abducted me from Boston! I didn't set up this expedition!"

Molly let Cavalcante wrap a bandage around her wounded arm, then the two left Kwiatkowski to recover his dead soldier and to contact Leveille-Gaus at Ur. They entered a lounge area jammed with people anxiously watching a television screen. A CNN reporter described the scene in An-Najaf.

"Despite a tentative accord between the American troops and the followers of Abdul Azim Nur, many people have taken to the streets unsatisfied with the results of the national elections which Nur had encouraged his followers to boycott. While Iraqi police have scrambled to replace retreating Americans, this is little comfort to the foreign nationals still holed up throughout the city. More disturbing perhaps was the discovery of the body of a French engineer kidnapped from Baghdad three days ago."

Food, was Molly's primary thought for the time being. She hadn't eaten since the night before at Ur. Molly grabbed a banana from a buffet table. Cavalcante picked up a tray and loaded it with leftover fruit, wilted salad, and dip. Then the two squeezed out of the crowded lounge and settled into a couch under two potted palm trees to wait for Kwiatkowski's return.

"Back to the map," Cavalcante said, as she swallowed a piece of dried fig. She was short enough to curl up on the couch, legs beneath her, and tuck herself into a corner like a happy cat. "What exactly did you find at Ur?"

Molly tried to separate herself from the chaos of the hotel. Ur had been so still, dark, and lifeless, she could well have believed herself to be on another planet, far less mad and unpredictable. "The jagged V made no sense to me at first," she said through cheeks stuffed with stale bread. "Jama believed that it connected Hannaniah's seven communities. Apparently, he was right. The shape, though. Why a V? Why jagged and not straight? The communities could have been placed anywhere, suggesting any configuration besides the one Hannaniah chose. Nothing I have found to date suggests that Hannaniah did anything illogically or without reason."

With a finger, Molly took a swipe of hummus and spread it onto the tray in the shape of the V. "What does this shape suggest to you?"

Cavalcante studied the rough drawing in ground lentils.

"Remember where I saw it. Ur. Where is Ur?"

And then Cavalcante's eyes widened with delight and recognition. "Molly! You're a genius! The Tigris and Euphrates Rivers! That's the V!"

Molly licked her finger clean of hummus. "God, I wish Hannaniah made things that simple. At Ur the symbol of the Jewish star was set directly beside the two rivers. Coincidence? An aesthetic decision? I don't think so."

Once again, Molly plucked the Star of David pendant from around her neck. The map to Hannaniah's tomb, the answer to her quest, was staring her in the face and she couldn't see it.

"Here's what I don't get. On the star, the jagged V is just one of six symbols. It would seem to have no greater significance than the others: the house, the squiggly w ..."

"If the w isn't meant to be a letter, mountains maybe. Then there's the dog's snout."

"And the two on the bottom, right, left. Houses? There's a Hebrew letter attached to each symbol."

"In the kabala, letters have numeric values," Cavalcante said.

"Possible. Hannaniah was definitely into mysticism." Molly placed the gold talisman back around her neck. "But I think I know what the letters in the hexagram inside the star symbolize."

"Lead and I will follow, mistress."

"Her children." Molly stood up. "*Lamed* for Leah. *Resh* for Rivkah. Always think family, Nina, when you think of Hannaniah. Religion at its simplest to her was family. It was for her father, too. After all, until children learn otherwise, who is God to them but their parents?"

"Then the Star of David is part of the map?" Cavalcante asked, trying to envision Iraq west of the two rivers.

"I believe so, and the heart of the star, the heart of David's kingdom, is where we should be looking for Hannaniah. In which case, we need to get our hands on a real map."

Molly looked around the lobby. Every reporter still in the city had to be living in this hotel. Men and women huddled in groups, an incoherent babble of languages. Staff appeared as frazzled as the guests, less interested in making beds and tossing out the trash than in cursing out their charges or arguing with one another. Molly left the couch and strode across the lobby to the front desk. Since there was no one behind it, she climbed over the counter and rifled the drawers for a map.

"How about a key?" Cavalcante suggested.

Molly shrugged. "Why not? Might as well be comfortable while we're here." She stole two, one for her and Nina, the other for Kwiatkowski. As she vaulted back over the counter, someone hollered her name.

"Molly!"

Her heart jumped. *Christ! Caught red-handed.* Her first instinct was to throw her hands into the air and beg forgiveness. Then she looked up.

"Father Ray?" She let out a breath of relief. Her bladder relaxed and she let him swallow her up in his arms.

"Molly, isn't this amazing!"

"What are you doing in Iraq, Father Ray?" She hugged him tight. "Jesus, of all places!"

The sixty-year-old Jesuit priest and college professor brushed his long white hair out of his eyes. In his hurry to embrace Molly, he had nearly lost his glasses. They swam in the perspiration on his nose and he held them to keep them from slipping off.

"It's no coincidence, Molly," he said. "We've been looking for you for days. My God, what happened in Poland?"

Molly glanced at Cavalcante, frowned at Teague. "You were in Poland, too?"

"The others were. Andrew Milstein. From Mt. Auburn. He said they'd arrived in Torun right after the attack on the castle." Teague nodded to Cavalcante. "You must be Dr. Cavalcante. I read your book *Queens, Amazons, and Witches.* Very Freudian. At least the two of you are alive. We couldn't be sure."

"Barely, Father Ray," Molly said, "but what are you doing here?"

Teague gave the lobby a quick scan before turning his attention back to his favorite colleague and student. "Let's get out of this madness," he said. "You have a room?"

"We just got here," Cavalcante told him. Teague glanced at the keys in Molly's hand. She blushed.

"Don't worry. We have a room," Teague told them. "We just arrived ourselves."

"We?"

"Yes. Come on. Let me explain upstairs. I can't hear myself think down here."

Placing his hand around Molly's waist, Teague led her and Cavalcante to an elevator. When it failed to arrive after a few minutes, they took the stairs. Teague was wheezing when they reached the fourth floor landing.

"Here. Thank God." Teague leaned against a wall papered in purple with white mosques and minarets. "Room 420."

"Out of shape?" Cavalcante asked.

"Too much lasagna."

The lightbulbs in the hallway flickered as though they felt each footfall on the fraying carpet. At room 420, Teague knocked on the door then opened it. Andrew Milstein was shaving. Seeing Molly in the corridor, he froze, eyes wide, razor to cheek, towel wrapped around his bare shoulders.

"Father," he stuttered, "you should have warned me."

"I didn't know they were here until just now," Teague said.

"Were you shaving for us?" Molly asked, smiling.

Milstein wiped the shaving cream off his face with his towel, retrieved a white shirt, and buttoned it up all the while uttering apology after apology. "I know this all comes as a major surprise," he said. "Please, sit. Have you eaten?" Then he noticed the patch of red on her bandage. "Your arm!"

"War wound. Something to show my students back home."

Milstein gestured to a table with platters of bread, pastries, fruit, a bottle of Chianti, ice cream red, white, and blue. "You did well," Molly said. She ignored the food and strolled to a plate glass window that gave a striking view of An-Najaf and the angry crowds occupying the street.

"We know each other, Molly," Milstein said to her back. "You wouldn't remember, but I attended Mt. Auburn College. We took a few courses together. Antiquities. History. Then, lo and behold, you publish a wonderful book on the Gospels of Hannaniah. And here we are."

Molly looked away from the window. "Why are you here, Mr. Milstein?" she asked. "With Father Ray. Obviously, this is not a happy coincidence."

Milstein stood with his hands crossed at his waist, not looking Molly in the eye.

"It all begins innocently enough," he said. "In the process of rounding up Iraqi criminals, we captured a man named Ghazi Al-Tikriti, who has subsequently escaped."

"More good news for us, I suppose," Molly said.

"Tikriti told us that he had been approached by the director of the Iraqi National Museum in Baghdad about a find made by a man named Mohamoud Jama somewhere to the west of here in the desert. Tikriti was a highly placed intelligence officer under Hussein, a relative of the dictator. The claim was, well, I think you know what the claim was. Unfortunately, Jama kept most of the information to himself, and now he is dead."

"What happened to him?" Cavalcante asked. The food remained on its platters untouched. Sunlight streamed warmly into the room and bathed the food. Since the noise below was somewhat muted up here, they could pretend they were enjoying mid-afternoon tea between seminars of an archaeological conference.

The truth was far different. "Jama was killed," Milstein said. "Looters. The museum official is also dead."

"Oh, great." Molly reached for a piece of flat bread and dipped it in a bowl of tahini. "And this Tikriti is on the loose. Could he have been responsible for Poland?"

"Maybe," Milstein said. He took the opportunity to gaze at Molly. "In short," he said, "we found out that Jama's discovery was related to your own. I am not an archaeologist by trade. Only an aficionado. My line is history, religion, Jewish, Middle Eastern. I taught at Amherst for a while, but I also served in the military. Intelligence. I was brought back to Iraq to help recover historical items lost in the first days of the war. Hence, my involvement."

"And you knew me?"

"And I am familiar with Dr. Cavalcante, as well. I apologize to both of you."

Cavalcante let the food go for the moment. Curled up on the couch, in the spill of the sunlight, the little cat looked cautious, as if eying a second trespassing feline. Her gaze fell on Teague. "What is your involvement?" she asked him.

"Unique at best." The Jesuit psychiatrist made himself comfortable on a chair opposite the platters of food and helped himself to a fig. "Molly can tell you, although I suppose as her therapist and Mr. Milstein's, I should consider our therapy sessions private personal business."

"You're here as a psychiatrist?" Cavalcante glanced at Molly, who dipped her shoulders.

"I told you I was crazy."

Teague said, "Not crazy. Brilliant, actually. Andrew, too. But the two of you have much in common beyond your intellectual interests.

I have regressed both of you."

Again, Cavalcante stared at Molly.

"Regressed?"

"Surely you're aware of the process, Dr. Cavalcante," Milstein said. "Your work entails the supernatural. What you do for the Vatican belies your true interests."

"I have a feeling," she said, "you know more about me than I am comfortable with your knowing."

"But you know about regressive techniques," Teague said.

"Yes. Regression opens up hidden corners of the mind, like dreams. The technique is merely therapeutic."

"True," Teague said. "In that therapeutic regard, it has its merits."

Molly's eyes lit on Milstein's, and she caught him, before he could avert his eyes, staring at her. He blushed.

"This expedition has been unsettling from the beginning," she said. "We've had people killed in Poland, Teodor's father among them. A soldier died here just a few hours ago."

Nina glanced at her colleague. "Molly, surely you don't think one of us …"

"I do. And I don't want to think who. We have two dead or disappeared Iraqi archaeologists, both of whom were intimate with the relics we are pursuing. Now Father Ray appears out of nowhere with a man who says he's been following us from Boston to Poland to Najaf. I have the Vatican on the one hand. Now U.S. Intelligence. I want to know right now what the fuck is going on, or I don't take another step!"

Someone knocked at the door. Teague got up and let a man in.

"Well, well," the Jesuit priest said. "Our numbers grow."

"Habib Al-Nazariiy," Milstein added by way of introduction.

"The expedition will need an Iraqi national familiar with the land and the issue we're dealing with."

"He's an archaeologist?" Molly asked. Al-Nazariiy was dressed in a brown suit coat with a white shirt and red tie. The gold rings on his fingers and the gold chain draped around his neck attested to a degree of success. He carried two suitcases, which he dropped on the floor in order to shake Molly's hand.

"You must be Molly O'Dwyer," he said. "My uncle Fawzi spoke in wondrous terms about you."

"Uncle Fawzi being …?"

"The curator of antiquities at the Iraqi National Museum. I was with him when he uncovered the baby's skull in Mohamoud Jama's basement. But I'm not an archaeologist, Dr. O'Dwyer. I'm an engineer by trade."

Accepting the paper napkin Habib handed her, Molly wiped hummus from her mouth and tossed the napkin on the table.

With a smile, Habib unlatched one of his suitcases. Out dropped an assault rifle in two sections, complete with a dozen cartridge boxes. "I," he said, "will be your guide. I worked the oil fields and did some exploratory work in the desert. I know the region better than any of you, I presume."

"That may be," Molly said, exchanging a glance with Cavalcante, "but how do you presume to be my guide? I already have a team, fully funded. We have a plan. I have a map. Do you?"

"Yes, we do," Milstein said quietly. "You."

Milstein left his chair to confront Molly. "Consider what we're going after, Dr. O'Dwyer."

"What are we going after, Mr. Milstein?"

"Only the greatest archaeological find in history," Habib answered.

"I asked Mr. Milstein," Molly replied. "Is Hannaniah so important to everyone but me and Nina that so many risks have to be taken and so many people need to die?"

"It's not just Hannaniah, Dr. O'Dwyer. Molly," Milstein insisted. He held her eyes with his own. "You heard Father Ray. He has regressed us both. Don't deny where he has taken you."

"Where I have taken him, you mean," Molly said. She returned to the window. While the mob seemed to have diminished, perhaps moving along to terrorize another neighborhood, armed men remained on alert in front of the hotel, Teodor's men among them. For the first time since having been introduced to him by Cavalcante, she felt a strong need for the Polish officer's presence. At first she had grossly underestimated him. Then she had simply taken him for granted. But through all she had endured in this whirling, spinning, confusing dash from the campus of Mt. Auburn to war-ravaged Iraq, he had been steady, constant, quiet, competent, even affectionate.

"Regression," she said, "is just what Father Ray says it is. A psychiatric strategy when nothing else works. I lost my mother when I was a child. I never knew my father. Regression is my way of finding them. That's all it is."

"And finding Hannaniah," Milstein declared.

"No, not and finding Hannaniah."

"Yes, Molly! Yes!" Suddenly his inhibitions seemed to desert him and Milstein approached Molly with exuberant eyes. "You think all of this is a coincidence? None of it is. Hannaniah's history is very much like your own. When I was first regressed, I thought the same thing you did. A quaint technique. A lark. Something to kill the time, but if it works, what the hell?"

"He was my first case, Molly," Teague said from his chair. "Even before you."

"I lost my parents when I was young just like you. My father was a quadriplegic. He died in a fire, trapped, unable to move."

"Stop it, Milstein!" Molly ordered him.

"A fire I caused."

"I said stop it!" This was too much. Had he pried into her own past and forged this idiotic story just to upset her? Rising on tiptoes, she stood eye to eye with the intelligence officer. He did not back down. "You're playing a damned game now!" she exclaimed. "Your father didn't die in a fire. You're making that up!"

"No. No. God, no. I wish I were. He was a wonderful man. Brilliant. He could have done anything he wanted, but he committed his life to people. He was known all over the country and in Israel as a voice of reason and faith. I didn't just love him, Molly. I worshipped him."

"And he died in a fire."

"Yes!"

"That you caused."

Tears trickled down Milstein's cheeks. He placed his hands on Molly's arms. "I wouldn't lie to you, Molly. That fire was the single motivating event of my life. All I have done since then has been to atone for what I didn't do for my father. Father Teague will tell you that my dreams, my regression, are simply Freudian escapades, fantasies conjured to relieve me of my guilt. But I know different. With all due respect, Father Ray, I have been there. So has Molly. You haven't."

"Milstein," Molly sighed, softening her tone. He was telling the truth, at least what he perceived to be the truth. But it clarified nothing.

"Look," she said, "life is what it is. I just want to know why you are here. What does regression have to do with this expedition? That's all I'm interested in."

Milstein smiled like the sun unexpectedly beating back the rain. "Regression is real," he said quietly, "and you know it." Standing beside Molly, he leaned against the window, gazing out at the afternoon in An-Najaf. He seemed more relaxed now.

"Father Ray took me back to a time long before my father was born. Nothing was planned. I had no preconceived notion of what was going to happen or where I might go. I just went. And where I landed was as far from where I expected as you can imagine. In Jerusalem. In the time of Jesus."

"Milstein," she said. She could feel all eyes on her but saw only Milstein's. He looked at her as a lover might, gently, anxiously. How could he have known, she wondered? Unless Father Teague had done the unthinkable and leaked private information spoken in therapy. That she had undergone regression. That she had traveled far back into history. That she, too, had ended in Jerusalem.

"All of this would have ended nowhere," Milstein continued, "if I hadn't seen your picture in the papers after you discovered Hannaniah. Your face was the face of a child I kept seeing in my sessions."

"A child?"

"Yes. But clearly yours. And in this ancient world of Jerusalem you know me well, very well."

"I admit, when I began experimenting with regression, it was an amusement," Teague said. "I had read articles about it—the famous cases—even attended a workshop or two. After Andrew, I had a number of patients eager to try it. As you were. I have maintained their privacy, naturally. But with their permission, I did a little investigating into some of the more compelling cases, where I felt detail they gave me under trance could be verified. A New Bedford fisherman was a Carthusian monk in France in the 15th century.

The name he gave me checked out, the dates, the description of the monastery and town. The man had never been to France, had never heard of the Carthusian monks. How did he come up with this story?"

"He read about them," Molly suggested. "It was a high school assignment he'd buried in his memory. Father, I appreciate what you're saying. But where is this getting us?"

"I think we can cut out a lot of hard work if you agree to go under, Molly, to be regressed." Molly looked about. "It all fits," Cavalcante told her. "The DNA markers on the test Jama took clearly indicate you are a descendant of ..."

"I am a descendant of the body we uncovered in Egypt! That's all! I grant you nothing else! The tissue samples didn't come from Hannaniah! They didn't come from Jesus!"

"Wait a minute," Milstein said. Teague and Habib stared at Molly now. "Jama took DNA tests?"

"Hundreds of them," Cavalcante said. She uncurled herself. "He was trying to find descendants of Jesus, people who carried enough genetic markers to tie them to his blood line. The body Molly and Jama uncovered in Egypt, just like the one Jama found here in Iraq, we believe was a grandchild of the Messiah. Molly's markers are almost identical to theirs."

"It's a crock," Molly said but could see in the eyes of the others in the room that they were inclined to believe otherwise.

"Molly, that would explain it," Milstein insisted. "That at least puts some science behind the phenomenon. Maybe it isn't past lives. Maybe you're just reliving someone else's past life."

"If you think I'm dredging up some fantasy for you people, you're crazy. Come on, Nina. We're finding Teodor and getting the hell out of here. Father Ray, if you want to find Hannaniah, regress

Mr. Milstein. Let him be your dupe. I'm a scholar, not one of P. T. Barnum's suckers."

At the door, she grasped the knob ready to slam the interlopers behind her. Habib called her back. "Dr. O'Dwyer, would it help you to know who Mohamoud Jama thought was buried out in the desert?"

Molly spun about. "I know who's buried out there," she hollered. "Hannaniah and her children, her followers, her family."

"And Jesus, Molly!" Milstein exclaimed. "For God's sake, admit it! That's who we're really after!"

Molly turned on the American intelligence officer. "I know who we're after! I knew it the moment Nina stepped into my life. It's you who don't get it. None of you. We're not going after Jesus! Not his bones anyway. We're after his soul and the soul of every other human being on this planet who believes in him." Molly headed out into the hall, Cavalcante at her heels.

Milstein ran after her. "Damn it, Molly!" he shouted. "You have no choice. You are Hannaniah. You are her flesh and her bones, breathing, walking, now, this moment. You are the key to all of this, and you can't keep us out. You won't. You won't be allowed to."

Molly stopped suddenly. "The hell I won't." Striding back full tilt at Milstein, she directed a punch at his nose. Her fist landed with precision, knocking the taller man off his feet and spraying his blood on the carpet.

"Anybody care to stop me?" she shouted. "I won't be intimidated, Mr. Milstein!" The American intelligence officer sat on the floor and held his nose. His fingers oozed with blood. He stared up at her. Cavalcante kept to the rear.

"Well, that took care of my migraine," he said through a cupped hand over his mouth. "I'm sorry. My intention wasn't to intimidate. I didn't know you were a boxer, Dr. O'Dwyer."

"I never had the need to be before this."

"My point was," Milstein said, "a find like this will be impossible to keep secret. I thought that would be obvious."

"Nothing is obvious about this expedition." Molly crouched. Pulling his hand away from his nose, she looked at the damage she had done.

"Get a wet cloth, will you, Nina?" Then she told Milstein, "Tilt your head back." She held him with the same hand that had struck him.

"You really didn't suspect, Molly?" he asked. "About why you've been having those vivid dreams?"

"Because I am Jesus' great-great-great-great whatever? I only knew what Jama told me about the results of the DNA testing. But think about it, Milstein. How would you feel if you were told you were the descendant of the man millions of people consider the Son of God, the man I considered the Son of God?"

"Considered?"

"My faith contradicts my reason. It's not easy giving up what you've believed in for so long. Now I've become the vessel of my own faith's destruction. What the fuck do I do?"

"Just exactly what you're doing, Molly. Seek the truth."

"Whose, Milstein? Whose?"

She glanced through the doorway into the room. Teague stood, hands thrust into his pockets. Habib was at the window studying the scene below, loading bullets into his pistol. By the time Cavalcante returned with a damp towel, Molly's anger had subsided.

"I will not be," she said, "a walking, breathing, time bomb in the heart of my religion." She looked up at Cavalcante. "Did you happen to bring the black binder when we left Ur?" she asked her friend.

"No," Cavalcante replied. "We were in such a hurry to get you to the hospital. Dr. Leveille will have it."

"Great. Do you mind looking for Teodor? We really need to get out of here. Not tomorrow. Now."

Cavalcante headed for the staircase at a trot, leaving Molly to check the flow of blood from Milstein's nose.

"All right, Milstein," she said. "I think you can walk again."

"Like Jesus, I am resurrected." Milstein's smile faded. Tears formed in Molly's eyes. He reached a hand toward her face, watched the dewy formation that clung without dropping from her eye. She averted his touch.

"I'm sorry if I underestimated your feelings," he said. "The mystery compels you. Why shouldn't it? You're an archaeologist, the best. But it doesn't have to be so bad, Molly. Maybe Jesus did come to earth to experience life as a man. That doesn't preclude his divinity. It just changes the story."

"Milstein, it doesn't just change the story." Molly felt her head begin to pound and her hands tremble. "Don't you see? If he wasn't divine, what does that make my faith? If he was divine, what does that make me?"

She dropped the bloody towel and got up. The tears flowed. Milstein rose unsteadily to his feet. Teague came over to comfort her, but she shook him off.

"Molly." Milstein grabbed her hand. "We're not out to subvert your faith, anyone's faith. People can believe Jesus is the Son of God, that he died for their sins, that he was resurrected after three days. None of that has to change. None of that has to be questioned. No one has to know anything. Except us. You and I. We need the truth. Stay here."

"I know the truth," Molly said. "I'm looking for Hannaniah.

Nothing else."

She started down the hallway to retrieve Teodor and leave Najaf. The lights flickered once and went out. Plunged into semi-darkness, she turned back toward Milstein who stood by the door to room 420.

That was when they felt the explosion.

In the movies, they would have waited until night and begun their operation under the cover of darkness and confusion. Many insurrectionists in and around Iraq's major cities preferred to set off their bombs early in the morning when civilians, police, and soldiers are groggy from sleep, when the day is just beginning and death somehow seems more horrifying. But Ghazi Al-Tikriti liked to cause mayhem around teatime. People were relaxed, weary, bloated perhaps, unprepared, easy targets. And his men weren't sleepy.

Tikriti had located the hotel where the foreigners were staying. He hadn't figured on catching the American woman in the same action, but it would certainly make things a lot easier. Nur's insistence on capturing her was indeed puzzling, given that the imam didn't seem to care at all about the true prize, Jesus. The trick would be getting them all out without killing them. But he had worked out a plan for that, too.

Behind him, as he viewed the hotel from a shop window across the street, the woman-hater Aden, whom he had retrieved from Abu Ghraib Prison, pestered him to advance now. But Tikriti was a patient man. The Americans would come to learn this. He was a businessman who could forgive and forget under the right circumstances.

"Aden, my friend," he said, as he turned away, "you will not kill the redhead. You will not kill anyone. Do you understand? We have a mission."

To make this mission easier, hopefully in and out quickly with no problems, most of his troops were outfitted as Iraqi police, thanks to a contact Tikriti had on the inside. In fact, most of the so-called terrorists doubled as police. The Americans were so desperate, they'd take almost any volunteer who'd patrol the streets with them. The false police not only were armed by the American occupation forces but could now relay vital information about American troop actions. But none of that mattered to Tikriti. He paused to purchase a Mariah Carey CD at the the audio shop. To the smiling cashier, he said, "My daughter will love this. American country music. Who can understand taste?"

The explosion that Molly had heard from four floors up shook the entire block of storefronts. The window to the audio shop caved in with a spray of glass that cut up stunned shoppers, including Tikriti and Aden. Racks of CDs and DVDs tipped over. People screamed. Plaster dust and fine particles of asphalt, brick, and wood filled the air. On concussion, Tikriti was thrown into and partly over the counter. Glass slashed his hand, but he hung on to Mariah Carey. Since the cashier was moaning and cradling her head in her arms, he didn't bother to pay.

"Habib, you idiot!" he cursed as he helped Aden, bleeding from his scalp and hands, to his feet. "Too much, too soon, too close! I'll wring his neck when I see him."

Moving on to the sidewalk, he saw that a crater had been dug out of the wide street about a block away and that cars fore and aft had been tossed about. But the diversion had worked. The few allied soldiers defending the hotel hurried from behind their iron gate toward the scene of the devastation. That left only a handful of

Iraqi police, and they weren't really police.

"Allah is good," Tikriti said. "Remember what I told you, Aden. Hands off the women."

The first screwy thought Molly had was, *You'll never get me on a balcony again.* Her second thought was, *Nina! Teodor!*

She lifted herself to her feet and felt her way through the darkened hallway. Clouds of soot, dust, and cinders hung in the air, all too reminiscent of a certain fire Molly had experienced as a five-year-old.

Milstein struggled to his feet with the aid of the wall. Teague had been thrown into the hallway and was coughing but otherwise seemed unharmed. Molly reserved her anxiety for Cavalcante whom, only moments before, she'd sent downstairs, and for Kwiatkowski, whom she hadn't seen since leaving the lobby.

At the thought of her friends, she scrambled down the stairs. At the third floor landing the flight of other frightened guests caught her in an impossible jam. People yelled in a dozen languages. Italian. English. Polish. Arabic. Like the Tower of Babel, Molly thought. With darkness behind her and panic below, Molly could do little better then hold her ground.

At least until the shooting began.

Kwiatkowski had hoisted his fallen comrade from the turret of the armored truck, lifted him onto a stretcher, and carried him into the hotel lobby past scared, curious civilians. A staffer pointed him in the direction of a makeshift infirmary through the dining hall and into the kitchen. A woman in a black burnoose attended to several wounded opposite the hotel's meat freezers. Kwiatkowski thought it might make a serviceable temporary morgue.

"Drive the truck around to the loading docks out back," he said to the corporal holding the feet of the stretcher, "I'm going to find the others. We're not staying."

They set the stretcher down on the floor. With his subordinate gone, Kwiatkowski turned to the Muslim woman. She was doing a competent job of bandaging an Iraqi police officer's leg.

"Do you speak English," he asked the nurse. She looked to be quite young, dark-complexioned, beautiful.

"I do," she said. "Your friend is dead."

"I know. There will be more. We may need you."

She nodded and continued her work.

Kwiatkowski looked out the back doors toward the loading dock. Several non-military trucks and a few cars were parked in an alley that led left and right to the main street. A brimful dumpster overflowed with uncollected trash. The alley was littered with garbage, scattered by the warm winds of Najaf.

He checked the parked vehicles for a forgotten set of keys or for easy access to hotwire an engine. Then came the explosion. Though it must have occurred some distance from the hotel, the shockwave dropped him to the ground at the driver's door of a red Chevy van. Hands cut, knees scraped, he experienced Poland again—the destruction of his home, the death of his father, the gunfight with the assassins who had tried to kill them all.

He hauled himself to his feet. Just then a van squealed into the alley and discharged half a dozen Iraqi police at the hotel's back doors.

Kwiatkowski ducked behind the Chevy until the last of them had entered the hotel. Something wasn't right. They were on the scene too soon. Way too soon. Why had they come here? The blast had not occurred in the hotel. Their leader, a mustached man who had paused in the doorway to glance behind before unholstering a pistol, looked familiar. Like a man he had met once in Baghdad when his father was working out one of his illegal deals. Like one of the American military's card deck criminals he had seen so many times. Like the eight of diamonds. Like Ghazi Al-Tikriti.

Cavalcante had reached the landing on the second floor when the explosion shook the hotel so violently she expected the stairwell to come apart and collapse on top of her. She wasn't alone in that fear. With the elevators inoperative, the staircase had become Highway 1. People went up carrying food and came down carrying their luggage. Hotel staff were noticeably absent. Everyone was stuck, unsure where to go, panic building to a boil.

Darkness of an unholy kind descended upon the hotel, and in the crying, screaming wake of the blast, Cavalcante had to wonder whether God Himself had decreed the disaster. Hadn't she been raised a Catholic in Italy, not allowed to skip a Sunday mass? And didn't she work for the Vatican on its most sensitive ancient documents? As much as she had spurned her faith to delve into the unusual, like any normal, inquisitive, intelligent person, she kept one small part of her mind open to superstition.

They were going after Jesus. She had known it all along even if Molly hadn't. They were going to find the corpse of the unresurrected Son of God, and they were going to put him on display, dissect him, test his DNA structure, weigh him, measure him, reduce him from godhead to a pile of interesting Discovery Channel bones. So why shouldn't God be enraged?

I must get to Molly, she thought. But struggling against the descending tide proved impossible. The surge of human instinct moved down toward escape. Cavalcante was forced to trip and stumble along with the rest of the half-blind lemmings toward the lobby one floor below. Uncharacteristically, she began to pray.

As soon as Tikriti and his men entered the hotel through the kitchen, they leveled their pistols and assault rifles.

From the night Imran Fawzi had approached him with Mohamoud Jama's find in the Iraqi desert, Tikriti had forged a plan to save his ass. As an intelligence officer close to Saddam, he could have told the Americans many things about the dictator's regime. Regrettably none of those things had anything to do with weapons of mass destruction or connections to Al-Qaeda, because there were none. With nothing to sell, Tikriti could expect nothing from the liberators but jail time. Fawzi's information then was a godsend. But Tikriti's good luck lasted about as long as the Iraqi defense of Saddam's regime. His Polish contact, Michael Kwiatkowski, had sold him out, preferring to deal with his Catholic masters. And then the Americans had cornered him in Nasiriyah, taken him to Abu Ghraib, and treated him worse than a dog. All of which he would forgive if he could capture his interrogators, Jackson and Milstein, the archaeologists, Cavalcante and O'Dwyer, and the son of the Polish traitor Kwiatkowski. Then he would locate Mohamoud Jama's holy relics, sell them to the highest bidder, and Ghazi Al-Tikriti, his wife, and ten daughters would live happily ever after.

Gun waving, he encountered a churning crowd of anxious, frightened residents in the dining area. Pushing them out of his way to clear a path, he shouted, "Move! Move! Everything is all right.

Give us room!"

He had divided his men into two units. The second came in through the undefended front entrance. Tikriti counted on people believing he was heading a police unit into the hotel. He had not counted on Kwiatkowski's Poles nor on Milstein's Americans, armed civilians under Richard Jackson's jurisdiction. One of them recognized the escaped eight of diamonds and shouted, "Hey, they're not police! That's Tikriti!" Chaos ensued.

Going down no longer seemed a good idea. Trapped on the staircase in a gray twilight further dimmed by the flour-fine cloud of plaster dust, Molly decided a detour was advisable. Against the relentless push downward, she looked for an exit door onto the third floor, but the impetus from above was too great and Molly was caught in a current she couldn't resist. Down toward the lobby she continued.

The shooting, when it began, took everyone by surprise. The police, for some unfathomable reason, tried to charge up the stairwell. Finding their way blocked by the hotel guests pushing them back toward Jackson's and Kwiatkowski's men, they fired into the mob to clear a way.

Such a mass of humanity has no leader. It simply shatters like porcelain on marble, pieces everywhere. The people at the bottom either dropped in streams of blood or pushed in vain against the people above them. Those at the top, unaware of what was happening below, kept coming. Molly, caught in the middle, could either fall under the weight of the mindless mob and be crushed beneath it, or she could fight her way free of it with as little regard for the mob as it had for her.

Jesus, she thought. That is what this is all about. Payback for even thinking of such a desecration. Payback because the scholar in her, the focused, driven intellect did not reject, even now, the possibility of doing just what Andrew Milstein had suggested.

The gunfire echoed all the way to the top floor, digging into plaster and wood or ricocheting off walls into flesh and bones. Molly dropped to her backside, covered her head against the railing, and let retreating feet step over her.

"The woman!" a man yelled. "The redhead! Take her!"

The dirty heel of a shoe ground into her cheek, scraping off skin. She struck out blindly only to have the hard leather sole of an army boot shoved against her forehead. Without thought, she grabbed it and yanked.

"Damn you!"

The Iraqi knelt motionless on top of her until a blast of gunfire sent him scrambling for the automatic weapon he had lost in his fall. Molly made the same move.

"Bitch!" he yelled.

Molly's curse was a guttural scream. She threw an elbow into the Iraqi's teeth, grabbed his weapon before he could, and bashed the barrel into his forehead. He reared back and threw a fist against her jaw. Molly blacked out and slumped against the staircase.

When she came to her attacker lay across her, his blood spilling from his shattered skull. Who had saved her? Teodor? Milstein? A stray bullet?

The firing had subsided, moved elsewhere in the hotel, she couldn't tell where. A trickle of blood ran down her face toward her lips. Gathering her strength, she pushed the man's body off her and picked her way past other fallen victims, some dead, some wounded, some in shock. Halfway down the final staircase, she stumbled over the body of another Iraqi policeman and, next to him, Nina Cavalcante. She lay on her side, face turned down, eyes closed. Her friend was not moving.

"Nina!" she yelled. "Nina!"

She shook the Italian, grabbed her shoulders and rattled her. Cavalcante managed to open one eye.

"Molly." Red foam bubbled between her lips. She tried to speak, but Molly shushed her.

"It's all right. You'll be all right," she said. There was no other blood. Molly looked for a bullet hole, but there was none. Someone in their flight had trod on her face and caused internal damage.

"Shit," Molly muttered.

When a hand grasped her shoulder, she practically tore it off at the wrist, twisting it and forcing the man to his knees.

"Molly! Jesus!" Kwiatkowski shouted.

"Teodor?" She threw her arms around him. "What happened? We have to get Nina out of here. She's been hurt. I think it's her ribs."

Kwiatkowski took one look at the frail archaeologist then scooped her up in his arms.

"Teodor, be careful with her!" Molly said.

"I'll be as careful as I can. This isn't Boston. There are no ambulances rushing to get here."

Cavalcante kept her eyes on Molly as Kwiatkowski carried her out into the lobby, through the dining area, and into the back.

"Will you help us?" Kwiatkowski said to a blue-eyed woman in a black burnoose. The woman looked at Cavalcante and smiled.

"Yes," she said. "I will help you." The woman followed them.

"Deeqa is a trained nurse," he explained to Molly and Nina. "She will ride with us to the military hospital where she works."

Outside, the sun still shone, a beautiful beach day. No Polish army vehicle waited for them, so Kwiatkowski pointed to the red Chevy van. "He was after you," he told Molly.

"Who?"

"Tikriti."

"Who the hell is that and why is he after me?"

"Former Saddam intelligence chief. He was the one who contacted my father about Mohamoud Jama. I suspect he wants you for the same reason we want you. We missed him. I think he got away."

"That's comforting."

Molly opened the back of the van. With Deeqa's help, they put Cavalcante inside on a blanket.

"Drive carefully. I think her ribs are broken," Deeqa said. "She could be bleeding internally."

"I'll do my best."

Kwiatkowski jumped into the front seat and fiddled with the ignition before starting the engine. "Where's Father Ray?" Molly asked.

"Don't worry about him. There's just us now."

Kwiatkowski pulled into reverse. He moved into the alley toward the main street away from the bomb area. All the while, Molly held Cavalcante's hand.

"Don't move. Don't say a thing," Molly told her. "We'll take care of you."

Cavalcante's smile turned quickly into a grimace as she tried to lift herself to say something. When Kwiatkowski turned a sharp left onto another main street, Cavalcante rolled closer to Molly.

"Be more careful, Teodor!" Molly insisted.

"I'm doing my best."

Cavalcante opened her eyes and tugged on Molly's hand. "Don't stop," she whispered.

"We won't, dear," Molly bent over Cavalcante to speak to her. "We're almost there."

"No. I mean don't stop the dig." Cavalcante pulled harder on Molly's hand, forcing Molly to drop to her knees to hear her better. "Listen to Milstein."

"Nina, he's crazy."

"No, he isn't." Cavalcante lay her head down to catch her breath.

"I can't do this, Nina. This expedition has taken too much of a toll on us already. I should never have left Boston."

Cavalcante's grip on Molly's hand tightened. "I have seen you, like Milstein, in my dreams."

"Nina, don't."

"It's true."

Kwiatkowski ever so slightly picked up the van's speed as he headed down a relatively fast, wide, and unimpeded roadway toward the American military camp called Eagle III.

Cavalcante raised her lips to kiss Molly's ear. "In my dreams, we were lovers, Hannaniah and I. Something magical is going on, Molly. This is not a sin. It was meant to happen. This expedition. Now. In this time. Because you are the one ordained to find your father."

"He's not my father. That's mystical nonsense, Nina." Molly stared into Cavalcante's beautiful eyes, wide and alive like a child's.

"You don't believe that, *cara mia*. You're Catholic. Unless you want your faith destroyed by the others, you must go on. They will find him if you do not. Do you understand?"

Molly gulped, thirsty for the coldest drink she could find. She couldn't respond to Cavalcante. At last Kwiatkowski pulled up to the heavily fortified entrance to the American military base. Leaning out the window of the van, he told an American guard what had happened in Najaf. The soldier quickly gave him directions to the camp hospital, and Kwiatkowski drove off.

By the time they reached the Eagle III tent hospital, Cavalcante had passed out. Kwiatkowski opened the back door of the van and let two American soldiers attached to the medical unit carry Cavalcante out on a stretcher. Deeqa followed them and they disappeared into the hospital.

"What was she telling you?" he asked Molly.

"Not to quit," she said.

"And?"

"I guess I'm not quitting."

Shutting her eyes and letting out a long exhausted sigh, she sagged to the ground in the shade of the tent. The temperature had to be somewhere in the nineties, and she wondered if she had the strength and commitment to go on. Kwiatkowski sat beside her and offered her a drink of Coca-Cola one of the medical staff had given him. She was taking a deliciously quenching swig when another man, tall with a thin face and a buzz cut, approached them. Dressed in white fatigues like a soldier, the man was not a soldier. He knelt beside Molly and Kwiatkowski and introduced himself.

"Talk about coincidences," he said. "We've been looking for you for some time."

"You are …?" Molly asked.

"Richard Jackson at your service, ma'am. I am going to be your escort into the past."

CHAPTER 13

André Leveille-Gaus was used to the desert. He had spent most of his youth in Algeria, had trekked across the Sahara, east to Egypt, south to Mali, west to the Atlantic. He could truly call it his personal sandbox. His leathery face was a result of the storms that blew across the dunes. His humor was as dry as the weather. His outlook on life had been fashioned by a world where borders were practically meaningless, where the earth and sky merged to infinity, and where humanity was unlikely to ever prosper or corrupt.

What lay beneath the timeless sands was of no interest to oilmen or diamond miners, only to men like himself, searching for the past. People who lived in the time of Christ had a greater appreciation for the world around them. They worshiped the gods of nature and lived or died by how deeply they bowed before them. These days, Leveille-Gaus thought, as he waited for the rest of his team to rendezvous with him a hundred kilometers west of Najaf, people tended to bow before foolish governments and mindless terrorists.

Leveille-Gaus never propitiated anyone. But he did have a boss to report to.

"Doctor, I see dust."

At the moment, Leveille-Gaus was sitting in the back of a Polish military vehicle that had left Ur earlier that day. He put back the radio receiver, breaking contact with those foreign masters, and put on his wide-brimmed straw hat. No matter how desert-trained a body became, the sun was never an ally. His permanently brown and chiseled face was a testament to that.

Jumping from the rear of the truck, he saw a cloud of dust approaching from the east, opposite the setting ball of fire to his rear. The sky was darkening. That afternoon, Kwiatkowski had radioed his soldiers and given them a rendezvous location west of Najaf at the intersection of two roads, one that went west to Jordan, the other that ran south to Saudi Arabia. A local weather pattern had created a desert dust storm, which had deposited sand onto the roadways. What Leveille-Gaus was looking at now was the throw of sand particles into the wind by a group of trucks easily visible across the flat terrain.

"There are three of them," he said to a Polish soldier standing to his right, gazing through binoculars.

"Yes, sir. Three."

"There should only be one."

The Polish soldier shrugged.

"Why three?" Leveille-Gaus wondered.

Their rendezvous point was a two-lane highway built for two purposes: to connect Iraq with countries to the west that ignored the American embargo and trucked goods into Baghdad, and to explore the desert for potential oil fields. A snakelike pipeline, in fact, ran westward just south of their position across the desert to Syria. A small village existed on this crossroads—shacks, hovels, a few one- and two-story buildings, a warehouse for storing oil equipment, not meant for tourism. The village was called by its inhabitants Al-Muthallath.

As the three vehicles pulled up to join them, Leveille-Gaus wiped his brow with a handkerchief and went out to greet his team.

Molly exited from the passenger side of the second truck, Red Sox cap perched on her head. She wore military fatigues and carried a folded map. The man who walked beside her was unfamiliar to

Leveille-Gaus, taller than Molly, dark-haired, not a native.

"Molly," Leveille-Gaus said, "you've had quite an adventure." He looked at the welt on her jaw.

He extended a hand. Molly didn't take it. "Not exactly over the rainbow," she said. "You know about Nina?"

He nodded. "She'll be all right, thank God. But you have guests."

The dark-haired non-native stepped up. "My name is Milstein," he said, offering his hand.

"Who are you?" Leveille-Gaus asked brusquely. "What are all these trucks?"

"We're here to support your dig," Milstein said.

Leveille-Gaus glanced at Molly for an explanation.

"It seems we've been commandeered," she said. "Mr. Milstein is American intelligence. Military. This is Father Ray Teague. You don't want to know what he does."

Teague smiled. Dressed in jeans, sneakers, and a *Burn this Bush* T-shirt, he hardly looked priestly.

"*Father* Ray?" Leveille-Gaus asked.

"I'm a Jesuit instructor in psychology at Mt. Auburn College, Molly's school. We go back many years. I knew Molly's mother."

"I wouldn't wear that T-shirt around here, Father," Leveille-Gaus suggested. Once again, he looked at Molly as if her non-committal expression would reveal something. It didn't. "So, we have a psychologist and a spy. How does this advance our expedition?" he asked.

"I advance your expedition," a new voice said.

Coming up to join the others, a khaki cap protecting his head, a gun holstered at his side, a tall man in military fatigues proffered his hand. Thick and calloused, it was hard for Leveille-Gaus to ignore. Still another man followed him.

"We've been trying to reach you since Boston," he said. "We were just a step behind you in Poland. From what I've seen so far, you should be thankful to have us. Richard Jackson at your service."

"Undoubtedly. A psychologist, a spy, and now a cowboy, is it? Alabama?"

"Tennessee, sir. You suffered casualties in Najaf. There's no telling what else lies out there. The Muslim bad guys know you're here. Ghazi Al-Tikriti. Abdul Azim Nur. They know what you're after. They want it, too. Am I making myself plain?"

Milstein said by way of introduction, "And this is Habib Al-Nazariiy, the nephew of Imram Fawzi who was director of the Iraqi National Museum." Milstein's glance fell casually onto Molly. "Can we sit down somewhere, get refreshments, talk?" he asked. "It's almost night. We aren't going anywhere until morning."

Unlike Baghdad or An-Najaf, there were no hotels in Al-Muthallath. No cafes. No water bubblers.

Jackson had come prepared. Of his three trucks, one carried men and provided a place for them to sleep. The second vehicle stored equipment for fighting or digging. The third, the most important, was the kitchen truck, fully equipped with two gasoline field ranges, cabinets for food storage, pots, pans, utensils, and an ice box in the small trailer attached to the rear.

Jackson cooked while the others talked under the stars. For the desert, he had provisioned typical military cuisine: pasta, rice, dried fruit, dried milk, powdered eggs, beef stew, chicken à la king. While he cooked in the back of the kitchen truck, the rest of the party circled around a campfire. An oil pipeline was visible in the moonlight.

Molly could almost relax. The evening temperatures had dipped and she wrapped a blanket about her shoulders, sitting in a circle around the fire with her colleagues in the hunt. She was a city girl, had never been a Brownie or a Girl Scout, but the allure of the primitive had always been with her. Perhaps it had been her mother's influence. She remembered dancing with her mother in a field, perhaps on a farm. She had been so young only vague perceptions remained—a huge bonfire, taller than three child Mollys, people with long dresses and long hair waving their arms, laughing, shouting, singing as they whirled like pagan worshipers around the fire.

Yes, it was true. In those days, her mother had been her night, her day, her spiritual center, her goddess of everything. Jesus had come along later. Sitting under the constellations, which had been such a powerful part of the ancient religions, Molly couldn't say that Jesus had been a poor replacement. On the contrary, He had been and was a significant part of her life. He was simplicity itself. Love. Tolerance. Something everyone in every religion could understand. What, then, was she doing out here in a desert in Iraq surrounded by people she didn't trust, looking for the one thing that could destroy everything she believed in?

"It doesn't matter who funded your mission, Dr. Leveille," Milstein said. "It has been decided by powers greater than I that it is in the best interests of the military presence in Iraq, and of Iraq itself, that we locate Mohamoud Jama's find and keep it under wraps."

"It has been under wraps for two thousand years," Teague said. "Perhaps it would be better if we simply left it there."

Molly chuckled. *It.* Did they even understand what this *it* was? "Supposing we find *it*," she said. "What do we do with *it*? We all understand what *it* is, don't we?"

"The remains of an early Judaeo-Christian community," Leveille-

Gaus said. "A cemetery. Perhaps the remains of Hannaniah."

"Oh, cut the crap, André." Molly wrapped the blanket tighter around herself as a cool wind blew across their encampment. "We're after Jesus. Nothing more. Nothing less. This is not Tutankhamon. This is not some minor prophet. This is the man much of the planet worships in one way or another. This is their Son of God. Assuming for the moment the unlikely—that his body actually exists—what in God's name do you expect to do with *it*?"

"The Vatican will protect it," Leveille-Gaus said. "It will not be desecrated. We will study it, naturally—who can't help being fascinated? But the rest of the world need never find out."

"Bullshit." Jackson entered the circle, wearing an apron and chef's hat. "You can get your food now. Spaghetti and green beans, biscuits and Italian wine. I figured we should inaugurate this expedition appropriately."

Kwiatkowski, who had been sitting quietly beside Molly, tapped her shoulder. "Let's eat." His eyes locking on hers told her that he had more on his mind than food. His four soldiers were already in line behind the kitchen truck. As soon as one of Jackson's civilian mercenaries dished them plates of pasta in tomato sauce, Kwiatkowski steered Molly off to the side.

"What's up?" she asked.

"Dr. Leveille is still talking about the Vatican as if your American friends aren't here. In fact, they outgun us and they have no intention of letting the Vatican get what is out there."

"At least we can now openly admit who's footing our bill." Molly looked around to see Father Ray, Milstein, and Habib standing in line for dinner. "I saw the Vatican license plate on the car that was destroyed in the explosion at your father's castle. You could have told me the truth."

"We couldn't be sure of your loyalty," Kwiatkowski told her. He walked away from the trucks, southward toward the desert and the oil pipeline. "I'm sorry, Molly. My father wasn't always an honorable man, but he loved his country, he worshiped our pope, and he would have done anything for the Holy Father. Your work on Hannaniah made you appear heretical in his eyes."

"Your eyes?"

"I kept my silence."

"I noticed."

Molly suddenly wasn't very hungry. Facing south into the desert, she could easily have been Hannaniah, recently fled from Jerusalem, scouting out a new and desolate land.

"As it is," Kwiatkowski said, "we don't know what is out there. We only think we know. Mohamoud made an assumption, based largely upon your work and Dr. Leveille's. And that is speculative, isn't it? You really don't know who Hannaniah was. Or if she was telling the truth."

Molly crouched and laid her plate on the sand. And yet, she thought, I could be her descendant. His. Jesus'. How do I protect my family?

Kwiatkowski leaned over and kissed her.

"Teodor," she said, but she neither moved nor complained when he kissed her again, gently on the lips. Then she kissed him back, briefly, eyes open, looking directly into his.

"I suppose," she said, "that means you trust me now."

"Oh, I always did, Molly. I'm not my father. I had no intention of following in his footsteps."

Molly smiled and on second thought discovered she was hungry enough to pick up a fork and start eating Jackson's spaghetti. "For a first date, this is the pits," she said.

"It can only get worse."

Molly laughed, but Kwiatkowski was completely serious. "At some point, we have to get away from these guys," he said. "If we are lucky, if you lead us to ... whatever ..."

"If I lead you?"

"Yes. You are the map. Cavalcante was right. And I don't believe in such things."

Out here in the desert, off by themselves, under the quiet night sky, she could take a good hard look at him for the first time. Blond hair had sprouted over his face. He was fair-complexioned and the Iraqi sun had reddened his cheeks, intensifying the blue of his eyes. He had dropped some weight in the short time she had known him, too, so that his face appeared thinner. Very kissable, she thought.

"What are you planning?" she asked. "Shoot-out at the OK Corral?"

"I don't know. Milstein I think is a reasonable man. You know Teague. Jackson is the one we have to worry about. The people he represents."

"Great," Molly said. "So, I should just sit my ass on this desert and not move a muscle?"

"That might not be such a bad idea. Until we can figure out what to do."

That night while the others slept in the trucks and in sleeping bags on the ground, Molly turned on the light in the cab of Kwiatkowski's truck and reviewed the Hannaniah material in Cavalcante's black binder. She fell asleep doing it, departing this world in the midst of a description by Hannaniah of her flight from Egypt. She awoke to the dawn. Rubbing her eyes and stretching her feet as far as she could in the cramped cab, she gazed out the windshield toward the village. A group of men and boys followed an old man who issued a call to prayer as the sun came up. But why did they come into the desert instead of to the village mosque?

Molly dropped from the truck's cab and followed the men into the barren flatland south of the village. She wiped the sleep from her eyes and kept a respectful distance as the men climbed a slight rise in the desert floor, probably the highest point of land for miles. Placing their mats on the rocky ground, they spread out in an irregular pattern before the village holy man instead of in the usual straight lines. The leader stood before them, a lone man knelt behind them, and four others stood in pairs on either side.

Even more astonishing was that the women had followed the men. Girls carried crying babies, older women brought pitchers and bowls of food and drink, which they spread on blankets at the base of the prayer hill.

"What do you think it means?"

Molly jumped. "Oh! Milstein! What do I think what means?"

Milstein's cheeks, like Kwiatkowski's, had grown stubble, only black. His hair was still unruly from a night asleep on the ground, and his eyes were invisible behind tinted sunglasses. "The women," he said. "I've never seen women in attendance during a Muslim prayer ceremony."

"You're an expert on religion?"

"I taught it along with history. Women generally aren't allowed around men at prayer," he said.

"Women generally aren't allowed to do a lot of things around men." Molly turned to face him. She could see her reflection in his lenses. The morning was rising hot and dry. She was famished and achy from nodding off in the truck but wanted to take advantage of the solitude to speak to Milstein in private.

"Jesus believed in the equality of men and women," she said. "So did Hannaniah. That's what made them revolutionary."

"The Jewish Sabbath service traditionally is constituted of at least ten males, representative of the ten lost tribes of Israel. At the Last Supper, the Passover seder, Jesus is portrayed with only men."

"Yes," Molly countered, "but who painted the Last Supper or described it in the gospels? Men. Hide-bound, conservative men."

She folded her arms across her chest as if to stiffen her position and prepare her defense, but Milstein wasn't interested in arguing with her. "You're right, of course," he said with a smile. Removing his sunglasses, he eyed Molly. "Jesus had too deep a respect for women to allow his faith to discriminate against them. He based his ministry on his own personal experiences. Either as a man of flesh and blood or as God come to earth, he drew conclusions from life and chose a new path over tradition."

"God is fallible?"

"Why not? Learning is essential to all things. You're a scientist. You know how experiments can go sometimes. Obviously, God isn't always happy with us."

Molly smiled. This Milstein was a far more likeable sort than the one she had first thought she knew, the military intelligence officer. "You speak as though you knew him personally."

"Not God. But Jesus. Yes, I did."

Whether it was fatigue, the stress of everything that had happened to her since she had departed Boston or the seriousness of Milstein's tone, Molly broke into such a fit of laughter that several of the Muslim women from the village turned to glare at her, fingers to mouths. Every time she looked at Milstein, who joined in her amusement, she burst into another gale of hysterics until she felt her belly would erupt.

"Sorry, sorry, Milstein," she managed to say. Tears rolled down her cheeks. She used Milstein as a prop to keep from falling over. She felt better, healthier, than she had in days once she was finally able to get control of her laughter.

"You're always beautiful," Milstein said, "but when you laugh you become transcendent. You should do it more often."

"Stick with me, Milstein, and I might."

Looking past Milstein she saw the rest of their camp rousing and preparing breakfast.

"You're going to have to choose soon, Milstein," she said. "Your people want Jesus. So do I. We can't both have him."

"I was hoping," he said, "it wouldn't come to that. We're responsible people. No one wants to turn this expedition into a farce."

"It's already pretty outrageous. Let's say we make a deal, Milstein." She could see how infatuated with her he was. "You seem like a reasonable fellow, an educated man. Jewish?"

"Yes."

"Let's agree to talk more when the time is appropriate. If we're lucky, if we find what we're looking for … Jackson's hard core. Jesus means nothing to him. An assignment. A contract. Money. We need to deal with this in a way that won't threaten anyone's faith. Agreed?"

Milstein took Molly's hand and shook it. "Spoken like Jesus' own child." He offered to escort her back to their trucks.

"Just one more thing," she said. "What did you mean when you said you knew Jesus personally? That sounds more fundamentalist Christian than Jewish."

The look Milstein gave her, long and searching, made Molly lower her eyes. Maybe she was wrong about him. Maybe he wasn't infatuated with her. Maybe he was in love.

"You'll find out," he said.

Over breakfast, Leveille-Gaus opened a black binder of his own translations. "You wanted a map," he said. "Here is a map." On a fold-up table set beside the kitchen truck, he opened an historical reference map of the ancient Middle East, covering the Mediterranean to Persia. Standing around the table, Molly, Milstein, Teague, Jackson, Habib, and Kwiatkowski focused on the pencil Leveille-Gaus used as a pointer.

"We are here, Al-Muthallath," he said. "There are the Tigris and Euphrates." He looked up at Molly. "Your find in Afghanistan was based upon fairly explicit scrolls you and Jama discovered in Egypt, but we don't have the luxury of such a detailed account."

"If Jama were still alive, we wouldn't have to go through all this guesswork."

"But he isn't, Mr. Jackson. What we do have are various pieces of a puzzle. Molly's Star of David talisman, the lamentation poem sent to us by Tikriti, and this tantalizing piece I translated from Hannaniah's gospels."

Molly moved beside Leveille-Gaus as he read. " 'Three travelers took a journey out of the Holy Land on the Day of Atonement.' Yom Kippur. So says Hannaniah in a letter to Peter in Rome. Each then went their own separate way."

"How do you know it was to Peter and not to one of her children?" Molly asked. "That's another document I'd like to read," she said.

"Patience. The letter also includes three horoscopes. Hannaniah believed in astrology."

Molly glanced at Kwiatkowski, himself an avid stargazer.

Jackson said, "What is your point, Doctor?"

"I believe the horoscopes were meant not only to direct people's lives, but to direct them physically. Her version of Mapquest.com."

"Do you have an example of one?" Habib asked.

Leveille-Gaus flipped through the binder until he found the appropriate page. Then he quoted, "'Her hair is as red as the setting sun, her eyes green like the sea.'" He paused to gaze at Molly who fit the description just as well as Hannaniah.

"'Strong of leg, she will stride like the Lioness of Judah, for her spirit is five parts from the house of her father and six parts from the house of her mother.'"

"Sounds like biblical genetics to me," Teague cracked.

"'*From* the house'?" Molly asked. "You're absolutely sure of the preposition?"

"I know how to translate Hebrew," Leveille-Gaus said. "'From.'"

"Fiddledy-crap," Jackson muttered.

"Bear with me," Leveille-Gaus said. "'Arms wide and giving, she will leave her mother to embrace her father on the road of the risen sun.'"

"Jesus?" Teague asked.

Molly shook her head. "Sorry, Father Ray. English puns don't quite work in Hebrew. She's talking about leaving her mother, Jerusalem, and walking east toward her father, Ur."

"Very good, Molly," Leveille-Gaus said.

"Can you be so sure?" Kwiatkowski asked.

"She uses the symbolism frequently." Molly frowned, wishing she could possess what Leveille-Gaus was holding, wishing she had had the five years to study and unravel the full mystery of Hannaniah.

Habib Al-Nazariiy, the engineer, produced a straight edge and placed it on the map. "So, she traveled east from Jerusalem to Ur." He drew a line on the map. "What next?"

" 'She is the third,' " Leveille-Gaus again began to quote. This time, he looked up in surprise as Molly mimicked him softly word for word. " 'She is the passage. From her father's kingdom. Past her mother's throne. Beyond the daughter's chained feet. There at last the three shall unite and point the way to the Fisherman.' "

"Peter?" Teague wondered.

"Unlikely." Leveille-Gaus eyed Molly. "How could you know the words?" he asked.

"I don't know." Molly searched her memory. "Three hearts, Hannaniah said, united in darkness. Nina's lamentation said the same thing. At her daughter's fingertips, the fisherman will plant his seed." Molly shook her head. "I don't know where it came from. Suddenly the words seemed so familiar." She glanced across the table. "Milstein, don't look at me that way."

"I'm sorry. I was only …"

"Spooking me out."

Teague, as well, watched her with interest. "I remember those words," he said. "Not verbatim, perhaps. You spoke them once under regression."

"Come on, Father Ray."

"You did. I remember. If I had my notes with me, I'd show you."

All eyes rested on Molly. She turned away.

Only Habib was focused on the map. "What are the houses she talks about? Five from her mother, six from her father?"

"Who knows?" the French archaeologist said. "But wait, there's more. Hannaniah, the daughter, is the third, the passage. 'There at last the three shall unite and point the way *to* the Fisherman.' "

"*To?*"

"Yes, Professor O'Dwyer. *To.*"

Molly frowned. Her focus was no longer on the map, but on the Star of David pendant hanging around her neck. Six points. Six unidentified symbols at each point with a triangle set in the center.

"Pointing the way," Molly muttered, and began mumbling the lines of Hannaniah's lamentation. Looking up, she saw they were all staring at her.

"Gentlemen, may I make a suggestion," Milstein said. "You're trying to decipher Hannaniah using twenty-first century logic, but her calculations came out of the period in which she lived. You need to access that mind, and you can do it because she's here. Right now. Right there. Molly."

"No, thank you, Milstein," she said.

Molly reached inside her shirt to remove the pendant. Many copies of the star had likely been made. Imran Fawzi had found a similar one in a funerary urn in Iraq. Molly figured Hannaniah had meant her children to wear them as a constant reminder of their faith and of their homeland no matter where the Diaspora took them. With absolute practicality, she had intended her children and her children's children to use it as a marker for a map.

Unhooking the Star of David from the chain, she slid it past her crucifix and held it up for everyone to see. "Do you have Imran Fawzi's?"

"Yes," Milstein said.

"Bring it to me."

Molly stared intently at the talisman, for the first time linking it to Hannaniah's lamentation.

"Two intersecting triangles," she said, "forming six points and a six-sided hexagram in the middle."

Kwiatkowski leaned in. "I never realized what an intricate work of art it is. It's beautiful."

"Made of gold. Made to last. And not a letter or symbol of it is irrelevant."

Milstein trotted over and handed her Fawzi's Star of David. It was identical to Molly's.

"You think those are maps?" Teague asked her.

"Unquestionably. The two symbols on the bottom right and left, the houses, one with the Hebrew letter *yud*, the other the letter *ayin*. I don't know why I didn't think of it before."

"Didn't think of what before?"

"*Yerushalayim*, Dr. Leveille, to the east. Ur to the west. And in between, the triangle, the three at last united, points to where we'll find Hannaniah. Plot your point, Mr. Nazariiy, five houses from Jerusalem and six from Ur. Then let's get going."

CHAPTER 14

By the time Abdul Azim Nur reached the village of Al-Muthallath, the Americans were long gone though the villagers could point him in the direction they traveled: south into the desert.

"Appropriate that our hunt should take us there," he told the Iranian Shamkhazi, who followed the imam like a dog its master.

Since he was a boy in a small village like this one, Nur had loved the desert. Often he would go into the wasteland like the holy hermits of old to seek isolation and to find God in the quiet and stillness of the empty land. Shamkhazi, too, knew of the desert, though he regarded the wastes with far less fondness. During the Iraqi war against Iran, Saddam's troops, armed by the Americans, had force-marched his family out into the desert and gunned them down. Shamkhazi had survived because even then, as a child lying among the dead, he knew how to keep quiet, watch, and wait.

"We're too late, Imam," Shamkhazi said. They had driven into Al-Muthallath in a black 1954 Aston Martin, the only car in Nur's marsh village, abandoned by a British army colonel a half century before. The blazing noontime sun turned the car into an oven. Shamkhazi had sat beside him in the backseat, as always, taking notes.

"Should we follow the Americans? Or send Tikriti?"

"Patience, Barid."

Nur's driver pointed toward the villagers mounting the desert hill for their mid-day prayers.

"We must not let them escape us again."

Nur left the car, ignoring Shamkhazi. *The dreams, the foolish, stupid dreams*, he thought. They should mean nothing to him, phantasms of his psyche, to be dismissed in the light of day, but these dreams seemed to have a tangible quality to them. Beyond dreams, they existed in his mind as memories of real events that had happened at some time, some place in his past. And why, *why*, did the redheaded American archaeologist, Molly O'Dwyer, inhabit them?

Nur's black turban and robes deflected the heat, but perspiration dropped down his cheeks into his beard. His men carried his prayer mat as they walked out into the desert toward the hill. At the foot of the rise, one of the village women greeted him with a smile and a bow of respect.

"Don't bow to me, woman," he said. "Bow to Allah." But when he attempted to join the prayer service, the woman held him back.

"You'll have to wait now, Imam," she said. "Once the men begin, they can't be disrupted."

Shrugging, Nur turned to ask his four guards to place the prayer mats on the ground so they could honor Allah apart from the villagers, only to notice that Shamkhazi had pulled them aside and was giving them his own instructions.

"You are being disrespectful," he told the Iranian. "Pray now, plot later."

"But we can't wait, Imam. Tikriti must be sicced on these foreigners now."

"Tikriti destroyed half of An-Najaf and still couldn't bring me the woman."

"Revolutions are rarely bloodless, Imam," Shamkhazi said.

Nur stood on his mat, dropped to his knees, and prayed, while thinking two things. First, that Shamkhazi was becoming a dangerous burden. Second, that as dangerous as the Iranian was, this red-haired woman named Molly O'Dwyer, was becoming even more disruptive.

Beyond the obvious, he wondered who she was, and why in the name of Allah he could not get her out of his mind.

There was no pavement in the desert south of Al-Muthallath, only sand, rocks, and dust. Each truck in the caravan tossed the sand into the wind, which in turn hurled it into each succeeding windshield as the expedition bumped along the flat terrain.

These were the times that Molly's heart pumped so fast she felt it might burst, when incidental intellectual concerns succumbed to the thrill of the hunt. Faith, fear, competitiveness, morality—all went the way of the wind, which blew her hair and made her laugh.

They had left the village four hours earlier. Two of the trucks took off on a westerly track, while her vehicle and the kitchen truck split toward the east. While they had a decent fix on a location for the site they were after, there were no absolutes. By coming at the presumed location from two directions, they hoped for a wider view, to spot any obvious visual irregularities in the land that would tell them where to start digging. Molly sat in the passenger seat squeezed against the door. Milstein sat between her and the driver. The land was so flat she could see dust rising into the air several miles to the west where Jackson's two trucks drove. Kwiatkowski rode in the kitchen truck with a half-American, half-Polish crew.

"You look carsick," Molly told the man in the middle. "Get used to it."

A sudden bump jolted Milstein whose attempted smile vanished as his head snapped back against the seat. "We shouldn't be going this fast, should we?" he said.

"We're doing twenty. You want to get out and walk? I thought you were a military man."

"Intelligence, not ground forces."

Molly's response was to stick her head out the open window and take the desert air full blast in the face. Her red hair cascaded behind her and her shirt collar ruffled in the breeze. "A few years ago," she said, "I traveled into Patagonia, into the Argentine interior to look for dinosaur bones. My boyfriend was a paleontologist."

"Was?"

"Life is fleeting, much faster than this truck, Milstein." Molly shrugged off his question as if in doing so she could dispense with those parts of her past she didn't like. Overhead, a jet left a white trail behind it.

"Ours probably," Milstein said. "We'll see a lot of flyovers but the ground troops are busy rooting out insurgents at the Syrian border. Out here we're on our own."

Lifting a canteen of water to her lips, she said, "Here's hoping."

"Look," Milstein said. He pointed eastwards at a distant cloud of dust.

"What is it?"

"Don't know." Milstein turned to the driver. "Stop here."

Kwiatkowski's truck pulled up behind Molly's and stopped. He had already seen the same disturbance in the sand. Once out of the truck's cab, he jumped onto the hood with binoculars.

"I suppose it's not the Tasmanian Devil," Molly said.

"Trucks."

"Whose?"

"Can't tell."

Kwiatkowski joined the others on the ground. He wiped the sweat off his forehead with his khaki hat. "They're heading in this direction, whoever they are. We can probably outrun them. But if we can see them, they can see us. And if they want us badly enough, they'll follow."

"So, what do we do?" Molly asked. "They could be friendly. Iraqi police guarding the pipelines."

"No pipelines out here," Milstein said. "Even our troops don't know we're here."

"We can stay and fight," one of Jackson's hired guards said. His finger was already fixed on the trigger of his assault rifle.

"We could," Kwiatkowski told him, "but I'm not about to risk these people's lives. Back in the trucks."

Kwiatkowski's truck pulled in front of Molly's and led them west toward Jackson's and Leveille-Gaus's two vehicles. Molly poked her head out the window. It was hard to tell, but she didn't think they'd gained or lost any ground to whoever was following them.

"Cindy-anna Jones," Milstein said. "That's what people call you."

Molly looked back at Milstein, then rolled up the truck window.

"People who don't know me call me that. I'm not a treasure hunter, and I don't own a whip."

"You may be missing out on a lot of fun." Milstein smiled. "When we find Jesus—if we find Jesus—what will you do, as a Catholic?"

"We can't let the fanatics get hold of him," she said, gazing at Milstein, letting her Irish green eyes rest on his, comfortably, lingeringly.

A jarring bump in the path tossed them against the dashboard. Molly landed in Milstein's lap.

"That's a fanatic for you," he said, having stolen a squeeze helping her off his lap. "Always getting in the way."

"You have to help me, Andrew." She touched his knee. She used his given name for the first time, another tactical maneuver. "I'm not going to let them have Him."

"Jackson?"

"Any of them."

Milstein looked straight at Molly. "Dr. Leveille didn't read Hannaniah's complete horoscopes," he said.

"When did you get the chance to read them?"

"I didn't. But I know them as well as you. 'Her hair is red …'"

"Andrew."

"'She is like the wheat in the field.'"

"If you didn't read them, then how can you quote them?"

"'She has the mark of the quarter moon on her left thigh.'"

When Milstein's gaze lowered to her lap, Molly reflexively closed her legs. "No," she said. "At least it doesn't look like a quarter moon. Milstein, what are you trying to do?"

Milstein braced a hand on the dashboard to steady himself. "Molly, please let Father Ray regress you."

"No."

"Why not?"

"Because it's unscientific."

"So?"

"It's irrelevant to what we're doing."

"You don't believe that, I know you don't."

"Well then, maybe it's just too damned personal. It's embarrassing to open yourself up like that."

"You mean, frightening."

Molly nodded. "Yes. All right. If that's what you want to call it, maybe there are some things I really don't want to know. Is that all right with you?"

"Of course, it is, Molly. But it's not irrelevant. It is by far the most relevant thing you could do."

Their driver suddenly swerved to the right, throwing Molly into the door and Milstein on top of her.

"You can get up now," Molly told him as the truck took an unanticipated descent in the desert floor. When she glanced out the windshield, Kwiatkowski's truck had already leveled out on the bed of a dry wadi. At one point, perhaps centuries ago, a stream had cut through this depression and an oasis had existed where weary travelers between Jerusalem and Ur could refresh themselves and camp out for the night before moving on. Now, nothing but rocks. With ten feet between former riverbed and the plain above, the two trucks might reasonably hope to hide here, shielded by the slope from would-be desert pirates.

Pausing to catch her breath from the jolting and unexpected detour, Molly started out the door only to have Milstein latch onto her arm.

" 'She will lie on the side of her father's throne and produce a multitude,' " he said. " 'They will gather once more from the corners of the earth and they will proclaim her the mother of all.' "

"Milstein," she said, "I'm not buying it." And out onto the wadi floor she jumped.

Ghazi Al-Tikriti stood on the hood of a military transport truck, binoculars trained on a cloud of dust to the south. Formerly British property, the truck had been confiscated by mujahedeen of the Iraqi jihad after they had wiped out the British soldiers who had occupied it. Now Tikriti contemplated wiping out the foreign scientists who had escaped him in An-Najaf.

Well, if I can't get the woman, he thought, I'll get them all. Then I'll get the woman.

Handing the binoculars to the woman-hater Aden, he winced as he jumped to the ground. He was still licking his wounds from the hotel in An-Najaf. He had lost half of his men, lost Molly O'Dwyer, and nearly lost his arm, a bullet cutting a gash that was still sore as hell. All in all, he was in no mood to be nice.

Aden said, "We can take them now, my general. They are no more than five kilometers from us."

"Habib is with them," Tikriti replied. "We can wait."

When Aden jumped from the hood of the truck, dust flew into the air coating the automatic rifle he never set aside. "Imam Nur wants us to take them alive. I don't think it will be possible," he said.

Tikriti grunted. He gingerly touched the arm he had nearly lost, the work of a Polish army bullet. He said, "I don't either."

Tikriti was not the only man who knew where Molly O'Dwyer and the other archaeologists had vanished into the desert from An-Najaf. Much farther away, a man in an army uniform sat at a radio console in a room filled with electrical equipment. He turned in his seat to a superior officer. The man said, "We have their position, sir. They are moving deeper into the Anbar Desert toward Saudi Arabia."

His superior officer, a man renowned for daring raids across national borders, rested a hand on a holstered pistol. He said, "Our mole will tell us when to fly. God help them all if they find what they think they'll find."

Two hours passed. And then three. Kwiatkowski had radioed Jackson and told them to sit tight and not draw attention to themselves by moving across the desert sands. Then he had positioned himself with his binoculars and the guards with their guns at the top of the wadi to keep their eyes on the advancing intruders.

But after three hours, the screen of dust to the west moved away and disappeared altogether having lost its quarry to the mysteries of the desert. Only then did Kwiatkowski radio the other half of the team and tell them it was safe to reunite.

"No way. You come to us," Jackson said. "We've found somethin' out here."

"What?"

"I'm sendin' Teague and Al-Nazariiy to get you. We'll join up tomorrow."

Indeed, night drifted across the desert and had settled over the wadi by the time Nazariiy and Teague had arrived in their truck. Molly leaped to her feet at the sound of their approaching engine and dashed from the trioxane campfire Kwiatkowski had made. Heart pounding, she wanted to know what the hell they had found in the desert.

"Well, I'm no archaeologist," Teague said, barely out of the truck before Molly was on him, "but Dr. Leveille is certainly excited. There's a mound and even some visible structures of brick and stone. Of course, we only got a very cursory look."

"Excellent," Molly said. "I'm surprised."

"There was oil exploration in this area," Habib said, "so this could be the place Mohamoud Jama was digging. The Americans launched missiles against our soldiers leaving Kuwait. It looks like one of them uncovered something. There is evidence of an impact."

"Good. Well, if we're lucky, we might know something in a day or two."

Molly could hardly relax, eat, talk, do anything normal as the others took supper around the fire. She would have reviewed the binder material, but Leveille-Gaus had kept it with him. Kwiatkowski sat beside her, encouraged her to eat.

"It's going to be a busy couple of days," he told her.

"Weeks. Months."

"Don't count on that."

"We may need to bring in more equipment."

"That's definitely out. As Jackson said, you've got what you've got."

Molly raised her knees, tucked them under her chin, and rested her head on them, wrapping her arms around her legs. "You can't imagine how it feels. When we opened up the sealed urns and found Hannaniah's scrolls, it was like, I don't know … What do you feel when you gaze at the stars?"

Kwiatkowski glanced skyward. "Ignorant."

Molly smiled. "You feel ignorant?"

"Of course. Don't you? How much is out there. How little we know about it. I prefer to look at the stars for their beauty. Everything else is too taxing."

"Are you an atheist, Teddy?"

Kwiatkowski nearly choked on a spoonful of mashed potatoes.

"You all right?" she asked him, pounding on his back.

"Nobody's called me Teddy since my mother died."

"Does that bother you?"

"No. You just caught me off guard." Kwaitkowski regrouped and took another spoonful of dinner. "I don't think anybody really believes in God," he said. "They want to. They may need to. But deep down I think we all know the truth."

"That's pretty cynical," Molly said.

"But honest?" Father Teague spoke from the far side of the fire. "When I entered the priesthood, I believed. Now I go to services and keep my mouth shut. The knowledge I gain from my job comforts me far more than false spirituality ever did. Every day, intelligence creeps up closer and closer to God's throne. Some day it will get to the seat of the Holy of Holies and find it empty."

Molly hugged her knees tighter. The night was cool and the fire small. "I've always believed in something," she said. "It's just not always the same thing. As you get older, you grow, you change, your needs change. I have a feeling Hannaniah is going to take me someplace I've never been before. For me, that's the saving grace of this expedition. That's why I'm still here."

"Then we share motives," Milstein said. "I've learned a lot about myself from Father Teague. From regression therapy. If you won't go, let me show you the way, Molly."

Milstein lowered himself on the ground, flat on his back on a sleeping bag by the fire. Teague settled in beside him.

"What are you doing, Milstein?" Molly asked him. "Don't do this. Please."

"If you're going to be stubborn, Molly," Milstein said, "Father Ray can regress me. Don't think it's an act. It isn't. It's a door opening. You'll see. You'll take it, too. You already have."

"It's a simple technique," Teague said for the benefit of the others. He wore a Mt. Auburn University sweater, purple and gold, to ward off the growing chill. The twitching flames of the campfire reflected off his glasses, which he pushed up the bridge of his nose. Kwiatkowski and Habib seemed amused, uncertain what Milstein was planning. Molly watched with unease. Above, on the bank of the wadi, their guards maintained an alert, scanning the vast dark desert with infrared night binoculars.

"No swinging watches or glowing lights," Teague explained, in the glow of the fire. "This is not the realm of the crystal ball. This is a real and verifiable phenomenon, as you will see."

"What brought Milstein to you in the first place?" Molly asked.

"I'm afraid that's confidential."

"Out here nothing's confidential," Kwiatkowski assured the priest. He set his supper dish aside. "If I'm to understand your premise, our success, our lives, may hinge on his, or Molly's, fanciful account of a past life. This expedition has already cost me my father."

"I don't mind telling them, Father," Milstein said. "I had a nervous breakdown, Mr. Kwiatkowski. The stress of the Gulf War. Other things. Father Teague was a fellow faculty member. He suggested, given my past history, this unique form of therapy."

"Which you, in your troubled state of mind, turned into a fantasy," Kwiatkowski said. "Isn't that possible, Mr. Milstein? A spiritual escape maybe, with Jesus of Nazareth."

Milstein closed his eyes again. "Actually," he said, "Jesus was not from Nazareth or Bethlehem. We grew up together in Magdala. That's how he came to know Miriam, impregnated her, and gave life to Hannaniah. No, Mr. Kwiatkowski, this was no fantasy, certainly none that I desired. I am, after all, a Jew."

Kwiatkowski picked up his plate again, glanced at Molly who said, "You could have read that in my translation of her gospel."

"Could have," Milstein said, "but you only corroborated what I had come to know."

Teague placed his hand on Milstein's head. "Focus on my fingers," he instructed, "as your eyelids get heavier. You are in your house back in Boston. On your couch. In the living room. It is warm, comfortable. Imagine your body growing, lengthening one inch then two inches from your head. Then slowly grow back. Now imagine you are growing two inches from your feet. And back again. Your eyelids are getting heavier."

Habib sat by Milstein's head, like a visiting surgeon watching an expert delve into a patient's brain.

Teague continued. "Expand yourself two feet around like a balloon. Blow yourself up to touch the walls of your home … the ceiling … the floor … Go back to your true size, and tell me when you're there."

"I am," Milstein whispered, barely audible.

"Speak up, please."

"I am."

"Good." Teague glanced at Molly, Kwiatkowski, Habib as if to say 'now the journey begins.' "Andrew, go quickly to the door of your house. Open it. Tell me what you see."

"Lawn. Flowers. A child on a swing. My child. A man is pushing him. They're laughing."

"Let them enjoy the moment. Now go to the roof of your house," Teague commanded. "What do you see?"

"Trees. All around," Milstein said. "A cat in a branch."

Teague lifted his hand from Milstein's brow. "As your lids thicken," he said, "rise above the house like a bird on a warm breeze. How does it feel?"

Milstein's giggle startled Molly who heard not an adult in the frivolous laughter, but a young child.

"Go higher now," Teague said, excitement creeping into his voice. Not all patients were susceptible to such suggestion. You almost had to long for it. The escape, the mystery. Milstein had departed reality into this unknown territory quickly, easily, from the very first. "A hundred feet. Two hundred. Make it a nice shiny spring day. The sun is bright. You climb higher and higher toward it, feel its warmth and comfort. Keep climbing until you can see the whole earth … Watch it spin … Slow it down … Watch the continents go by … Now come back to earth. You will find yourself in another existence in a life that has relevance to you. Tell me when you land."

Milstein licked his lips, twisted on top of his sleeping bag as though trying to break invisible ropes wrapped about him.

"Where are you?" Teague asked. "Tell us what you see. Where are you now? Speak clearly. Where are you now?"

"A desert. Hot. Dry."

"That's appropriate," Kwiatkowski mumbled.

"A trail. A caravan route. From Qumran toward the cities of the Parsi."

"How do you know?" Molly asked. "How can you tell?"

"I've been here before. Many times. Yeshuah lived here."

"When you say Yeshuah," Molly asked, "whom do you mean?"

"Yeshuah," Milstein said, as if she had asked a ridiculous question. "My brother. He is talking to James."

Kwiatkowski's loud sigh did not go unnoticed. Molly ignored it. "Is Yeshuah the one people know as Jesus?"

Milstein grunted. "Yeshuah is Yeshuah."

"Can you hear what they're talking about? Yeshuah and James?"

"They don't trust me." Milstein frowned. "Whenever I come near, they stop talking."

"Why?"

Tears formed at the corner of Milstein's eyes. "I don't know why!"

"What does …?"

Molly and Teague raised their voices, contesting for Milstein's attention. Molly had been regressed by Teague, but not into a different or earlier incarnation. She had simply re-experienced an event that had occurred earlier in her own life. But now that Teague had sent Milstein on a voyage of a singularly different kind, Molly found herself compelled beyond scientific reason to go with him.

"What does he look like?" she asked him. "How old is he? How is he dressed?"

But Milstein had his own motives, his own agenda in allowing Teague to regress him. "They don't know," he said.

"What don't they know, Andrew?" Teague asked. "Tell us. Tell the others who you are."

"She has a birthmark on her thigh. I've seen it, touched it. She points at me and they stop talking." Milstein clenched his fists and went still.

Then all was silent. The night. The desert. The tiny encampment in the wadi. Milstein. Until Molly asked him, "Are you in love with Hannaniah?"

"Yes," came the whispered response.

"Your cousin."

"Yes."

"And who are you, brother of Yeshuah? Who are you? Can you tell us your name?"

Not that Molly believed any of it, not that she assumed anything other than that Teague had compelled Milstein to create a fantasy, one that Milstein would have invented to suit his own psychological needs. Even so, she couldn't help herself, much as she imagined her friend Cavalcante would have been unable to resist prodding, probing. And so she asked one last time, "What is your name?"

She wasn't totally taken aback when Milstein raised himself up on his elbows, stared her in the eye, and said, "Judas the Blade. Judas Iscariot."

Morning broke over the desert, a quiet quick animal on the hunt. One moment it wasn't there. The next it had snagged its quarry in its super-hot grip. Molly awoke in the back of the kitchen truck, forgot that she had moved her sleeping bag inside, and nailed her forehead on a shovel strapped to the side.

Damnit! It hadn't been a good night. She had tossed and turned, unable to slip into a dream state despite fatigue. Nobody had mocked Milstein when he returned to the present from his paranormal trip to ancient Judea, but the mood around the campfire had changed, most noticeably her relationship with Kwiatkowski. He absolutely discounted Teague's treatment and Milstein's journey.

"For God's sake, Molly," he had told her when they were alone. "It's obvious. Milstein suffers from a guilt complex. For what, I don't know. So who better to become in his mind than Judas Iscariot? I warned my father he was throwing away his money. Now he's thrown away a hell of a lot more than that. And for what? You people are as gullible as children."

And hadn't Molly lit into him? Which was one of the reasons she slept in the truck while everyone else snored outside. But she refused to let his cynicism deter her. Dr. Leveille-Gaus awaited, and God knew she didn't want to leave him alone at the discovered site any longer than necessary.

Before dressing, she sponge-washed. Water was a precious commodity not to be wasted. Molly had washed her clothes by hand in a pot of water and hung them up to dry at the rear of the truck. She had only one change of clothes. Slipping them on, she already felt the intense heat of the day. She injected her insulin into her abdomen then returned the metal container to a refrigerator and jumped from the truck. Heat or no, she was ready to dig.

"Breakfast?" Habib asked her. As designated cook for the morning shift, he was preparing powdered eggs. Molly brushed him off.

"I'd like us to get going. What time is it?"

"Five-thirty."

"How far is Dr. Leveille from here?"

Habib gazed westward in the direction they would soon be headed. "About twenty kilometers," he said. "Relax and eat, Dr. O'Dwyer. We have the shovels."

But she couldn't, at least not until the trucks were on their way. Then she could take down some Cheerios and dried figs while sitting beside Milstein. He was quiet, thoughtful, for a few minutes after the trucks began to head west, and looked up only when Molly spoke to him.

"Judas?"

"I didn't ask for it," he said.

"You know, if you had chosen Jesus, I could have understood it," she said. "But Judas? I hate to say it, Milstein, but I have to agree with Teodor. You've conjured this identity because you committed an act in your own life which you consider a betrayal."

"So, voila, I became Judas, the most renowned betrayer in history?" Milstein sighed. "How condescending of you. Don't you think that was my first thought, Molly?" he asked. "I took Psych 101. I didn't discover Judas's identity until the third or fourth time I went under. After that, Father Teague and I met every day with the specific purpose of exposing Judas as a creature of Freud. It didn't work. Every time I went under I learned more about myself. In other incarnations, I existed as people who didn't suffer guilt or shame. Only Judas did. And this was before your published accounts of Hannaniah."

Milstein turned to Molly. "Don't you see? Through Judas I knew about Hannaniah before you did. You corroborated my regression. You were the final proof that I couldn't have conjured or fantasized Judas. I was him, Molly. And you were Hannaniah."

If Molly even for a moment considered laughing at Milstein's suggestion, the urge caught immediately, a belly laugh stillborn, snagged on the unexpected sight of a gun barrel pointing directly at their truck. Instinctively, Molly cursed and ducked before realizing on second hurried peak that the gun barrel was mounted on the metal hulk of an Iraqi tank, burned and blistered and left to rot in the Al-Anbar. Behind it, a troop transport truck had apparently taken a direct hit from an American missile. The back had been eviscerated as, no doubt, had been the troops it was transporting. Its remains had been scattered left, right, and every place in between. The trail of debris, in fact, spilled across the desert the length of a football field and ended at what appeared to be the skeletal remains of a half-completed oilrig.

All of this flew past at thirty-five miles per hour, a quick reminder of American wars gone by, until Molly caught sight of something that far exceeded her interest in the rest.

"Stop the truck!" she yelled and nearly slammed her own foot on the brake pedal.

By the time Kwiatkowski in the lead truck had braked to a halt and joined Molly, Milstein was already crouched beside her and she was digging into the sandy soil of a hummock about twenty yards west of the oil tower. Teague and Habib came right behind.

"Just what the hell do you think you're doing now?" Kwiatkowski demanded,

"This may be the site!" she exclaimed without looking at him.

"But Leveille ..."

"Fuck Leveille!" Molly's digging tool spurned patience. She threw her whole body into the effort of uncovering the top layer of soil on the mound, her feet planted firmly in the ground, her right shoulder, elbow, and wrist set in a powerful rhythm of dig hard and fast while she had the chance. "Jama said the site was near oil exploration, right? Well ..." She jerked her head toward the rusted oil well. "An American missile strike at retreating Iraqis." She didn't bother pointing this time.

"Yes? So?" Kwiatkowski said. "Dr. Leveille has found something, too. We can't dig at two sites. Equipment aside, we can't defend two positions if we come under attack."

That argument at least got Molly's attention. She stopped digging. Her breath came in quick, shallow gasps. "A missile missed its target," she explained, "and exposed something that Jama was brought in to investigate." She pointed to the left descent of the hummock into the desert floor. "He tried to cover it back up when he found out what he had uncovered. A burial ground, perhaps of Jesus' extended family and disciples fleeing Israel. If you look carefully, you'll notice that part of the mound has sunk in over time. The desert has reclaimed the hill, buried it in more sand and debris since Jama was here, but it still bears signs of having been worked on by human hands."

"Damn, you've got good eyes," Teague said, peering blankly at the site. "From a moving truck you saw this?"

Just then a familiar loud concussive noise brought everyone's heads around from the hummock westward toward Leveille-Gaus's site. The terrain was so flat, the air so still, that even at a distance of several kilometers, the explosive sound wave compelled Kwiatkowski to run back to the trucks.

"Everyone in!" he shouted. "Hurry! Now!"

Even Jackson's men obeyed without hesitation. Molly cursed under her breath and followed, giving one final reluctant glance back before joining Milstein in the cab of their truck. Then they were off, bouncing across the desert. Milstein gripped Molly's thigh, ostensibly to keep from being launched through the roof.

A thin plume of smoke rose into the air then diffused. The convoy headed for it as to a beacon and reached Leveille-Gaus's site in a little over an hour.

She had expected to fly into the midst of a raging gun battle and wondered at Kwiatkowski's lack of caution. There was no sign of Iraqi militants or insurrectionists even though Jackson's truck was destroyed, ripped apart by the explosion. Jackson stood over Leveille-Gaus, whose arm was being tended to by a Polish medic. A headless torso lay in the sand where it had been flung twenty yards by the blast. Jackson's southern confection of foul language greeted her the moment she jumped down to the ground.

"It was an accident!" he raged. "A goddamned accident! One of your Poles, Kwiatkowski. Don't they teach you people how to handle explosives?"

"One of my men?" Kwiatkowski's eyes widened. "Which one?"

"What the hell does it matter now?" Jackson held an automatic rifle and used it to point out into the desert. "We're all gonna be in it in no time. We might as well have waved a red flag and shouted, 'Come an' git us!'"

Kwiatkowski ignored Jackson's ranting, grabbed a shovel from one of the trucks, and handed out two more to his remaining soldiers. Then he set about to look for body parts to give his dead trooper a burial worthy of a good Christian.

Molly knelt beside Leveille-Gaus. "What happened?" she asked.

"We found the site!" he exclaimed, his focus elsewhere. "Look at the way the desert rises here. It's an obvious circle. Has to be artificial. The desert couldn't form dunes in that shape."

Indeed, Molly noticed a series of sand-covered mounds of varying lengths and shapes with gaps in between. They clearly formed a circle or oval approximately a hundred feet in diameter. As if the desert wind had been trapped within the circle and swirled about its circumference, a pit had been dug out of the southeastern wall of the unknown structure, exposing even more obvious clues to trained archaeological eyes. Bricks lay scattered across the circle, perhaps uncovered by time and the wind or by the explosion of the U.S. military truck. Better yet, what appeared to be the bottom of a cairn stuck out of the ground in the very center of the circle. Its mud bricks had collapsed and decayed but were clearly of human origin.

"Well, what do you think?" Milstein asked her.

Molly didn't know whether to be excited or frustrated. Two sites? How had Jama missed this one? How had everyone missed it? She had been so sure her site had been the correct one. What the hell could this be?

"I don't know," she said. "Let's hope we have time to find out."

General Jim Eisenstadt didn't envy the archaeologists crossing the desert under the sweltering sun of an Iraqi noon. But locked as he was in his air-conditioned office in the Green Zone of Baghdad, he should have felt far more comfortable than he did. Sweat poured out of him like a man with Nile fever. This Jesus thing was getting out of hand. Jackson had misled him. People were dying left and right. Iraqi insurgents were now involved in the hunt. And somehow, one of his superiors in Washington had found out. He wanted the whole thing squashed, and by that he meant in the old CIA way of squashing things.

Eisenstadt looked out his window at the brilliant sunny afternoon in Baghdad and regretted, as he had never regretted anything quite so much in his life, that he would have to be the one to issue the orders to kill.

CHAPTER 15

They dug in earnest at Leveille-Gaus's circular site that day after lunch. The French archaeologist had surveyed the area the day before, and he and Molly agreed that they would dig two trenches, one in a north-south direction from the central cairn and one in an east-west direction, creating a cross whose arms would reach the walls of the circle.

Stonehenge on Salisbury Plain in England was the most famous circle of antiquity, but Molly had never heard of a similar structure in the Middle East. Of course, Stonehenge had an astronomical function, and Hannaniah, the intellect, had loved and studied the stars, so anything was possible. But Molly's gut instinct kept getting in the way of her enthusiasm. Something was wrong with this site.

Pausing in her work mid-afternoon to take a drink of army-issue Gatorade, she wiped the sweat from her brow and studied the brick cairn in the center of the circle. It rose to the level of her waist. A scattering of material spread out beneath the sand was being exposed by the excavators. It was as yet unclear how deep the cairn went and whether it had been a pillar holding up a long vanished ceiling or if it stood isolated. The mud brick and the bitumen mortar certainly merited a close look. The stepped pyramid of Ur had been constructed of similar material. But local craftsmen could have built this place with the same materials a hundred years ago.

"You don't look happy." Kwiatkowski approached her from behind. His men and Jackson's Americans had been put to work doing grunt labor with shovels and picks. His khaki shirt was stained dark from perspiration. He borrowed her canteen for a drink.

"If this is another Essene outpost," Molly said, "something Hannaniah would have been familiar with, we should see walls. Within the walls, there should be buildings, buried several feet beneath us now, centered around a courtyard. Homes, perhaps communal in nature. Halls for worship. Stables. Shops for baking or pottery-making. Wells. That's one problem. Where's the water?"

"That was two thousand years ago, Molly. Streams dry up. The whole coastline has receded since then."

"I know this is right," Milstein said from the first trench, already three feet into the ground to Molly's right. He was on his knees in the trench, trowel in hand, looking up at her. "I feel it. He came here to escape the Romans and the wrath of his own people, but he was never far away."

Molly looked about at all the hard work that normally she would have thrilled at. This time all she could muster was a slight shake of her head. "It's a site, all right."

"But?" Kwiatkowski asked.

"If we're looking for scrolls hidden in jars, buried in the desert, we could be looking for a very long time."

"Yes, but we're not looking for scrolls," Milstein reminded her.

Shortly before evening, Molly's trowel struck floor, a hard surface beneath the shifting desert sand three feet from the surface. Her call brought everyone to her trench at a run. Leveille-Gaus jumped in beside her and brushed away detritus with his hands.

"See!" he said. "I told you. This is unmistakable evidence of occupancy, ancient occupancy."

"Maybe," she said. "Look at the bricks, Dr. Leveille. They're mismatched. It's like a patchwork quilt."

"You've only uncovered a small sampling. Time corrupts the most elegant architecture."

"Yes," Molly argued, "but there's stone mixed in with brick. Even in this small area, you can see the builders didn't even bother with any kind of sustainable mortar. It's as if somebody cannibalized an older site, occupied it for a short while, then deserted it."

Leveille-Gaus glanced up at Molly who stood in the three-foot-deep trench, her khaki shorts filthy. "Look, Dr. O'Dwyer, you yourself said that Hannaniah had deserted Ur. Perhaps they abandoned this site, too."

"If they were ever here."

"They were. Your own interpretation of the Star of David medallion and Hannaniah's lamentation corroborates our decision. Try not to be so fickle. Give us time to dig deeper."

"We don't have time."

Molly left the trench only to have her Red Sox cap blown back in by a sudden gust.

"A storm's coming in," Habib said to the others. He pointed to the northeast. "Coming down from the mountains."

"A big one?" Leveille-Gaus protected his eyes from the sun as he gazed in the direction Habib had indicated. Already grains of sand in invisible volleys of wind targeted the eyes and faces of the archaeologists.

"When they come down from Turkey, they can kill," Habib told them. "They move fast and hard. We'll need to cover everything. Cover tight and prepare to dig out in the morning."

"*Merde.*" Leveille-Gaus was not a happy man.

Molly O'Dwyer was not a happy woman. Kwiatkowski helped her unload canvas sheets from one of the trucks.

"This is wrong," Molly told him.

"We've only been here one day."

"Hannaniah set up communities for her people, to have children, live, die, be buried. We've guessed at two of the symbols on the star, Jerusalem and Ur. But what do the three on top mean: the house, the jagged v, the squiggly w? And Nina's dog snout on the bottom? Perhaps the triangle in the middle is pointing to that and not to the line connecting Ur and Jerusalem."

"Maybe this is just an outpost," Kwiatkowski said. With the help of one of his soldiers, he stretched the canvass sheet over the length of the north-south trench. Molly hammered stakes into the ground as the wind curled waves of sand over her bare arms.

"Dr. Leveille's being blindsided by greed," she said in between hammer strokes. "I still see no source of water."

"An underground spring?"

"Maybe. But I took an accurate measurement of the circle after lunch. The circumference is almost exactly three hundred meters."

"A nice silo for storing food."

"A thought," Molly said. "But the ancients didn't measure in meters."

By the time the last of the covering had been laid and roped down over the trenches, the canvas of the kitchen truck billowed like the sail of a desert boat. To the north, the landscape darkened as storm clouds gathered and the wind sweeping down from the Turkish highlands picked up millions of cubic feet of sand. This arid topsoil would be re-distributed over the desert landscape. Thousands of years of such weather had buried Ur and Babylon. In the next few hours, it would do a job on Site 1.

Molly hunkered down in Kwiatkowski's truck unmindful of the sand and gravel that pelted the camp. Habib advised everyone not to venture outside the trucks at all.

"If you get lost, we might not see you again."

Molly concentrated on the Star of David and Hannaniah's six-verse lamentation even to the exclusion of dinner, which Kwiatkowski made and Milstein brought to her, corned beef hash and green beans covered by a bread pan to keep the sand from peppering it. Milstein didn't interrupt her but sat quietly listening as the intensifying sandstorm drowned out everything else.

"I know what you think of me, Molly," he said at last. "Or at least what Kwiatkowski thinks of me. But I told you. I didn't ask for any of this. I was a Doubting Thomas myself."

"Milstein, do you honestly believe …?" Molly rubbed her tired eyes. The tent flap pitched a fit at the rear of the truck, fighting vainly against the wind and sand. Molly leaned on her knees. Outside, the day had become utterly dark. "We're not talking about an anonymous galley slave here. Judas Iscariot! It's too coincidental. You and me. Judas and Hannaniah in search of Jesus? What are you really up to, Milstein? Are you CIA? Be honest with me."

"I am telling you the truth," he insisted. "I was Yeshuah's lifelong companion, his youngest brother. Only I was more militant—the sicariot was a short dagger Judas always wore, trying to raise money from the Jewish communities to build an army, to promote insurrection, to make Yeshuah king. His will was otherwise."

"His will? You mean Jesus? Or is Teodor right? This is all fabrication."

"Kwiatkowski is wrong. Dr. Leveille is wrong. Only you are right." Milstein moved beside Molly, took her hand, stared into her eyes. "I think I committed suicide," he said. "My last memory of Judas is being alone in the desert with a dagger. If so, I died by my own hand, not guilt-ridden over what I had done to him, but because I had lost you. Forever."

"Milstein, if you died, how could you have passed along the

memory of dying?" Molly tried to pull her hand free of his grip, but he wouldn't let go. Her eyes skirted the constantly shifting truck flap hoping someone would intervene. Finally, Milstein dropped her hand.

"Let me regress you, Molly," he said.

"Absolutely not." Certainly not while they were alone, she thought.

"I would never harm you. Look, I don't pretend to understand any of this. By training I am an historian. A teacher. Maybe there is such a thing as past lives. Maybe our soul doesn't die with our body. Maybe it is capable of moving on from one karmic state to another until it finds peace. If you believe in God, then anything is possible."

That, then, was the issue. The real one. Molly lowered her eyes, troubled by what she saw in Milstein's. He believed. That much was obvious. He was no threat to her, not at all. He loved her, had loved her, perhaps, if he was right, would go on loving her beyond this life into the next, and the next after that, and so on until something in nature, God or whatever, was satisfied that their fates had finally entwined as they were meant to. It was she who was faithless, she who, despite all the church services attended, all the prayers uttered, all the confessions made to priests like Father Ray, was afraid of what the truth might really be. Hence, the search, the constant endless search, that was her life.

Calmer, quieter, yet as determined as ever, Milstein caressed her face. The palm of his hand came away wet from her tears. "Maybe it isn't anything so foolish as past lives," he said softly, so softly she could barely hear him over the wind. "Maybe you're right. Somehow we pass on our memories to our children through our DNA, generation after generation, our minds acting as a library, books available only under hypnosis. We'd go crazy if we could dredge up all that information any time we wanted. It has to be suppressed. It would be system overload otherwise."

"And you see no coincidence in our coming together?" she asked him.

"After all these centuries, maybe this is the first time. Desires buried deep within us, things we can't control, needing fulfillment, driving us together. There are no blackboards out here, Molly. Just timelessness, where anything is possible. Let me regress you. I can do it as well as Teague."

For a moment, Molly almost considered saying yes. Then her eyes fell back on the Star of David, on the mysterious symbols that held the clue to the whereabouts not only of Hannaniah but of her father, and suddenly she let out a shout of discovery.

"Jesus, that's it!"

"Molly, what? What about the regression?"

"Fuck the regression!" Molly grabbed the black binder in which Hannaniah's lamentation was written. "Listen," she said and began quoting the poem.

"Once more, O City of Life, your daughter cries for you. Seven tears.
"Mother, your children fly before you. Six children.
"Blow the ram's horn, Father. Five notes.
"Upon the back of the horse. Four legs.
"In the corpse of the night. Three hearts.
"Rest where he casts his nets. Two lamps alight."

Molly looked at Milstein. "The numbers, Andrew," she said. "Now look at the symbols on the Star of David. The jagged *v* has seven dots. The squiggly *w* has six. The house has five. Jerusalem and Ur each has four. The triangle, three. But, damn ..."

"What's the matter? What are you two giggling about?"

Jackson peered in at them through the back flap of the truck.

"We aren't giggling," Milstein said. "Molly just made a discovery. There is a correlation between the Star of David and Hannaniah's poem."

"Goody-two-shoes. So what?"

"So, I don't know," Molly admitted. "Nina's dog snout at the bottom has more than two dots, so what do they mean? *Two lamps alight.* Shit, it's right there and I can't see it!"

Jackson turned away. "Well," he said, "hunt for Hannaniah and her father tomorrow. Teague's missin' tonight, and we can't find him."

Father Ray Teague was not a beach person. From childhood on, every time he visited one of the great Cape beaches or those along the North Shore, he invariably came away with a sunburn that sent him to the hospital. He never learned to swim very well, and the Atlantic water was too cold to enjoy anyway. Without an umbrella, he couldn't get comfortable enough to read, the bikini-clad girls had no interest in him, and his tuna fish and potato chip sandwiches, no matter how many layers of Saran Wrap he used, always became impregnated with sand.

No matter how sunny the summer day, no matter how warm and beautiful, Ray much preferred the dark movie theatre, almost any kind of movie, to the outdoors. The eighth of eleven children, he was fortunate to have an older sister who also loved film. An unattractive child doomed to dreaming of a life she would never live, she enjoyed her younger brother's companionship. Her death of an overdose of sleeping pills at the age of nineteen was what had led Ray into the ministry. He was a shy, intellectual Catholic with few skills but an uncanny ability to listen to people in time of need and to help them. His parents had hoped he would go into medicine. He chose the ministry and never really regretted it despite his lack of a true religious vocation. Teaching at Mt. Auburn College was the ideal life for him, and as long as he kept his mouth shut about his unorthodox way of practicing his faith, he could spend the rest of his life there.

Jackson had warned him not to leave the truck even if he were only planning to walk twenty feet to the next truck. Father Ray was like a beach ball, short and round and easily blown off course. He had promised Milstein that he would try to convince and then lead Molly into a past life far beyond her childhood. There was something to this phenomenon of past life regression that he had stumbled upon that excited him. He had thought it a good therapy tool but little more until Milstein began to recount his past lives. Ray wanted to regress them all. Molly, Kwiatkowski, Leveille. Good Lord, if Milstein was right, he thought, you could travel through time without a time machine. You could talk to all the great figures of history, resolve all the mysteries. If Milstein had been Judas, or if he simply had Judas's memories by way of ancestry, and if Molly, similarly, were connected to Hannaniah, then, by God, somebody had to be Jesus and what a dialogue that would make.

But Father Ray never made it to Molly's truck. The wind really wasn't so bad, so much as the particles of sand that it raised, an endless fog of it that took away sight and sound and breath. Ray held onto his truck, forced to close his eyes. He opened them only when he realized that his fingers were no longer grasping anything. Then he looked up, shielding his eyes with his hands to look off to his right.

A ghost moved. He was startled by the sight for he hadn't expected to see anyone else out in this weather. He tried to call to the obscure figure, but his voice was lost to the howl of the wind. Staggering into the weather, he tried to follow the gray shape hoping it would lead him to the next truck. He really should have turned around and gone back to shelter or just sat down and stayed where he was. But novice adventurer that he was, he didn't understand just how dangerous a position he was in.

He plodded on, head buried in his chest, eyes every once in a while defying the storm to look right, left, and forward. Unbelievably, he could see nothing of the trucks. And then the ghostly figure abruptly reappeared, this time almost on top of him, face to face as if the man had gotten lost himself and had circled back. He was talking not to himself nor to anyone else Ray could see. The figure held a radio to his face and spoke loudly above the wind in Arabic.

"Hey!" Teague shouted at the man to make himself heard. "Who are you talking to?"

The man pointed. "The trucks," he said. Teague turned to look, saw nothing, and was startled when the man pushed him in the back and shoved him forward into the nothingness.

"Hey! What are you doing?" Ray yelled. "Who were you talking to?"

But the man only pushed him harder, forced him farther into the storm. Ray tried to turn around, but the next shove sent him face first into the sand.

Jesus, he thought, what is this idiot trying to do?

He found out a moment later when the man jumped onto his back, pressed his face into the desert floor, and used his thumbs to crush Ray's windpipe.

Father Ray was well and truly gone. Their camp was small enough to begin with, no more than three hundred meters in circumference, and he was nowhere within those limits, not in the trucks, under the trucks, or stuck in the sand between the trucks. The storm passed during the early evening. Molly wandered out into the desert, now graced by a starry canopy, with Kwiatkowski, Leveille-Gaus, and Habib. They circled the camp, wandering away from Site 1, and she called for her friend, shining her flashlight into the newly deposited sand.

"Now what?" she asked Kwiatkowski, who didn't let her stray as Teague had done. "Where could he have gone? Why would he have left the camp?"

"People can easily get disoriented in a sandstorm," Kwiatkowski told her. "I heard he was looking for you. He never made it?"

"We didn't see him. We found something else."

"What?"

"The Star of David, the poem, they do relate, they are a map. Just not to here I don't think."

"Great time to find out."

At that moment, Jackson's voice echoed over the desert like God's over the Sinai. "Over here!" he shouted, bringing everyone else on the run.

Molly's boots crunched on rocks as she raced ahead of Kwiatkowski. Habib and Leveille-Gaus lagged behind. Jackson called once more, directing her over a dune. Jackson was below with Milstein and the remaining Polish and American forces. They stood in a semi-circle. The beam of Jackson's flashlight illuminated something sticking out of the sand at the base of the dune. When she reached the bottom and aimed her own light she saw the back of a clothed human body, the rest, including the head and appendages, completely buried.

"Jesus," Molly muttered.

"Not yet," Jackson said. "That's later. Grab a shovel, boys. Better still, a bodybag. We won't be needin' shovels."

Dropping to her knees, Molly watched two of Jackson's men burrow into the sand with their hands to remove the corpse. The remains of people long dead didn't disturb Molly. Those of the recently dead were too ghoulish. She hated death and could only deal with it from a distance. And Father Ray had been her friend. She had to shut her eyes and let the tears trickle, otherwise the sand would instantly blind her. Kwiatkowski, on the other hand, had seen enough death that it didn't bother him. He gave Molly a quick comforting touch on the head then pushed one of Jackson's men aside to turn Father Ray's body over, face up.

"Why don't you just get him out of the storm? He's dead, for God's sake!"

"Sorry, Molly," he said. "We need to find out what happened."

"What?" Jackson crouched beside him. "He got lost, he fell, the sand did the rest. We're not equipped to do autopsies out here."

"You brought bodybags?" Molly said from the far side of the corpse.

Jackson gazed at her. "This is Iraq."

Kwiatkowski studied Teague's lifeless face, stuck a finger in the priest's mouth and probed inside.

"You've done this sort of thing before?" Leveille-Gaus asked him. He stood behind Kwiatkowski, peering over the Pole's shoulder.

"I took my training as a physician," Kwiatkowski replied, now rolling the body back onto its stomach to study the nape of the neck. "My father wanted me to be many things since I was his only child."

"And you ended up, what, a soldier?" Leveille-Gaus asked.

"A mathematician actually, Doctor."

Kwiatkowski stood up without saying a word.

"Well, Doctor K?" Jackson asked. "What does CSI Anbar have to tell us?"

"He is dead, that's for sure," Kwiatkowski said and turned away. Only when he pulled Molly aside did he tell her what he really knew. "Father Teague didn't die accidentally, Molly. He was killed. Somebody straddled his back, forced his face into the sand, and choked him. There are obvious finger marks on the neck, throat, and base of the skull."

"Christ. Poor Ray." Molly swiped at a tear.

"I don't think we can blame Muslim insurgents for this one."

"But why? Why Father Ray of all of us? He had nothing to do with this expedition." Molly watched in numb silence as her friend's body was lifted out of the sand and placed into a black bodybag, zipped inside, and carted back to the trucks.

"There's no way of knowing," Kwiatkowski said. Facing the rest then, he told them, "From this point on, I'm taking charge. Mr. Jackson, you are not a soldier. I am the highest-ranking person here. This was our expedition to begin with. You intervened, and I don't give a damn who you take your orders from. From now on, you take them from me."

"I don't think so," Jackson replied. "I outgun you." And with that, the civilian security contractor pointed his pistol at Kwiatkowski's belly. "Half my country believes the Second Comin' of Christ is at hand. Crazy, you say? Don't matter, so long's they run things, and I get paid to protect their interests. They figure all signs point to His return, and without their commitment in Iraq, our mission folds. Milstein says one of us might just be Jesus. Buried somewhere in our heads. Fine and dandy. I don't think he'd be Polish this go-around. I think he'd be American."

"And Republican, no doubt," Molly said. "Put the gun down!

Put it down, Mr. Jackson!" Anger reanimated her like a shot of hot black coffee, which, if she had had it, she would have thrown in his face. "I can't believe we're fighting over Jesus. The Son of God is not American, or Polish, or anything else. He is most certainly not a pretext for war. Right now we don't even know we have Him. We have a theory, very likely a crackpot theory."

"It's not crackpot, Dr. O'Dwyer." Leveille-Gaus stood with Milstein between Molly and Jackson, taking neither side. He, too, carried a gun, but it was holstered. "You wouldn't be here if you thought that."

"I wouldn't be *here*, is right," Molly answered him back. "This isn't the right site. I'm this close to cracking Hannaniah's code. We need to go back to the oil rig."

"We need time here."

"If we hadn't come here in the first place, Father Ray might still be alive. I don't intend to be next. You can stay here if you like, Dr. Leveille. You, too, Mr. Jackson. At daybreak the rest of us are leaving." She turned and disappeared over the dune.

Jackson holstered his Glock pistol. "Maybe she's Jesus," he said with a grunt.

"No," Milstein told him. "She's Hannaniah. Every corpuscle and molecule of her."

"Hannaniah!" Nur yelled in his sleep. And when he bolted upright on his bare cot in his nondescript mud-brick headquarters, her pretty face was still in his vision, drenched in blood. His.

Barid Shamkhazi gaped at his mentor. He had been writing by the light of a kerosene lantern when Nur shouted the foreign name and shot up as if he'd been stung by a wasp. "Hannaniah," Nur repeated, then lay back down to sleep, without ever realizing that Shamkhazi had witnessed his nightmare.

For a few moments Shamkhazi kept his eyes trained on the holy man, half expecting him to sit up once again, smile, and put him at ease. But Nur never moved. Troubled, Shamkhazi left the little house to look for a radio with which to contact Ghazi Al-Tikriti. Whoever this red-headed woman is, he thought, she must be dealt with. Permanently.

CHAPTER 16

True to her word, Molly was ready to go at first light. As testament to their belief in her, everyone else was willing to abandon Site 1 except Leveille-Gaus, but he had no choice in the matter. Three military vehicles set out for Site II as the sun bathed the desert in warmth. Father Teague's body lay in the back of the third truck. Molly sat in the cab of the lead vehicle next to Kwiatkowski, eyes never wavering from the passenger side window southward.

"This is it?"

"Yes."

"You're sure?"

"Like Bush in Iraq."

"What the hell does that mean?"

"I'm optimistic, but the planning ain't so hot."

Molly tried to lighten the mood between them, but her heart wasn't in it. Ever since he had kissed her, a wonderful, spontaneous moment, she had looked for five minutes here, ten minutes there, to be alone with Kwiatkowski. This just wasn't the most convenient time or place to engage in romance, even if the thought had been strong enough to divert her focus for a while.

"I know you don't believe this," she said to him, "but ever since I came into contact with Hannaniah, my life has changed. Things that I had long forgotten, feelings I'd done my damnedest to suppress, all came back to me. It's like being swooped up by a tornado that won't let go."

Kwiatkowski kept silent, eyes on the road ahead, in the rearview mirror, anyplace but on Molly. "Do you mind if I say something that you're going to take wrong?"

"Probably," she said. "But go ahead. I'm a Sox fan."

"You're having the same experience Milstein's having. You're playing off each other. You desperately want to believe, so you do."

Hadn't she thought that very thing? Except she had felt this way about Hannaniah long before she'd met Milstein. "Now you sound like me trying to convince Milstein he's full of shit." Molly finally relaxed enough to look away from the desert to gaze at Kwiatkowski. He hadn't shaved in days and his cheeks had become a blonde forest, pleasant and manly enough to want to caress. But his mood had deteriorated. No longer the silent, disinterested partner, he had been forced out of his isolation into a world that scoffed at mathematics, logic, and the stars.

"All I can tell you," she said, "is that what I feel is real. Don't you ever have dreams, Teodor? So real, you feel they can't possibly be dreams? The people who inhabit them you've never seen before, and yet you have. And the things that happen in them can't possibly be contrived. Nina Cavalcante said she began having dreams like this after she encountered Hannaniah. That makes three of us: me, Milstein, and Cavalcante. Have you had them, Teodor? Anything like them?"

Kwiatkowski was quick to say no. Too quick.

"You have had them, goddamn it!" she said. "I see it in your face."

"Don't be ridiculous."

"Why repress it? It could be important. Tell me."

"There's nothing to tell." Kwiatkowski set his hands firmly on the steering wheel. "There's your oil rig," he said.

"Lucky you."

Molly was out of the truck seconds before the engine had shut down, already padding across the sand as the second and third trucks pulled up behind. Twenty meters to her left lay the ruins of the Iraqi army convoy that a decade earlier had met its fate at the hands of American military technology. The ruined oilrig stood to her right. Sand had blown against its rusting legs the night before. No less touched by the sandstorm, the mound that held Molly's greatest interest had been reburied. Two thousand years of such storms had entombed the site under several feet of sand, easy enough to dispose of if recognized as an archaeological point of interest.

Molly stood before the mound. Leveille-Gaus strode up to her with Milstein close behind.

"Well, it's a mound, I'll give you that," Leveille-Gaus told her. "How do you know this site has anything to do with the Star of David?"

"Women's intuition. Mine. Hannaniah's. But it won't take long to find out." She pointed to her left. "There's a slight depression there. I pointed it out to Teodor on the way past the other day. I suggest we start there. We have enough strong bodies. I'd put two other teams to work, one on the right and one in the middle. We'll dig three trenches straight into the mound and out perhaps ten feet. Let's get some fluid into us and start digging," she said. "Mr. Jackson, if you've equipped us as well as you say you have, I would like tents staked up right at the dig site. Fruit and beverage and shade. We'll need lots of that. It's going to be a hot one."

"They all are," Jackson said.

To Kwiatkowski she said, "Teddy, I'll take your boys. You, Milstein, and Mr. Nazariiy will work the right trench. Jackson, your people can help Dr. Leveille in the center. Any problems?"

"Who's gonna stand guard?" Jackson asked. "They're out there watchin' us, stalkin' us. The mujahedeen. I can't see 'em, but I know they're there. And I don't like bein' stalked."

"You'd much rather be the stalker, is that it?" Molly couldn't help looking to the horizon north of the site. Since the first dusty encounter with the invisible enemy on the road two days earlier, they had seen no sign of human activity. Given Father Ray's demise, she was more worried about the enemy at home.

"Post one guard, if you want," she said. "No more. I'm more concerned about my back."

As the crew unloaded tools for the dig, Molly set up a small fold-up table at the site and drew a rough sketch of what she intended the team to do. Leveille-Gaus leaned over the table and watched her pencil in three trenches on the thick pad of sketch paper.

"You're good, Molly. Don't let my attitude suggest otherwise. I think you're the best. But we need to talk in private some time. Mr. Jackson is a serious problem."

"He's not the only one, Doctor."

"Milstein?"

"You." Molly gave the French archaeologist a long steady look. "You're still withholding information from me. That has been your pattern from the beginning. Why? More important: what?"

"I have a very special relationship with the Vatican," Leveille-Gaus said. "I haven't spoken of it before. But given what has happened since we have been in this country, I think I owe you this explanation."

"Go ahead, Doctor."

"Dr. Cavalcante has their respect, most certainly. But not their entire trust. She comes from a good Italian family, aristocratic, wealthy. Her brother is a bishop, highly placed in Vatican circles. But Nina is a little too … loose. Scientifically and sexually, if you get my meaning."

"She's gay? So?"

"So was Imran Fawzi. Whenever he visited Rome, she saw to it that he was well entertained. That is essentially how we became involved with this mission. Because Fawzi thought so much of Nina, he contacted her first. But the Vatican would prefer to entrust their deepest, darkest historic secrets to men of discretion. And, trust me, there is a lot to be discreet about. Wouldn't you say that the truth regarding the divinity of Jesus might be one of those things?"

"I have never questioned Jesus' divinity, Doctor," Molly said. "That doesn't mean I don't have my doubts. I'm a scientist. It's faith that matters, faith that rises above all else. Without it, everything else is irrelevant. Nina and I are good Catholics. Whatever we find here stays here with us. But we are driven to know, just as Galileo was driven to know, as Columbus was driven to know. We're human. That's our nature. I want to know everything you know. I've earned that right."

Hands on hips, Leveille-Gaus scanned Site II in silence before turning to Molly.

"It was disease," he said.

"Disease?"

"That forced them to leave Ur. That is my best guess at least. Vatican letters from Hannaniah to Paul indicate that members of her family had contracted some disease. Several died. They might have moved into the desert to escape. Perhaps, ultimately, that is what killed Jesus. And Hannaniah."

"I would like to have had that information before now, Doctor. That might have saved us a trip to Ur."

And a lot more, she thought but didn't say. There was so much to think about. Too much. Beyond what or who she might find. Just as important, what to do with him or them if she found them.

Molly put her whole body and spirit into the dig. That was what she did best. Gripped with an excitement that reduced religiosity to a dank dark corner down a long corridor and several flights of stairs to the deepest levels of her cognitive mind, she grabbed a shovel and helped the men dig where she thought Mohamoud Jama might have begun his search more than a decade ago.

As the sun rose and the trenches deepened, Molly's adrenalin flow kept her hard at work. Hannaniah could be just a few feet and a few spades full of dirt away. A body only, perhaps, another good reason for Jackson's bodybags, but so much more as well.

Into the late afternoon, the three teams of workers dug their exploratory trenches, while guards watched for signs of movement in the desert. One of the trucks at some point would have to return to civilization to get water and supplies. She had no sense of doubt or foreboding as her shovel bit into the sand. Even when none of the teams had come up with anything by sunset, she felt in her heart that this was the right site.

As the light faded, Milstein bowed out to take his turn in the kitchen truck. One of the Poles stood guard on the hood of another vehicle, binoculars up and scanning the horizon to the north. Infrareds would keep them usable during the night. Molly intended to dig until someone handed her a dinner plate. She was tired but happy. The dig could make her forget and overlook many things. Pausing to sit at the edge of her trench, which now stretched four feet deep for twenty feet, ten away from the mound, ten into the mound itself, she removed her Red Sox baseball cap, wiped her brow, and reached for her canteen. As the advertisement said, this was how life was supposed to be.

As she tilted her head back to take a swig, one of the last fading rays of the day struck something in the hole near her feet. It glittered faintly like a distant star. Molly cast her canteen aside and was on her knees in the hole, scraping at the dirt with her fingers. She tossed aside several stones before she gathered into her palm a tiny relic, not of the desert but manmade. Her heart rate picked up. She held the object up to the light between two fingers. It was a nail. Not one she'd purchase at Home Depot either. This one was so old, she believed, it could have been brother to the nails that had crucified Jesus.

"Dr. Leveille!" she shouted. "Teodor! Andrew! Get over here!"

Leveille-Gaus, who had been working the middle trench, was the first to scramble up the mound to her side. "What have you got?" he asked, breathing hard with the effort of his run.

Molly was on her knees looking for more evidence. She reached up to hand him the nail. And then she found something else.

"Jesus!" Her hands clawed at solid material that just kept going.

"Wood," she said. "I think I've found wood."

"Timbers?"

"Maybe."

Leveille-Gaus joined her in the trench as Kwiatkowski, Habib, and Jackson came to surround them above. "Gold?" Jackson asked.

"Better. Grab a shovel," Molly told him. "Start digging over there toward me."

"It's getting dark, Molly," Kwiatkowski said. "Maybe we should hold off until tomorrow."

"We've got twenty minutes at least and lanterns in the trucks."

"But we're not robots. Twenty minutes. As soon as Milstein says supper is ready, we're done for the day."

Molly glanced up. She was so close! Timbers. A structure. Afghanistan flooded her mind, the temple and burial chamber that she discovered. This Iraqi site could be a duplicate. Tomorrow seemed much too long a wait.

When dinner did come, meat loaf and peas, Molly reluctantly

thanked Milstein, who'd carried it out to her personally on a plastic plate, and lay down her trowel.

"Join us," he said. "Think of it as Christmas. The anticipation makes the receiving all that much more enjoyable."

"She might be right beneath us, Milstein. Are you sure you want to wait?"

"I think we have no choice."

Under a clear night sky, it was restful to eat a decent meal. But once she was done, as the others relaxed, she sat at a folding table lit by a lantern, opened up the black binder to the page of Hannaniah's lamentation, unclasped her Star of David pendant, and set about deciphering Hannaniah's most important clue.

"Do you see her?" Milstein asked. "Hannaniah."

"Milstein, I'm trying to concentrate."

"What do you think she was like?"

"A very modern woman. Blue jeans, cell phone, lap top computer. She's had a tough day, a tough life, and she's preparing a best seller. She's going to teach us all the truth."

"That'll go over big," Milstein said.

"She was the daughter of the Son of God after all," Molly said. "She ought to know a thing or two."

"If, indeed, there was a Son of God." Leveille-Gaus cleaned off his plate and came to look over Molly's shoulder. "So? May I look?"

"So long as you don't touch anything."

"Numbers. Letters. Dots. Milstein could be right, Molly. You may never understand what Hannaniah is trying to say unless you go under."

"I'd say that's rather moot now. Father Ray is dead."

"Milstein will do it."

"No."

On a blank paper Molly drew the Star of David with all its symbols, hoping that in the process of laying it out she would see what the original designer of the pendant had intended.

The others had drifted away when an explosion in the desert ripped her focus away from the paper.

"Jesus!" someone shouted.

A brilliant orange-yellow light erupted on the horizon.

"What is it?" Molly cried.

Kwiatkowski darted past her, Milstein and Jackson right behind. At the edge of the camp, facing north, they watched the fiery light dissipate. A thunderous noise briefly followed the flash, leaving utter stillness in its passing.

"Insurgents?" Leveille-Gaus asked coming up breathless behind the others. "A firefight?"

"Sabotage more likely," Jackson said. He raised binoculars to his eyes. "An oil pipeline. If it were a fight, we'd see and hear more action. Choppers."

"How far?" Molly asked.

"Hard to say. Could be five miles. Could be twenty."

"Damn," Molly said. "They're closing in on us." She took the binoculars from Jackson and studied the horizon.

"You don't know who it is," Kwiatkowski said at her side.

"I've been pursuing Hannaniah for too long to lose her now. At first light we dig, and we don't stop until we find something.

"Yes, ma'am."

"What the...?" Molly studied the horizon.

"What is it?" Jackson asked her. "What do you see?"

"A dust cloud. Wind-blown sand, maybe."

"I don't think so." Jackson grabbed the binoculars from Molly. "Where's the wind? Sand don't move like that. Might be our troops.

Might be someone else. Everybody grab a gun who knows how to use one. And sleep with one eye open."

Molly dragged her sleeping bag outside and set it beside the table she had been working at, but she had no intention of drifting off. Instead she poured her effort into the intricacies of the Star of David, drawing each symbol, locating each letter and dot with the preciseness of the originator until her eyes could no longer focus and, despite herself, her head sank onto her work.

When at last she dreamed, she did so of her mother, but her mother's face merged with another woman's, no longer distinct and recognizable. The one common factor that remained in her dream world was fire, shooting out of the darkness to engulf child Molly. It burned and choked and isolated until she awoke with a scream that should have roused the entire camp. Bleary-eyed, she raised herself on to her elbows to see the sun brightening the desert and Kwiatkowski sleeping on a blanket behind one of the trucks. Her scream from sleep had bothered no one.

"Dr. O'Dwyer."

The whispered voice made her start. She sat up and looked around, half expecting to find Milstein hovering over her. She was surprised to see Habib keeping a respectful distance. He wore Adidas sneakers, Levi jeans, a green Gap shirt, and Ray Ban sunglasses, a walking commercial for the Americanization of Iraq. The gun he held, however, was Russian made.

"Come with me," he said.

"Why the gun?" she asked. "Are you going to shoot me? Did you kill Father Ray?"

"I thought the desert killed Father Teague. If one of us, I'll keep this at my side, thank you."

Already the desert air was a humid soup, a drop of which hung from Habib's black moustache. "I've found something you should see."

"And you need a gun to show me?"

"Oh, this?" He tucked the gun inside his Ralph Lauren leather belt and gestured for her to follow him to the excavation. "I couldn't sleep," he explained, "so I returned to your trench. I've been up for a couple of hours."

"I hope you were careful, Mr. Nazariiy. You're not a trained archaeologist." Molly strode through the sand, up the bank of the hill, to the trench she'd been working on the day before. Her muscles ached from the labor and from sleeping on the hard ground, but her heart raced with the anticipation of Habib's discovery.

"I knew Mohamoud Jama," Habib said as they approached the trench. "He was a friend of my uncle Imran. Only one time did I ever hear him mention a lost site out in the desert. He called it heaven's cemetery. Do you think this is it?"

"I don't know. Show me what you've done."

Habib lowered himself into Trench I and pointed to where he had dug deeper into the hill and exposed more of the wooden structure Molly had uncovered the night before. She wiped the sleep from her eyes, brushed back loose strands of her unbrushed red hair, and sank her already dirty knees into the sand.

"So far as I know," Habib explained, "there has never been a forest here in the desert. Even two thousand years ago. So whoever built this must have transported the wood."

"My thought, too. Go on."

"The desert climate, as I'm sure you know, will preserve wood fairly well, particularly if it's been under several feet of sand. No rain. No wind. No termites. I assumed this was the ceiling of some structure and I was just planning to remove as much dirt from it as

I could."

"Thank you. You did a lot."

"Do you recognize the wood?" Habib asked.

"Initial guess? Cedar."

"Really. There would have been none of that at Ur."

"Probably not. But there would have been in Jerusalem," Molly said. "Not necessarily native to it, but brought in from Lebanon by the upper classes to build their estates. Hannaniah grew up poor but married into wealth."

"Then we have something in common. Some day I'll marry into wealth."

In his two hours of toil, Habib had cleared away a rectangle of earth about five feet by two feet, four feet in depth. The hard work showed on the palms of his hands where incipient blisters had formed.

"There's something else you should see," he told her. He pointed from where he sat on the lip of the trench, and Molly crawled to the spot he indicated. "I'm an engineer," he said. "But I've also done some building, carpentry. It was my father's line of work. That piece of wood where your right hand is does not belong on a roof. It's wide and thick and was used to support something heavy. Stone, perhaps. I'd say it was part of a door frame."

"Good work, Habib! I think you're right. But used here as a roof beam." Molly unraveled a tape measure attached to her belt and measured the width of the timber. The wood was firm enough to be used by modern scavenger/carpenters. Laying the tape measure aside, Molly scraped away more debris until her trowel struck metal and she discovered something else.

"Holy shit!" The words blurted out.

Habib nearly trampled her in his hurry to peek over her shoulder.

"What is it?"

Molly brushed away the last of the detritus to reveal a two-inch-long rectangle nailed into the cedar timber. Hunkered so low she could blow sand grains off the thin metal, she reached back a hand. "Habib, your flashlight."

She trained the light on the metal.

"It's gold," she said. "Somebody had money. Hebrew letters."

"Somebody was Jewish."

"It would seem so. I think this is a mezuzah, a good luck charm set into a door frame." Molly blew off more dirt and shifted her body within the narrow trench to get a better look. The excitement in her voice was like that of a kid on Christmas Day, constructing a train set, on top of her toy, all over it, protecting it from the grasping hands of other kids.

"My God!" She sat up to gather her wits before sinking down again to make sure she wasn't mistaken.

"What is it?"

"My God!"

"Dr. O'Dwyer, what?"

"Another Star of David. Just like in Egypt, Afghanistan."

"Like Mohamoud Jama's find."

"This is the right place! Habib, wake up the others! Tell them to get their asses up here. Now! We've got work to do."

Oh, thank you, Hannaniah, she thought. For leaving this sign. For showing me the way.

Once her enthusiasm was unleashed, it was hard to curb. After an hour of painstaking labor following up on Habib's success, however, she felt the familiar nausea and dizziness that told her she needed to eat something and take her insulin. Damn the medicine! Damn the diabetes! Damn the interruption! At least by then she could turn the reins over to Leveille-Gaus and Milstein. Jackson was now solely consumed in watching the desert. Kwiatkowski was consumed solely by Molly.

"You're sure?"

"Yes, I'm positive. At least …"

"At least?"

"At least she was here, Teodor. So you can stop clinging to me like Milstein. Grab a shovel and put those strong Polish shoulder muscles to work." She graced him with a smile, which, judging by his smile back at her, sent waves of excitement through his body similar to those she had experienced upon finding the gold mezuzah.

The expedition had quit Trenches II and III to concentrate on Molly's site, but the number of laborers was reduced because of Jackson's insistence on increasing his guards. He formed a semi-circle with the trucks then completed the circle using the mound as their defensive bulwark between the first and third vehicles. Kwiatkowski might be the only legitimate military officer on site, but Jackson was the only one who had experienced real combat. Then, reasonably well protected, the team worked through the morning, broke for lunch, then continued in the afternoon, expanding the trench, removing wheelbarrows full of dirt and rocks.

Under Molly's direction, the trench took on a U form. If this wooden structure was a building, there had to be an entrance. Molly was reminded of the underground sod houses built on the American plains. Her own find in Afghanistan was a buried temple and mausoleum. But that had been constructed in a more hospitable environment with water and forest. It was hard to imagine that whoever had built this mound had meant to put down roots here. Hannaniah wasn't about creating monastic communities set in unforgiving conditions. She was an early urban scientist trying to structure her far-flung Jewish communities around family.

"I'm guessing," she told Milstein during an afternoon break, "this wasn't meant to be permanent. If Dr. Leveille is right, her people fled from disease. The desert acted as a purifier, but some people died along the way. Jama found a burial urn. This could be a cemetery."

"Then where did Hannaniah's community go? Or do you really think we'll find her here?"

"I don't know, Andrew. I hope so."

Enthusiasm abounded in the camp. Molly didn't want to spoil it, particularly after she had insisted they abandon Leveille-Gaus's site for hers. But what if he had been right all along and Hannaniah's community had settled at a close but different location?

By the time evening rolled around again, the excavators had removed over a ton of dirt. They were exhausted and had managed only to expose more timbers. The architects of the building had used stone to reinforce the structure. It was crude construction, built in haste and out of necessity with whatever materials they had been able to carry with them, then buried to protect the dead from the elements and vandals.

Their own dead, Father Teague, lay in a less permanent state in a plastic bag in one of their trucks. His soul may well have traveled heavenward by now, but his remains would decay and begin to reek if he were not spirited back to Baghdad and, thence, back to the States.

As night fell, Molly worked by lantern light, having taken a quick dinner before compulsion drove her back to the trench. Around nine o'clock, on impulse, she took a compass reading, then laid out a forth trench heading downslope in a westerly direction.

"What are you doing?" Kwiatkowski asked, having followed her.

She pointed west. "Jerusalem." Then she pointed east. "Ur. The entry to the structure will face Jerusalem."

"I think you've used up your quota of hunches. Time for bed." He took her elbow, but she shook him off.

"In a minute," she said. "Come with me."

Molly hiked up the short stretch to the top of the small hill, Kwiatkowski so close behind that when she abruptly turned around, she was instantly in his arms. He pulled away only to have her grab his belt and pull him back.

"We could be dead tomorrow," she said.

"I've thought of that. That's why I haven't let you out of my sight."

Molly glanced toward the camp where the rest of the crew were preparing for sleep. Overhead, the stars shone in such unobscured multitude that Molly could almost lose herself in the vastness of God's realm, become one with the stars herself, no longer human but, like Father Teague now, part of some greater whole. Grabbing Kwiatkowski's hand and laughing like a woman with a plan, she tugged him down the far slope where only the open desert to the south and God above could see what they were up to.

"I'm supposed to be standing guard up here," Kwiatkowski said.

"You will be."

When she suddenly dropped to the sand, Kwiatkowski had to follow. She lay back, her head on the sand, a girl again, relaxing on a beach, the sky above, her mother beside her. Only it wasn't her mother but a man whom she trusted almost as much.

"Teddy Ballgame," she said.

"What?"

"Teddy Ballgame. Ted Williams. He played for the Red Sox. He was a war hero and a great baseball player. You remind me a lot of him."

"I never played baseball, and I've never fought in a war. How am I like him?"

Molly's fingers slyly forced their way between his. "You strike me the heroic kind," she said. "Unique. Tell me what you know about the stars."

"Not a lot really. I like to look at them, that's all."

Molly turned onto her side, the better to study the man who had saved her life in Poland and again in An-Najaf. "Someone once described the sun as a baby, a second generation star, whose mother star had long since died. Think about what that means. If our star is the child of another older one, there could have been other planets, too, other races of beings who lived, died, and left nothing behind. Do you think that will happen to us sometime? We'll just run our course, and no matter how well we've done, how much we've achieved, we'll simply cease to exist?"

"That's why people believe in God," Kwiatkowski said.

"Milstein thinks we have lived before. All of us. And at least once, in the time of Jesus, we lived together. Teddy, could it be? Do you think that what has drawn us here, don't ask me how, is that we are buried here, right beneath us. Not us, of course, but the people we were two thousand years ago?"

Kwiatkowski sat up. "Be careful what you wish for," he said, avoiding her eyes. "No, I don't think it's real. I think it's a ridiculous idea. I told Nina that, too."

"You dream about her, don't you?" she probed.

"No. Yes. So what? It's the stimulation of the expedition, that's all."

"When did you begin?"

"Molly!" Kwiatkowski sighed. "A few weeks ago. A few months ago. I don't remember."

"And in your dreams, who are you? Milstein says he is Judas. I'm Hannaniah. Great casting. What about you?" Molly moved her hand out of his and along his bearded cheek. She hoped she knew the answer. "Were we lovers, Teddy? Is that what you dream?"

For the longest moment Kwiatkowski said nothing, didn't move, became a rock. When at last he turned to face her, he brought up his hand to mimic her caress, only her cheek was far softer than his. His answer was gentle as he leaned into her and kissed her lips. He broke contact, then kissed her again, and again, three times, four, hungrier and hungrier, tugging on her lips, groaning, drawing out the pleasure only to come back for more. By their sixth kiss, Molly had her hands under his loosened belt. His were tracing the flesh of her hips, exploring her supple curves with the loving and thorough patience of an archaeologist.

We have been lovers before, Molly thought. We have been. He could not know her this well if he had not touched her so wonderfully in the past, even if it was in another life. Kissing him deeply, she lost herself in his artistry, drifted into ecstasy, never heard the approach of the enemy.

When the first mortar shell blasted into the sand not twenty feet from where they lay, Molly crazily thought nothing of it. Kwiatkowski was on his feet, pants back up, belt tightened, gun drawn.

"Jesus Christ!" he shouted. "I should have been on guard!"

The second blast came almost on top of the first. It threw Kwiatkowski off his feet and spattered Molly with his blood. She screamed, and then down they both went, suddenly, down, through the sand, through the timbers, through the roof of Mohamoud Jama's long-buried crypt, like two startled worms caught in a sinkhole that appeared out of nowhere and dropped them into the earth.

Milstein had settled in for a quick game of chess with Leveille-Gaus. He was considering a move with his knight to check the archaeologist when the mortar shell whistled overhead and exploded on the hill a hundred feet away. Leveille-Gaus was on his feet so fast he sent the chess board flying and the chess pieces tumbling onto the ground.

"Mr. Jackson!" he shouted. "We are under attack!"

"I can see that, goddamnit!"

Jackson had been preparing his people and Kwiatkowski's remaining Poles for just such an event all day. Regrettably, he had taken his one break just a few minutes before to relieve himself. He was zipping up his fly as he ran past Milstein and Leveille-Gaus screaming orders to his troops.

"Infrareds on! Use your anti-tank launchers! Two men to every openin'! Where the hell is Kwiatkowski?"

"On the hill the last I saw," Habib said. He grabbed an assault rifle and followed Jackson around the camp as the American deployed his troops behind the cover of the trucks. Between Kwiatkowski's men and Jackson's, they could count on a dozen armed defenders.

"Go and find him," Jackson yelled. "I'll be damned if I'm gonna lose this command to a bunch of towel heads."

Habib's radio communications had kept Tikriti informed from the moment he left Al-Muthallath until he had arrived with his troops a mile away from the excavation, far enough away to be unseen, close enough to launch an attack. Nur had given him permission to protect the historic remains. He had not instructed him how to do this. But then Tikriti didn't need directions. Nor would he need Nur, for that matter, once the remains of Jesus of Nazareth were in his possession. Whether or not he would kill the Americans remained to be seen.

With thirty mujahedeen, fully armed with rocket launchers, Kalashnikov rifles, grenade launchers, mortars, some of which had been commandeered from dead Americans, Tikriti was fairly confident that he could overrun a camp of archaeologists even if there were paid mercenaries among them.

Lying on his belly in the sand, binoculars in place, he watched as the first mortar rounds were lobbed up and over the trucks, and in one instance scored a direct hit. At a distance of a hundred yards he saw the bodies of two men fly apart along with their truck. Then he rose to his feet and yelled, "Allahu Akbar!" and off his men raced on foot and in trucks toward the Americans.

At first everything was so dark she couldn't see a thing. She coughed and spluttered in the dust their fall and the mortar blast had caused inside the ancient tomb. Then she was on her hands and knees searching for Kwiatkowski.

"Teddy! Teddy!" she hollered. His blood still trickled down her cheek. She felt around wildly with her hands until she heard him groan. "Teddy? Where are you?"

His sounds directed her in the blackness to his side only a few feet away.

"Don't talk," she ordered as she felt his head then lifted it onto her lap. He coughed, cursed, then spoke for the first time.

"Molly. Okay. I'm okay."

"No, you're not. Sit still. We're under attack."

"My leg, my butt, a little head wound."

"Then rest your butt. It's too nice a butt to waste."

But Kwiatkowski wouldn't listen. Bracing himself on her shoulders, he sat up, yowped in pain.

"You see?" she said.

"From the fall. I think I twisted an ankle."

"I'm covered in your fucking blood!"

"Head wounds bleed a lot," he insisted.

"And large head wounds bleed a lot more. Sit still. Let me see where we are. You had a flashlight?"

"Somewhere."

Molly slithered like a cobra in the sand, breathing in and coughing out dust, until she bumped her head against a wall. "Ouch! Damn! Do you know where we are, Teddy?"

"In a grave. Ours if we don't get the hell out of here."

"Hannaniah's," she said. "Maybe Jesus."

"Find the flashlight."

"I'm trying."

Above them more explosions, then small arms fire. Molly figured that as long as it lasted it meant that her side was fighting back. Once it stopped, then she'd really worry.

"Got it!" she cried as her hand latched on to it. She flicked it on and sucked in her breath. "Oh, my God!"

Kwiatkowski turned around to face her. Blood dripped from a gash above his right eye. His shirt and pants had been torn by pieces of shrapnel exposing wounds in his back and legs. When he tried to move, his ankle gave way and he grunted with pain. "Oh, my God, Teddy," she repeated.

"I'm fine. I'll live. What are those things?" he asked.

The room was full of earthen jugs. Twenty, thirty, like the hull of a Roman ship carrying flagons of wine.

"Burial urns? I'm not sure." Her flashlight beam flicked from floor to wall to ceiling.

"I can't tell how far back this room goes, but, Jesus!"

Kwiatkowski said. "We need to get out, hide. We can't stay here."

"I don't see as we have much choice."

Molly checked Kwiatkowski's scalp wound. A concussion from above knocked debris down on their heads but Molly never moved.

"You'll live," she said.

"I already told you that."

Molly moved away from him and shone the light on the closest of the urns.

"Now what are you doing?"

"Just looking."

"Molly!"

Paying him no more mind than she did the fighting above, she aimed her beam on the unadorned urn. Then she moved on to the second and third. "These have no markings on them."

"Molly!"

"It's like we dropped into a warehouse. These are unfinished products."

"Molly, listen."

At last, Kwiatkowski got her attention, at least enough of it for her to pause, lower the beam onto the ground, and do as he said. The fighting had stopped.

"Shit."

"We need to move. We need to get out of here."

"Wait a minute."

With the stubborn compulsion of a treasure hunter, she excitedly traced a circle of light on the wood-supported ceiling.

"Look!"

"Molly, stop it."

She moved away from him until she reached the opposite wall, then she extended her hand. "Come here. Quickly."

"Damn it, Molly." He glanced at the hole above and the night peeking through, then hopped on his good foot as far as it would take him before he collapsed against the wall behind her. With an aggravated whisper, he said, "What is it? This better be good."

In his younger, rasher days, Richard Jackson had dropped out of veterinarian school and joined the army, attaining the rank of captain in the First Gulf War. He prided himself on his combat experience, but in fact his experience amounted to little more than rounding up Iraqi prisoners after the Air Force and the Navy had bombed the hell out of them.

In all fairness, he had positioned his men as well as he could, given their small number, but he had not equipped them as well as he might have. And when the opening salvo took out one of his remaining trucks and two of his civilian associates, he figured the jig was up.

Grabbing Milstein by the collar and Leveille-Gaus by the arm, he shouted, "Let's bail!"

"Where's Molly?" Milstein demanded. "Kwiatkowski. I'm not leaving without them!"

"And I'm not losin' my ass lookin' for 'em!"

At the truck that contained Father Teague's body, Jackson jumped into the cab and behind the wheel. Bullets pinged off the metal, but Milstein would not follow Jackson, even when Leveille-Gaus slid into the passenger side seat and offered the intelligence officer a hand.

"You go. Go!" Milstein yelled at them. He turned to run. A spray of bullets tore into the canvas of the truck above him. Milstein ducked and was hit, not by the mujahedeen missiles but by the truck itself as Jackson tried to make his escape. The vehicular swipe sprawled Milstein on the ground, fortunately for him, for the next round of machine gun fire struck Jackson's rear tire, blew it out, and left the truck, passengers included, sitting like a big fat deer in Ghazi Al-Tikriti's headlights.

The man himself arrived moments later, barreling into camp at the wheel of an American Humvee. The rest of his forces rushed in behind him. Jackson and the other survivors threw down their guns, raised their hands, and hoped the mujahedeen would treat them better than the Americans had treated the mujahedeen at Abu Ghraib.

Tikriti stepped out of his Humvee, walked over to Milstein who lay on his face in the sand, and helped him up. "Mr. Milstein," he said. "Fancy meeting you here."

"Don't do anything foolish, Mr. Tikriti," Milstein said. "This is an archaeological expedition, not a military engagement."

"Oh, I understand that. I don't know if Mr. Jackson does." Tikriti looked up into the cab of the truck and waggled a finger at Jackson. "Come on down, Mr. Jackson. It is the day of the dog."

Without a word, Jackson joined two Polish soldiers and two Americans, along with Milstein and finally Leveille-Gaus, in a circle surrounded by Tikriti's troops. Some of the Iraqis went through the archaeologists' trucks looking for booty. The woman-hater, Aden, gave one glance at the circle of captives and said, "Where's the woman?"

"I think if you find Habib," Tikriti said, "you'll run into her."

While the fighting was still going on, Habib walked up the side of the excavation to the top of the hill. Kwiatkowski was armed and good at using his weapon. After all, Habib had been the lone Iraqi survivor in Poland after they had bombed the Kwiatkowski estate. Not that he was angry with the Pole for doing what he had done. That was the nature of the beast. Habib just didn't want to be mistaken for an unfriendly mujahedeen and shot. He, naturally, wanted to get off the first shot. After that he would deal with Dr. O'Dwyer.

At the top of the hill, he crouched low and couldn't understand why he had seen neither the female archaeologist nor her guardian. Perhaps they had taken to their feet at the first sound of battle and disappeared into the desert. Slowly he moved ahead, his eyes moving left, right, ears trained for any telltale sound.

As he descended the opposite side of the hill, he saw something weird, like a dark hole in the desert floor, a drop-off. He crept toward it. He was not about to be taken by surprise. When the ground beneath him gave way, he gasped and let go of his gun as he plummeted into darkness. He landed hard, his gun clattering somewhere nearby. Dazed, he lay still for several minutes unable to move, looking up at the sky and the stars looking down. Bizarrely, a face looked back down at him. Foolishly, he moved.

Aden the woman-hater, not knowing who it was and not being of rational mind, shot at the first thing that entered his sight. That it was Habib was unfortunate because the Iraqi engineer took a bullet in the brain and died instantly. But at least that made Aden pause, whisper, "Habib?" and not shoot so quickly when the next movement caught his eye.

Molly's flashlight beam orbited the black sky of the tomb, the yellow star pausing every ten feet to focus on the peculiar markings that had been carved into the wooden beams.

"See?" she told Kwiatkowski, who had followed her into the core of the hill. "The mound might be oval, but the center was built into a circle. It looks unfinished, so we can't say how many rooms they meant to build."

The lightless space they had entered was like the hub of a wheel, filled with more of the nondescript clay urns and with the tools and debris that went with the manufacture of such ware. What fascinated Molly was the series of smaller chambers that led off from the hub. Above each entry, the ancient artisans had crafted wooden lintels, and in the center of each lintel had carved markings, different on each beam. One of them, the one she was studying now, looked exactly like the jagged V she had seen in Afghanistan and on her Star of David pendant.

"I *know* what this is," she said, not quite knowing but wishing the hell she did.

"You said it was the Tigris-Euphrates Rivers before."

"Maybe I was wrong. It happens once a century. The daughter's seven tears from Hannaniah's lamentation. The seven dots composing the jagged V. The V is the daughter, Teddy! The house, the five notes, that's the father. And the squiggly W is the mother! They were intended for burial here!"

Molly moved along the walls, using her hand as a guide.

"Christ." she said, "they all have symbols, all twelve of them!"

At a second entry, Molly moved over one of the urns, set it, with Kwiatkowski's help, on its flat bottom, then carefully tested whether the body of the vessel would support her weight. Seeing that it did, she boosted herself up and perched on the circular lip of the urn where she could now view the symbol at eye level.

"This one is different. Another symbol. Maybe for a child."

Then something fell through the hole in the roof and landed with such a crash that Molly lost her balance and toppled backwards into Kwiatkowski. He slid to the ground with Molly in his lap.

"Someone's here!" she whispered.

"Don't move," Kwiatkowski ordered her. "Say nothing."

Within moments of the rooftop falling in, gunfire shattered the quiet of the tomb. A man screamed. Molly rose quickly to her feet and grabbed Teddy's arm. She could see that Kwiatkowski was in no condition to move. Whoever had fired down into the tomb would be joining them soon. Her thoughts were no longer on saving the urns, the magnificent archaeological treasure, but on making sure Teddy stayed alive. The catacomb was a finite space. There was no place to hide. So Molly retrieved her flashlight and dragged him deeper into the tomb's darkness.

"Molly, what the hell are you doing?"

"Stay put!" she whispered. Better me than both of us, she thought. She kissed him quickly and said, "Head to Ur when you can."

"Ur?"

As she made her way back toward the opening, someone jumped through the hole and landed on the dead Habib.

She called out, "Hello! Don't shoot! I'm coming out!"

The man hesitated when Molly's flashlight beam struck him square in the eyes. He blinked, backed out of the path of the light, and raised his weapon.

"I said don't shoot," Molly said. "I'm giving myself up."

"Where's the other?" he said.

"Dead." Molly burst into tears.

Drawing near, gun pointed at her breasts, he grabbed her hair, yanked her head back, and stuck the barrel of his weapon under her shirt.

Molly could hear his harsh, excited breathing, smell dinner on his breath. Though her Arabic was not up to snuff, she didn't need an English-Arabic dictionary to lay out a definition of what he intended to do. So she took her flashlight, and hit him on the head with it.

"Sharmuta!" he yelled. "Bitch!"

He fell back but not far or hard enough. In an instant, his Kalashnikov was aimed at her face and his finger was pulling the trigger. Was he going to kill her first, then fuck her?

Ghazi Al-Tikriti stopped him. Peering down through the hole, he said, "Aden, it occurred to me you might do something stupid. Put down the gun. I told you we need the woman alive."

"But ..."

"Alive!"

Molly sagged, shut her eyes. She didn't move until several other Iraqis had dropped down to retrieve her and Habib.

"She killed him!" Aden insisted.

Tikriti rolled his eyes. "The Pole?"

"He killed him!" Molly pointed at Habib and let loose another volley of tears.

Back in the camp above ground, the stars shone as if nothing out of the ordinary had transpired. Molly was shoved in amongst the other prisoners, Milstein, Leveille-Gaus, Jackson. Other foreigners, kidnapped by insurgents throughout Iraq, had faced execution live and on the worldwide web. Molly had no doubt that Tikriti planned a similar fate for them. But there was one chance and she took it, jumping into Tikriti's face.

"This is the wrong site," she said.

"What?" That brief interrogatory was shouted not only by Tikriti but by Leveille-Gaus and Jackson as well.

"My dear," Tikriti said, "if this is your attempt to buy time, it's pretty thin."

"We have to go back to Ur. Right now."

"What about Kwiatkowski and Habib?" Jackson asked.

"Dead," Molly said.

"Habib was your man, Tikriti," Jackson said.

"Yes. And I could have been yours. Now I'm not. Let that be a lesson to you in Iraqi politics."

"But you don't have Jesus. And we might."

"You, Mr. Jackson?"

Jackson pulled a small black book from his windbreaker pocket and held it out for Tikriti to see.

"Mohamoud Jama's diary," he said.

Molly gaped. "What? Let me see that!" She tried to grab it, but Jackson was too quick. Tikriti was quicker and snatched the book that had been stolen from him at Abu Ghraib.

"Why didn't you tell anyone you had his diary?" Molly yelled.

"Didn't seem necessary," Jackson said. "You and Leveille-Gaus had everything under control. Or so it seemed. Now it doesn't."

"Give it to me," Molly said to Tikriti.

"Why?"

"Are you an archaeologist?"

"Can you read Arabic?"

Tikriti held onto the diary and flipped through several pages while one of his men shone a flashlight on it.

"Well?" Molly asked.

"There are maps, drawings. There is a hill. It could be this one. There is an entrance. It could be the one you fell into."

"Could be," Molly said. "But it isn't."

Or, at least, she hoped the hell it wasn't. First, because she didn't want to die here. Second, because if this was the site Jama was so impassioned about, he, and not she, had made the big mistake. This was not Hannaniah's tomb.

Tikriti turned his green eyes on Molly. They twinkled kindly. "Ur," he said.

"Is that Jama's opinion?" Molly asked.

"He says that the site he uncovered was only the doorway. The house lies elsewhere. Where the father and mother were born. Unless I am mistaken, you interpret that to be Abraham and Sarah, the father and mother of the Hebrew race. You were there once before. Ur."

"Yes, and misunderstood what I found."

"And won't misunderstand this time?"

"I never claimed to be Jesus. Only his daughter."

Tikriti chuckled. "Let us hope so. Otherwise I will unleash Aden and let him take his pleasure." Then he signaled to one of his men. "Bring me a radio." And to Jackson. "You're my prisoner now. If you want to avoid what you did to me, get on the line to your General Eisenstadt. Tell him to remove his troops guarding Ur. Jesus is there. No one is to know who doesn't need to know. I don't want Professor O'Dwyer disturbed. Yes, Professor O'Dwyer?"

She stepped forward again. "There's one other thing."

"Only one?"

"Milstein is to regress me. At Ur."

Milstein beamed. Tikriti frowned. The term puzzled him.

Leveille-Gaus sighed. "She intends to find Jesus. Here," he said, indicating his head.

At which point Tikriti burst into such laughter that his men couldn't help being drawn into his happy mood. Tikriti himself ended it, withdrawing his pistol. "At Abu Ghraib," he said to Jackson, "your people had a fondness for the gun and the knife." He stuck the barrel of his weapon in Jackson's groin. "Humiliation was key to your torture. Emasculation. Sometimes your young soldiers got carried away. Especially your young women soldiers." Tikriti looked around at his men then fired. But not at Jackson. At Molly. Just over her head. She gasped and ducked instinctively. "You see, Professor O'Dwyer," he said, "we Iraqis are civilized, respectful. More subtle than you Americans. But our patience has limits. The next time, the bullet will be fatal. Do not fail me."

A gunshot also startled Abdul Azim Nur, disrupted his evening prayers and sent his male gathering of Shi-a Muslims leaping from their prayer mats and scrambling for their guns. Out from the mosque they rushed, prepared to defend their leader who was much slower to rise than they.

Nur had been making his way in triumph from village to village in Southeastern Iraq much as an American politician on the campaign trail. Only a few kilometers from the border with Iran, he had returned to the birthplace of his mother and father to renew old ties, gather old friends, and prepare for a political march on Baghdad. Like Jesus entering Jerusalem, he intended to challenge the democratically elected secular government of Iraq with an organized Islamic force they had not yet encountered.

The gunshot came at a fortuitous moment because Nur had not really been praying. He had drifted off into a light sleep and begun dreaming of his guardians and followers. But in a perverse role reversal typical of his dreams lately, they turned on him and tore him to pieces. Indeed, they would have killed him had the beautiful young woman of his previous dreams not appeared to gather him in her arms and carry him to safety.

She leaned forward to kiss him when the gunshot emptied the tiny village mosque and brought him back to reality.

"Imam! Imam!"

The sound of Barid Shamkhazi's voice hurried him out into the darkening sky. The young Iranian had collared the gunman who had fired the lone shot.

"They've found her!" Shamkhazi shouted. "This man has just come from Ur. Tikriti has them all!"

"Including the woman?"

"Yes."

This excited Nur, for he believed that this woman, this beautiful American archaeologist whom he had encountered in Baghdad and who somehow inhabited his dreams, could explain what was happening to him and dispel his fears. He believed that his visions were God-sent, after all, and that Barid and the men around him were the very same disciples who plotted to kill him in his dream.

"To Ur then," he told Shamkhazi, wondering who might die there.

CHAPTER 17

Kwiatkowski waited beyond endurance before he dared move. Inside the earth, he had no sense of place or time, could see or hear nothing above him. Only when dawn brought its lightening did he force pain aside to venture out of the hill core and climb out of the hole with the help of the clay urn that the mujahedeen had thoughtfully left in place.

The camp was empty. The only traces of the trucks were the tread marks in the sand. Kwiatkowski might have despaired but for two things. First, he trusted Molly. She had risked her life for him and would never desert him. Second, the careless mujahedeen had left behind one truck, the one hit by the first mortar explosion on the camp.

Several bodies, all from the expedition, were scattered about the camp. None of them, thank God, was Molly's. His cuts were healing. His ankle remained a source of annoyance. But with Molly leading the enemy back to Ur, he knew what he had to do. Looking at the forlorn surviving truck, the roof and windshield of the cab missing, one front tire flat, and the fuel tank leaking, he wondered how the hell he was going to do it.

Despite everything, the moment Molly saw the pyramid of Ur rise out of the flat plain, her heart raced to meet it. Her demand of Tikriti to return here was not a thin attempt to buy time. She had been wrong about where to look for Hannaniah and her father even if the Star of David medallion had led them, perhaps by sheer luck, to Mohamoud Jama's original site. Jama's diary seemed to corroborate her belief. Nor was her request for Milstein to regress her a diversion or fancy. The answer did lie in Ur. She needed to get back, and she needed a way to find the missing evidence without alerting Tikriti, Jackson, or Leveille-Gaus. It was a gamble easily wagered, especially if it kept Kwiatkowski safe.

At the gates of the ancient city, deserted now by its American watchdogs, Molly exited the Chevy minivan. She stood hands on hips, her red hair pulled up under her Sox baseball cap, the frames of her sunglasses dangling from her mouth, and wondered what to do now. Without Hannaniah's ghostly help, could she find that room again where Jesus' illegitimate daughter had guided her before?

"Well, you're here," Tikriti told her, coming from the front of the oil-powered caravan, "and you didn't have to buy the gas. What now? We are all in your lovely hands."

"I will need the help of your men, all of them," she said. "They're no longer mujahedeen. They're archaeologists. Ur is an extensive site. They should be arranged into four teams, one per quadrant. I'll lead one. You, Dr. Leveille, and Mr. Milstein will lead the others."

"What are we looking for?"

Kneeling, she traced two symbols in the dirt, one a Star of David, the other a jagged V. She said, "Any symbols like this or similar in nature, carved into the building material. Don't be hasty. Take your time. They may be in fairly inaccessible locations. Be thorough. And call me as soon as you've found anything." She looked up at Tikriti. "You have radios? Good. Then let's move."

Tikriti acted as if her idea was his, her orders likewise his. Dividing his men into four groups, he made sure Aden was assigned to Molly's team of amateur archaeologists. He kept Jackson with him, and around eight in the morning the hunt for Jesus began.

Evening brought blessed relief from the heat of the day. Such temperatures typically reduced productivity, so that the four exploration teams Molly had created that morning searched and rested, searched and rested, and found nothing. Molly was no help. She had no memory of her walk through the maze of Ur to find the chamber with the circular hole in the roof. She had been in an insulin-deprived daze and had been following a ghost. And those who found her had not bothered to map the routes they had taken in their search.

They set up campfires among their many vehicles and set guards at the gates to the Chaldean city. The mujahedeen were lax in watching the archaeologists, who had no place to go and nothing to go there in. Molly took her turn and prepared dinner from the expedition's food supplies, treating the Iraqis to soup and dinner rolls. It gave her the chance to think and plan.

The jagged V was not a symbol of the Tigris-Euphrates Rivers, or, at least, not just a symbol of the rivers. Had it stood alone, she might have continued to believe so. But it was only one of six symbols on the Star of David and one of twelve at Mohamoud Jama's excavation. The key was understanding the symbols.

She ate dinner by herself, her back to her captors, face to the ziggurat. Otherwise, every time she looked up she would see Aden staring at her as he would at the last piece of meat on his plate. Only when Tikriti came to her did she turn her gaze away from the city.

"Are you ready?" he asked.

"Ready?"

"You said you were going to have Mr. Milstein do something to you that would help you see into the past. I presume a trick, but my men are gullible and intrigued. And I am unopposed to entertainment.

What do you need to do this thing?"

"Just me and Milstein," Molly said. She almost regretted having to stand and go back into the camp. To some degree Tikriti was right. Regression was not scientific and hardly an accepted way to conduct an archaeological expedition. Molly was used to hard work, to making important discoveries only after weeks and months of exhausting labor. None of that bothered her. In fact, the nitty-gritty time-consuming toil always brought forth the most incredible finds. If you didn't mine the details, you missed the gold.

But curiosity motivated her, and she had promised a show. So avoiding Aden's stare and taking her last slurp of pea soup, she handed the plate to Tikriti and said, "Let's give it a shot."

Milstein insisted that it could not be done in front of such a large, gawking audience. Tikriti could watch, Leveille-Gaus, Jackson, but no one else. For her part, Molly wanted him to do it in Ur, within the walls, within the city. While the intellect in her disputed regression, the pagan was more than ready to be dipped into the mystical sea and come out on an ancient shore.

"How about there?" Milstein pointed to an alcove off a brick courtyard. A fat silver moon shone overhead and the ziggurat loomed behind them. Plenty of light reflected off the stones and brick and it was quiet as only a night in the desert can be. Tikriti had allowed Molly and Milstein to choose their site, but he had insisted on bringing several of his men, including Aden, even if they had to have one wall of bricks between them and the regression.

Molly carried a blanket and laid it down on the dusty floor of the alcove that might once have borne the likenesses of gods and goddesses of the Chaldeans. Milstein folded a blanket and placed it under her head.

"I'm not sure how old Judas was when he died," Milstein said. "My sessions with Father Ray never got so detailed as dates, ages. But I think Judas was still a teenager, a young boy, about Hannaniah's age, when he killed himself."

Milstein sat beside Molly, ignoring Tikriti and Leveille-Gaus. He had his own story to tell before he regressed Molly. "I only know," he said, "that in none of my experiences as Judas is he older than a young man. And as a young man he was clearly suicidal. He loved Hannaniah, was rejected by her. He was reckless and foolish, and did everything he could to win her approval but never succeeded so far as I can tell. He did not accompany her and Yeshuah out of Jerusalem."

With a sigh, Milstein leaned forward to whisper to Molly. "You must believe," he insisted. "I have never seen Jesus' face in my regressions. I don't know why he eludes me. He won't elude Hannaniah, his daughter. Do you understand that? Do you understand that when I regress you, you may be seeing things in your past that no one could ever imagine seeing?"

Molly laid her head on the folded wool blanket and took one last glance at the stars above before shutting her eyes. "Milstein," she said, "don't scare me. Just regress me."

The ghosts of Ur may have gathered around to watch the spectacle. Certainly, Leveille-Gaus, Tikriti and Jackson hovered as close as Milstein would allow. Aden and the mujahedeen guards kept their distance but stood close enough to hear Milstein as he began the procedure.

Molly floated through time and space, deep into the recesses of her mind. Awake, she could envision the past like a child descending into fantasy. In a semi-hypnotic state, she lost herself completely, flew gently through a dark sky that grew lighter and lighter, until Milstein's soft voice and steady directions led her into a different land.

"Wash. Wash," she whispered.

"Watch? Molly, we can't hear you."

"Wash. Want to wash his face."

"Whose face, Molly? What do you see? Where are you?"

In this different land, Molly was a girl of about thirteen, slender and vibrant. Her curly red hair blew in the wind, free of headscarf or shawl. Around her, anxious crowds milled about, talking and whispering. Hannaniah is angelic, solemn, aloof from the commotion. Other children stare at the three men being raised onto crosses on the hilltop outside the walls of Jerusalem, but Hannaniah stands apart.

"Molly." Milstein couldn't wait. "What do you see?" he asked her.

"He wants me to watch him," Molly said. "But I won't."

"Who?"

"Yeshuah."

Milstein gasped. "You see him? His face? What does he look like? Molly, what does he look like?"

"He is raised," Molly said. "He is in pain."

"Yeshuah is in pain?" Milstein asked. "Please, go on. Hannaniah, tell us what you see."

"You expect us to believe you are witnessing the crucifixion of Jesus?" Leveille-Gaus scoffed. "Please, Dr. O'Dwyer, some respect here for your peers."

"Three men are raised above the people. They suffer terribly. They hammer the nails into their hands high on the wood. Their bodies sag. They are so thirsty! Why don't they put them out of their misery? It is so cruel, I don't want to look."

"Who are they, Hannaniah?" Milstein asked.

"Shimon is the one on the right, the high priest."

"And Yeshuah?"

"And Yehudah."

"Yehudah?" Milstein went white. He tried to speak, but his words failed to find life.

"You mean Judas?" Leveille-Gaus said. He glanced at Milstein. "I guess that would be you, Mr. Milstein. And what of Jesus, Hannaniah? If he is the third, what does he look like?"

"I will not watch! It is too much! James! James can save them."

Molly as Hannaniah rolled on the ground with such fervor that her motions snapped Milstein out of his daze and he held her still.

"Move her forward a few hours," Leveille-Gaus suggested. "Go forward a few hours, Molly, Hannaniah. Leave the pain behind. What is happening now?"

She settled, breathing deeply, her eyelids fluttering as they would in dream state, her hands clenching and unclenching.

"Have they died?" Milstein asked. "Has Yeshuah died?"

In Molly's mind, through Hannaniah's eyes, the hill of the crucifixion is now deserted. Hannaniah remains alone with the man she calls Father. Raising her hands to the sky in imitation of the condemned, she feeds the crows who would otherwise feed off the dead.

"Tell us," Jackson said. "For Chris' sake, Dr. O'Dwyer, tell us. Is he dead? Jesus? Why are you smilin'?"

Indeed, a beautiful smile brightened Molly's tear-stained face. What Hannaniah saw was the sunlight high above Jerusalem reflecting off an object that Yeshuah wore about his neck, a Star of David pendant. And when Yeshuah opened his eyes and spoke, Molly uttered his words.

"The blood of my blood shall rule."

"Is he dead, Hannaniah?" Leveille-Gaus demanded, for Milstein had lost control of the session and sat by Molly's side aghast and unable to say anything. "Is the man on the cross, the Messiah, Yeshuah, is he dead?"

In her trance, Molly licked her lips, for Jerusalem was in its rainy season and the clouds had begun to deposit droplets on Calvary. Molly/Hannaniah tasted the refreshing water, as James, Yeshuah's oldest sibling, appeared.

"They are taking him down," Molly said.

"But is he dead?" Leveille-Gaus begged an answer.

"If you think that, you have no faith, child," Molly said. Her cryptic remark made Tikriti chuckle, Leveille-Gaus frown, and Jackson fall to his knees. Milstein held his hands over his eyes as if unable to look.

"She's blocking us," Leveille-Gaus said. "Intentionally, I'd bet. I hope this is not a joke, Dr. O'Dwyer. Milstein, bring her forward. Bring her to Ur. We know Jesus survived crucifixion. That's why we're all here. We need to know what happened to him after. Come on, Milstein. Snap out of it."

Milstein refocused when Leveille-Gaus shook his shoulders, then, with a deep intake of air, he reasserted his control over Molly and advanced her in time to when Hannaniah and the rest of her community, perhaps including her father, had entered Ur in their flight from the Holy Land. This time they were not alone. A stranger, a visitor from the future was with them. When Molly opened her eyes, she was back in Ur, lying on the ground amidst the ruins of the uninhabited city, but it wasn't Milstein, or Leveille-Gaus, or Tikriti who stared down at her. It was Hannaniah.

"Molly, are you there?" Milstein asked.

She was there. Ur was in ruins, but not as the city had become by the 21st century. The ziggurat and the surrounding plaza and town were not yet buried. Enough of the ancient Chaldean capital remained above ground that Hannaniah and her followers could easily trespass and make a home for themselves.

"Molly," Milstein urged, "what is happening? What do you see?"

In silence, in solemn wonder, the two women gazed at one another, Hannaniah and Molly. Then, with a smile, Hannaniah turned and led Molly into the city, deep into the heart of the past, as she had once before. Down the twisting and turning alleyways, through open spaces where merchants of old once sold their goods, along pathways that sheep and goats and chickens once occupied. Molly longed to speak, but something in her heart told her that if she did, as in a dream, she would break the spell, destroy the magic, and be returned to the present no wiser for this wondrous experience. With dread and exhilaration, she let Hannaniah take her wherever the child of Yeshuah bar Yushef wanted to go.

"Molly? Come on!" Leveille-Gaus insisted.

"The father is ever forgiving," she told him in response.

"What?"

"Light and darkness made one. The one guarding the other for eternity."

"What do you mean? Stop speaking gibberish. Is Yeshuah, Jesus the Nazarene, is he buried where you are? Is he at Ur?"

With a simple "Yes," Molly propelled Leveille-Gaus onto his feet.

"Can you take us there?" Tikriti asked. "When Mr. Milstein brings you back to the present, will you be able to take us there?"

Silently Molly spun Tikriti's wheels in the mud of her deception. She could hear him, she could hear him very well even from so far away. More importantly, she could understand him. Sitting up so abruptly she nearly cracked heads with Milstein, she startled them all.

"Well?" Tikriti repeated, asking the question they all wanted to ask. "Can you take us there? Where Jesus is buried?"

Molly played for time, rubbing her head, weak and woozy from her inner journey. "Not now," she mumbled. "Let me rest. I need sleep."

"I didn't bring her back properly," Milstein told them. "She came back on her own. I don't know what that means. Molly, did you get anything?"

She nodded. "Let me sleep. Let me think on it. I saw Hannaniah. In the morning, I think I can find the way."

Tikriti sounded doubtful. "You won't forget?"

"Not likely."

"Don't, for all of your sakes." Then Tikriti brought Aden and the other mujahedeen into the alcove. "Watch her. She goes nowhere tonight. The same for the rest of them. Tomorrow we dig."

Milstein wrapped an arm about her and whispered in her ear. "Do you believe now?"

"More than I did this morning."

"Can you—can you really lead us to Jesus?"

Molly took a quick look about to check the lie of the land. Aden was behind her beside Leveille-Gaus but far enough away that she could whisper back. "He's not here."

"What? Then where?"

"You have to help me, Andrew. Give me a chance tonight. I need time by myself. And I need a truck. I'll even take Jackson's help, but we need to get away."

At the camp, where the rest of Tikriti's men relaxed among their trucks and cars, eating, drinking, and watching two of their number play an intense game of chess, Milstein placed a blanket around Molly's shoulders and hugged her.

"Andrew, aren't you married?"

"I was. I blew that, too. Sorry." He let her go but kept his eyes fastened on hers. "During their evening prayer something will happen. Head into Ur. If I can follow you, I will. Don't be wrong this time." Then he kissed her, long, as a lover. "What I would have done for you," he whispered when he parted. "Anything."

"You have a way with men," Tikriti said, having watched the embrace with great interest. "Aden will be glad to hear it."

Molly made a bed for herself on the ground. Uncomfortable as it was, she fell asleep quickly. The last thing she saw before drifting off was Milstein creating his own makeshift bed near the kitchen truck.

She dreamed that she was back in Ur, but her mother was with her this time. A child again, she showed off the city to her mother, pointing out the sights—the temples, the wharves, the stalls and shops. Her mother was dressed in green robes and white sandals and looked wonderingly at everything Molly showed her. Molly smelled lamb cooking over open fires, the wonderful perfumes from the Arabian peninsula, the dank smell of wild animals roaming the tight alleyways. For the longest time, mother and daughter roamed to their hearts' content, tourists of an ancient land, until they came to a room. In the entrance to the room hung a white and blue cloth that stirred gently with the breeze that followed in their wake. On the stone lintel was carved a Star of David.

Molly was about to pull at her mother's long green sleeve, excited and anxious to show what she had found, when, out of her dream she burst awake at the sound of an explosion.

The camp was in uproar. Fire raged in one of the trucks and exploding shells sent the mujahedeen running for cover. Molly sat bolt upright and wasted no time. She looked about to see what had become of her omnipresent bodyguard Aden. Seeing no sign of him, while the rest of the camp was in a tumult, she threw off her blanket and darted past the gates of Ur into the labyrinth of the city.

Milstein watched her go while he helped the mujahedeen fight the fire. The relaxed watch while the mujahedeen were at prayer—Tikriti may have been strictly secular in nature, but his men were not and insisted on obeying the will of Allah—had been Milstein's opportunity to sneak into the kitchen truck, retrieve and douse the truck with cans of cooking grease, and set the truck ablaze. The fire, in turn, had spread quickly to a neighboring automobile whose trunk contained hundreds of clips of ammunition and boxes of explosives. It was the fire in the Camry that turned the mujahedeen camp into a Fourth of July fireworks display.

Two others caught sight of her fleet form disappearing into the night. Leveille-Gaus decided it was a convenient time to disappear himself and took off into the darkness away from the city into the desert. The second man, the woman-hater Aden, could have alerted Tikriti to his escaped prisoner but chose instead to bring her back himself after, naturally, he had taken his pleasure with her.

Molly did not run blindly through the maze that was Ur of the Chaldees. First, except where walls and roofs intercepted her light, the moon provided guidance through the web-work of alleys and lanes. Second, Molly had her dream to guide her.

Under Milstein's regression, she had awoken to Hannaniah. Skeptics, non-scientists, heretics, Freudians would have declared that she had experienced an induced fantasy based upon her psychological yearnings. Maybe. But Molly had found Hannaniah's occult symbols before. They were legitimately here in Ur, so they could be found again. And in her dream, as in her insulin-deprived stupor the last time she had been in Ur, Hannaniah had shown her the way.

Unfortunately, Molly wasn't dreaming now. She was fully awake, alert, and all too aware that before long someone would realize she was gone and come looking for her. She had minutes, perhaps ten, twenty.

Molly stopped to listen. In the distance, the fireworks of Milstein's sabotage popped and banged. If someone was on her trail, she couldn't hear him. Above, the stars were oblivious and beautiful. Ahead the narrow street bent this way and that, a bit of random construction created as new buildings were added piecemeal by the Chaldean occupants. But she was sure it was the path Hannaniah had taken her on, so that was the way she went.

Molly kept to the moon-generated shadows. At times, she closed her eyes to better envision where Hannaniah had taken her. Then, eyes open, she would trust her instincts to guide her down this lane rather than that one, up that path rather than the other. Right, not left. Across, not back. At last the ancient ruins began to look familiar, to resemble the walls and homes they had once been, white-washed and lived-in, alive with humanity, devoid of the desert sands.

Her heartbeat picked up. She was closer, she could feel it.

She heard a sound behind her, quite distinct from the chaos in Tikriti's camp, the crunch of feet on the alley stones off, she thought, to her left.

She glanced over her shoulder. The moon had moved almost directly over the top of the ziggurat, forming a mystical conjunction that the priests of Ur had worshiped in their day, prostrate to the moon goddess, much as Tikriti's soldiers had been praying when their world exploded.

Whoever followed her was closer now. He stumbled over bricks and stones, cursed her and the darkness. He turned into the alley in which she hid and saw her.

"Sharmuta!" Aden yelled.

Molly ran. She spun to her right down a lane so narrow she could touch both sides with her arms extended only a few inches. Dislodged bricks scratched her bare skin. She stubbed her sneakered toe on the corner of a building as she rounded it to head onto a slightly wider pathway. With her pursuer only yards behind, she raced like an Olympic hundred-meter champion, but the course she ran wasn't smooth and straight. It took her on a helter-skelter, last-second-decision quickstep right or left as the need or gut reaction took her. Her breath rushed out of her. Her head reeled. Her knee ached where she had banged it against a wall.

At last Molly made a fateful choice. She was banged up, bruised and winded, needed water and felt nauseous. When she spun into an alley that came up a dead end, she dived into the nearest doorway. The room was a rectangle about ten feet in length. When she looked up, she saw a familiar circular opening. She might have let out a yell of celebration, for the moonlight filtering in gave her a glimpse of one of the magic symbols on the ceiling. But before she could turn to see what had become of her stalker, he was on her.

Aden grunted, satisfaction and lust bursting in his veins, and lunged at her. His wicked curved blade sliced down at her. With all her strength she grabbed his wrist with both hands as they went down, his weight jarring the breath out of her. Her head struck stone, but she forced his knife-hand back.

"Bitch!"

"Bastard!"

He lost the knife but grabbed her hair and slammed her head into the ground then shifted his weight to pin her down. Bucking and twisting and scratching at his face, she rolled him off and jammed her knee into his groin. He cursed and was back on her like a wild animal, sinking his teeth into her shoulder.

It was Molly's turn to cry out. His teeth had drawn blood. When he punched her in the face, he drew more. Molly snarled, every bit as crazed as he was. Without regard to her own pain, she smashed her forehead into his teeth. He screamed, and she stabbed at his throat with the chewed fingernails of her right hand.

Retrieving his knife, he crouched like a cat and prepared to pounce. There wasn't a hell of a lot she could do. She was wounded, exhausted. He was bigger, stronger, and willing to kill. As he leapt across the short space that separated them, she thought, This is it. I am dead. Good-bye, Hannaniah.

But he never made it.

Someone leapt from the shadows behind. With a grunt, Aden fell on top of Molly who was too winded to move him. She shut her eyes in disbelief, not even wondering who had come out of nowhere to save her life. When she heard Nina Cavalcante say, "Molly, is that you?" she nearly fainted.

Cavalcante stood before her, an archaeologist's pick-ax in her hand.

Her companion, Deeqa the Iraqi nurse from An-Najaf, pushed the unconscious Aden off Molly, then brushed a gentle hand across Molly's forehead.

"I'm all right. I'm all right," Molly insisted. "Nina, I never thought I'd see you again."

"Nor I you, dear. Mr. Milstein told us to expect you. But not this way."

Molly tried to rise but a wave of dizziness brought her back down. Deeqa held a canteen to her mouth, and Molly took a grateful swig of lukewarm water.

"You remember Deeqa," Cavalcante said. "She agreed to bring me here."

"Your ribs?"

"Aren't feeling very good, but I wasn't going to stay away. It wasn't as bad as it looked. I hoped I might find you here."

Once again Molly forced aside pain and rose to her elbows. The Iraqi girl was lovely, with blue eyes set in a framework of pitch-black hair and thick dark brows. Molly wondered if the girl was more than just a friend.

"We left Ur," Molly said, rising to a sitting position, her eyes skirting the prone Aden, then upward to the ceiling and the circular opening that gave her a view of the sky above. "We thought we'd found Mohamoud Jama's location. We didn't. I think he was purposefully misleading people with his diary. So we came back here."

"With help."

"We didn't ask for it. Give me your flashlight."

Cavalcante handed it to Molly then helped her to her feet. Molly shone the light along the ceiling looking for the spot where she had first sighted the familiar Jewish symbol and its mysterious sign of the V.

"We don't have much time," she said. "Milstein created a diversion."

"We heard."

"We'll have the rest of them after us in no time."

"We have a truck."

"You do?" Molly said.

"An ambulance. We swiped it from the hospital. Deeqa drives like a madwoman." Cavalcante cast a proud glance at her shy friend who so far hadn't uttered a word. "Mr. Milstein snuck us some food and water. We were pretty well done without it."

"Mr. Milstein is busy making amends," Molly said. "Help me up. Quickly."

With help from Cavalcante's silent companion, Molly slid a stone block to the center of the room. Shining the flashlight onto the stone frame of the opening, she immediately found what she was looking for. And more.

"I didn't see all of this the first time."

"What?"

"The symbols. One, two, three, four, five, six ..." Molly counted. "Seven, eight, nine, ten, eleven, twelve. Just like at Jama's site."

"Twelve what?"

"That's the million-shekel question. You want to look?"

But before Cavalcante could supplant Molly on the stone perch, Deeqa, who had moved to the entry, whispered, "I hear something!"

"Great." Molly refocused the light onto the fallen mujahedeen. "He had a gun. Better get it. You know how to use it?"

"I do," said Deeqa.

Molly wasn't surprised. She said, "If it ain't Milstein, shoot it." Then she turned the beam back on the ceiling. "I'm not leaving until I know what the hell these are."

Jackson's first impulse upon watching the kitchen truck go up in flames was to follow Leveille-Gaus into the desert to get as far from Tikriti's mujahedeen as possible. Milstein's gumption shocked him. He saw his Jewish colleague pouring the incendiary liquid over the truck but made no move to assist. If the plan worked, great. If not, Milstein alone would pay. But it had worked magnificently. And when Milstein, rather than dart for freedom headed instead at a run back into Ur, Jackson figured he better follow, stopping along the way to claim a rifle one of the Iraqi fire fighters foolishly left behind. If Jesus was in Ur, Jesus was coming home with him.

Milstein had hoped to light up all the Iraqi vehicles and use Cavalcante's truck for their escape. Heroic as he had been, though, reckless like Judas, fear at the last had gotten the better of him. Too many Iraqis. Too little time. The diversion would have to do. If they could make their escape in the desert, there was no reason Tikriti should be able to find them again. Jesus had taken a backseat to saving the woman he loved.

As the kitchen truck burst into flames and the fire miraculously spread beyond Milstein's dreams, he dashed back into the ruins of the Chaldean city hoping the hell he could find Cavalcante and that Cavalcante had found Molly.

Now, like a pair of wind-up lovers embracing as they turned atop a mechanical toy, Molly and Cavalcante stood on the stone block, their attention directed at the twelve symbols carved into the frame above them.

"Twelve," Cavalcante said. "Certainly not for the Tribes of Israel. Nor for the books of the Old Testament."

"Jesus had twelve disciples," Molly said. "One for each? But why? God, could they all be buried in one place?"

The notion astounded Molly. Such a find would magnify the wonder, or folly, of finding Jesus alone.

Cavalcante said, "Peter and Paul died in Rome. After Jesus' death, the disciples scattered."

Of course. A frantic Molly couldn't help being diverted by Deeqa hovering in the doorway, nervously cocking and uncocking the trigger of Aden's Kalashnikov rifle.

"You still hearing noises?" Molly asked her.

"Yes. But I can't tell from where." The girl had acted marvelously so far but was beginning to show signs of nerves. Molly was reminded of Afghanistan when her friend and colleague Anicet Kashimura had warned her that tanks were approaching their dig site. Disastrously, Molly had ignored her. Anicet had nearly died. So had Molly. So when Aden began to awaken, moaning his way back into consciousness, Molly angrily jumped down from the stone block and gave him one resounding slug with her flashlight. He never moved again.

"I think you killed him," Cavalcante said.

"In the line of duty," Molly replied, too distressed by other matters to care that much.

"At the very least he'll be seeing stars."

Molly's head shot up. "What did you say?"

"I think you killed him."

"No. About seeing stars. Jesus, Nina! That's it!"

In an instant, Molly was back on the stone block. Cavalcante had to step off as Molly, in her excitement, claimed the perch for herself. The beam of her flashlight stopped on each symbol one at a time.

"*Fuck!*" she said. "Why didn't I see it? We talked about the stars—I need Teddy."

"You want a stuffed animal?"

"Kwiatkowski. Nina, these are stars! Constellations! The zodiac! Hannaniah wrote horoscopes, she loved the stars. She must have navigated by them."

"On land?"

"Why not? Each constellation symbolizes something. The poem!" Molly recalled lines from one of Hannaniah's lamentations on the loss of Jerusalem. There was a connection between the star symbols and the specifically articulated and structured verses. But what?

"Shit," she said. "Your black binder with Hannaniah's writings. Who knows where the hell it is now? *Shit!*"

"We better be going," Deeqa warned from the doorway. "*Now!* Someone's coming!"

Molly didn't move. Instead, she traced the beam of her light one by one on the twelve star signs.

"*Now!*" Deeqa urged.

"I need to memorize these symbols! There's no time to write them down."

But Cavalcante grabbed Molly by the hand and pulled her out of the room. "This way!" she insisted. To the right. Two blocks, then another right down a wider avenue toward the city gate.

Molly took a quick glance behind her. The moon, which on the occasional evening could be quite romantic, tonight was playing look-out for the gods of war and mischance. Someone was racing after them down this Chaldean boulevard. More than someone. A lot of someones. And when one of them, shouting in Arabic, fired his weapon at her, Molly guessed it wasn't Milstein.

"*Hurry!*" she shouted. But the gap was closing. She was exhausted, and, worse, Cavalcante was groaning, holding her side, slowing to a halt.

"Nina!"

"I can't!"

To her everlasting glory and Molly's eternal gratitude, Deeqa, Nina's twenty-year-old pick-up, whirled, aimed Aden's Kalashnikov down the avenue and gave Tikriti and his men something to think about. Once her finger hit the trigger, it sent an entire clip up the avenue, sending the Iraqi mujahedeen belly down in the moonlight.

"Go!" she yelled. "I'll cover you!"

"I think not," Molly said. Such a brave girl would be carnal fodder for Tikriti's men when they got theirs hands on her. And they would soon enough. Already they were shooting back. One bullet winged Molly's shoulder. A second would have hit Cavalcante if Molly hadn't pushed her friend down just a moment before it whisked over their heads.

Deeqa screamed, "I don't have another clip!"

Molly said, "Wonderful."

That, thankfully, was when she heard the ear-piercing noise of an ambulance siren, looked back, and saw the flashing red lights of the hospital vehicle Milstein had commandeered for their rescue. He screeched to a halt beside them, bullets shattering the windshield. He leaned out his window, ducking glass, and hollered, "Back door! Let's get the hell out of here!"

"What about Dr. Leveille?"

"We can't go back!"

Then in reverse—Molly, Cavalcante, and Deeqa barely in the door and on the floor—Milstein hurtled back down the roadway, spun a circle to face forward, and sped at a body-jarring clip out of the city and down the highway into the desert.

"West!" Molly shouted above the siren, which Milstein had forgotten to turn off.

"Why?" he shouted back.

"Teodor! We need him!" From the back of the truck, where she, Cavalcante, and Deeqa had been lying, panting, she crawled to the front cab of the ambulance. "And, Milstein?"

"Yes?"

"Turn off the damn siren."

With a guilty smile, he did. Only then could Molly collapse in the seat beside him and, after a few minutes of quiet driving, lean over and reward his cheek with a kiss. His smile broadened.

"It doesn't take much to please you men, does it?" she said, smiling back at him. "Thank you, Andrew. I think you can justifiably shed the Judas coat."

"That remains to be seen. Do you know where Jesus is?"

"Not quite. Teodor might, although he doesn't know it."

"Kwiatkowski?"

"The astronomer. And Hannaniah. I need her poem. But we lost the damned binder somewhere."

"We lost the binder, yes. But …" Cavalcante joined Molly at the front of the ambulance. "Naturally," she said, "I always keep a copy."

Tikriti regrouped as best his temper would allow. Had his troops been Iraqi Republican Guards, none of this would have happened. The case would now be closed. Jesus would be his. The Americans would be dead and no one of any consequence would be the wiser. Unfortunately, Allah had called mujahedeen to his service who were little better than shoemakers and pimps. Aden had survived his brush with the three women only to have Tikriti put a bullet in his head as encouragement to the rest of his men to fight better the next time. Then he got behind the wheel of his Humvee, waved his arm like a wagon master in the old American West, and started out on the trail of the escaped archaeologists. This time when he caught up with them, as he surely would, he would make no mistakes.

CHAPTER 18

Leveille-Gaus stumbled around in the darkness for two hours before he found a highway heading east toward the city of Nasiriyah. He waited until daylight before moving and kept his eyes peeled for the first friendly vehicle to pass. Fortunately for him, it was British, because he didn't want American military interference. Giving the English soldiers a half-truth about what happened at Ur, he finagled a ride into the city, into a military encampment where, upon his first opportunity to be alone, he placed several phone calls. It was the last, at eight in the morning, that was the most important.

"I've lost them," he said to his superior. "But I think I know where Dr. O'Dwyer will take them. She won't leave her Polish lover in the desert."

"And then?"

"Rendezvous with me. Can you keep surveillance on them from a distance once we've located them?"

"We have been tracking you from the very beginning," came the heavily accented response. "By satellite."

"Then Jesus is still ours. It will be up to you what happens to the rest. I think you know my advice."

The army officer who had killed in many countries on several continents knew exactly what Leveille-Gaus meant.

As for Jackson, he kept well hidden within the bowels of Ur. Luckily, Tikriti had lost all interest in him and, instead, chased after

Milstein and O'Dwyer. Which was fine by Jackson. He'd been a nose guard in college. A little hardship didn't bother him. He'd trek to the nearest American military base at Nasiriyah, contact General Eisenstadt, and bring in reinforcements. People who were willing to kill for freedom, Jesus, and America. And it wouldn't be that difficult to find the wayward archaeologists either.

Scrounging through the burnt wreckage of the kitchen truck, he found a bottle of Poland Springs Water, took a sip, and began his march eastward. Not having much trust in Milstein, he had slipped a tiny tracking device in the Jewish intelligence officer's pants pocket. If it was still there, he'd be able to locate the archaeologists in short order.

You gotta love American technology, he thought and headed down the road to success. An hour later a convoy of American military trucks picked him up.

Driving west along the highway in the middle of the night, Molly sat in quiet concentration over a blank page of white paper. She drew from memory the constellations she had seen in Ur and in the Al-Anbar, trying to do it in the order they had been carved into the stone.

Cavalcante and her new Iraqi friend researched the copied sheaf of Hannaniah material, until Molly, at last, rested a weary head against the ambulance wall and said, "Want to take a look?"

"You bet."

Molly stretched and handed the Italian her work of art. Deeqa looked on in interest while they traded Hannaniah's poem for Molly's perusal.

Once more, O City of Life, your daughter cries for you. Seven tears.

A lone flame, darkness's guide, shines in the desert
Leading her, the king, his queen, to the Father of all.

"Jesus, I'm stupid," Molly muttered. She dropped into the passenger side seat beside Milstein, clasping the Star of David pendant in her hand. The road was theirs, nothing in front, behind, or in the lane heading east. Just the stars above. Milstein floored the accelerator.

"How so?" he asked.

"I've focused my whole scientific life on the past and don't know squat about the stars. This was so obvious!"

"Don't blame yourself. Nobody else got it either."

Molly spoke the first verse of Hannaniah's poem. " 'A lone candle, darkness's guide.' " Staring through the bullet-cracked windshield, she could discern the constellation of the Little Bear and at its tail Polaris, the North Star. "Hannaniah was telling whoever read this poem where to look for the survivors of Jerusalem, those who followed her father."

Mother, your people fly before you. Six children.
Romulus and Remus breathing fire upon the king's crown.
We are lost. We are separate. We are rootless and mad.

"I figured the second line referred to Rome chasing the children of David out of Jerusalem. But maybe Hannaniah only wanted us to think that. What if she really meant the constellation of the twins, Gemini?"

"You drew it here," Cavalcante said from the back of the ambulance, indicating one of the twelve symbols Molly had penned on the blank page.

"I did?"

"I thought you didn't know astronomy," Milstein said.

"I don't. I read the horoscope first thing in the morning. Just before the obituaries." Molly took the drawing from Cavalcante and read it. Knowing she was forming constellations, she had connected the star dots to create pictures. Her Gemini, with the twin stars Castor and Pollux, looked more like a daddy long legs without the daddy.

Blow the ram's horn, Father. It is Yom Kippur. Five notes.
Your daughter plays the lute. Your wife sings her song.
Praise the shepherd who dies, she sings. Adore the world that
is born.

Upon the back of a horse the savior rides. Four legs.
The fisherman sinks, the bearer of life disappears.
What rises is the Trinity to welcome home the reborn.

In the corpse of the night we unite again as one. Three hearts.
Mother, Father, your children have come home.
At their daughter's fingertips, the fisherman will plant his seed.

Rest where he casts his nets. Two lamps alight.
And where your daughter's arms reach out to her people
There in the heart of David we wait for you in silence.

"Are you sure that's Gemini?" Molly asked, holding up the Star of David.

"It's my star sign," said Deeqa. "You must be an Aries."

"Born Easter morning." One sign confirmed, Molly studied her crude sketch work. "So, if Romulus and Remus are Gemini, we might reasonably assume the king, his queen, their daughter are not

Jesus, Hannaniah, and her mother but are also constellations, the three symbols on the top points of the star."

"And on the bottom?" Cavalcante asked "The dog's snout?"

"Another constellation, I suppose. The fisherman isn't Peter. It's Pisces. Or, at least, what he's caught in his nets." Molly moved the star closer to the overhead light.

Now that it began to make sense, Molly wondered, what sense did it make?

"That sign," Deeqa pointed to the simplest one, containing only three stars, "is definitely not from a horoscope. It's just a triangle."

"True. But it's the middle symbol in the star, and Hannaniah is nothing if not consistent."

Maybe it was just a triangle. But clearly that sign was the most important one of all. It was the needle of the compass, the directional beacon. But toward what? The fisherman's catch? Pisces? How did that direct Hannaniah's children, her followers, to wherever she had ended her days?

Refocusing on her crude star map, Molly remembered one other important clue Hannaniah had left. One dot, one star from each constellation, was larger than the rest. With a quiver in the pit of her stomach, she glanced at the Star of David medallion then back to her map, enlarging the appropriate star in each constellation.

Damn it, Hannaniah, what are you trying to tell us?

"Wait a minute," she suddenly said to Cavalcante. "There's one other piece to the puzzle."

"That being?"

"You remember what Dr. Leveille said when we were trying to figure out how to start? We each had a piece of the puzzle. The star, the poem, and the horoscope. The horoscope, Nina! What were the words?"

"Five houses from the mother, six from the father," Milstein said.

"No, no. Something else." Molly concentrated on the road ahead, into the darkness of the desert. "'She is the third.' That was it. 'She is the passage.' Do you remember now?"

"'From her father's kingdom,'" Milstein said. "'Past her mother's throne. Beyond the daughter's chained feet. There at last the three shall unite and point the way to the Fisherman.'"

Molly's heart quickened as she drew a line from an enlarged dot in one constellation to one in a second.

Jesus, she thought and gazed out the side window toward the night sky and the stars above. Is that it, Hannaniah? A map not out of gold or paper, but an eternal one?

"Al Muthallath," Deeqa said quietly.

"What?"

"The triangle. That's how we say it in Arabic."

"Al Muthallath!" Molly exclaimed. "The Triangle! Jesus, we were standing on Him!"

She had seen the villagers celebrate their morning prayers on a sand dune south of the town. She had wondered briefly, disinterestedly, why they would carry their prayer mats into the desert and why they would pray in an unusual form, in a pattern unlike any she had ever seen before.

Tradition, she had thought. An odd ritual handed down to the people of that village because it had been performed that way in the past when it had meant something more to those who offered their prayers to Allah. But in those long-ago days, perhaps as long ago as two thousand years before, the people hadn't been praying to Allah at all. They had faced westward not toward Mecca, but toward Jerusalem.

She might have ripped the steering wheel out of Milstein's hands then and there, spun the ambulance off the road to head in the direction they needed to go, if she weren't suddenly blinded by the headlights of a truck coming smack down the center of their lane at a speed to kill.

Despite his injuries, Kwiatkowski put his life experience to good use reanimating the military truck damaged by the mujahedeen mortar shell. His father had been an auto mechanic many years before he became one of the richest entrepreneurs in Poland. He had also been an imaginative and successful blackmarketeer under the rule of the communists, a human magnet for the tiny filings of information that adhered to his life as he pushed and crawled his way to the top. He was a devout Catholic and a loyal bureaucrat. He was a super-patriot and a mobster who loved collecting the finest in underground archaeological prizes. Having successfully climbed the financial and political ladder of Polish society, Kwiatkowski was determined that his son, his only child, would inherit his wealth the hard way, by learning as he had, by trusting in his own skills, which would have to be many and broad-reaching given the duplicitous nature of the world, and, therefore, by depending upon no one but himself.

Teodor Kwiatkowski had learned so much from his adored father that he was able to forget his own pain, focus solely on his feelings for Molly, and do what he had to do to replace the flat tire, patch up the gas tank, and set out after Molly in a dawn-of-the-dead, bare-bones army truck. Unfortunately, the labor had taken so much out of him that, by the time he approached the neighborhood of Ur, his eyelids drooped, his head sank, his truck swerved into the wrong lane, and a siren blasted him awake .

Kwiatkowski sat bolt upright, flattening his brake to a tire-rending stop that left chunks of rubber on the highway. He was still shaking when Molly jumped out of the ambulance and ran to his window.

"Kwiatkowski? Jesus! What were you trying to do?"

"Sleep. Bad timing. Sorry."

Molly pulled his door open, climbed up beside him, and took his face in her hands. "You look a mess. Lucky we have an ambulance." Then she gave him a long, deep kiss, before hauling him out of the truck.

"We have to hurry," she said. "Al Muthallath. Remember that desert village we were in? It means triangle in Arabic. That's where Hannaniah is!"

"Huh?" Kwiatkowski was still shaking off the effects of fatigue. He placed his hands on Molly's shoulders, felt her essence so close to him after they had been apart for so many hours. He couldn't resist a kiss either. Gentle, probing, good enough to disorient her briefly.

"Teddy, not now," she said, and her eyes said, *But definitely later.* "Is there anything in the truck we need to salvage?"

"Father Teague. Unless you want to leave him. Not much else."

"No. We'll bring him. Then you rest. I need your astronomical expertise. I need you to be sharp, Teddy. The game ain't up yet."

With Milstein's and Deeqa's help, Molly carried the bodybag holding the remains of Father Teague into the ambulance. Then Deeqa directed Milstein to the first exit that would take them northwest toward the Triangle, Hannaniah, and, perhaps, to her father, called Jesus the Son of God.

Kwiatkowski slept for a little more than an hour. A pre-med student before the American liberation, Deeqa attended to his wounds when he woke up. Impatient and excited, Molly was less deferential and thrust her constellation drawing into his hands.

"We figured out what those symbols meant at Ur, at Jama's excavation, and on the Star of David. They're star signs, constellations. Hannaniah's poem, the horoscope, everything corroborates what should have been so damned obvious. Her references to people and things were references to stars."

Molly jumped up and poked Milstein in the shoulder.

"Stop the ambulance!"

"What? Tikriti could be on our asses right now!"

"I don't care! Pull over!"

Milstein obeyed, and as soon as he had parked on the shoulder of the road, Molly leapt from the back of the truck, her attention skyward.

Once Kwiatkowski was beside her, she said, "In one verse Hannaniah says, 'Upon the back of a horse four legs strong the daughter rides.' There's a horse constellation, isn't there? Pegasus or something."

"You drew it here." Kwiatkowski pointed to one of Molly's creations on her star map. "And that one is Cepheus the king," he said, indicating another.

"The king!" Molly and Cavalcante cried in unison. "Then what is the one at the bottom?" Molly asked.

"Andromeda, Cepheus's daughter."

Molly's heart leaped like a student who had just aced her final exam. "Then that's it! You're a genius, Mr. Kwiatkowski. Pop the cork. We have lift-off." She hugged Kwiatkowski, then high-fived Cavalcante. "Let me guess," she said. "The one to the right of the triangle, the squiggly W: the queen?"

Kwiatkowski nodded. "Cassiopeia, Andromeda's mother. They belong together in an ancient myth. Andromeda was chained to a rock until she was rescued by Perseus, another constellation."

"Thank you, my dear Perseus!" Molly wrapped herself in her own arms to keep warm in the chilly desert night. "Point them out to me now, Teddy. Up there, in the sky."

"You can't see them at these latitudes this time of year. They're autumn constellations."

"Autumn as in Yom Kippur, the Day of Atonement, when Hannaniah began her journey."

Molly took Kwiatkowski's chin in her hand and turned his face to look up at her. "Can you draw a star map?" she asked.

"You mean a real one?"

"Is there another kind? Exactly as they are configured in the sky. Cepheus, Andromeda, Cassiopeia, Pegasus, all of them that I've drawn. 'Where the daughter's arms reach out to her father, There in the heart of David we wait for you in silence.' Hannaniah and her father."

Of course, she already knew where they were going. Al Muthallath. The Triangle. But she wanted confirmation. She had already made three mistakes. First at Ur. Then at Al Muthallath. Finally, believing Jama's site was the correct one. She couldn't afford to make another error. Tikriti was after them. Leveille-Gaus and Jackson wouldn't be far behind, and she didn't intend any of them to desecrate that holy site or the holiest of remains that might lie within.

Back inside the ambulance, resting against the wall as Milstein started the motor, she reined in her nervous excitement and gazed at the sealed remains of her friend Father Teague, offering a silent prayer to those she was about to disturb after two thousand years.

Hannaniah, forgive me, she prayed. Jesus, forgive me. I know exactly what I am about to do. Forgive me for doing it. No disrespect meant whatsoever. Amen.

After thirty minutes, Kwiatkowski came to sit beside her. He handed her his rendering of the zodiac.

"The king, his queen, their daughter," he showed her. "The Horse, Perseus the Hunter. Andromeda seems to be raising her arms to him rather than to Cepheus."

"Yes, but ..." Molly took Kwiatkowski's map and his pencil and connected three dots, one from the father, one from the mother, and one from the daughter. Extending that line, though, took her nowhere, into a gap in the constellations between Perseus the Hunter and Pisces.

"What's out here, Teddy? Nothing? There must be something. Hannaniah clearly says the three shall meet once again, be united, and point the way to the fisherman."

"Well, yuh, there is, but it isn't much of a constellation. It's this." And in the vacancy between the hunter and the fisherman's fish, Kwiatkowski drew a triangle. "Triangulum," he said.

"Now draw straight down from the apex of the triangle to Pisces, and where does it take us?"

Kwiatkowski's line through the tip of Triangulum did not lead, as Molly had expected, to the second star in the chain of the constellation, but to the fourth. Kwiatkowski saw the disappointment in her face. "Well, wait a minute," he said, and drew in a second star close to but apart from the constellation of the fish.

"What's that?" Molly asked.

"The M74 galaxy. Hannaniah might have confused it for a double star, part of Pisces," he said. Molly's face lit up as bright as any constellation and she kissed him hard and happily.

"You're a genius, Mr. Kwiatkowski!" She took in a breath. "If the stars are our map," she said, "if we assume Andromeda the Daughter, the jagged V, is also a map of the Tigris and Euphrates, then the second star in Pisces, west of Ur on an earthly map, is where we'll find Hannaniah. Al-Muthallath."

"At this point anything's possible," Kwiatkowski said. "Might I suggest that if Al Muthallath is wrong, we leave it alone, go home, forget this ever happened?"

"You might. Except for one thing."

"That being?"

"I'm not wrong. Not this time. The only question is, what will we find when we get there?"

Al-Muthallath appeared out of the desert plain like a mirage, an apparent illusion of mud-brick buildings catching the first dim rays of the morning sun. The world was still and peaceful, as yet too early even for the devout Muslims of the village to leave their homes and march to the sandy mound to utter their prayers.

Everyone in the ambulance had taken a turn at getting some sleep. They had left the highways behind several hours earlier and crossed the last hundred miles of Iraq through desert waste. The ride was bumpy but didn't cost the exhausted passengers any shut-eye. Molly alone had trouble sleeping. She couldn't get out of her mind where they were going and what they were about to do.

The world had changed two thousand years ago. Out of the backwaters of Judea had been born a child who would become the most famous and followed man in the history of the human race, a man worshiped as God by hundreds of millions of people, a man revered even by those who didn't believe in him as a prophet of goodness and love.

In the two thousand years since he had departed this earth, either through death or resurrection, nothing happened on the planet that was not somehow connected to his mission. Human faith changed. Governments and empires flourished or failed because of his word and the power and might of his loyal followers. Even in the lands where Jesus was not worshiped as the Son of God, where Mohammed or Buddha or Moses were given greater emphasis, even there people could not live out their lives without the shadow of the Western Jesus cast upon them.

And yet, if Molly and the others had their way, if they succeeded in digging up the ancient prayer hill of Al-Muthallath, people would never look upon Jesus of Nazareth as they had before his body was raised for public witness, before his physical remains were exhumed and exploited for tabloid gratification.

It was a somber and thoughtful Molly who drove the last miles across the barren Iraqi landscape toward the triangle. I believe in Jesus, she thought. And yet I need to know.

"Tired?"

She looked at Milstein who had done most of the driving but had given way to her in the past two hours so he could get some sleep.

"How long have you been awake?" she asked.

"A bit. I didn't want to disturb you. I could see you were deep in thought. You and Kwiatkowski have a thing going, huh?"

Molly had to smile. She knew what Milstein was thinking. A little bit of her felt some regret that she could not get to know him better. "Jealous?" she asked. "Don't be. I've never committed to a man before. I love my work too much."

"I think that's about to change." Milstein yawned and gazed out a jagged hole in the windshield. The remaining shards of glass reflected the sunlight. Ahead, Al-Muthallath appeared out of the dawn as a line of small rectangular bumps in the desert. "When … if we find Hannaniah and her father, not all the security in the world will keep it quiet. You will be hailed and reviled. We all will."

"Judas all over again." Molly sat up and stretched while gripping the steering wheel. She had thought the same things as Milstein. That was why she was still thinking, plotting. "It doesn't have to be that way," she said. "We need to be fast, efficient, smart. I'll give you this, if we don't find them and move them, one of the others will. Jackson, Leveille, Tikriti. Are you with me, Andrew?"

"One hundred percent. I just want to say one thing before all this unfolds, however it unfolds."

"Yes?"

"When I started this, I was doing it, like you, out of profound scientific curiosity, maybe as a way to hunt down my own ghosts. You know, dead father. Guilty as charged. Now, frankly, I'm doing it for you." Milstein sighed, looked away, then back again directly into Molly's eyes. "Because I love you. You. Not Hannaniah. I hope you don't find that strange or upsetting. I just needed to let you know. In case."

Molly smiled, blushed even. A tear formed in the corner of her eye. She ignored it and reached out to touch Milstein's shoulder. "Not that it matters, Andrew. But I hope we stay friends. Then, who knows? I'm such a fickle woman."

Milstein laughed, which was just what Molly wanted to see. She had raised his spirits. She had given him something to look forward to. And with his spirits buoyed, so were hers. At least for now. God knew they would need to be at their best in the next hours. With the sun on the ascent, with Tikriti at their back, and the world awaiting, they would all need to perform like gods or be damned for the rest of their lives.

A single face peered out an open window in one of the mud-brick dwellings when Molly parked the ambulance at Al Muthallath. It was a little girl's face. She was about four years old and wore a simple robe. She came to the entrance and leaned against the doorframe to watch the strangers exiting the truck. Deeqa approached her and spoke to her in Arabic.

"What time is it?" Kwiatkowski asked.

Cavalcante turned over her wrist to glance at her Powerpuff Girl wristwatch. "Five-thirty. Time for bagels and coffee."

"Almost time for sunrise prayers," Molly said. "I wonder what the people will think when we start to dig up their hill."

"I don't think they'll like it at all," Milstein said. "In fact, they will probably try to stop us."

Molly watched Deeqa talk now with the little girl's mother and father. The father pointed down the street.

"I'm sure they will," she said. "Unless we can convince them we're not going to destroy the site, just take a quick peek."

"How do we do that?" Kwiatkowski asked.

"The same way we were going to do it at Jama's site before we blew our way in." Molly turned to face southwest. "Jerusalem is that way. Why don't we make the bold assumption that Hannaniah placed her entrance into the hill in that direction and start digging there?"

"Except for one thing," Cavalcante said. "What do we dig with?"

Deeqa solved that problem. When she returned from her discussion with the family, she said, "There are tools in a shed up there. Shovels. Spades. I think if we pay them, they might even be willing to help us."

"They don't care if we desecrate their hill?" Milstein asked.

"Apparently, your Mr. Jama was here many years ago. But he only dug a short way into the mound before covering it up again. The people don't know what he found. Just as long as they can pray on top of it, we can do what we want under it."

At least that was what the little girl's father said. But as the word of the archaeologists' return to the village spread and their intention became clear, at least one other villager thought it best to radio Abdul Azim Nur to ask for his opinion.

Nur, on his way to early morning prayers, said, "Let them dig, but don't let them leave." Then, to a lieutenant, he said, "Contact Tikriti. But tell him to do nothing until I arrive."

Molly couldn't begin the excavation fast enough. The people of the village fed them a breakfast of bread and fruit. Then Molly and the others loaded the ambulance with tools and drove the truck directly to the site. It was only seven in the morning, and the sun already tapped streams of perspiration on her brow.

"All right," she told everyone. "This is not going to be your prototypical archaeological dig. This is a huge mound, I'd say two hundred feet long by seventy-five wide. We haven't time to map things out. We're not looking to be overly careful to prevent corruption of the site or anything buried within. We're looking for an entry into a chamber, probably a burial chamber. Once we're inside, then we'll worry about what's there. Deeqa, if there's another truck in the village, we'll need it. Can you try to round one up?"

"What for?"

"To remove bodies."

Apparently, Jama had solved the riddle of the Star of David but couldn't bring himself to open Pandora's box. Molly had no choice. Hannaniah had been consistent so far. In Egypt. In Afghanistan. Here in Iraq. A community of her followers may well have existed at Al Muthallath two thousand years ago, a community of Jews who had passed down their traditions through many generations until those rituals and practices melded with the newer religion forged by Mohammed fourteen hundred years ago. Amazingly, those traditions persisted here at Al Muthallath to this very day. If Hannaniah had built a community beyond the mound, it was no longer visible, but the hill that may have served as a marker for visitors and a holy burial chamber for herself and her father had been protected by the villagers who used it as their mosque.

With less rigorous logic and careful surveying than she had ever used before in her fieldwork, Molly measured a location equidistant from either end of the sloping hill and sank the first shovel into the ground. She and Kwiatkowski dug in one area. Cavalcante and Milstein worked about ten yards away. The plan was to dig toward each, creating a large square trench and increasing the odds of their making a discovery quickly. When members of the village joined them after their morning prayers, the effort multiplied in intensity and speed, and Molly had high hopes of making a find during the morning hours.

Immediately, however, it became clear that this site was not like the first one Mohamoud Jama had investigated. At that archaeological site, Hannaniah's people had constructed a building and covered it up in sand. Here at Al Muthallath, the hill was natural, built of dirt and rocks and sand. If Hannaniah had used it, she would have had to dig into the hill itself, hollow out a portion of it, and construct her burial chamber within. Not at all unfeasible. It just meant that Molly and her crew had more work on their hands with an unknown amount of time in which to do it.

At noon, Molly rested briefly. Thank God Deeqa had brought sun block. The village water was tepid, but the food was nourishing.

She had enough insulin for a few more days. She didn't expect to be in Al Muthallath in a few more days. As the villagers worked with surprising enthusiasm, she took the time to study the star map that Kwiatkowski had drawn for her.

All the stars of the constellations could represent places, towns, landmarks, in the Holy Land and beyond. Travelers could easily lose a papyrus map or Star of David pendant on the arduous journey across the desert or mountains, but the stars remained fixed in the night sky. They might not make an exact map, but they could certainly give the unschooled traveler some direction and would never change or disappear. Ages, generations after Hannaniah's passing, descendants read the stars and returned to their ancestral home.

I love you, Hannaniah, Molly thought. I have lived with you so long, you are a part of me. Whether you are my lost mother or a great ancestor or even myself in a past life, I will find you and I will take care of you.

If Milstein could admit his feelings for Molly, then Molly could do the same for Hannaniah.

With a final swig of warm water, Molly returned to the dig, relieving Cavalcante whose injured ribs ached. She stepped into the expanding trench, approximately ten square yards, stuck her shovel into the gravelly soil, and almost immediately hit gold. "Here! Here!" She dropped to her knees. "I've hit something!"

Cavalcante, Milstein, and Kwiatkowski jumped into the hole beside her. "What is it?" Milstein wiped at his forehead, breathless from his labors. Their faces glowed red, sweating oceans, wide-eyed with excitement.

"Help me dig." Molly's hands shoveled with the speed of a dog uncovering a bone. Like ants following their queen, the villagers dropped what they were doing, rushed to Molly's side and ripped up the soil with their own dirty fingernails. So much for the sanctity of the prayer hill. Even the women and children who had delivered food and drink to the laborers joined in the recovery effort.

Molly widened the area she dug in at a depth of about two feet and exposed an artificial layer that was certainly not a natural part of the hill. "Wood," she said. "Timber. A beam."

"Good work, Molly," Kwiatkowski said.

She dug faster, tearing open the ground with a trowel. Below and to her right, one of the villagers called out.

"He's found something!" Deeqa exclaimed.

In an instant, Deeqa was up, loping like a gazelle, Molly right behind her.

With the force of a powerful magnet, the lucky villager brought everyone down to where he had been digging. Molly quickly supplanted him without any apology. "This is brick," she said. "All right. Dig carefully now. This is flatland. We may have hit a path into the structure, which could lead to a door. From here on, we expand five feet on either side and up into the hill. Let's see if we can find that door."

In earnest, as if they were about to uncover the tomb of Mohammed the Prophet, the villagers eagerly followed Molly's orders. More than two dozen people, divided into two opposing lines, worked their way slowly into and up the hill. They removed more dirt than they could possibly wheelbarrow away.

Even so, as morning gave way to mid-afternoon, the hole in the trench bore archaeological fruit. The original clay brick became a veritable yellow brick road into the interior of the hill. It was at least eight feet wide and on one side ended at a brick wall that rose parallel to the slope of the hill. From there, they dug straight into the hill, as Molly visualized a six-foot-tall entryway into the structure. At about four in the afternoon, she was proven correct.

"Doorway!" Milstein hollered bringing Molly at a run from the ambulance where she had paused to get a drink. Cavalcante was already knocking at the metal entrance with a trowel.

"Copper on wood," she said. "And look here. At the top."

"Oh, my God. Oh, my God." This was it! This was definitely it! No more mistakes. No more blunders. Molly placed her fingers on the Star of David carved into the stone at the top of the door and felt Hannaniah touching it two thousand years before. "This is hers," she said. "Look. The jagged V. Only it isn't a jagged V. It's Andromeda the daughter. And here. To the left of the star. Cepheus, the king, her father."

Molly could have dropped to her behind and bawled like a baby. Tears streamed down her face. She closed her eyes and pressed her hands against the ancient door to regain control. When she opened her eyes again, it was as if she had been transported in time, as she had been through regression, transported to a place where none of the others could go. Kwiatkowski. Cavalcante. Milstein. They were no longer here. They and the villagers of Al Muthallath had stayed behind. When she regained her senses, she was crouched alone at the entrance to the underground chamber. Its door was open and a messenger stood within, beckoning her to come inside.

"I will not hurt you," said the red-haired woman waiting in the shadows of the earth. "Come with me. Let me show you."

She didn't have to tell Molly twice. Molly was on her feet and in the mound in a second. But once inside, she could go no farther. The woman reached out with an open hand as if to touch Molly.

"You are beautiful," she said.

"You are a dream."

The woman moved her hand upward and rotated it in a circle.

Molly followed the gesture and looked up at the ceiling. The perimeter was circular. Lowering her gaze, she saw that eleven doors opened off the central chamber. Above each door was a symbol, a star sign. The woman, moving bonelessly like a ghost, abruptly appeared in the doorway of one of the smaller rooms. The constellation Cepheus was carved into a wooden crossbeam directly over her head. Once there, she chanted in Hebrew.

"Sh'ma Israel, Adonai Elohaynu, Adonai echad." *Hear, O Israel, The Lord our God, the Lord is one.*

And then she faded. Molly rushed forward to grab her, to embrace her, to keep her alive only to end up clutching empty space.

When Kwiatkowski shouted in her ear, "Molly, are you there?" she stared at him, not sure where she was, or when. After a moment she cleared her head of her vision. Then she realized that she had not budged. She crouched before the closed door. Not a minute had passed. Not a breath had she taken.

"God," she muttered. "That was crazy." Then just as suddenly, "Get this door off! We're going in!"

Tikriti was ten miles away, driving full tilt for Al Muthallath. He had recovered from the embarrassment of Ur, but if Nur thought he was going to do nothing when he reached Al Muthallath, then Nur was sadly out of touch with reality. Molly O'Dwyer hadn't returned to the village called The Triangle for nothing. She had discovered something at Ur and slipped away hoping to steal the prize for herself. Tikriti had other plans, a fabulously wealthy contact in Beirut, and a ticket to punch, possibly for oil-rich Bahrain or the Italian Riviera. Many tickets actually. For Tikriti had ten daughters, and he wasn't a selfish man.

Jackson figured he'd have to put every ounce of muscle, political savvy, plus a rewarding retirement package together in order to convince General Eisenstadt, Army Chief of Operations in Baghdad, to lend him one lousy helicopter. Surprisingly, Eisenstadt had told him, "Go with God. And do whatever you have to do."

Armed to the teeth and with a license to do whatever he deemed necessary to complete his mission, that was what Jackson intended to do. He had been raised in the evangelical world by devout parents, although he had never taken faith as seriously as they had. But now that he was confronted with the very real possibility that the remains of Jesus lay under the soil of Al-Muthallath, he began to reflect upon his life, the sins he had committed, and he realized that this might be his one last chance to redeem himself. Nor could he shake the terrible image left in his brain many mornings after he woke up, the blood of Christ on his hands. Fearing the meaning of these nightmares, he would make sure that the Son of God would not be profaned by disbelievers, be they Muslim, Catholic, atheist, or Jew. And if, on the odd chance there were a few dollars to be made in the bargain, well, it could go to charity.

As the UH-60L military helicopter lifted off from the US airbase outside Baghdad, Jackson fingered the trigger of his XM8 Lightweight Assault Rifle, capable of firing 750 rounds per minute, and thought, if only Jesus had had these babies with him at Gethsemane, the Romans woulda been shit.

Leveille-Gaus did not have mixed feelings about what he was about to do. A scientist, he had a profound interest in what lay beneath the mound at Al-Muthallath. He wanted it intact, undamaged, and in his possession. But he had other loyalties as well, very deep and very old, far older than Jesus.

Per orders from his masters, he had persuaded his British army rescuers to escort him to a small town south of Nasiriyah where he would rendezvous with another helicopter. His superiors had tracked Molly to the village in the desert that Leveille-Gaus had previously visited. He cursed himself for failing to see the obvious then sat in the shade of a palm tree and did the only thing he could do: wait. His people were not used to failure, did not fail, would not fail. Jesus was as good as his already. In the time remaining before the helicopter scooped him up and off to Al-Muthallath, Leveille-Gaus imagined how he would dissect the remains of the Nazarene and how he would use the DNA to change the world.

CHAPTER 19

They pried open the two-thousand-year-old door with crowbars, Kwiatkowski levering from the top and Molly from the bottom. Wood splintered, mortar sprayed, stone broke into tiny pebbles and flew into Molly's eyes. With a quick swipe of her hand, she cleared her eyes and kept working. Several attempts and fifteen minutes later, the door surrendered to the efforts of the archaeologists.

Milstein and Cavalcante kept the villagers at bay. The last thing they wanted was a mad rush into the ancient tomb. Deeqa spoke to the people in their native tongue and kept them apprised of what was happening. The patient men, women, and children sat on their haunches in the sand or on blankets as if they were on a picnic by the sea and ate dinner as the sun made its westward journey toward night.

When the door gave way, stale warm air blew past Molly's face, Jewish spirits escaping into the light of day for the first time in twenty centuries. Molly almost felt their essence, saw their faces, heard their delighted voices. She hesitated to go inside and stumbled back against Kwiatkowski.

"Are you all right, Molly?"

She stared into the darkness beyond, mute, expressionless, like a child who has witnessed something so appalling she can't speak.

"Molly?"

"Do you know what is in there?" she whispered at last, breathless, wondering.

"Maybe nothing."

"No," she insisted. "There is something. I feel it. This is it. I felt it coming out when we opened the door. I felt it brush by me. She's inside."

"You're imagining things."

Molly shook her head. She looked back into Kwiatkowski's eyes, touched his hand. "Non-believer," she kidded. She wrapped her fingers about Kwiatkowski's, gripped them tight. "Take my hand," she said, pulling him forward. "I'm not sure I can go in by myself."

Day quickly vanished. Inside, the chamber was cool. Milstein and Cavalcante came in behind her.

"There's a passageway," he said.

Cavalcante shone her light as far into the darkness as it would go. "A long one. I don't see an end."

"No markings." Uptight and nervous as Molly was, she kept her professional wits about her and focused on the walls of the mud-brick corridor and on Cavalcante's light. "I feel a breeze. Up ahead."

Dropping Kwiatkowski's hand, she took the flashlight from Cavalcante and pressed on, feeling her way with one hand while the other created a line of light along the floor, up the wall, and along the ceiling.

"It goes in very deep," she said. "They may have hollowed out the entire hill."

"Can you make out anything? Any carvings or symbols?"

"No." Her voice sounded dead in the narrow confines of the hallway. The ceiling was low enough that she could touch it with her hand, and the walls were a mere four feet apart. The structure was built of the same mud bricks and bitumen mortar as the ziggurat of Ur.

"Be careful," Molly said. The arc of her flashlight had shifted from ceiling to floor. "There are steps ahead. Three, four, going down."

Before she reached them, another surge of air, cooler than the first, rushed past her, spooking her. She shot her beam of light into a much larger open space, half expecting to see Jesus of Bethlehem Himself standing in the darkness, admonishing her with silent reproach for her blasphemy.

"How dare you enter this House of God," he might have declared. "You who have sinned, faithless and forsaken."

"I don't dare," Molly would have replied, then fallen to her knees and begged his forgiveness.

Of all times for her to smell smoke, this was not the best.

"*What is that?*" she shouted, her senses suddenly pricked back into reality, panic rising in her voice. For a fleeting moment, she was five years old again, cringing from the flames that had taken her mother's life.

"What?" Kwiatkowski said behind her.

"*Smoke!* I smell smoke!"

"You're imagining it."

"No, I'm not!" She sniffed the air, a cat sensing an enemy. As an archaeologist, she had entered tombs many times before and had never felt such a compulsion to flee for her life. She trembled. *Why now?* Kwiatkowski's strong hands on her shoulders calmed her, while Cavalcante's tiny, lithe frame stepped past her inside, more daring than she.

"I smell something, too," she said. "But I don't think it's smoke. It's musty. *Dio mio!*" She turned a circle. "Molly, toss me the flashlight."

Cavalcante held it aloft and exposed a vast circular space, with smaller rooms opening from the larger. Eleven in all. "Do you know what this is?" she asked with awe.

"The pot at the end of the rainbow," Milstein said. He stepped past Molly who could not bring her shaking knees to move. As Cavalcante directed the light, Milstein counted the rooms. "Eleven.

Why eleven and not twelve, Molly? The zodiac should have twelve. Shine there, Nina."

Milstein pointed, and Cavalcante followed his finger with the flashlight. What finally got Molly to move, what finally snapped her out of her frightened stupor, was the sign on the wood on the lintel above the exposed entrance.

"Andromeda," she whispered. "The daughter."

It was at that propitious moment that Ghazi Al-Tikriti drove into Al-Muthallath. Some of his mujahedeen were native to the village, others had friends who lived here. As a result, rather than take up arms or rush to shoot somebody, the members of the insurrection and the men, women, and children of The Triangle embraced, joked, and shared their food. None of which pleased Tikriti, who gathered up the few of his soldiers he could count on, and was about to enter the tomb of the hill, when he heard a familiar sound.

Turning to look over his shoulder, he saw the familiar sight that went with the familiar sound. "Shit!" he swore in perfect English, as he was raked by the rotary winds of Richard Jackson's UH-60L helicopter with its armed crew of eleven American mercenaries and its advanced American technology.

He considered standing up to the Americans and fighting them. He considered the possibility of running for his Humvee and trying to escape. Surrender was unthinkable. But by then it was already too late. Jackson had no intention of letting anyone do anything. For the second resurrection of Christ Jesus, there could be no living witnesses.

Leveille-Gaus waited and waited, hovering in the air over the Al-Anbar desert, still thirty miles from The Triangle. So close, and yet so far, he felt like a frustrated commuter on a passenger train that had inexplicably stopped to make him late for a vital appointment.

"What? What?" he demanded of the operations officer in command of the helicopter.

"We've been ordered to stand down, to wait."

"But why? We're so close?"

"Another helicopter has gotten there ahead of us. Something's going on. We don't know what yet, but we're not flying into a trap."

"Christ Almighty! Who?" But then, of course, Leveille-Gaus figured out who. Jackson. The Americans, Goddamn them! Which left him with one unanswered question. How far would his people go to resurrect the man they had been accused of killing two thousand years before?

Molly stood transfixed before the jagged V that was really the constellation Andromeda on the lintel above the doorway that was surely the entrance to the tomb of Hannaniah.

Well, old girl, she thought, this is it. At long last we meet. But she still couldn't bring herself to move.

"How do you feel, Molly?" Kwiatkowski asked her.

"Like lunch is about to come up."

"What do you want to do?"

"Go home."

"Really?"

"I don't think we're supposed to be here."

"Of course, we are, Molly," Milstein said. "We're family. Leveille-Gaus has been here. He'll figure out the puzzle eventually. Jackson won't give up on it either. We've got to move them. We have no choice."

"Move them? How? We've got one fucking ambulance!"

Molly took a step into the cavernous core of the hill. Her anger and desperation scattered whatever hesitation remained. God, she thought, as much as she didn't want to admit it, Milstein is right. This is no longer an issue of archaeological ethics. Do we profane history, or do we let someone else do it?

No. Now it was a matter of preventing the desecration. But that didn't answer the question. How?

Deeqa, who had been standing watch at the entrance to the hill, abruptly ran in. "Mujahedeen!" she cried.

"Oh, great." Molly looked about the dark expanse of the oval. "And we're armed with a flashlight."

She took several steps forward, toward Andromeda, toward Hannaniah, with no thought or plan in mind, simply drawn toward the woman she had bonded with five years before. When the dirt floor beneath her feet gave way and she tumbled into a hole smack in the middle of the oval, she thought briefly that God was paying her back, dragging her into hell. Instead, she landed with a thud on a coffin.

"Jesus!" she heard someone shout. And they probably weren't too far off.

"That's why there were only eleven doorways," she whispered to herself.

"Molly! Are you all right?" Cavalcante shone her light through the rotted timbers Molly had stepped on. She had fallen only a few feet but with enough impact that her elbow had caused an indentation in the pliant old wood of the coffin. Situated on her hands and knees, she stared down onto the coffin which likely contained the remains of the being she had worshiped as God from the moment she surrendered her adoration of her mother. She couldn't breathe.

"Molly!" Kwiatkowski called as if from a great distance. "We have no time!"

"We better make it," she said through clenched teeth and despite trembling arms and legs. *"Flashlight! Now!"*

Cavalcante lowered it. "They're fighting. We hear shooting."

"Bring up the ambulance if you can. I need a crowbar."

Milstein raced up the stairs and down the lightless hall, which rang with the sound of battle beyond. Deeqa followed.

Molly trained the flashlight on the coffin. The artificial sun wavered with the shivering motion of her unsteady nerves. Even so, she held her doglike pose and forced her professionalism to take control.

This cannot be it, she muttered, heart pounding. How could anyone, let alone Hannaniah, his own and only child, bury Yeshuah in such a paltry and pitiful grave? The wood wasn't simply decayed with age. It had never been of quality material. It was a pauper's sepulcher, not the Son of God's. The coffin of a human throw-away.

Molly shuddered. Her beam struck something carved into the wood, letters in Hebrew. She realized then that she faced the foot of the coffin not the head. She refocused the light on the words, still legible in a blue dye after all these centuries.

Oh, my God. At last she understood whose coffin she had landed on, neither Jesus' nor His daughter's.

By the time Milstein and Deeqa reached the entry to the tomb,

Jackson's helicopter had raked the mujahedeen and the villagers indiscriminately with so much fire power, machine guns and grenades, that the dead lay like an unholy prayer blanket over the desert floor from the sacred hill to the outskirts of the town called The Triangle.

"God bless America," Milstein muttered. Then he gripped Deeqa's arm. "Crowbar," he said, picking one up and thrusting it into her hands. "Ambulance," he added, showing her the keys he had pocketed. "Go!"

Pushing her in one direction, he ran in the opposite. The panic and flight of the villagers had led the battle away from the hill, so that his path to the ambulance was at least for the moment unimpeded.

He jumped into the cab and jammed the key into the ignition. Once. Twice. The damned engine snorted and laughed but didn't catch. "*Shit!*" Milstein yelled. A sudden wind stirred the sand around the vehicle. Accompanying it, the horrific sound of a huge mechanical killing bird in flight.

Milstein glanced out his side window as the army UH-60L approached from the north. Gunning the motor, which abruptly sprang to life as if it finally understood the danger it was in, Milstein drove forward. He skirted the hill, hoping to lead the helicopter out into the desert. Anything to buy Molly time.

If he hadn't had to slam on the brakes to dodge a panicked Iraqi mujahedeen, he might have made it, too. But even if it meant saving the life of Ghazi Al-Tikriti, Milstein's instincts forced him to swing the steering wheel sharply to the left. The ambulance careened into the hill the other way. At that point, the tires simply spun in the sand, which meant Milstein was dead in the water.

Which was when the U.S. Army attack helicopter focused its deadly machine gun fire on the ambulance, riddling the van, the cab and Tikriti with hundreds of rounds of ammo. Milstein had joined Tikriti in death before he had been able to shut off the motor.

Molly read the carved inscription on the aged wooden coffin. *Yehudah bar Yushef. The Father is ever forgiving. Light and Darkness made one. The one guarding the other for eternity.*

"These," she said to the others standing above her, "are the bones of Judas Iscariot."

"Buried in a shallow grave," Cavalcante said, "in a fisherman's crate, without any glorification, set apart from the rest of the family, who are buried in these other rooms."

"Which leaves us with twelve bodies to remove in an ambulance while the Army of the Mahdi is killing everything in sight."

"Teddy," Molly said, "you're not helping."

She tried to push herself up and out of Judas's grave using the ground above as leverage. Ever the archaeologist, she cursed the lost opportunity to exhume Judas, to study the entire catacomb. But the mujahedeen had given her little choice. There were only two bodies she cared about now. One should be located in the chamber Andromeda. The other in Cepheus. She and Deeqa would bear the daughter. Kwiatkowski and Cavalcante would have the sacred honor of carrying out the remains of the father.

But first there was the slight problem of the mujahedeen. And, second, when Molly attempted to push herself off Judas's coffin, instead of going up, she went farther down. Her feet plunged through the top of the coffin, down and through the stale cavity of the box, and ended cracking through something else below it.

"What the hell?" she said.

"Molly?"

"I'm stuck! There's something beneath Judas's coffin. Space. I feel air coming up."

"That might explain what you felt before," Cavalcante said. "The breeze and the smoke. Maybe Hannaniah prepared an escape route for us. Maybe there's a back door."

"Don't count on it."

Molly tried to untangle herself. When Deeqa proffered the crowbar to break her free, Molly told her, "No." She extended her hands and let Kwiatkowski grab her by the wrists and pull her out.

"Lose weight," he grunted.

"It's coming off faster than sweat, trust me," she said. A quick scan of the chamber lintels showed her Andromeda and Cepheus. "There and there," she said. "I'll take Hannaniah. Nina, check out Cepheus. Teddy, Deeqa, see if you can lift Judas out of his hole without damaging the coffin any more than I already have, Then pray. I think we've got one chance out of here."

Not if Jackson could help it. His chopper circled the ghost town of Al-Muthallath several times to make sure none of the mujahedeen had escaped.

"What about the villagers?" one of his men asked.

"There are no villagers. They're all mujahedeen."

"Even the women and children?"

"I didn't see any women and children, did you?"

In fact, some of the women and children had fled the battle and cowered within the village, but Jackson didn't care about them. He'd leave them alone. Death occurred all the time in Baghdad and the other Iraqi cities, and no one ever heard about it. Who would care about a remote desert backwater straight out of the Stone Age?

After the third reconnaissance, Jackson was satisfied he had destroyed the enemy without sustaining a single casualty of his own. With a brief command into the radio operator's speaker, he ordered the flying fortress down.

The UH-60L carried a penetration team of eleven men. With Jackson, that made an armed force of twelve, a particularly apt number. Just before jumping ship onto the desert carpet of Al-Anbar, he turned to his men and thought, *We are Christ's new disciples.* Then he cocked the trigger of his pistol. Regrettably, he knew the killing wasn't done.

Leveille-Gaus's helicopter had set down in the desert, too, now only ten miles from Al-Muthallath. Frustrated beyond words, moving like a herky-jerky toy whose battery was winding down, he cursed his masters in vain.

At the bleep-bleep sound from the chopper's radio, he ran and leaned into the belly of the unmarked, undesignated Israeli helicopter. Should the mission fail after all, no one would be able to tie it to Tel Aviv. With anxious eyes he watched the commando leader talk into the machine. Magically, wonderfully, he issued a thumbs-up when he got off.

"We go," he said.

"And Jackson?" Leveille-Gaus asked. "And the others? What do we do with them?"

The Israeli major, a Mossad agent like Leveille-Gaus, stood up to scan the horizon of the approaching night. "For two thousand years, we have been blamed for Jesus' death. Let us from now forward be proclaimed his savior."

CHAPTER 20

Each room off the central core of the catacomb contained a single wooden coffin, far sturdier than Judas's, set on a base of mud brick. An inscription carved into a stone plaque was set into the coffins at their heads. When Molly read the name Hannaniah bat Yeshuah on the coffin in the Andromeda chamber she had entered, she froze.

'Bad timing,' she thought. Frozen like a child, frozen as she remembered being years before when her aunt and uncle, who had gained custody of her, took her to her first confession. They thought it would be a way for her to relinquish her demons. She was scared to death the priest would discover her guilt and cast her straight into hell.

"Molly?"

"I can't do it."

"We have to." Cavalcante strode past her with the crowbar. "It's too dark in Cepheus. Let's open this one first."

"Nina, don't!" Cavalcante glanced at Molly, the Italian's face yellow from the light in Molly's hand. Indecision would kill them, she knew. Worse, indecision would place Hannaniah and her father in the hands of the false faithful, the holier than thou hypocrites, killers and exploiters. Molly had no choice.

"Give me the crowbar," she said. "I'll do it."

While Molly pried at the lid of Hannaniah's coffin, Kwiatkowski and Deeqa raised the surprisingly light burial container of Judas known as the betrayer. Molly supposed that Judas may have died in Jerusalem long before Hannaniah's death or her father's. Under regression, she had seen Judas hoisted beside Yeshuah on a cross, but she still wasn't ready to concede the validity of those descents into the past. Half truth, half dream, who could say what they really were? But given all that she did know, and accepting biblical accounts, Judas may well have preceded his older brother in death and his body may have been exhumed and reburied here years later. Hence the poor quality of the wood. Or Hannaniah might have had another purpose altogether.

What excited Kwiatkowski after he had lifted the decayed coffin to the floor above was not the occupant of the grave but what lay beneath it. Dirt and rocks scraped the soles of his feet, but there was something else under the natural deposit from the hill. Shifting his feet in the darkness, he felt a hard subsurface only inches below the dirt.

"Deeqa, I could use some more light."

"Molly has the flashlight," the Iraqi girl said. She breathed deeply and every few seconds looked behind her toward the corridor, anticipating at any moment the appearance of mujahedeen fighters.

"In that case …"

The soft sound of cotton ripping, then the flick of a cigarette lighter, and Kwiatkowski's blazing shirt gave him temporary light.

"There's a trap door!" he shouted. "Look!" But his makeshift torch singed his fingers and he tossed the scrap aside. Another tear, another flick later, and Kwiatkowski dug with one hand around the edges of the dirt floor of Judas's tomb.

"Here!" he said. "A latch!"

When the light extinguished again, Kwiatkowski stepped to one edge of the hole and pulled the trapdoor open. A rush of air caught him in the face. Deeqa shouted to Molly.

"We've found something!" she cried.

Kwiatkowski didn't wait. Removing his entire shirt, he shouted to Deeqa, "Get me the crowbar!"

"But ..."

"Just do it!"

The girl disappeared. Kwiatkowski waited in darkness. Months before when his father had first expressed an interest in this mission, Kwiatkowski had advised him it would be a colossal waste of time and money. It was unlike his father to behave frivolously on a mythological hunt for an over-hyped biblical figure, even if he was the so-called Son of God. Michael Kwiatkowski had startled his son by exploding in a furious rage. Kwiatkowski had never realized how deep his father's faith was. It had held him together when his wife, Kwiatkowski's mother, had died. After that, Kwiatkowski had had no choice but to obey his father. Now, standing in the tomb of Jesus' betrayer, in a hidden subterranean cave in the middle of the Iraqi desert, even he felt something mystical beyond anything that mathematics could explain or describe. And even if capture and death were moments away, he needed to know what lay in the tomb within the tomb and what the hell Hannaniah had been doing setting this trap.

When Deeqa returned and handed down the crowbar in the darkness, he wrapped his shirt around it, tied the shirt on with a lace from his shoes, and created a torch with his Bic. He was astounded by what was revealed.

"Molly!" he yelled up. "Get your ass in here!"

Jackson didn't bother with Al-Muthallath. He let a squad of his men filter through the town and make sure they wouldn't be ambushed by hidden terrorists. He set his sights on the hill mount of The Triangle, which he could see had already been excavated. His gun was unholstered. The sun was going down. It was time to end this.

"They're inside," one of his men told him as they approached the entry that Molly had exposed to the light of day.

"Could be," Jackson said.

At the opening to the hill, he peered into the darkness. "Damn," he said. "Get flashlights. I can't see shit."

When his man raced back to their chopper, Jackson called into the hill, "Dr. O'Dwyer. Milstein. For your own safety, come on out. Now."

No sound came from within the hill. "Did you hear me?" he yelled. He looked back toward the UH-60L, anxious, impatient. He was standing on the most important find in the history of the human race. Once he brought it to light, he would be honored, ennobled, perhaps enriched. Except for one goddamned thing. For all the frigging technology they had packed onto their multi-million dollar flying machine, they hadn't thought to bring any flashlights. Jackson fired his weapon into the entrance of the hill.

"Fuck it!" he shouted and charged in. "Who needs a goddamned light?"

Before Deeqa came to Molly, before Kwiatkowski had yelled about the trap door, Molly had opened the sarcophagus containing the remains of Hannaniah bat Yeshuah.

Within the cedar coffin lay a body wrapped in a shroud. Molly was no forensic scientist but certainly knew enough about human anatomy to determine that the skeletal remains that lay within were not, could not, be Hannaniah's. They were the remains of a child, a girl child, she thought. Long strands of red hair clung to the small skull. A slight wooden doll lay in the crook of her arm. Molly was pulling a bronze ring off a bony finger, when Cavalcante joined her.

"Not Hannaniah," Molly said, disappointment in her voice.

"No? Then you think Yeshuah is a fake, too?"

"I don't know."

Molly felt like weeping. *Hannaniah, how could you do this to me?* But there must be an explanation, she thought. *There has to be.* Deeqa came at a trot.

"Molly," she said, panting, "Hannaniah's not up here. She's down there!"

"What?"

"Mr. Kwiatkowski has found a way out. There are more tombs down in the hole."

"Holy shit!" Molly and Cavalcante shared one brief look of disbelief then were out of the false chamber and down into Judas's hole faster than two prairie dogs chased by a hawk. Kwiatkowski was nowhere to be seen.

"Teddy?"

"Down here. Hurry!"

Beneath Judas's grave lay a larger cube-shaped cavity. The sacred hill was coming to look more like an anthill with passageways leading every which way. Four separate entrance tunnels, one in each wall of the cavity, led off into darkness. One of the passages was slightly lit. Kwiatkowski's voice came from there.

Ducking her head, Molly scooted inside, with Cavalcante right behind. The skill involved and the time commitment to construct so complex a network meant that Hannaniah's community must have settled here for some significant period of time. Perhaps it had never vanished.

About twenty feet into the left-hand passage, Kwiatkowski's head popped out of a side chamber. Molly took a quick glance at the lintel above, recognized the Andromeda symbol, and shoved Kwiatkowski aside to take a look at what he had found. With tears filling her eyes and a laugh of joy rising in her throat, she threw herself at the casket that Kwiatkowski had pried open. Inside, exposed to view by the beam of her flashlight, lay the remains of the real Hannaniah, daughter of Yeshuah, tall, bones broken apart, disintegrating, yet still robed in tattered white, fingers bejeweled, a crown of gold near her head, still bearing strands of red hair.

"Oh, my God!" Molly cried, "It's her!"

Unfortunately, it was at that very moment that Richard Jackson stumbled blindly into the tomb of the ancients.

Leveille-Gaus had been advised to keep his head well inside the body of the helicopter. Americans were notorious for being fast on the trigger, and the Mossad commando chief couldn't afford to lose his archaeologist from a stray shot. But the scientist couldn't resist a peek out and down at the approaching village of Al-Muthallath. Even from a quarter mile away, he could see the dead littering the dry landscape.

"Bloody idiot," he muttered and wondered if his former colleague Molly O'Dwyer lay among the dead.

Leveille-Gaus was prepared to kill, too. Like many a European Jew, he was the product of survivors of Nazi Germany. Much of his extended family had died in places like Auschwitz or Bergen-Belsen. In Algeria, where the Levy survivors settled, they had been targeted by the Muslim insurgents against French rule. He had defended himself then, carrying a weapon wherever he went, using it when he had to. For him and for many Jews like him, Israel was more than a country. It was mother's womb, God's gift, the last sanctuary on earth, inviolable sacred ground that every Jew should kill or die for.

The Jewish people had been waiting for nearly two thousand years to return to their homeland, the place Abraham had left Ur to colonize. For almost as long a time, the followers of Jesus had used this Jewish son of David as an excuse to hunt them down and convert, condemn and massacre them. Now Leveille-Gaus had the opportunity to bring Jesus home to his own people.

"Yeshuah," Leveille-Gaus whispered into the wind of the helicopter's rotary blades. "That's his real name. A Jewish name."

Perhaps the world would never know of this resurrection. Perhaps for the sake of Christendom, the Jewish leaders of Israel would say nothing. But Leveille-Gaus would know. And if the world ever tried to do to the Jews what they had so often tried to do in the past, Jesus would be resurrected, all right. Just not in the way so many Christians expected.

"We're going in," the Israeli officer told him. "Buckle up and stay inside. We have been ordered to secure the package no matter what it takes."

As soon as Kwiatkowski heard the crash from above, he extinguished his torch. In silence, he, Molly, Cavalcante, and Deeqa waited for all hell to break loose. When it didn't, Molly whispered, "Follow me."

The gust of air that she had sensed upon entering the core of the hill felt even stronger in the lower passages. Grabbing Kwiatkowski by his hand, she tugged him out of Hannaniah's tomb and down a lightless tunnel farther away from Judas's burial space. The tunnel rose gradually, steadily after about twenty feet. She could make out the sides of the clay brick walls thanks to a source of waning daylight up ahead.

Finally, the passage came to an abrupt end in a widened space. Four brick steps led seemingly nowhere, directly into the hill. But upon closer inspection Molly found a door of rotted timbers that slanted from the ground at an eighty-degree angle. The light that had guided them came through cracks in the wood.

Molly looked about. "Crowbar?"

"Got it." As soon as Cavalcante handed the tool to her, Molly chopped at the aged wood. The others dug in with their hands and fingernails, tore at the wood and the soil surrounding it. In moments, the door began to give on its own as if something above were pressing down on it. The wood splintered and debris and desert sand came pouring in, spilling into Molly's mouth and eyes. Gagging, she backed away, fearing a cave-in. Instead, the shower of rubble came to a stop as abruptly as it had begun. In place of the door, a large, round rubber object poked through the shattered shards of timber.

"Uno *pneumatico!*" Cavalcante exclaimed. "A tire!"

"More precisely," Kwiatkowski said, "the ambulance tire."

The metal hub of the wheel was visible. Kwiatkowski cleared off a layer of dirt to prove his point. "I don't know what the hell it's doing here," Molly said. "But I have a thought."

"It better be a good one," Kwiatkowski told her. "We have company."

Jackson worked his way cautiously through the darkness of the passage into the hill, impatient, deadly and foolish. He never saw the steps leading down into the central chamber, so he tripped over them and tumbled head first into the darkness where he landed against something that tore a hole in his left leg. With a curse, he kicked out at the unseen object and sent it toppling out of sight.

"Dr. O'Dwyer!" he yelled. "Milstein!" He was tempted to spray the darkness with gunfire, particularly when he heard a sound coming from behind him. He spun around, still on his butt where he had landed, and pressed his finger to the trigger. He was stopped only by the sound of a familiar friendly voice.

"Dick? You in there? You all right?"

"Yeah. Bring a light."

An artificial sunrise spread slowly across the large cavity, from the entrance to the tunnel and across the sky of the tomb's ceiling. Several heads and several flashlights followed, shining this way and that to give the newcomers a complete perspective of the space they had entered.

"God!" one of them whispered. "What is this place?"

"Never mind," Jackson said, getting up, dusting himself off, checking his leg wound, which bled but not badly enough to warrant a transfusion or an amputation. He aimed his revolver at each of the eleven rooms that exited off the central chamber.

"Dr. O'Dwyer! Hidin' is useless. Thank you for your efforts. The relief crew is here to recover your find."

Directing his men with his pistol, he ordered them to search each room. Even he, when time allowed him to calm down a bit, held his breath in awe. If the archaeologists were correct, he was standing in the catacombs that held the remains of Jesus of Nazareth and perhaps a number of his disciples or family. The light that now filled the oval clearly showed the symbols carved into the lintels above the doorways and the markings in Hebrew that adorned each of the burial caskets.

"Goddamn," someone muttered. "Lookie here."

"Coffins, Dick," his friend said. "How old you think?"

"Two thousand years," he said. Then he looked behind and saw the hole that Molly had fallen through, the coffin that had been raised, and the bone fragments scattered along the floor where he had lashed out and kicked them. He tore away the last of the floorboards that had covered Judas's grave. There was enough light for him to peer down into it, but all he saw were the rest of Judas's skeletal remains, part of the decayed coffin, and dirt.

"Nothing there but bones," his friend said, shining his flashlight into the opening. "Whose you think?"

The thought crossed Jackson's mind at that point that they could be those of Jesus Himself who Jackson had meanly booted like so much skeletal trash. With a sudden surge of guilt that would take years of confession and a couple million Hail Marys to eradicate, he fell to his knees and crossed himself.

"Good Lord!" he said. "What are we doin'?"

"Dick?"

"Get everybody. We may need another chopper. Get Eisenstadt on the horn. I want all of these coffins removed. Delicately. Gently. Does anybody here understand Hebrew?"

Rising to his feet again, Jackson felt dizzy and giddy. There were those who, having lived lives of disrepute and apostasy, abruptly claimed to have seen the light, to have found God, to have been reborn. Sometimes they were sincere. Sometimes they had ulterior motives. When Jackson tottered on weak knees into the Cepheus chamber, the chamber of the father, he felt his legs buckle beneath him. Nobody had ever been reborn so fast and so hard as Richard Clark Jackson Jr.

The room was by far the largest of the eleven. In its center, lying on a raised brick bier, sat a lovely cedar wood coffin with a Star of David embossed in the center of the lid. Above it, or below it depending upon perspective, was carved a crucifix. Jackson didn't have to understand Hebrew to recognize whose coffin he was staring at. Falling to his knees and laying his head against the side of the tomb, he did something he hadn't done since he was a child. He prayed.

"Dick. Dick!"

"Shhh!"

"Mr. Jackson!"

"Quiet!"

"But Mr. Jackson," came the persistent interrupter, "there's another chopper coming in. And it ain't ours."

Pushing her head out from Hannaniah's hidden egress from the hill, Molly couldn't believe her luck. What she couldn't immediately figure out was how the hell the ambulance had come to be rammed into the side of the hill. It was only when she levered herself up and came out directly beneath the front of the ambulance that she began to suspect something bad.

Glass and bits of metal littered the area around the vehicle. So many rounds of ammo had been fired at the ambulance from the sky that the ground was riddled with little craters. Molly could scoop bullets out of the sand like pebbles. One had a coat of congealed red to which the sand of the desert had collected. Squeezing out from underneath the ambulance, she emerged from the hill on the side between ambulance and mound, blocked from view of the village and its denizens by the truck. One look into the cab told her why she had found a blood-covered bullet.

"Oh, no." Gagging, she fell back on her knees to vomit into the sand.

Cavalcante appeared next out of the hole. She darted out like a mouse only to come up short when she saw Milstein's disfigured form sticking half-in, half-out of the ambulance, face unrecognizable, body torn apart by so much military might.

"*Jesu Cristo,*" she said. "It's Mr. Milstein."

"Debt paid in full, damn them to hell!"

Molly staggered to her feet. From here, Molly faced south toward the open desert. The village and Jackson's terrorists were obscured by both the ambulance and by the burial mound. But Molly didn't figure that to last long. She dared a peek at poor Milstein. Then, holding back tears, she opened his door and hauled his body out.

"Molly, what are you doing?" Kwiatkowski asked as he appeared out of the darkness below.

"I said I had a plan," she told him, gruffer than she meant to be. Then she turned, brushed his cheek with her hand and said, "It's time."

The arrival of the Mossad helicopter took the Americans by such surprise that Jackson's men stood about, hands in their pockets, sitting ducks to the Israeli machine gunners. They were luckier than they knew. Had Leveille-Gaus been in charge of the operation, the Americans would have been as dead as Milstein. As it was the commando leader ordered one of his men to be prepared to disable the American helicopter. He hoped he could deal with the Americans. He hadn't reckoned with the born-again Jackson.

From the air, Leveille-Gaus could see that the Americans were moving something out of the hill south of the town. They had created a killing field out of Al-Muthallath and had parked their UH-L60 a short distance from the mound.

Those idiots will ruin it all before it leaves the site, he thought.

Flying in from the east, he paid no attention to the destroyed ambulance at the western side of the hill. He jumped ship and raced for the mound, pistol waving at his side, even as the rotors of his helicopter spun the desert floor into spirals of sand.

"Jackson! Jackson, you idiot!" he shouted. "What in God's name do you think you're doing?"

Jackson emerged from the hill at that moment bearing one end of the most important coffin of all, the one he presumed belonged to Jesus of Nazareth. He wouldn't lower it even when Leveille-Gaus waved the pistol in his face.

"Dr. Leveille, you stick that gun up my nose one more time," he said, " and I will personally hose you down with a semi-automatic. This site belongs to the government of the United States. Stand down, I warn you."

"You impertinent jackass! You're not talking to one of your Muslim prisoners now." Leveille-Gaus planted himself in front of the coffin.

Jackson might have shot him then and there if the chief of the Mossad commandos hadn't come running at a gallop. His men had Jackson's under guard, but Jackson wasn't done yet. Lowering the coffin he was helping to carry, he strode up to Leveille-Gaus, disarmed him with a sudden knee to the groin, then placed his own revolver up against the archaeologist's head. To the well-armed Israeli commando, he said, "Stand-off."

"Not quite," the Israeli said. Then lied. "CIA."

"No way!" Jackson exclaimed. His gun didn't waver. "You're bullshittin' me."

"Regrettably, no," the Israeli said, all traces of an accent gone. "The president is on this one himself." He produced identification and documents that seemed to corroborate his story.

"But he wasn't supposed to know," Jackson said.

"Well, he does. So, lower your gun, step away from the coffin, and let Dr. Leveille do his job."

Leveille-Gaus didn't rush to the two-thousand-year-old casket because he was still feeling the pain Jackson had administered. But he had no problem slapping Jackson across the face first. "Did you open it already?"

"What if I did?"

Leveille-Gaus limped over to the casket and felt at the lid with his fingers. There were obvious marks of desecration caused by one of the crowbars Molly had left behind. He glared at Jackson before lifting the lid ever so slightly so that he could look in.

"Exposing such old remains to the open air like you did can destroy vital information. You should at least have waited for someone more appropriate than yourself to investigate."

"Are you kidding?" Jackson said. "Look at the markings on the top. A Star of David and a cross. Do you know who that might be?"

Leveille-Gaus took a longer, harder look. "Not Jesus," he said.

"What!"

"How do you know, Doctor?" the Israeli commando asked.

"See for yourself." Now with less caution, Leveille-Gaus opened the casket completely to the wind and forces of the desert. The sun had descended to the horizon by this time, so that a reddish tinge colored the skeleton within, a small skeleton, that of a child. "Unless Jesus was about four or five years old when he died, this is not Jesus."

"Then where is He?"

"Could that be Him going that way?"

The Israeli commando pointed towards the south at a rising cloud of dust hurled into the air by the escaping ambulance.

Leveille-Gaus took one step forward before realizing what was happening. "O'Dwyer!" he screamed. And the chase was on.

This time Kwiatkowski took the wheel. Molly sat beside him. They sat in Milstein's blood and fragments of glass and metal, while Cavalcante and Deeqa stayed in the back of the ambulance keeping two ancient coffins company. The first was of cedar wood inscribed with the name 'Yeshuah bar Yushef, the Father'. The second, similar in make and design, contained the words in Hebrew 'Hannaniah, his daughter'.

"You know, we're almost out of gas," he said.

"That's a pessimist's perspective. I'd say we're nearly full of air."

"Great, if this were a dirigible." Kwiatkowski looked through the hole in the roof. "Even if it were a dirigible, it couldn't out-fly a helicopter."

"Just drive it as far as you can," Molly said. "Until it runs out of gas."

"And if they shoot at us?"

"They won't. They know who we have with us."

Molly glanced back at the two coffins. Cavalcante held one down, Deeqa the other, to keep the shaking of the ambulance from damaging the wood. Normally, they would have handled the remains wearing surgical gloves and a facemask to prevent contamination. This was not normal.

Even so, inside the tomb, Cavalcante had cajoled, begged, prodded Molly to look inside the father's casket while they had the chance. Molly had balked. Cavalcante had not.

At first, Molly couldn't even peek. Cavalcante gave a forensic anthropologist's quick and utterly cold analysis of the remains. Between five feet eight inches and five feet ten in height. Weight probably proportional to height. Red of hair like his daughter. He had been buried in a shroud and wore only a Star of David ring on one finger.

When Molly dared look, trembling and quivering like a frightened lamb, she noticed something else buried with him, nestled against his side. A stone bas-relief of two people, a father and daughter, facing each other, gazing into each other's eyes. Molly wept when she saw it, coveted it, but knew she had no right to steal it from the father.

Kwiatkowski patted her knee as the engine of the ambulance sputtered and died. "I'm afraid," he said, "this is as far as we go. I suggest we step outside the ambulance, put our hands high in the air, so they don't shoot us on the spot."

"They might shoot us anyway."

"Here or back there, what's the difference?"

Molly reluctantly stepped out into the darkening desert.

The wind of the descending helicopter almost knocked her down. It landed so close to the gasless ambulance that Leveille-Gaus reached the ambulance in ten steps and threw open the doors.

"Aha!" he shouted. "Just what I thought! Dr. Cavalcante, you?"

"Me," the slight Italian woman said, sliding out of the van, followed by Deeqa.

But Leveille-Gaus wasn't much for preliminaries. He jumped

into the truck and immediately scoped out the two coffins inside. "Yes! Yes!" he said. "Beautiful! Wonderful! You haven't opened them yet, have you?" he asked.

"I am a scientist," Molly said lifelessly from behind him. She had entered the vehicle, too, to make sure he didn't violate the remains of Hannaniah and her father in his intellectual avarice to know what lay within.

"And you're sure this is Jesus and His daughter?"

"They were hidden beneath the grave that held Judas."

"Iscariot?" Leveille-Gaus drooled as his hand swept over the coffin of the father as if he were feeling the living flesh of the being within.

"Apparently we have uncovered a family plot. I think Hannaniah dug up Judas from an older grave in Jerusalem and carried him with her. Before her father died, she prepared a secret burial chamber underneath the others, having learned from Egyptian grave robbers not to be too obvious about where you buried someone. Dr. Leveille, what are you going to do with this?"

Leveille-Gaus was breathing rapidly.

Surprisingly to Molly, when he turned to face her, he, too, had tears in his eyes.

"You do me an injustice if you think I would desecrate these bodies in any way. I am not a Christian. I am not a particularly religious man. But I understand the importance Yeshuah has for the world. He will be treated with utter respect, and no one, *no one*, will ever know we have him. He will not be put on display. He will not be abused. He will be studied. He will be kept safe. And he will be kept with us."

"Us being ...?"

"The people of Isreal, of course."

Leveille-Gaus looked up as the Israeli commando leader, who had created the CIA cover, joined them. "It's time to go, Doctor," he said. And to Molly, "We apologize for the inconvenience. You will have to walk back to Al-Muthallath. We've got what we want. Whatever is left you may study at your leisure. But I would advise against seeking publicity. Nothing will be gained from it."

With that, Molly and Leveille-Gaus moved aside to let the commando team remove the two coffins from the ambulance and carry them to the helicopter. Just before it took off again, Leveille-Gaus glanced out of the belly of the craft and shouted above the roaring of the rotor blades, "I respect you, Dr. O'Dwyer. I will send you what I can. Sorry. Truly."

And then the helicopter without any markings was gone, up into the evening sky, leaving the desert and its guests behind. When it was far enough away that Molly felt comfortable, she dropped to her knees and sobbed. "How far do you think we drove from Al-Muthallath?" she asked Kwiatkowski.

"We forgot to bring any water."

"Too bad. I hope you do piggyback."

CHAPTER 21

Five miles. Two hours. Molly, Kwiatkowski, Cavalcante, and Deeqa dragged themselves through the desert until they reached Al-Muthallath with the moon directly overhead. Molly clutched her bas-relief of Hannaniah wrapped in the blanket in her arms. Jackson's helicopter was gone. The tomb had been raided, and none of the coffins had been left behind. Whether Leveille-Gaus got them all or whether they were shared with the Americans was unclear. All that Molly knew was that the desecrators had come and gone and gotten what they wanted.

Or almost.

Heading straight down the village's only street, the four companions stopped at a well constructed of the same brick that had built the tombs of Hannaniah and her father. The shaft descended deep into the ground. Kwiatkowski unreeled a leather sack that disappeared into the darkness below and rose a few minutes later filled to the top with cool water.

"It's gotten cold," Molly said.

"You're shivering. Why don't you wrap that blanket around yourself."

"No. It's not the night. It's everything else. We came for Jesus and brought nothing but misery."

"Not true, Molly," Cavalcante said. "If anything, you saved our souls."

"Molly, sleep," Kwiatkowski advised. "In the morning we can figure out what to do."

"No," she said. "Not yet anyway. I need to check on our friends."

Molly took a last swig of water from the hide container and headed toward the hill beyond the village. The survivors of Jackson's attack had gathered their dead and laid them in neat rows between hill and town, preparing them for burial. Molly counted about two dozen, among them the father of the little girl who had first introduced Al-Muthallath to the archaeologists. The child and her mother kept the father quiet company, causing Molly to pause briefly on her way back to the catacombs.

"They should bury their dead in the hill," she told Deeqa. "Tell them. It's unoccupied now. It's holy ground. They deserve that much."

She took Kwiatkowski's hand and walked the last few yards under the starlight to the final resting place of the Son of God. However, it would not be his final stop. Shortly before they had taken off on their dash across the Al-Anbar with the coffins of Yeshuah and Hannaniah, Molly and the others had made a little exchange. Leveille-Gaus may have thought he was flying the remains of Jesus and his daughter to Mossad headquarters or wherever he was going. Quite soon, he would discover, to his great shock and fury, that he was carrying instead the remains of Father Ray Teague and Andrew Milstein. Yeshuah and his daughter had never left Al-Muthallath.

Molly ducked her head to enter the catacombs. Kwiatkowski came in behind her. The full moon lighted their passage into the tunnel but only so far. As the narrow decline took them to the cavity beneath Judas's grave, Kwiatkowski used his lighter to give them minimal direction.

The first time Molly had stumbled into the hole, she had followed the incline up toward the burial chambers of Hannaniah and her father. In attempting to save them, she, Cavalcante, Deeqa, and

Kwiatkowski had wrapped the remains in the burial shrouds and carried them deeper into the underground before closing the coffins with the new occupants. Molly was certain that both Milstein and Father Ray would appreciate their roles in saving the holy father and daughter from desecration.

In the core of the hill Molly had discovered a room filled with the clay urns she had seen at three other sites. Most of them were sealed, finished products, ornately designed, lovingly crafted, and bore inscriptions of those buried within. Leveille-Gaus and Jackson had been too greedy and in too great a hurry to bother searching the rest of the archaeological site believing the prize was already in their hands.

In a far corner of the chamber, squeezed and hidden between a wall and a row of burial urns, the shrouded remains of Yeshuah and Hannaniah lay undisturbed. Molly fell to her knees beside them in worshipful pose.

"Turn off the light," she told Kwiatkowski.

"It's cold in here, Molly. You're sweating from the walk. It's not healthy."

"I'm all right. Wait a minute," she said, suddenly taking his wrist and moving it so that the tiny Bic flame he was holding would focus on a finger bone protruding from one of the shrouds. "Here lies the man who gave us the Sermon on the Mount, Teddy. Doesn't that mean anything to you?"

"Yes, of course, it does." He closed the flame and left them in darkness. Then he knelt beside her.

"My faith has been challenged throughout my life," she said to him, reaching again for his hand. "I guess that's what makes faith what it is: how we meet those challenges and whether or not we come away better or worse."

"If these bones truly belong to Jesus," Kwiatkowski said, "then at the very least the resurrection never happened. His body is here with us. That fact would be a hell of a challenge to anyone's faith."

"You miss the point, Teddy." Shivering with the cold, Molly snuggled into her lover's body. He gathered her in, kissed her cheek, laid his head on hers. "When I first learned what we were after," she said, "I expected the worst. My faith would hit my intellect head on. My intellect would win out, and my faith would be destroyed. I'd be left with this amazing knowledge that would do me absolutely no good. But I was wrong. My faith is stronger than ever."

Molly trembled in Kwiatkowski's arms. "It's something in the bones, the strands of hair. It's the man in him that makes him more real to me, that makes me feel stronger. He experienced what I experience, whether as a man or as the son of God. Love. Loss. Deep, deep sadness. You understand? The distance between us is gone, and I can appreciate him more than I ever did. He was resurrected, Teddy. Tonight. In me."

Molly sighed, felt a tear roll down her cheek. Now they had to figure out what they were going to do with Hannaniah and Yeshuah. They certainly couldn't leave them here. Ghazi Al-Tikriti's mujahedeen had left behind their vehicles for transport. That was one good thing. What Molly had to decide now was where to take them.

Her prayerful silence was broken by Deeqa who scrambled through the darkness yelling. "Molly! Molly! Quick! Someone's coming!"

"Damn," Molly said. "Now what?"

Once out into the night air again, she saw from the top of the hill a string of bright headlights making their way to Al-Muthallath. Five cars, six. She had half a mind to retrieve the weapons the mujahedeen had no further use for, but that would only be further desecration of the site. Rather, hands on hips, she stood her ground and waited for the newcomers to approach her.

Abdul Azim Nur left the rickety confines of his Aston-Martin, stretched his tired aching arms and legs and stared at the bodies of the dead mujahedeen and villagers, all one now thanks to the liberators. Among them was Tikriti.

They had arrived at Ur too late, finding the burning remains of Milstein's sabotage and a few scattered remnants of Tikriti's forces who directed them west. Now, entering Al-Muthallath, seeing the dead and dying, Nur recalled his own dreams of death and destruction and saw in this chaos the fulfillment of his worst nightmares.

As the survivors of the village gathered around him, clung to his trousers and begged for answers, he watched Shamkhazi casually, grimly writing notes to be forwarded by courier to the theocrats of Tehran. Just a few short days from his planned march to Baghdad, Nur could foresee the collapse of his mission into violence and his own death at the hands of his most trusted men.

He cast his eyes south, to the prayer hill and to the figure framed in the moonlight on top of it. *I must draw the dagger first,* he thought, *before someone draws a dagger on me.* Surely someone ought to pay for the slaughter at Al-Muthallath.

"Who is that?" he asked pointing toward the hill. "One of the killers?"

"No," said the child who had lost her father. "She's nice."

"She?"

Nur quickly blessed the crowd, promised them Allah would reply to the murders righteously, then set off up the hill to confront this mysterious woman who dared rise above the dead of Al-Muthallath without fear. If Shamkhazi was a threat needing to be deterred, perhaps, Nur thought, one sacrifice might need to be made.

But halfway up the hill he was struck by a wave of chills that shook his body. When he saw Molly, he stopped cold in his tracks.

"It is you!" he said.

"From Baghdad," Molly replied. "Do you remember me?"

If only she knew, he thought.

"The woman who risked her life to save an Iraqi girl. Yes, I remember." Nur studied the face he had seen so many times in dreams whose origins he couldn't conceive. She was indeed lovely. But what, in the name of Allah, was she to him?

Kwiatkowski, Cavalcante and Deeqa stood their ground with Molly, despite the angry looks of Nur's guardians and the way they eagerly fingered their weapons. Shamkhazi trudged up behind Nur and whispered in his ear. "This is the perfect solution. They have slaughtered our people, innocent women and children, in the name of their prophet. Their faith is false, their presence in our land a sacrilege. Execute them in the name of Allah, and our people will rise behind you in jihad."

"Our people?" Nur asked, all too aware of the cold bureaucratic brutality that lay beneath Shamkhazi's flawed faith. "They are my people, Barid." Then he turned to Molly.

"They say you're an archaeologist. I never realized this hill was so significant, though I myself wondered why the villagers would come here to pray. Are you responsible for the deaths of these people?"

"No, sir."

"Why are they dead?"

"This hill contains something that other people desperately wanted to find." Molly tried to approach Nur, but Shamkhazi intervened and pushed her back. "I was desperate to find it, too, I admit. But we didn't kill your people. Let us go."

Nur did not respond immediately to Molly. Instead, he eyed her over Shamkhazi's shoulder like a portrait artist studying his model's every feature before he captured her beauty and humanity on canvass. He shook his head in disbelief. "You are she," he said. His eyes beheld her in wonder.

"I am an archaeologist, that's all."

"It is uncanny." He stepped past Shamkhazi to touch her cheek, then thought better of it and lowered his hand, not knowing how his men would react. He was a holy man, after all, who denied the flesh of women for his own gratification. Indecision played into the Iranian's hand.

Molly said, "We're terribly sorry for what happened here. If we had known … You're looking at me like I have horns. Believe me, I'm not the devil."

"No? What did you find?"

"Bones. Bodies. Nothing else," Molly said.

"You're lying to me! Don't lie to me! Your life depends on your being honest!"

Molly flushed. "I'm sorry. You're right. We found very special bones, very special bodies. But the bad guys got the prize."

"Which was?"

Molly was reticent to speak. Nur could see in her look the same sense of déjà vu that she had seen in his.

"Do you dream?" she asked suddenly.

"What?"

"Dream. But not ordinary dreams. Strange ones."

Nur's eyes widened. At first he couldn't speak, wouldn't speak in front of his people. How could she know this, he wondered? What was she doing? Testing him? Probing him?

"Perhaps in a way what has happened here at Al-Muthallath is my fault," she admitted. "We came here based on information gathered from past expeditions in Egypt and Afghanistan. But not just from that. From dreams, too. Dreams brought me here. It may sound ridiculous, but it feels as if I lived in this very spot many years ago and died here."

Molly's last words brought a gasp from Nur's throat. He took a step back and had to ward off his soldiers who stepped forward to his aid. They grabbed her and the others. Shamkhazi might have had them all killed on the spot had Nur not shouted, "Stop, Barid! Move away!"

"Imam!"

"Move!" Only when the Iranian had released her did Nur step forward and take her face in his hands. Then he scanned her eyes, riveted by them. His hands shook.

"What do you want?" he asked her suddenly. "Who are you? How dare you?"

Tears filled her eyes. "I don't know!" she cried. Her face still cradled in the palms of his hands, she blurted, "Hannaniah. I think I am, I was, in another life, his child."

"Whose daughter? Whose child? You're not making sense."

"Yeshuah bar Yushef's! Jesus'!"

Barid Shamkhazi had been shoved aside but not so far that he didn't hear their conversation. "Enough of this! Imam, get a hold of yourself! She is manipulating you, can't you see that? Strike her dead now! She will ruin everything!"

"Shut up, Barid!"

"She must die!"

"I said ..." Nur's hands found Shamkhazi's throat. And in that moment, when he had come closer than ever before to killing a man, when he saw the confused and frightened faces of his people all around him, the mujahedeen, the women and children, Nur had an epiphany. He released Shamkhazi, pushed him out of his sight.

"Put this man under guard," he ordered.

"Imam, don't be foolish!" Shamkhazi begged, but Nur ignored him.

He turned to his men. "See to the villagers. Leave me alone with the woman."

"Imam, she is poison! Your mission has failed!"

Nur blocked out the Iranian's words. Then, aware of his men's staring eyes and indecision, he signaled to Molly. "Why don't we take a walk, and you can show me what the bad guys didn't get."

With a tentative smile, Molly shrugged, descended the hill, and led Nur to the entrance of the tomb. Neither said a word. The next few minutes would decide their fate. Kwiatkowski had lent her his lighter, but one of Nur's followers had a flashlight, which Nur used to enter the tunnel and to reach the core of the hill.

Molly shook. Nur followed her lead, amazed by what he was seeing.

"No wonder," he mumbled. "No wonder the people came to pray here."

As they descended farther into the hill, Molly explained Hannaniah, the flight of the Jewish people from Jerusalem, what brought them here. Throughout all her lecture, Nur studied the strange markings, considered the heretical story, and for some reason found none of it hard to believe. He trusted Molly because, incredibly, he was beginning to feel as she did, that Al-Muthallath a long time ago had been his home.

Deep beneath the hill, in the darkness of two millennia, Molly pointed out the shrouded remains of Yeshuah and Hannaniah. Her hand shook.

"*Abba v'bat,*" she said.

"What?"

"The father and the daughter."

"Jesus?"

Molly nodded. "That is our best guess."

Nur dropped to his knees. "You've looked?"

"Yes. And I can't anymore. We need to hide them. Surely you understand."

"And you're sure this is …?"

"Not positively," Molly said. "Not scientifically. Dreams. A feeling. I had done research in Egypt and discovered scrolls written by his daughter Hannaniah. I've been dreaming about her ever since. And of her father."

"Yes, of course." Nur bowed to the remains of the father and the daughter as if he were praying to Allah. The dreams, the madness of them, flooded his mind. In them he saw the woman, and when he looked at Molly, he saw the same face. And the man in his dreams, the man who was not Nur, the man who suffered yet survived, he recognized his face at last, too.

"Allah, have mercy," he whispered.

"Mr. Nur?"

Then he crossed himself. "Abba v'bat," he said. "It seems I am equally at fault for what happened here at Al-Muthallath."

Molly glanced at the Muslim holy man, studying him much as he had her. Where, indeed, had she seen his face? He was more than familiar to her. His presence, so close to her, produced a sensation akin to déjà vu, powerful, mysterious. Behind the beard, behind the mustache, she wondered, *how do I know this man?*

"Do you then believe in the efficacy of dreams, Ms. O'Dwyer?"

he asked her.

"Do I believe in the supernatural? Is that what you're asking me?"

"For several months," he said, "like you I have been having bizarre dreams. I am no longer Nur. I am someone else. I am no longer in this time and place but somewhere else. These dreams have frightened me, crippled my work. You, Ms. O'Dwyer, are in all of them."

"In what capacity, if I might ask?"

Nur bent forward and stretched out his hands to touch the shrouded remains of Hannaniah. A stream of tears ran down his cheek. "I would say," he told her, "as a daughter."

Molly squeezed her eyes shut, felt a pounding of blood rushing through her head. "Exactly what are you trying to say?" she whispered.

"I don't know. These dreams are new to me. I don't know what they mean. I am a religious man. When I saw you standing on the top of the hill, it was like being struck by God. Everything all at once became apparent and yet remained completely unknown to me. I don't know how to explain it any better than that. Who are we, Ms. O'Dwyer? What are we?"

At first, Molly couldn't find the words to express herself. From the first moment Father Teague had regressed her … no, even before that … in Egypt with the newly discovered Hannaniah scrolls, Molly had tapped into a realm of experience she would never previously have believed existed, even with what fellow archaeologists called her romantic and vivid empathy for the dead. But the past five years had torn away the curtain of scientific disdain and inexorably prodded her either toward madness or toward making the most profound of personal discoveries. Looking at Nur, she finally understood why he looked so familiar to her, understood what his words meant. She had known. Somehow she had understood even before this but hadn't wanted to believe. Now she had no other choice.

Crouching beside the Muslim cleric, Molly pointed at the shrouded human remains. "Please don't consider me utterly unprofessional, Mr. Nur," she said. "I think you know the answer. Unless I am wrong, that is me, or was two thousand years ago. And that, sir, is you."

"Then it is real." Nur looked as though he'd just been lifted off his feet, the ground falling fast below him. Molly thought he was going to be sick. He fell prone before Hannaniah and her father but said not a word, not even in prayer, and stayed that way for ten minutes. When at last he got up, he stumbled out of the catacombs with Molly chasing after him.

Neither spoke again, not as they descended the hill, not as Kwiatkowski came to take her in his arms and the Al-Muthallath villagers pulled at Nur to tend to their needs. Under a watchful moon, beneath a canopy of stars that had borne witness to the full extent of human drama from the instant human life had begun on earth to this very moment, Molly and Nur gazed at each other one last time. And each knew, though neither would ever say it, that after two thousand years apart, Hannaniah and her father had once again come home.

EPILOGUE

As a devoted scientist and as a Catholic faithful to her belief in her own way, Molly struggled with the idea of surrendering Hannaniah and her father to Abdul Azim Nur. But what other choice did she have? She could never hide them. Her notoriety would ultimately bring them to light. And then she would be forced to reveal everything, killing so much in the process, too much.

Nur was the logical caretaker. She trusted the holy man would find a place where none would ever disturb them again. Not only was he as good as his word, he embraced her upon their parting and pledged that when indeed he returned to Baghdad, he would go with the full knowledge of who he had been and what he had meant to the world. The Iranian Shamkhazi he sent packing back to Tehran.

Only two days later, through Kwiatkowski's connections, she and Kwiatkowski, Cavalcante and her delighted new interest Deeqa Hassan, boarded a plane and left Baghdad for Rome. If anyone could show Molly the real City of the Caesars, Cavalcante could. And Molly had to admit, the few days she spent with Kwiatkowski in Rome, free of so much emotional baggage, were the best of her life.

Cavalcante came from a wealthy Italian family and had a lakeside country home in the Italian Alps to prove it. Kwiatkowski had intended to drive from Rome to Warsaw to show Molly that his native land was every bit as beautiful as Cavalcante's, but he certainly found no reason to complain at the sight of the lake, moon-lit past the pine-covered slope. The porch, the hammock, the woman curled up beside him: all was pretty good with the world.

"Do you think you'll ever hear from Dr. Leveille? Or the American?" he asked her. The hammock rocked lightly with their weight against a pleasant evening breeze.

Molly grunted. "They'll call. I'll hang up. That'll be the end of it. What are they going to do? The last thing they want is me talking to the press."

On impulse, Molly sat up, swung her legs to dangle over the side of the hammock, then pushed off onto a dark trail that led to a boat house on the lake.

"Where you going?" Kwiatkowski called to her.

"For a little walk," she said. "Do you mind? You can come, but give me a few minutes alone, okay?"

Against a backdrop of mountains, forest and stars Molly could pretend briefly that she was Hannaniah, young and beautiful again, walking down from the Galilean heights to the shores of the lake where her father preached and gained recruits. In the reflection of her own face in the water, Molly could tell what Hannaniah looked like.

How much of what had happened in Iraq was real? Had she truly been Hannaniah in a past life? Was she an ancestor with Hannaniah's memories somehow gifted to her through the marvel of DNA? Or was something else at work? Coincidence. Fate. The work of some unseen hand.

Bending, Molly picked up a stone and tossed it into the lake, watching the ripples spread across the surface just as the gospels had traveled across the world.

Who did we find out there in the desert of Iraq? she wondered. Jesus? Someone named Yeshuah? Truth is everything to me, yet I have proof of nothing. Nur has buried the answer. All I have left is the dream.

She turned at the sound of rocks crunching under foot, smiled as Kwiatkowski joined her, holding out something in his hand. It was a ring, a very old one, taken from the tombs of Al-Muthallath. Molly's eyes widened.

"Hannaniah's!"

"It was meant to be passed down generation to generation," he said. "Don't lose it."

"I'll take it with me to the grave."

With tears in her eyes then and with little regret at her lover's theft, she kissed Kwiatkowski, fully, hard and deep. Then she gazed up at the sky and the stars, as beyond human inquisitiveness as they could possibly be.

Stripped of all its pomp and mystery, she thought, faith is a very simple thing. Like a lover's kiss. My faith calls for me to be honest. I owe nothing else to anyone. Let Leveille-Gaus and the rest do their worst. I can still look up into the night sky and see God.

ABOUT THE AUTHOR

Born in Portland, Maine, **Peter Clenott** began writing his first fiction after graduating from Bowdoin College. A prolific author of novels and screenplays, he is particularly drawn to issues of conflict and spirituality, faith and responsibility. Having lived in South Africa during the time of Apartheid, he has written about insurgency in Africa, upheaval in the Congo, and the relationship between a Jewish father and son in Johannesburg.

Hunting the King is his answer to those who believe that they have exclusive knowledge regarding God and faith. A past member of the Harvard Square Scriptwriters in Boston, Mr. Clenott has also written about revolution in Europe and the last survivors of World War 1.

For the past fifteen years he has worked in social services helping out local survivors of fire, flood, domestic abuse, and lost employment to find new homes. He currently lives in Haverhill, Massachusetts with his wife, Lisa and three wonderful children, Leah, William, and Stephen.

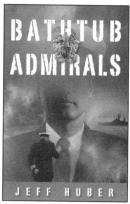

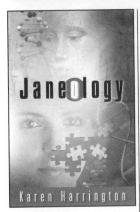

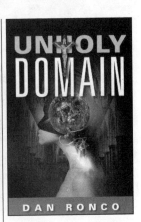

Provocative. Bold. Controversial.

Kunati hot titles

Available at your favorite bookseller

www.kunati.com

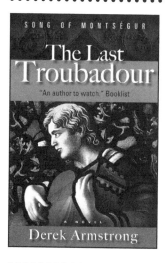

The Last Troubadour
Historical fiction by Derek Armstrong

Against the flames of a rising medieval Inquisition, a heretic, an atheist and a pagan are the last hope to save the holiest Christian relic from a sainted king and crusading pope. Based on true events.

■ "... brilliance in which Armstrong blends comedy, parody, and adventure in genuinely innovative ways." *Booklist*

US$ 24.95 | Pages 384, cloth hardcover
ISBN-13: 978-1-60164-010-9
ISBN-10: 1-60164-010-2
EAN: 9781601640109

Recycling Jimmy
A cheeky, outrageous novel by Andy Tilley

Two Manchester lads mine a local hospital ward for "clients" as they launch Quitters, their suicide-for-profit venture in this off-the-wall look at death and modern life.

■ "Energetic, imaginative, relentlessly and unabashedly vulgar." *Booklist*
■ "Darkly comic story unwinds with plenty of surprises." *ForeWord*

US$ 24.95 | Pages 256, cloth hardcover
ISBN-13: 978-1-60164-013-0
ISBN-10: 1-60164-013-7
EAN 9781601640130

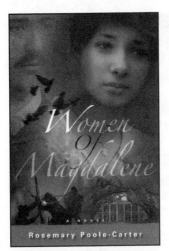

Women Of Magdalene
A hauntingly tragic tale of the old South by Rosemary Poole-Carter

An idealistic young doctor in the post-Civil War South exposes the greed and cruelty at the heart of the Magdalene Ladies' Asylum in this elegant, richly detailed and moving story of love and sacrifice.

■ "A fine mix of thriller, historical fiction, and Southern Gothic." *Booklist*
■ "A brilliant example of the best historical fiction can do." *ForeWord*

US$ 24.95 | Pages 288, cloth hardcover
ISBN-13: 978-1-60164-014-7
ISBN-10: 1-60164-014-5 | EAN: 9781601640147

On Ice
A road story like no other, by Red Evans

The sudden death of a sad old fiddle player brings new happiness and hope to those who loved him in this charming, earthy, hilarious coming-of-age tale.

■ "Evans' humor is broad but infectious ... Evans uses offbeat humor to both entertain and move his readers." *Booklist*

US$ 19.95 | Pages 208, cloth hardcover
ISBN-13: 978-1-60164-015-4
ISBN-10: 1-60164-015-3
EAN: 9781601640154

Truth Or Bare
Offbeat, stylish crime novel by Richard Cahill

The characters throb with vitality, the prose sizzles in this darkly comic page-turner set in the sleazy world of murderous sex workers, the justice system, and the rich who will stop at nothing to get what they want.

■ "Cahill has introduced an enticing character ... Let's hope this debut novel isn't the last we hear from him." *Booklist*

US$ 24.95 | Pages 304, cloth hardcover
ISBN-13: 978-1-60164-016-1
ISBN-10: 1-60164-016-1
EAN: 9781601640161

Provocative. Bold. Controversial.

The Game
A thriller by Derek Armstrong

Reality television becomes too real when a killer stalks the cast on America's number one live-broadcast reality show.
■ "A series to watch ... Armstrong injects the trope with new vigor." *Booklist*
US$ 24.95 | Pages 352, cloth hardcover
ISBN 978-1-60164-001-7 | EAN: 9781601640017
LCCN 2006930183

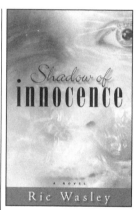

bang BANG
A novel by Lynn Hoffman

In Lynn Hoffman's wickedly funny *bang-BANG*, a waitress crime victim takes on America's obsession with guns and transforms herself in the process. Read along as Paula becomes national hero and villain, enforcer and outlaw, lover and leader. Don't miss Paula Sherman's one-woman quest to change America.
■ "Brilliant"
STARRED REVIEW, *Booklist*
US$ 19.95
Pages 176, cloth hardcover
ISBN 978-1-60164-000-0
EAN 9781601640000
LCCN 2006930182

Whale Song
A novel by Cheryl Kaye Tardif

Whale Song is a haunting tale of change and choice. Cheryl Kaye Tardif's beloved novel—a "wonderful novel that will make a wonderful movie" according to *Writer's Digest*—asks the difficult question, which is the higher morality, love or law?
■ "Crowd-pleasing ... a big hit." *Booklist*
US$ 12.95
Pages 208, UNA trade paper
ISBN 978-1-60164-007-9
EAN 9781601640079
LCCN 2006930188

Shadow of Innocence
A mystery by Ric Wasley

The Thin Man meets *Pulp Fiction* in a unique mystery set amid the drugs-and-music scene of the sixties that touches on all our societal taboos. *Shadow of Innocence* has it all: adventure, sleuthing, drugs, sex, music and a perverse shadowy secret that threatens to tear apart a posh New England town.
US$ 24.95
Pages 304, cloth hardcover
ISBN 978-1-60164-006-2
EAN 9781601640062
LCCN 2006930187

The Secret Ever Keeps

A novel by Art Tirrell

An aging Godfather-like billionaire tycoon regrets a decades-long life of "shady dealings" and seeks reconciliation with a granddaughter who doesn't even know he exists. A sweeping adventure across decades—from Prohibition to today—exploring themes of guilt, greed and forgiveness.

■ "Riveting ... Rhapsodic ... Accomplished." *ForeWord*

US$ 24.95
Pages 352, cloth hardcover
ISBN 978-1-60164-004-8
EAN 9781601640048
LCCN 2006930185

Toonamint of Champions

A wickedly allegorical comedy by Todd Sentell

Todd Sentell pulls out all the stops in his hilarious spoof of the manners and mores of America's most prestigious golf club. A cast of unforgettable characters, speaking a language only a true son of the South could pull off, reveal that behind the gates of fancy private golf clubs lurk some mighty influential freaks.

■ "Bubbly imagination and wacky humor." *ForeWord*

US$ 19.95
Pages 192, cloth hardcover
ISBN 978-1-60164-005-5
EAN 9781601640055
LCCN 2006930186

Mothering Mother

A daughter's humorous and heartbreaking memoir.
Carol D. O'Dell

Mothering Mother is an authentic, "in-the-room" view of a daughter's struggle to care for a dying parent. It will touch you and never leave you.

■ "Beautiful, told with humor... and much love." *Booklist*
■ "I not only loved it, I lived it. I laughed, I smiled and shuddered reading this book." Judith H. Wright, author of over 20 books.

US$ 19.95
Pages 208, cloth hardcover
ISBN 978-1-60164-003-1
EAN 9781601640031
LCCN 2006930184

• •

Rabid

A novel by T K Kenyon

A sexy, savvy, darkly funny tale of ambition, scandal, forbidden love and murder. Nothing is sacred. The graduate student, her professor, his wife, her priest: four brilliantly realized characters spin out of control in a world where science and religion are in constant conflict.

■ "Kenyon is definitely a keeper." STARRED REVIEW, *Booklist*

US$ 26.95 I Pages 480, cloth hardcover
ISBN 978-1-60164-002-4 I EAN: 9781601640024
LCCN 2006930189

HPARW CLENO

CLENOTT, PETER.
    HUNTING THE KING

PARK PLACE
08/08